Tony Groom is a former Royal Navy Mine Clearance Diver, what the public used to call a frogman. He served in the Falklands Conflict, where his missions included the defusing and recovery of unexploded Argentinean bombs from Royal Navy warships. Tony has also served in other arenas, about which he wrote his bestseller life story, DIVER. He now lives and writes in Portsmouth. As he says, his experiences in real life make thriller-writing that much easier.

Tony Groom's best-selling memoir *Diver* is available on-line at www.amazon.co.uk. Copies signed by the author may be had from: www.deep-sea-diving.com

# IN2DEEP

## Tony Groom

A La Puce Publication

IN2DEEP

Published by La Puce Publications

e-mail: info@la-puce.co.uk/georgeeast@orange.fr

website: www.LaPucePublications.com

© Tony Groom 2010

This paperback edition 2010

ISBN 978-0-9562691-1-9

The author asserts the moral right to be identified as
the author of this work

Printed and bound in Great Britain by
imprint*digital*.net
Set by Red Dog Books  www.reddogbooks.com

## Author's Note

Dedicated to Harry and Snowy.

First of all I have to thank *the* George East for his tireless help in making me a better writer. He has been my editor, publisher, confidant, friend and guiding light. Were it not for him and La-Puce Publications, this story may never have seen the light of day. Also I'd like to thank Harold Mewes of Red Dog Books, for his observations and for the look of this publication. I'd like to thank B.B. for all things special, you know who you are. Thanks also go to Rikke Bhathena for the cover art and to Paul Morris for his Hercules flying tips. My gratitude also goes to Mazin Albaggou for his guidance, to Phil Lindsell for his gruesome ideas, and my parents for their love and belief in me. And last but not least, my wonderful wife and son, without whom, I would be wordless as well as soul-less.

The specific terrorist 'spectacular' described has not happened, but that does not mean it could not. My thanks are due to all those who have, by their actions, contributed to this story. They will know who they are, and would perhaps not thank me if I named them.

To 'Miles'

# 1

The alarm brought him quickly back to reality. Louder than usual, it had to be something large.

Very large.

The green light on the handle of the detector winked, confirming the find. It was definitely metal. The sound never failed to bring with it that buzz of excitement and intrigue. Utter silence for hours on end, then... that sound; the sound that meant it wasn't all a waste of time. If this was the right shipwreck, only one piece of proof was needed. He was looking at a shallow depression that had to be the bronze cannon.

Nick never had trouble with his conscience when recovering items like this. It wasn't stealing, it was retrieving. After all, this piece had been on the seabed for hundreds of years and if he didn't rescue it, who would? This was an area no one else would dive, it was too sensitive. He wasn't justifying his actions. It was lost, now it's found, simple. Nick struggled to keep his excitement down. He had a buyer who would pay a quarter of a million pounds for a Spanish bronze, 'Long Nine' cannon. Just a few more nights' work were required to retrieve it.

Nick's breathing started to tighten; the oxygen was running low. He reached down and gave a squirt of the pure $O^2$ from the emergency bottle into the counter-lung on his chest. Every diving regulation in the world said this was the time to stop, but Nick had reasons for ignoring the rules. Maybe a quarter of a million reasons. It was time to head up to the surface and come back the following night. It was four in the morning anyway.

Instead, he dug away with the trowel, working to expose that classic cannon shape.

Small fish darted in to snatch and search the sand and sediment as it drifted up around his headlamp. Even if it wasn't a cannon, it was a large lump of brass or bronze and was worth money. It wasn't exactly what he was looking for, as pirate booty would always be preferred. But there was something romantic about the history, the violence, the sheer beauty of these old weapons that collectors around the world couldn't resist. Then, something interrupted his dark, submersed world of absolute silence.

Nick flicked the ear-piece off and froze.

Holding his breath and standing motionless on the seabed, he listened.

There it was, in the background, the distant sound of an engine; the almost imperceptible murmur of an inboard diesel. This was something big: not big as in a big ship with slow ponderous revolutions or the oh-so-slow thump of a fishing vessel, but something with higher revs; a faster, more powerful craft. It was getting louder. That's why he always used a re-breather. No noise, no bubbles.

*Shit! Time to move.*

A quick clove-hitch around the cannon, then release the buoy, but not all the way up. It was made to sit three metres off the bottom, invisible from the surface, but there were ways to find it again.

The compass told Nick it was north to the anchor, hand-over-hand along the cable to the quick release. Keeping the mouth-piece clamped in his teeth, he took the diving set off, then clipped it to the anchor cable. He attached his tiny military metal detector to the diving set.

One final look around. Good. With one hand on the rope leading up, he knocked the quick release off with a rock. The rope and anchor cable slowly drifted apart. Taking a good breath of oxygen, he turned off the quarter-turn valve on the mouthpiece, making the diving set watertight, then spat it out. Nick moved slowly up the rope to the surface, unflustered and breathing out all the way. Less than thirty seconds. Easy when you'd done it so many times.

Near the surface, the ghostly shape of his yacht loomed into focus above. He took in the strange, almost flat hull just abaft amidships and the two-furled propellers behind which hung the long rudders. She was fast and... unique.

Having anchored stern-to for this very reason, he released the rope and swam to the ladder. Up and onto *Orelia's* bathing platform at the rear and off came the face mask.

Turning out the headlamp and taking great care to stand on a towel, he snatched another from the pulpit rail. The radar repeater by the wheel revealed the offending blip. The collision alarm was sounding its rhythmic warning; it was set to ten miles. Whatever it was, was still two miles away to the South. Close, but enough time... just.

Slipping out of the fins and shorty wetsuit, he pulled up the boarding ladder and jumped naked into the cockpit. Then he hit three digits on the auto-pilot: 285 degrees. The gentle whine of the auto-helm kicked in. The wheel came alive, searching port and starboard, trying to keep the course but, as yet, *Orelia* wasn't making any way.

Nick pulled on the self-furling mainsail halyard. The large triangle of white sail magically appeared from the mainmast. A quick pull on the out-haul to set it tight, then steal a look at the radar. One and a half miles. Whatever it was, it wasn't hanging about. It was on a collision course with Nick's slow moving yacht. Maybe it was heading from the Moroccan coast to the Isla De Alboran. Unlikely, he decided, as the island was a military protected area.

It looked like those aboard the approaching craft knew he was there, so he reached down and switched on the sailing lights. He then jumped back onto the bathing platform and undid the anchor line that was streaming out slowly astern. He clipped an old water container full of rocks to the wetsuit, mask and fins and lowered the lot gently over the side. It sank and was gone, about twenty metres north-west of the ditched anchor. *I might even get that one back*, he thought. There was now no evidence that anyone on board had been diving.

Picking up the towel, he jumped back in the cockpit. The vessel was a little over a mile away and Nick could see the port and starboard steaming lights bearing down on his position. *They have only just switched those on as well*, he thought. This was not looking good.

*Orelia* was beginning to pick up her course now that she had a little drive from the mainsail. A glance at the instruments told him there was only about five knots of north-easterly wind. He let the main sheet out a tad and she began to slip along. A quick pull on the roller-furling jib sheet and she was just touching two knots. The cockpit was dry enough, so he slipped below to pull on some shorts and a T-shirt. Nick had taken to shaving his head so that his wet hair couldn't give him away. Putting the towels into a pre-filled sink of water, he settled into the navigation seat and studied the chart. He looked at his watch and wrote 04:11 next to *Orelia's* present position, then drew a 'cocked hat' next to 03:10 and 02:10. To the casual observer, it would look like the yacht had just been on a normal passage.

Finally, it was off with the waterproof headlamp, drying it on the paper towel and hanging it up on its home, a cup hook by the radar screen. Everything on board must have a home, then you just had to pick it up, not look for it first. The foreign engine noise was getting louder. He did some quick calculations, ten or so minutes to cover the two miles; whoever it was, was making twelve to fifteen knots. He squashed his face and scrunched up his eyes with his fists to make it look as though he was just a tired mariner on a long passage.

Bump. Someone was alongside; Nick's cue to go up on deck. Looking through the porthole there was a glimpse of dark, wooden hull alongside. He switched on the saloon light and went stumbling on deck looking sleepy, with just a shade of anger.

"What the...!" he shouted, until he saw the guns. Then his mood changed, hands raised, non hostile.

Two Moroccan customs men were on board, pointing their ancient, wooden-stock rifles at him. He could see the younger one had no magazine, and no bolt. So, this one was harmless. The other had a bolt, and was sporting a rusty bayonet. *Nice touch*, he thought. *The blood poisoning would probably kill you. He may have one up the spout as well.*

They were both sweating profusely and motioning him back down into the saloon. Nick just had time to glance over at the launch; it was old, tired and dark, with a dated fisherman's wheel-house. One thing was for certain, its speed didn't match its appearance. He led them down the companionway stairs; easy does it, no sudden movements. Once below, the boat rocked to starboard; was that another passenger boarding?

Nick looked up through the companionway. Someone used a dull torch to search around the cockpit and peer over the stern to the bathing platform. Then a naval officer of a sort came down into the cabin. Four gold rings on the shoulders, gold leaf on his cap. A bit over-kill for the skipper of a launch. He wore a side-arm in a leather pouch. Nick humoured them, played along. The launch revved its engine again. So, a fourth one had stayed on board. The yacht rocked as it motored away.

"What can I do for you, officer?"

Nothing. The man's eyes were everywhere, moving all around the cabin. He clocked the bottle of Johnnie Walker in its home in a recess above the saloon table; his eye lingered on it for a moment. Nick nodded at the bottle: "Would you and your men like a drink, sir?"

The tiniest inclination of the head, and Nick took it to mean yes. Seeking permission to move, he went over to the saloon table, reached into the well in the middle and brought out four plastic glasses.

He poured two generous measures and was about to pour the next one when the boss said "Two!" That made it clear. Only two would be indulging tonight; maybe his boys weren't old enough? Nick picked up the glasses and offered the biggest to the boss. He nodded, meaning, put it down there. Nick had a decent pull on his glass then placed it on the table.

The boss had four medal ribbons on his chest. Looking like an Admiral of the Fleet, his hands were behind his back like all good officers; his chin was slightly raised in a superior manner. He had the look of the desert about him, combined with that modern, more wealthy appearance and the golden skin colour; North African/Arab, Nick guessed. He was about 5ft 10ins, his hands were small and, if not exactly manicured, they had never done any labouring work. He had a thin and perfectly straight scar on his forehead above his right eye, like a knife wound, not an accident. Under his immaculately tailored uniform he was probably quite fit, a good shape to him if not exactly a muscle bosun. Nick realised the man was not as young as he first thought; he was difficult to age, maybe 35.

Over at the navigation table, his visitor turned on the flexible light and looked at the chart carefully; bending down close to it he examined *Orelia's* position, checking maybe, to see if someone might have made notes about where they were heading or what they were up to. *There's nothing for you there, mate*, Nick thought.

The officer opened the log book and studied the pencil shorthand for course made good, speed and wind. Turning his attention to the brass chart dividers he picked them up; instead of squeezing the top part to make them open, he pulled them apart as a kid would with a compass at school.

*This guy's never been to sea*, thought Nick. The officer then made a show of walking the dividers across the chart, but hadn't set them on the latitude scale next to *Orelia's* position. So what was he measuring? Nothing; this was all for show, for Nick and his boys to see. The man nodded as if all was well, keeping the dividers in his hand as he proceeded with his tour. He picked up his whisky and downed it in one. He didn't flinch, and that was also for show.

"Passport." The man spoke in heavily-accented English.

"Oh, yes sir, of course, right away." Nick moved to the chart table and opened the drawer. Immediately, the officer's hand was on his arm, guiding him backwards out of the way. The man rummaged through the drawer although the passport was right on top. He had a quick look at the back pages, but Nick suspected he was looking for something more interesting, some sort of trophy. Perhaps he would settle for a bottle of J.W?

The intruder rummaged around inside the drawer and reached for a packet of unopened Marlboro. He looked over at Nick.

"Please, please help yourself."

The man opened the cigarettes, put one in his mouth and slipped the packet into his trouser pocket, along with the brass dividers.

That's two things he's managed to pilfer and he's only been on board a few minutes. From his top pocket, the officer pulled a Zippo and proceeded to light up. Nick decided to let his strict no-smoking rules go on this occasion.

The thief put the Zippo down on the chart table and continued his detailed study of the cabin. Lifting a cushion here, opening a drawer there, he looked into the sink full of washing and curled his lip up in distaste.

What or how much does he want, apart from what he can half-inch? Nick decided to try and open up communications and cut to the chase.

"Would you like a...?" A palm came up in the international sign for stop, shut up. Nick started to get peeved. How long was this imposter going to keep this up?

The man moved forward to the heads and shower. He switched on the light inside the tiny compartment and Nick could hear him rummaging around. Didn't these people know about running on batteries? Nick took the opportunity to look at the two decidedly nervous guards; they hadn't taken their eyes off him. He smiled at Bayonet Brains, but got no reaction. If it got nasty, he'd be the one to watch. He had the eyes of a shark: soul-less black pits without a hint of humanity.

The younger one was a puppy, trying to look tough. His gapped, almost gawky teeth were permanently on show. Nick could break this one in a second, and the guard knew it, too. He could tell by the way Gappy kept a safe distance. Nick was fit and solid, built like a rugby player, with the scars showing all over his shining pate and on most parts of his body. He knew he looked lived-in. Nick smiled at the young man and he looked away. *Good*, he thought, *he's beaten already*.

The pretend Admiral made his way further forward searching and rummaging around. In the forward cabin, just above the anchor locker, he found the safe.

"Bring." Nick was encouraged forward. The boss signalled for the safe to be opened.

Nick shook his head, pleading, "Why, what have I done?"

The boss uttered his first recognisable sentence. "Open, Mr. Nick."

Nick opened the combination safe, but before he could put his hand in or step back his vision swum in confusing swirls. He collapsed to his knees. Up until then, there had been no warning of violence, no hint of trouble. Now his eyes were watering and he could feel something warm running down the back of his neck.

There was a loud exchange between Bayonet and the Admiral. Nick, slumped on his knees, could feel the anger rise in him as his vision started to clear. He tried to come to his feet, but stopped as the bayonet was pushed hard into his back. Had it not been so blunt it would have pierced his skin. All three were talking excitedly and the boss was pulling everything out of the safe.

Through the mist of his water-filled eyes Nick could see that the boss already had his old Navy Rolex on his wrist. In the meantime, Gappy was in the safe and had something in his hand. The boss whacked the guard's arm with his now-drawn pistol.

From his knees, Nick watched as the Admiral trousered the 1,560€ he knew the roll of money amounted to. He and the boss made eye contact, then Nick saw him nod towards Bayonet.

"Hey!" was as far as he got in protest. He heard as well as felt the thud of heavy rifle butt on the back of his head.

Nick lost all interest in proceedings as the floor raced up to meet him.

# 2

Nick drifted slowly into consciousness, then opened his eyes and tried to move. The pain was so intense he had to lie still again. White noise filled his head and hissed like an angry cobra. He focused on a fire extinguisher and slowly realised he was lying under the chart table. He remained in the recovery position, thinking about his situation. His ear was in something wet and sticky; the smell of blood was close. Something covered one of his eyes and it was damp. Things began to make sense again. Gradually the images and events replayed. The Admiral, his Rolex, the man with the bayoneted rifle; it must have been Bayonet Brains who'd hit him. And they'd taken his money.

Waves of nausea rose from deep inside. He tried to swallow, but there was no moisture in his mouth; it felt like it was stuffed with cotton wool. Taking slow and deep breaths, he lay still until the sickness abated. Looking along the deck, he saw his wrists were tied around the corner leg of the chart table. Water gurgled along the fibreglass hull like the sound of a free-flowing stream over rocks; that meant the boat was still under way. He had to get free, and soon. What time was it? The Bremont was gone from his wrist. How long had he been out? They couldn't have been gone that long as there was no daylight coming through the companion way.

They had used some old sail ties to secure him. He edged forward on his hip towards the knot he could see, then realised his ankles were also tied to the ladder down to the cabin. He could just get his teeth to work on the granny knot. The tears came as he moved. A rest, then as the throb subsided he tried again. Soon, there was a loose bite in the knot and he undid the first half-hitch, then the next. He eased his wrists out, and was free of the table leg.

The next move proved to be a mistake when he tried to sit up. The excruciating squeeze behind his eyes was so intense he thought he would pass out again. He let out a loud, gut-wrenching animal yell to help him stay awake. His eyes felt like they were throbbing in time to his heartbeat, which was pumping away like a sprinter's legs. He cupped his hands to his face and felt the wet towel bound around his head. Hands red, red and wet, he lifted it off and was shocked to see the volume of blood. It was all over the cabin floor. Whoever had put the make-shift bandage round his head had saved his life.

Nick freed his feet and shuffled over to the galley on his backside for fear of standing and repeating the agonising stabbing sensation. Opening a drawer, he got out a new tea towel and wrapped it tightly around his head. Delicate exploration with his finger tips revealed a lump the size of a tennis ball. It wasn't so much the lump that hurt; it was more that his brain felt like it was pulsating.

With the tea towel tied on, he shuffled back to the companion ladder and contemplated getting to his feet. If he got this bit wrong and collapsed again he could be out for hours. *Orelia* could run aground, or worse, he could bleed to death. He swivelled round and swapped position from arse to knees, and had to wait again for the sickness and pain to recede. Steeling himself for what would be the considerable challenge of standing up, Nick grabbed the saloon ladder with both hands and tried to pull himself upright. His knees were wobbling as he was bent over in a half-crouched position, head bowed, like an old man leaning on two walking sticks. Nearly upright, with lights still flashing in his tightly-clenched eyes, he yelled: "JESUSSSS!"

Sheer bloody-mindedness had him grip the ladder and refuse to let go. He waited; the flashing lights started to diminish. His breath came in short, sharp urgent gasps. The back of his eyes now ached, his head felt as though there was an ocean of surf sloshing around inside. He decided to hold on and wait, frightened to open his eyes in case that unbearable sensation came back. The sickness seemed less when it was dark. Upright and hyper-ventilating and with his knuckles white with the effort of hanging on, he risked opening one eye. To his left he could see the radar screen above the chart table, but it was off. Above the navigation station the clock read 05:41.

One step at a time, up the ladder then into the cockpit. The wheel was still moving in small increments to keep the course. Gingerly stepping over the coaming he looked around; no near lights in the pitch dark. No sight of land ahead or any ships nearby, thank God. All that was visible were the four, white, quick flashes from astern, the lighthouse on the island of Alboran.

It looked as though they had not touched the autopilot and *Orelia* was still ghosting along on the same heading of 285 degrees. Next he moved to the helm and looked at the radar repeater, they had left it turned on. The 360 degree sweep revealed no ship echoes nearby. There was Isla de Alboran almost dead astern, right where it should be. With bloodied fingers he switched from ten to twenty-mile range: a few huge ships way out to starboard, nothing else. They'd gone.

On to the thirty miles range, and... *what was that*? A smaller blip at twenty-six miles, moving away towards the African coast, heading straight for a bigger ship. Soon the two contacts merged into one. If that was the boss and his mates, he had made a big error and headed west, the same direction *Orelia* had been sailing whilst he had been out of it. Had they gone south-east, or straight into the Moroccan coast, they would have been out of his radar range or lost forever in the scatter of the African coastline. If that was them, of course, and it was a big ask. Now he had just one big echo, but it was something.

Apart from that, the Med was pretty dead so early in the morning. He switched on his GPS and could now see exactly where he was. The echo sounder showed deep water and the breeze had dropped even more throughout the night.

He punched in 250 on the auto-helm. The self-furling main was now a godsend; he rolled it neatly away into the mainmast, then completely furled up the jib.

For some reason, it didn't seem to hurt so much with only one eye open.

He chastised himself aloud: "What a fucking state to get yourself in, Carter."

Nick checked that both throttles were in neutral, pushed the two start buttons for the main engines and listened to them cough into life. No time to let the diesels warm up.

A quick glance below to be sure his lifting keel was up, and he pushed the twin throttles to full ahead. The yacht dug her tail in and the white water churned up behind. She was the only forty-footer he knew that had twin, lightweight, turbo-diesels.

*Orelia* was a one off. Built by Macgregor yachts in California, she had performance under sail and engine. He opened the transom valve and just over a ton of sea water ballast poured from the hull. As the water emptied, the yacht grew lighter and the speed kept on climbing. He couldn't kid himself that it would make a pretty sight; a yacht was never going to look right motoring so fast. By definition it had to have a lot of weight down low so she could carry the sail area. She was working hard to reach ever increasing speeds. Twelve knots and the bow wave was huge; fourteen knots and it was like she was trying to drive herself under water, pushing out a massive wake.

Then, with the ballast emptied, the nose started to lift, very slowly as the flat hull amidships started to come into play. She laboured away until she climbed up onto the surface of the water. With less wetted area and less drag, the engines were no longer struggling. The black smoke she was making faded.

Finally she was planing, skimming over the dark surface, and the shackles were off. The engine note eased and she bumped along on top of the near flat calm sea instead of through it. He had once had twenty-two knots out of her like this. Nick loved to see other yachties' faces when he passed them at this speed in a flat sea and no wind. The noise was doing his head no favours, though. He would also be eating up fuel at an alarming rate, and now he only had credit as a means of paying for it. He set George the auto-helm, and checked it could hold a steady course.

Nick adjusted the radar and narrowed the angle that the alarm would go off to just ahead of midships on both sides. Now if anything got in that area ahead of him, he would hear the high-pitch warning.

"If I ever get hold of those thieving..." he muttered, and stared into the darkness as his imagination acted out what he would do to the piratical trio.

*For now, look after yourself*, he thought. Checking the radar again and sure there was no craft or danger ahead, he went to patch himself up. He would never normally leave the helm going at such a speed and especially in the pitch black, but these were not normal times.

Water must come first. Lacking a saline drip, he needed lots and lots of fluid to start to replace the volume of blood he'd lost. He guessed his blood pressure was already low, hence the dizzy spells. Tentatively, he went down the steps to the galley, got a two-litre bottle of water and drank as if his life depended on it – which it did. He then shuffled over to the chart table and switched on the main radar screen, turned the alarm volume up to full and turned his sailing lights off.

"Darken ship please, Carter."

Next stop was the heads, where he caught sight of his reflection; it stunned him. One eye was puffed and swollen, his face was covered in varying stages of dried and wet blood, and his shaved head had a few more battle scars.

"Bastards!" he said bitterly. Opening the cabinet, he took out the pain killers, and popped two, then another two.

Still in shorts he stood under the shower and turned it on. The cold was a real shock, but certainly livened the senses. Carefully un-wrapping the tea towel, he put his head under the flow. The water in the white shower tray turned red and for the first time his head no longer felt like it was on fire. The blood spiralling down the plughole reminded him of the shower scene from *Psycho*. Watching his reflection in the mirror, a semblance of the person he knew began to appear. Turning to try and see the back of his head, he could just see the huge lump; it had a deep, half moon shaped gash in the middle, but it didn't appear to be bleeding badly now. The red blood cells were finally doing their bit and starting to clot.

"About bloody time," he muttered.

Nick stared at his sorry, beaten reflection and spoke aloud again: "You've been robbed, son; I can't believe you've allowed yourself to be mugged, and on your own boat. How did you let this happen?"

As he stood looking at his mirror image, a stark thought overwhelmed him. He froze and stared at himself. He was consumed with the sort of feeling that comes when you realise you've left your wallet on the train; the shiver they say you have when someone walks over your grave. That startling, horrible dawning, that something was seriously amiss.

Nick dropped his soap in the shower, and ran slipping and skidding in a cocktail of water and blood, forward to the safe. It was a big mistake. His head felt like someone was blowing up a balloon inside it. Grabbing both sides of the door to the forward cabin and with eyes screwed tight, he waited. The noise in his ears subsided. He opened his eyes and peered through the fog as his vision slowly cleared.

The safe was empty. On the floor, there was paperwork everywhere, with smatterings of blood on them. *Orelia's* owner documents, his yacht master certificate. Nothing else. His body tensed up.

Her pendant! It had definitely been in there. He looked at it almost every day. Now it was gone. Sod the money and the watch. Mariyah's pendant had been the most important thing on his boat, and maybe in his life.

Whatever happened to him, he would get it back.

# 3

When sailing the length of the Mediterranean from Cyprus to Alboran a few weeks earlier, Nick had worn the pendant every night whilst on watch. Sometimes he would catch himself tumbling it between his fingers, re-living some cherished moment. He had found it on a wreck dive seven years before in the Mediterranean. It was just after his Navy and North Sea escapades. He'd given it to her as an engagement present about a year before they got married, and she'd loved it.

Mari never went anywhere without it. He knew it was very old and probably worth a lot of money, but as soon as he met her, he knew it was for his girl.

The pendant also had a secret. Nick first suspected it opened not long after he'd found it in its near-perfect state. It seemed to have an almost indiscernible rattle. Maybe not even a rattle, an inner movement, a slight vibration when it was shaken. There were random wavy lines etched into the shell, but no apparent way that it opened. It had frustrated him for years.

In the end, he'd taken it to Musto, a street gold vendor come-jeweller he'd got on well with whilst working in Cyprus on an EOD job for some ex-Navy lads. Sometimes Nick would take on minor Explosive Ordnance Disposal jobs. This gave him the chance to catch up with the lads, to make some money, and, most importantly, to cadge more diving gear.

Whenever Nick was in town, he would sound out Musto by taking him little pieces of gold and jewellery he found on the dive site. Never once did Musto break Nick's trust or disappoint with his workmanship. He was always amazed at the old boy's knowledge of antiquities, and the work he turned out with such ancient hand and pedal-driven tools.

Whenever Musto presented him with a finished piece and the final bill, they would barter for half an hour or so. Then Nick would give him roughly double what they'd settled on. In these sort of situations, some people paid only what they were asked and thought they had had a result. Nick's reasoning was different; if you find someone good, pay them well and keep them on your side.

He had already returned twice to Musto's and on both occasions the old jeweller had just shaken his head. On the last visit he had intended asking for the piece back. Maybe it was all in his mind. Maybe it didn't open. It had been three months since his last visit, but when he walked into the shack, Musto was beaming. Clearly, he had cracked it.

Musto summoned his petite wife to fetch the piece, and she came back carrying it on a blue velvet cushion as if she were delivering a crown to her king. But it was still in one piece. Nick's heart sank. Then Musto dismissed his wife and performed a little miracle. He opened it. Theatrically he shielded his movements with his delicate, almost feminine, jeweller's hands. Then he showed Nick the trick of it. It was brilliantly simple and yet unfathomable at the same time.

Nick then presented the piece and its secret to Mari. She eventually took to wearing it all the time, but at first took some persuading to even put it on.

"It's too nice to wear everyday."

"Right, I'll have it back then."

For a long time, Nick, Mariyah and Musto alone knew that it opened. But one other person had the total trust of the couple, and they would both enjoy the teasing of Smudge.

Mick Smith, or Smudge (as he was inevitably known in the Navy), was Nick's partner, his best buddy and his shipmate. Their trust in each other was total. They had dived for mines and sat alongside 1000lb bombs during air raids together in the Falklands Conflict in 1982. Then they had found themselves working as a team again in the first Gulf war of 1990-1, where they were caught up in some pretty hairy mine clearance operations. Also, in the Navy, they had spent months living in cramped decompression chambers undertaking deep saturation dives. They knew each other's likes and dislikes, weaknesses and strengths. At one time they knew one another so well they could finish each other's sentences. Smudge stood a few inches taller than Nick at six foot one. He was tall and fit although Nick took great pleasure in calling him a lanky streak of piss.

Like Nick, Smudge was now out of the Navy - or officially anyway. It seemed to Nick that the only difference was that he no longer wore the uniform. Smudge now worked for the MoD in the secret back offices of Northwood in London. He was meant to put together naval procedure diving and mine warfare books, but Nick knew he spent most of his time scouring ancient charts and documents looking for virgin wrecks. It started out as a bit of a hobby but it was now how both of them made their fun-money.

Although Mariyah was the only person he would allow to call him 'Mickey,' he would make a pretence at not liking it, but secretly he would melt, especially when she used her high-pitched little-girly voice.

Both of them had been in love with Mariyah. If Nick was struggling to get some chart or sensitive information or equipment out of Smudge, her head would go to one side and she would flutter those huge dark eyes, saying, "Oh, Uncle Mickey - pleeease tell us, go on."

The time for the unveiling of the secret was not organised; it just happened. The three were sitting on the boat in Malta. They'd just had Christmas dinner and were wearing party hats made from old charts. They had also done some damage to a shipping order of cheap local plonk.

After twenty or so attempts, Smudge had reached the point where he was convinced it was one big wind-up, and that, what he called, *the mysterious gonad,* did not open. He had fiddled with it for two hours before announcing:

"That's it. It doesn't open. You're winding me up."

"How much?" asked Mariyah coyly.

"How much what?"

"How much do you bet I can open it?"

"You can't open it because it doesn't open."

She smiled, "How much?"

Nick was too drunk to get involved, but was happy to sit and watch the two people closest to him go through their ritual. Mari looked over at Nick and, although no words were exchanged, he knew she wanted his blessing to open it for their closest buddy. Nick just nodded; they understood each other.

They finally settled on a bounty of £100. She was only allowed to shield her hands with the logbook, and he was not allowed to cheat by moving the book, or from his seat. If he broke these rules while she was doing her magic, he would forfeit £200. Smudge had proposed she have two minutes to get it open. Then he wanted his cash. They agreed, and shook on the deal. Nick had to be the judge and jury. Mariyah was smiling as Nick started the stopwatch.

"Go!"

Nick counted down the last five seconds. Mari was still looking serious and fiddling with the pendant behind the logbook.

With one second to go, she shouted, "Stop!"

Nick stopped the watch.

Smudge was jubilant, "See... see! I told you it was a wind-up. It doesn't open. I knew it, I knew it."

Mariyah let him enjoy his moment as he rolled about on the saloon settee. When he sat up, she lowered the logbook with a satisfied grin. There it was, lying on the table, not in two, but four pieces.

If that wasn't shocking enough for Smudge, in the middle of the four pieces was a perfect ruby, the size of a large pea. It was gently rolling about the table with the motion of the boat. Mariyah's hands made a cup around the pieces so that it couldn't escape. Smudge was stunned. Nick and Mari looked at each other. She put her hand under the table searching for his; they gripped each other tightly. She was loving it. Smudge slowly reached across and picked up the four pieces.

What really threw him was that it was solid gold inside. He had known it was metal because of the weight, but he hadn't expected that. Now Smudge looked at the outside and could see what Nick had done. He had simply dipped it in some kind of dark blue stain or dye. It had the effect of making it look like a cheap oval trinket.

Smudge was suddenly sober. He looked up at Nick.

"Where the fuck did you find this?"

# 4

Not finishing his shower, Nick went as fast as his muzzy head would allow from his ransacked safe to the cockpit and stared, through one eye, at the dark horizon. It was 06:15 and sunrise would not grace the Mediterranean until 07:32. Looking at his radar he could tell the ship, and hopefully the launch, were still barely making headway. Maybe they were customs men, boarding a bigger ship. Nick doubted it, but this close to Africa, nothing would surprise him.

*Orelia* was half bouncing, half smashing her way along at an impressive twenty-one knots. It was not comfortable, but it was effective. Then the minor blip parted company from the bigger one. He watched the screen as the small craft left the ship and took off towards the African coastline.

Which to follow, the big blip or the small one? It was unlikely that the Admiral and his henchmen were still on the ship, if indeed it was them. Nick had to be sure. He'd have to follow the smaller craft. He could be dashing around the Mediterranean after the wrong boat half the night but he was not going to let this drop. If they were Moroccan customs men, he would have them hung, drawn and quartered. If they weren't, he'd make it up as he went along; either way they would pay.

Nick quickly extended an imaginary line on the radar screen of the suspect craft's heading and extended it South. It was heading for Morocco, and now the ship looked as though it was making headway again. It was making its way westwards towards the Straits of

Gibraltar. If he had guessed wrong and they were all on the big ship, they could be away into the vastness of the Atlantic, never to be seen again.

The only land on the radar at full range was the island of Alboran, now fourteen miles behind, and the tip of the huge peninsula that dipped its nose out into the Med and went by the name of Cabo Nuevo.

One thing was for sure. The *Orelia* was gaining on what he thought was the elusive launch. He had no idea whether it was them, or if they had radar; he had to assume they did, being this far out to sea. They were now about fifteen miles ahead and had altered course a touch more southerly. He reduced the yacht's engine revs and *Orelia* dropped back into the water instead of on it, and altered course to dead south. If they did have radar, he didn't want anyone on board thinking they were being followed. *Orelia* was now matching their speed, but he only had quarter-full tanks of diesel. This couldn't go on for much longer.

Going below to finish his ablutions, Nick had time to think about his actions. If it hadn't been for her pendant, maybe he could've let it go, put it down to experience. No, he was kidding himself. The value of the pendant was both sentimental and financial. As for his Navy Rolex, that stood him for about thirty-five grand on its own as they had recently become collectors' items. Plus, there was his cash and the state of his head and face. They would have to pay for that. He was getting into something best avoided but this had gone too far already. Perhaps he could get away with stealing it back and disappearing off into the Med. That would be the best solution. On the other hand, he didn't entirely trust himself to do the best thing. He would want revenge.

*What if Mariyah had been on board?* He shuddered at the thought. There is no way he would have let anything happen to her. He would have had to fight, and people would have been hurt, badly hurt. Not that they'd given him a chance to fight, or a hint of their intentions. They just wiped him out, from behind.

What would she do? She would tell him to leave it. Perhaps he would just leave it; that was obviously the best, the most sensible option. But he still found himself steaming headlong towards the African coast into God knows what. He promised himself he would just go and look, to see if the launch was there. If it wasn't, he'd go on his way to... to where? Nick knew he was lying to himself and grew angrier every time he thought about what they'd done.

Feeling slightly more human after a wash and re-dressing his battered head, he went on deck and thought about how he might change the look of *Orelia*. Nick figured it was going to take his target three hours to reach the North African coast. Looking at the large-scale chart of the western approaches of the Med, it was clear they were heading towards one of the little bays of Morocco or a port he knew called Al-Hoceima.

At last, the painkillers seemed to be having an effect. He could move about that bit quicker and with both eyes open without them welling up with foggy tears. Nick was still unsteady on his feet and suspected he was suffering from concussion. It wasn't just the deck moving under his feet, his head was decidedly woolly and he was still feeling sick and unbalanced. What he should do was lie down and rest, but there was no chance of that.

He made his way for'ard, up onto the deck to the main mast, making sure he had two handholds for every movement. He then had to think hard about how to manage his spinnaker pole, which on any other day he could've done blindfolded. He lowered the long pole to the deck, moved aft to the cockpit, then pulled it down into the well with him. Taking out a reel of four millimetre rope from one of the seat lockers, he began to fashion a jury rig.

He managed to change the yacht's appearance by adding a short aft mast, turning her from a sloop with one mast to a ketch with two. Eventually, he had a wobbly and slightly off-centre mizzen-mast. Standing

back he thought it might look alright from a distance...
to a land lubber.

Periodically he checked his radar. The target blip was
nearing what Nick thought was their target destination
of Al-Hoceima. He had kept the blip about ten miles to
the west of his position. It was almost 10:00 when Nick
lost his target in the scatter of the Al-Hoceima headland.
He now felt sure they didn't know they were being
followed. They probably had no suspicions whatsoever.
Not only had they knocked Nick severely on the head,
tied him up, and left him sailing on a westerly course,
but from their point of view, no yacht could possibly
follow a launch around the Mediterranean at twelve or
more knots, never mind catch up with them.

Killing both engines to save fuel, Nick sailed past the
Ras Tarf headland and set a course across the Bay d'al
Hoceima towards the Point De Los Frailes, just north of
the town. He then went below and broke out some of his
Army/Navy ration packs. Selecting two packs of chicken
curry, and boiling some water, he forced down the calorie-
laden, energy-giving food and drank as much water as
his stomach would carry.

For all he knew he might sail straight into full view of
the launch, which would not be clever. Just in case, he
rooted around for a pair of aviator sunglasses, an old
Captain's hat and a shirt, tie and blazer. The disguise
might make him look older, and perhaps more
prosperous.

He went up on deck and sucked in his surroundings.
The Rif Mountains stood away to port, and he took in the
perfect clear-blue sea and the cloudless sky. He adjusted
the sails and sat listening to the silence. The background
smell of the desert intermingled with the sea in his
nostrils. Even the VHF radio was quiet. The
carbohydrates he'd just taken in started to work and he
realised how weary he was. Not wanting to get into port
until near dark, he settled down. He was still sitting up,
but gravity soon hauled on his heavy eyelids.

As he drifted in and out of his restless, sleepy state, his mind wandered back to a previous visit to Alboran, last nights dive site. He'd been there with Mariyah in early March '04. It had been a happy time, only weeks after their honeymoon on board *Orelia*. Nick had borrowed a towed magnetometer from the Navy divers at Gibraltar, and had to buy a tiny, experimental side-scan sonar. This was so new and so sneaky he knew it was going to cost him. It incorporated a piece of kit in the towed fish called, in military parlance, an SBP, or Sub-Bottom-Profiler. It could look under the seabed as well as above it. Best of all, having been developed for the Navy, it was idiot-proof. No need to pore over complicated data sets; it gave it to you in colour pictures.

The use of such equipment involved no exchanging of money; just a bar bill that still made Nick cringe weeks later. The session had gone on for three days, in one form or another. Mariyah had wowed the bubbleheads with her looks, her sense of humour and her uncanny ability to stay the course. She had cried out laughing at some of the bar games the younger divers had got up to. When she joined their ranks and ran up the Rock with them in formation on the Sunday morning, she had been promoted to goddess status.

Despite Mariyah's protestations, Nick had paid the island of Alboran a short visit on the first night. Having circumnavigated it as close-in as he dared, he declared it safe to invade. These round-the-island trips didn't take long, as Alboran was only about 600 metres long and 300 wide. The island was composed of red, volcanic rock, and was the top of a long-dormant volcano whose head just cleared the surface of the Mediterranean. The coast was mainly of jagged, sixty-foot-high cliff faces, with two coves on the southern side. Nick had chosen one of these for a landing in his dark green inflatable canoe. As he had suspected, there was no one living there. The lighthouse was completely automated and unmanned.

And there was no sign anyone had been on the island recently.

Back on board, he told Mari that he had accidentally broken the island's ancient radar.

"What do you mean, accidentally?"

"Well, I slipped and some superglue ran down into the bearing and then I dropped some volcanic sand on top of it. It sort of stopped turning, and smoke came out of it," he had said, grinning.

No one had turned up the next day, or the day after that to fix it, nor had anyone asked the couple to move their yacht on. They had spent the second day there pretending to have engine problems and sheltering from a force six gale. They thought they had been rumbled one day when a Spanish military helicopter had flown over, but nothing came of it.

They had been dragging the two bits of kit around the island of Alboran in the dead of night for the whole week, trying to nail down the position of a wreck Smudge had given them. According to Smudge's latest hunch/guess, or, "After months of exhaustive maritime research, with much skill, determination and above-average knowledge of the job," as he put it, this was the big one.

"But Mickey, they are all The-Big-Ones, according to you!" Mari had cried back to him over the phone.

According to Smudge, in 1540, a Berber pirate who went by the catchy name of Mustafa ben Yusuf el Magmuzed Din, or Al-Borani to his few friends and fellow cut-throats, had thrown the Christians living there over the cliffs into the treacherous waters, and claimed the island for himself. By doing so, he had claimed sovereignty over the only small island in the middle of the western approaches to the Mediterranean and had the perfect bolthole to raid trading ships of all nationalities. Or so he thought.

The Spanish, having lost two of their ships in the area in a year, had sent three frigates to investigate. Al-Borani had seen the approaching Spanish warships and loaded his considerable booty on board his skull and cross-boned vessel. The pirate, confident he had the fastest ship in the Mediterranean, immediately ordered his anchor hawsers to be axed through. According to the ancient Spanish account Smudge had unearthed, the pirates were barely making way, when a fluke cannonball took down their main mast. The Spanish fleet then homed in and pounded Al-Borani's vessel into submission.

The Spanish seaman's account, told of the events as they boarded her. They ran Al-Borani through with a boarding pike and forced open the hold to recover the gold and other treasure. The sailor's story told of them filling the small boats to the gunwales with loot, but as they were unloading their cargo onto the Spanish frigates, Al-Borani's ship had turned turtle and sank. With air-supplied diving many hundreds of years away and the island being the tip of an underwater mountain that dropped off to crushing depths, there were no records of any attempt to recover the remaining treasure that had been lost with Al-Borani's ship.

The side-scan sonar, had shown an area of higher than normal volume just south of the island on the screen that came with the towed fish-like scanner. When this was overlaid with the readings from the magnetometer, it was clear something was there, something with metallic echoes and man-made, despite being on the opposite side of the island they'd expected it to be. The good news was that it lay in only 32 feet of water, which meant it was within oxygen diving depths, hence long bottom times with no need for decompression.

Nick and Mariyah had dived all over the Mediterranean but never had they witnessed marine life so abundant and as varied as that which gathered around the island.

The Alboran Sea, as the western-most reaches of the Med are known, is where the Mediterranean and the Atlantic Ocean crash together. It is the life blood of the Med's eco-system. The nutrient-rich Atlantic can only come in through the relatively narrow opening known as the Gibraltar straits. Without this gateway, the Med would be no more than a huge pond, another dead sea. Deep underwater, the Atlantic pours through the gap and tumbles over the submerged cliff face between Europe and Africa. The colder Atlantic waters drop from around 150 metres to over a thousand in just a few miles, and mix with the warmer and more saline Mediterranean. This turns the Alboran region into an oceanographic motor in the Mediterranean basin. This easterly-flowing, cold, food-bearing current is then eventually forced to the surface by an underwater mountain, 55 miles long and 4,500ft high. The top of this gargantuan edifice just manages to poke its head above the waves in the form of the Island of Alboran.

It was as if fish knew they were safe there and that food would constantly well up from the depths. No trawler could pass within twelve miles of the place; even rod fishing was illegal. It was whilst on their very last night dive that Mari had made the first significant discovery.

The plan was to finish the survey dive and then sail to Gibraltar to put her ashore so that she could make her way back to the UK to receive her degree. It was midnight and they'd been in the water for an hour. Nick had pointed out that they might discover things of financial value if she spent more time looking and searching for artefacts, and less time thinking about her Marine Biology degree. She had spent one whole dive studying a large area of *corallium rubrum* (a rare red coral) then examining a group of *patella ferrunginea*. Nick told her it was only a limpet, but she informed him it was so rare to see in the wild that it was on the verge of extinction.

He had to threaten her with a purely supervisory and lookout role on board the yacht to re-focus her on the job in hand. It appeared to work until one night, when having started grid-searching a marked area with the metal detectors they were surrounded by a school of bottle-nose dolphins. It had stopped all work. A young dolphin, intent on playing all around Mari was closely chaperoned by its mother. Even Nick couldn't work on through such a display of agility and affection. Through her mask Mariyah could not hide her bursting enthusiasm for the beautiful creatures. Nick knifed open a clam and gave it to her. She stood on the bottom and tried to entice the baby to take it from her hand. It wanted to, but caution won. So Nick slowly moved over to her, turned off her headlamp and the metal detector, then moved away again. The young dolphin circled nearer and nearer until with a gentle pluck, it took the mollusc. As quickly as they had arrived, they disappeared and Nick had to come over to her again, to do some further re-focusing. She hugged him in the water, and even with the mouth-piece in, she had been smiling broadly.

*

When she looked down, she was no longer in the search area Nick had painstakingly marked out for her with red and white poles. She had drifted out of it while keeping pace with the dolphins. When she switched the detector back on, it bleeped loudly in her earpiece; too loudly. She winced, looked down at the controls and turned down the elimination control. This had the effect of weeding out unwanted echoes, such as aluminium ring pulls, lead or small pieces of rusting metal. Still it whined in her ear, so she turned the volume down and down until it was near zero. Still, she could hear the constant noise.

*What's wrong with the stupid thing?* She thought, shaking it. She moved the metal detector off of the rock, and the noise stopped. She put it down next to the rock, and it started again. The rock was an odd, long shape, and had a green tinge to it compared to its surroundings. She traced the length of the rock with the metal detector, the noise constantly in her ear. Either the detector was broken, or this was no rock. Mari looked across the clear, dark water to where Nick had his head buried in the volcanic sand, about twenty feet away. A cloud of smoky

36

sand and silt rose where he was digging with his trowel, a pair of fins were waving about above his head in the eerie glow of his headlamp. She looked back down at the long, straight rock and traced it again with the detector's magnetic hoop. The noise whined on, and every time she moved it away, it stopped.

She looked up and over at Nick again. He was now standing on the bottom looking over at her. She beckoned him. When he arrived at her side, she just gave him the detector and pointed. Her eyes were wide with excitement at what she had found.

# 5

Nick jumped awake to the *squawk* of the VHF. He'd been dreaming of her again. Mariyah's silky voice slowly faded as the inevitability of reality bit. Thankfully, it was the laughing, happy, face that had come to him. Not the torn, ravaged and burnt effigy that sometimes visited during darker times. He shook his head free of the image. Time was meant to be a healer. How much time *did* it take to heal a memory?

It was this place that was doing it. Al-Hoceima was where he had said goodbye to her. He would look around at the radar, make sure everything was alright, then nod off. Sometimes it was only for a moment, at others maybe five minutes or more, but it recharged the batteries.

When the headland was in full view, about two miles away, he stood up and saw stars. They taunted and danced a jig against the back drop of a perfect blue sky. When he felt marginally better, he laid out his ropes, broke out some fenders and prepared himself for entering harbour in his bastardised ketch. But there was one more job to be done to create his new vessel. Breaking out a pack of black stick-on letters, Nick took them to the bathing platform and sat down next to the name of his yacht on the transom. The capital 'O' peeled off easily enough and he stuck it back into the pack. Selecting another couple of letters, he wiped the transom with a dry cloth and, RELIA became RELIANT. This exercise was entirely for the Admiral and his friends. If Moroccan officials came on board and noted the paperwork didn't match his boat name, which was highly unlikely, he'd be right in the dog-house.

As he admired his handiwork, the seaside town came up on *Reliant's* port bow.

At first, Nick barely recognised the ancient and familiar place. Then he realised that a walled harbour had been stuck on the outside of the old port. A large white ferry was berthed in the outer harbour, together with some tugs, and what looked like a new customs launch. This confirmed that he'd been done over by a bunch of pirates rather than what counted as officialdom. What made it worse was that he had been taken in by them.

He was right, there was nothing in there. Maybe there was nothing anywhere? He didn't know if what he had been following was his target, but he still didn't turn out to sea; he had to keep looking.

Steadying his powerful ex-service binoculars, he scanned the port to check there were no obvious hidey holes or official berths for his prey to lie up in. He began to have the feeling he had been wasting his time, energy, fuel, and everything else. He wanted to find the bastards and their boat, but then, he didn't. If he did, he had no plan; if he didn't, then what would be his next move? Nick flashed up both engines and dropped all sail. He sighed and said out loud, "It's no good putting it off; go in there and have a look, you soft bastard. You're just looking for a berth for the night."

He was early. It was only 20:12 and still not dark. The sun was disappearing over the high Rif Mountains to the west, and the dark red velvet curtain of the now hidden sun cast its long shadow over the marina. What little wind there'd been had died and it was now the most balmy of evenings. It was so still the palms hung limp and lifeless around the marina, casting their mirrored reflection on the red-blue water. The glare had ghosted away and the setting scene was easy on Nick's sore eyes. The plan was to look around, then sleep like the dead.

Real sunset was not until 21:30, but he could find excuses to postpone the inevitable all night. Motoring in along the end of the newly-built breakwater, Nick peered anxiously along the yachts. Every time he saw a vaguely dark hull he would lift the bins to look at the craft in detail. Nothing resembled the launch in the outer harbour, so he motored in around the green-topped rock that used to mark the outer limits of the old fishing port.

Passing the rock, he went as slowly as he could towards the fishing part of the shelter. There was hardly any activity at this late hour and darkness would soon be upon him. Nick's experience told him to always buy fuel where the fishermen bought theirs, and never where yachties gathered. The price could be double. He could see a dozen large oil drums on the jetty and decided that is where he would have to top up *Orelia's* hungry fuel tanks. Paying for it would be another matter; credit cards were not universally accepted in Africa. Hard cash would always rule.

All tension had left him, he would not find them here. They were gone, he could relax. He would try to stay in the fishing part of the harbour. There were, after all, two other yachts there, even if they were obviously Moroccan. He knew he was in for an early and rude awakening as the fishermen departed in the early hours, but there was no way he wanted to go through the immigration signing-in process in the marina. This, in turn, would mean paperwork and questions, maybe a bit of bribery, and signing out again in the morning. From his point of view, it was always better to stay out of the system altogether. If *they* weren't there, he might as well spend the night anyway, life would be a lot clearer at daybreak.

Nick went into the fishermen's haven, put *Orelia's* engines astern, and spun the wheel over. The yacht stopped in her own length. Two children on a small Moroccan trawler were fishing over the stern and waving to him. He waved back and tried to smile but suspected it turned out more like a grimace.

He picked the trawler nearest the oil drums; a once white, high-bowed, wooden vessel, covered in bright orange buoys. As the yacht edged in closer, an old man appeared on deck and looked suspiciously at him and his vessel. Nick motioned he was coming alongside, and got a stone-faced response.

"Suit yourself," he said, and crabbed his way in beside what he had decided would be his host trawler. He bumped gently alongside and tried again to make sign language contact with the fisherman to take his ropes, but to no avail.

"Ah sod ya!" said Nick and tied up anyway. He clambered over the stinking vessel and immediately saw why the fisherman might not have been too pleased to have any European for company. He was frantically trying to hide his illegal monofilament driftnets under tarpaulin. Nick stood on the quay and tutted loudly, shaking his head to make sure the man knew that he knew. He then made a point of watching as the old man shuffled off round the back of the wheel-house and tried to stuff a net down his engine room access.

Even as the evening faded, Nick was still stiflingly hot. Standing on the quay, he looked down at himself and realised another reason why the fisherman might have given him such a cold look. He was still in his Posh Nick outfit. Without making eye contact with his new neighbour, he jumped back aboard the fishing boat and climbed over to *Orelia*. Standing in the cockpit, he took off his shirt, tie, hat, trousers and ridiculous sunglasses and threw them down into the saloon. He followed the clothes and sought the comfort and familiarity of his shorts, his oldest T-shirt and a pair of battered deck shoes. Tucking his passport in his pocket along with his pocket telescope, he came back on deck and hopped across the fishing boat.

The old man, now ensconced in his wheelhouse, gave him a double-take, perhaps unsure if it was the same person. Nick just nodded and picked his way amongst the fishing nets, pots, rusty wire and ground gear that would be familiar to trawler men anywhere in the world. The oil drums he had been drawn to were definitely diesel; he could smell it, and the ground was black and slippery underfoot.

Turning right towards the mountains, he sauntered past the pleasure craft to the natural central rock slap bang in the middle of the harbour, then climbed up the well-trodden, ancient steps cut into the volcanic sandstone. There he found a vantage point, sat down and scanned every craft with his tiny telescope. There was nowhere to hide a forty-foot dark-hulled vessel. She would stand out like a sore thumb amongst these white, expensive pleasure craft. He scanned the marina repeatedly, then the anchorage by the beach. It wasn't there. He sat back with his head on a rock and winced as his lump hit the immovable object. That was it, it was all over. They could be anywhere by now; they may have gone north or east after knocking him senseless. You've followed the wrong radar echo, mate; they're long gone.

Nick's head lolled sideways. He woke from a micro sleep - that horrible feeling that most people have had when driving or watching a late-night film. Not here you soft git, he said to himself. Get back aboard; leave is cancelled.

As Nick clambered over the adjoining fishing boat, the old salt was still in his wheel-house smoking something that smelled suspiciously like the famous Rif Mountain hashish. The old devil, he must be seventy. Nick smiled and wondered if *he'd* still have the mind to smoke marijuana if he ever reached such a ripe age. He nodded again as he crossed the man's reeking craft and thought there was just a hint of an inclination back. *Maybe he's mellowing with the weed*, he thought.

Nick went below with the full intention of going to bed, but Johnnie called. He poured himself three fingers and felt the warm glow as the black-labelled liquor burnt his throat. He knew if he sat down that would be it; his eyes would go, and he'd be out. So he went back out on deck and stood taking in the clear dark sky. Looking out towards the breakwater, he became aware of the fisherman looking out of his smoke-filled wheelhouse towards him. Nick looked back, and this time, they fixed on each others glares. Then Nick cracked a grin and raised his glass. This time, the old boy definitely nodded.

"Right, it's now or never." He went below and filled another tumbler with a generous tot, took it back to his cockpit and raised the glass to the man, and beckoned him. The old man just stared back like a suspicious dog being offered a biscuit by a stranger, so Nick gingerly climbed between the vessels with the two glasses and took them up to the wheelhouse.

He smiled and took a sip from his own tumbler. The old man moved towards the window, removed a wooden wedge and the window slid down. He took the glass, smelled it and gave Nick a smile that had barely any teeth involved; it reminded him of a row of bombed houses. The man then offered Nick a pull on his giant joint. The end was wet and nicotine-stained and didn't fill him with enthusiasm. He shook his head.

The fisherman had a leathery, deeply-lined face that had clearly been at sea all its life. His nose looked as if it was being kept up by the support of what resembled a two-legged table: a Mexican bandit type moustache. He still had a full head of grey-black hair, and the biggest ears Nick had ever seen.

They both had a good pull at their drinks and looked at the moon. It was just poking its head over the western mountains. Then Nick decided to try and break the ice with his rough Spanish:

"This - your boat, YOUR BOAT, captain, errr capitan, you?" he pointed.

"Si, si mi barco," my boat.

"Argh, good - bueno."

With that, the old boy got up and disappeared down below and came back with a plastic mug full of ice.

"Buen hielo," he said, good ice. It sounded like a statement, but Nick knew that ice was like gold dust tonight. The whisky tasted better instantly. This might be a good night after all.

"Qué sucedió?" asked the fisherman, pointing at Nick's head.

"Oh, this? An accidente, the boom." Nick pointed to the boom on *Orelia* and motioned it smacking him on the back of the head with the palm of his hand. The old boy thought it hilarious.

"El auge. Heh heh, Inglés." It obviously made it all the more funny, Nick being English. He just kept saying 'Inglés, Inglés.'

As he laughed, Nick felt sure the smog of his breath could bring small children to tears and fell trees at a hundred paces.

English may be the world's preferred tongue, but no one told the Moroccans. The official language is a bastardised Arabic, with a bit of the indigenous Berber thrown in for good measure. Being so close to Spain, nearly all the Northern Moroccans have a smattering of Spanish as well.

An hour passed with the two old salts having a broken, gesture-ridden, conversation about the sea, fishing, women and whisky. As far as Nick could gather, his new friend didn't rate women, as they made rubbish fishermen. He positively scoffed when Nick pointed to his wedding finger and posed the question of marriage. He liked the whisky though, for sure. Nick had reined back his intake, but kept his guest's glass topped up. The cocktail of drugs and alcohol had the old boy rambling on in a strange mixture of Arabic/Spanish, with some French thrown in. Nick tried once to steer the conversation to fuel, but failed to make any headway. Eventually, he went back aboard the yacht and came back with a whole bottle of J.W. The breath-monster's eyes lit up. Nick then walked across the trawler and onto the jetty and plonked the scotch on the barrel which had a brass siphon pump stuck in the top.

Fish Breath wobbled out of the wheelhouse, and for the first time, Nick realised he was about five foot tall.

He came up onto the jetty and stood shaking his head, pointing up at the hills, saying, "No. El jefe, El jefe!" The boss, the boss. Nick tried to indicate he only needed a small amount, but he just shook his head, mumbling on. Nick tutted and made to go back aboard with the scotch until, with a surprisingly strong grip, the fisherman grabbed his arm. Nick looked down at him and realised the rank odour may not have been just his boat. It was him. His whole being oozed dead fish. Guts, bits of fin, scales, and blood were all over his smock, in his moustache. It was... part of him. It was who he was. The maritime overtones now entwined with the smell of whisky, marijuana and strong tobacco. Nick swallowed hard. No wonder he never got on with women.

"Cinco," he said, pointing at the bottle.

"FIVE!" said Nick in as exaggerated a manner as possible. Shaking his head he weakly tried to walk off again but was restrained by the vice-like grip. He just looked up at Nick with a questioning look.

"I'm meant to barter, I really haven't got the time, inclination or will-power for this," he said. So unpicking his fingers from around his forearm, Nick broke the grip and headed back to the boat. The man was distraught, jabbering away in the background. Bartering is a way of life in Africa and Europeans will never get it. Nick disappeared below and could hear the old boy still rambling on the jetty.

He came back out with four bottles and lifted them high into the air. The breath monster was back. He tried to nod as if he was resigned to defeat, but his glee shone through. He retrieved a bunch of keys from somewhere inside his fishy tunic and unlocked the padlock on the hand-driven pump. Then with surprising agility he hopped back on board his boat and returned with a coil of filthy plastic hose.

Whilst the old man was winding the pump, Nick shot off and filled his glass. When he gave it to the fisherman, he offered to take over the winding so as not to interrupt his drinking time. Fish Breath was now full of himself and chatting away about God knows what as Nick wound the handle faster and faster.

Nick became aware of a deep rumbling beneath his feet, turned and saw the ferry behind him slipping away from its berth. He turned back to his task and kept nodding and encouraging his companion to keep talking, then he could keep winding and *Orelia* would have a few more miles of fuel in her.

*I could change her name back to Orelia, tomorrow*, mused Nick as he swapped pumping arm. Then he looked again at the ferry and saw it was lit up so brightly that it was impossible to see her navigation lights. This was true with all passenger liners nowadays, he thought.

Meanwhile, Fish Breath lit a normal cigarette and continued another story. Nick had to keep ushering him away from the fuel while he smoked, and he seemed genuinely puzzled as to why.

Still idly watching the ferry leave port, his eye was drawn to a red navigation light making its way around the large rock he had sat on just before sunset. He couldn't see what kind of vessel it was until it ran past the lit-up pontoons of the marina. The boat had a dark hull, and was about 40 foot long. Nick stopped winding and felt in his pocket for his 'scope. After he had fumbled for a moment, the single, magnified picture leapt into focus.

"Would you Adam and Eve it?" he said.

"That... could... just... be... it!"

# 6

Staring through the tiny telescope, Nick strained to see the outline. The vessel left the glow of the pontoon lights and was quickly swallowed by darkness. The craft rounded the rock and was heading straight for him. Snapping the telescope shut, he stepped back into the cover of the buildings. It looked familiar. If it was his launch, it would have to come into the fishing half of the harbour as it would not look right berthed amongst the white pleasure yachts. It was a pure coincidence that just when he thought he had lost his prey, he had moored right where she was headed.

Fish Breath was still jabbering away and took Nick's pause in winding to mean it was his turn. Stepping up to continue the transfer of fuel, he looked at Nick, now so obviously cloaking himself in the obscurity of the dark, then out to the launch, then back at Nick. He finally shut up as the launch drew closer. The old man then said something he didn't immediately understand.

"Guerrillas."

Perhaps he'd had a run in with these not-so-gentle men. As it motored slowly past their position, he knew it was the boat. The engine pitch, the deep throbbing note of an over-powered diesel. There was nobody on deck.

Back-lit by the shore lights, the faint silhouette of the helmsman flickered like an old movie through the glass of the wheelhouse. The launch passed close to *Orelia's* starboard side. Nobody had given his boat a second glance.

47

Nick watched it motor towards the end of the enclave, then, he heard the engines kick astern. Right at the end of the harbour and on the opposite side to Nick, was a large boat under refurbishment. Earlier in the evening he had walked past the bamboo scaffolding that hid it from the elements. The launch turned to starboard to go alongside the ugly lash-up, then disappeared from view.

Nick left his new pal muttering to himself. Staying in the dark, he made his way to the end of the basin. Creeping between two open-topped potting boats on the quay, he edged towards the water to look across at where the boat should be.

It was gone.

There was no launch beside the tarpaulin hovel, and no mooring beside it. Then he heard the sound of an engine. The launch was inside the tented structure. The still luminescent wake bubbled white and revealed the path of a vessel. The boathouse was built over the water, over a berth. There was a curtained door to seaward to hide its innards.

*Very clever, very sneaky.*

It became quiet as the engine was shut down. The sudden silence carried the murmur of voices from within the tented structure. Then Bayonet Brains appeared and struck up a hushed conversation on a mobile phone.

*Please let the Admiral be on board.*

Bayonet was soon joined by Gappy, then, a teenage boy. Nick hadn't seen him before, but, he remembered, there'd been a boat driver that morning; he'd just never laid eyes on him.

Bayonet was no longer dressed as a customs man but wearing the full-length traditional white gown called a *djellaba*. It looked like a kaftan with a hood. The other two were dressed in jeans and dark shirts. The boy was wearing a baseball cap. The youngster snapped shut the padlock on the door to the launch's home, and they all gathered outside. When Bayonet had finished his call, they walked off, towards the town. Nick crouched in the shadows. There was nobody else on board, he was pretty sure of that. He waited another fifteen minutes hidden amongst the boats, watching, waiting, listening, before he headed back.

Fish Breath had gone. The pump was still in the oil drum, but it was locked. Nick pushed the top of the drum and it was light, empty. Whatever he had on board would do. He crept over the trawler and onto *Orelia* and after doing up his fuel filler cap, went below. In the saloon he paced forward aft, forward aft. *Now what?*

The Admiral had gone. Where, he had no idea, most probably onto the larger ship the launch had linked up with in the early hours. Jesus, had that been today, this morning? It was around twenty-one hours ago that it had all started.

The Admiral may not even be on that ship. The launch had gone missing for a few hours that evening. Where did they go?

The only link Nick had with the Admiral and his pendant was through these thieving bastards. It was possible, however unlikely, that the Admiral had left Nick's stolen belongings on the launch. They could be in a safe. He didn't believe it for one second, but now realised he had to look. What harm could it do?

It was time to go swimming again.

*

In the darkest corner of the harbour, opposite the launch's shack, were some stone steps worn smooth by the path of countless fishermen. Sitting on the last step with his fins in the water, Nick took a bearing with his hand-held compass on the launch's hidden home. He had been hyper-ventilating for fifteen minutes, taking in large gulps of air to flush out the carbon dioxide from his system. He drank in the largest breath he could hold, dropped into the water with hardly a sound and sank to the bottom of the harbour. Wearing his mask, shorts and only one lead weight, he looked at the compass and pushed off from the wall behind him. Long slow finning movements sent him arrowing diagonally across the gap that was, he guessed, no more than forty metres. He had toyed with the idea of nonchalantly walking round the jetty and trying to gain access, but dismissed it just as quickly. The jetty was well lit.

The water offered him a way in, and it was his element. It was where he had spent most of his life. Where he was at home.

Keeping close to the bottom of the harbour, Nick swam unhurriedly across the gap, his dull red head light casting just enough light to show the bearing on the compass. All the while, he had the picture of his intended target firmly in his mind. He was trying to hit the left hand of two pontoons that poked out from the end of the ramshackle boathouse. The pontoons had to be centred on a pile, like all the others along that pier that weren't hidden from view.

Even at the harbour's deepest point of about four metres, there was a hint of moonlight. As the contour of the seabed began to shallow, the moonlight faded. Something was blocking the moons milky light, he was under something. Nick stopped swimming, and looked around. There, to his left, was a square wooden pile. *You've not lost it.* Then, holding onto the pile, he turned out the headlamp and shimmied up as though climbing a tree. The distorted air/sea interface grew closer in his mask until, slowly and silently, the very top of his head broke the surface. There was just enough headroom to breathe under the floating pontoon and Nick filled his lungs.

In front was the dark shape of the launch. He was now inside the floating hidey-hole; the hanging garage tarpaulin curtains hid him from the outside world. On the surface, he moved over to the hull and gently put his ear to it. He listened like a suspicious parent eavesdropping on a teenage couple left alone for the first time. There was nothing.

Nick could reach one of the lines sagging close to the water. He pulled down on the rope and the boat moved.

When it stopped, he went under and, pulling himself up on the rope, came high out of the water until he could lock his arms straight. With a knee over the pontoon, he was out of the harbour.

He removed his jet fins and mask, took a carabina from his belt and hung his engines over the sagging rope. He grabbed a paint-stained rag, wiped his wet body over, then stood on it. The water from his shorts now dripped onto his makeshift bath mat. That noise and the sound of his own breathing, was the only thing he registered. He twisted his headlamp on and surveyed the scene.

The jumbled mess around him had all the hallmarks of a major boat overhaul. There were wood, tools, paint, fittings and work-benches all over the place. The wheelhouse door on the far port side was slowly moving as it hung open.

Its owners obviously felt secure enough to leave the launch open, maybe because the outer door to the boathouse was locked and no one went swimming around there in the middle of the night; until now.

Nick turned his waterproof LED headlamp from red to white and gingerly stepped over the wooden guard rail onto the launch. It was a heavy boat, and hardly moved when his weight was transferred onto the deck.

She had once been a trawler, he was sure of that. There was a large round metal hatch on the port side that would have been used to pour tons of ice below to preserve the fish. Creeping forward, just aft of the anchor windlass, he could see a pair of short double doors that led below. One side was open. The deck was of thick, pitch pine. Looking over the bows, the stem-post hung over the jetty, which was covered in boat repair paraphernalia. He crept towards the wheelhouse. Amidships was a large square hatch which would once have given access to the fish hold. Nick felt himself drawn to the open wheelhouse door, but before he went in, he continued his upper deck search.

Then he heard a voice.

He moved instantly towards the starboard side and his exit route. It was a deep, man's laugh, coming from the marina area. He switched his headlamp back to red.

He made his way down the starboard side towards the stern. Just aft of the long wheelhouse was a closed hatch. He lifted it slowly and peered below. The smell of diesel lead to a metal ladder running below, and he stepped on the first rung. Crouching down with his head inside the engine room, he switched his light back to white. What sprang out at him was not what he expected to see in a battered, 1930s, ex-trawler. The Perkins engine was brand-spanking new; far too big and powerful for this vessel, and bloody expensive. There was a petrol generator down there, some scuba bottles and a host of brand new spares.

Back on deck he moved round to the open wheelhouse door. Peering through the glass windows he stepped inside and was hit with the alluring smell of strong coffee. There was an old-fashioned, spoked, ship's wheel, which contrasted starkly with the state-of-the-art electronics on board. Radar, sonar, GPS, Sailor VHF, electronic chart navigation - the works. He turned the Global Positioning System on. Aft of the wheel was a large fixed table and a chart of the western Med lying on it. The position where the launch had linked up with the bigger ship was marked in red biro. There were no other marks. Nick tapped the rendezvous point, "A bit lax with the old chart work, boys."

The GPS beeped to announce its readiness. Nick scrolled through the way-points stored on the memory. One was the liaison position of the larger ship, one was Al-Hoceima and one was Gibraltar. There was also one with no name that was a lot further east in the Mediterranean. Nick picked up a pencil by the ship's wheel and read out the latitude and longitude that was stored as Way-Point-9.

"32 degrees 56 minutes and 42 seconds north." He turned and put a faint mark on the large chart behind him. Then he read out the second part of the vector, "13 degrees 12 minutes and 15 seconds east." He then moved two fingers across the chart until they merged. "Tripoli... Libya?"

Then he went through the menu and selected: *Reset-Clear All WP's*. With a grin he selected: *Yes*. And that was it, the memory was wiped clean.

To the right of the wheel was a set of steps. At the bottom he walked straight into the galley area to port. There was the strong smell of Turkish coffee and eight cups on the side. Moving forward into the main saloon area, there was a large dining table with seating all around and a pilot berth to starboard.

Hanging just forward of the single berth were some Moroccan customs uniforms.

*Gotcha.*

Nick rifled through the pockets but there was none of his gear and nothing of interest. The Admiral's uniform was missing. The forward cabin was split in two, port and starboard. He searched through the drawers under each bunk and in one were some cards, a single bullet for a large calibre rifle and an old French novel: *Le Comte de Monte-Cristo*, by Alexandre Dumas. Sticking out from under the book was his Bremont Super Marine watch.

"Exhibit one, your honour."

Nick hung the deep diving watch over his wrist and saw the familiar dent in the titanium strap. It read 01:06.

Without realising it, he was making a mental plan of the boat. It was an old habit. Finding your way around a mine in nil visibility at the Defence Explosives Ordnance Disposal School (DEODS) always had you making a drawing in your head. It was the way he always did it, and it worked. He would do it whilst visiting warships and more recently, mapping out an underwater wreck site in his head, or even looking around yachts.

Lifting bunks and being careful to put everything back as it was, he continued his search, silently, meticulously, in the surreal light of his dull-red head lamp.

One bunk smelled different. The scent of perfume and a woman, perhaps?

He now knew he would not find Mariyah's pendant. The boss was away, and with him the money and the Rolex. He may have given the crew a sweetener of Nick's cash, but he doubted it.

The black Bremont was back in his possession; now he wanted the rest back.

Nick suddenly stopped his search. The layout plan in his head was finished, but something was amiss. He went into the saloon and studied the old square fish hatch in the roof, and then moved forward to the port cabin. Even on the other side of the wall, looking up at the deck head, he could not see the underside of the metal ice hatch. He went up the forward steps from the cabin and out onto the deck and stared at the round, metal ice-shoot lid. So where did it come out? There was no sign of it below?

Going below he could now see what was wrong with the virtual plan in his head. Someone had built a false bulkhead. It was cunningly done. Between the saloon and the forward cabin was a wall around four feet thick. It looked equally old on both sides and there was no way in. Access, he decided, must be from the metal hatch on deck.

He crouched and studied the hatch. There were two rusty holes where a key or wrench had been used to open it. Nick jumped up and moved aft and back down the engine room access. There, hanging on the bulkhead over the petrol generator was a rusty, long-handled key, with two small protrusions. *Bingo.*

The key fitted. He forced it to move anti-clockwise, first with his knee, then by hand; it then unscrewed easily. With the lid off the entrance hole, it was clear it would be a tight squeeze for a man of Nick's size to get down there.

Lying on the deck for a closer view, he shone his head torch inside. There were four, long, wooden boxes with rope handles stood on their ends. One had been opened and the lid lay discarded. The others were held in position by a ratchet-type strap. On the deck below was a large bundle of brown waxed paper. Also, what looked like a large biscuit tin and a smaller wooden box lay discarded. There were no ladders down, but there was a worn shelf on one side that previous visitors appeared to have used as a step.

Nick lay there, looking and thinking. There was something familiar about the large boxes. He had seen them before - they were definitely military. He had to have a closer look.

Acutely aware that if anyone came back on board, he was done for, he went down anyway. He lowered himself in until his foot found the step on the bulkhead, then bent his knees until his shoulders jammed in the entrance. He lifted his arms above his head and tried again. He took some skin off the lateral muscles under his armpits on the rusty edge, then he was in.

As he suspected, the open crate would once have held rifles. It had been opened down there, and the weapons passed up. These were not any old rifles, but wooden stock Armalites, AR-10 semi-automatics. The boxes had been coated in matt black, like the launch, but the painted-over white AR-10 writing could still be seen. Each box would carry four, standard stock military assault rifles. Inside the lid was a black stamp that read:

Fairchild Industries
Manufacturing licence
Artillerie
Inrichtingen
Holland

He could see the other three had not been opened, at least not for a long time, so they still held their deadly contents. Squatting down and looking around, he wondered why the men would need assault rifles. And if they had them, why didn't they use them last night? Nick rocked back on his haunches, and his bottom touched something. It was a small black wooden box.

There were no tell-tale paint marks to give away the contents of the smaller container. The lid had four brass screws securing it; all were undone and protruding out of the top. Nick pulled one and the lid lifted easily. Inside were six professionally made hand-grenades. They were egg-shaped, a drab, olive-green, and smooth-skinned, except for a ridge around the centre where the two halves were joined. Under one grenade was a Russian operator's manual. On the top of the yellowing leaflet was written RGD-5. Nick looked up at the entrance hatch and racked his brains. He had seen these scattered about the ammo dumps and ambush houses in Kuwait and Iraq during the Gulf campaign.

He picked one up. It was a Russian anti-personnel fragmentation grenade. If his memory served him correctly they were old, but still in service around the world. They were filled with about 110 grams of TNT. He placed it back in the box - carefully.

Then he noticed a recess on the deck, a shelf, set-back. There were nine more of these boxes, some a slightly different shape, all held in place by bolted wooden battens to stop them moving. One was painted army green and had NFDD M84 stencilled on the side. That was military talk, but for what? He'd heard it somewhere.

By the shelf was the biscuit tin he had seen from the deck level. Nick was about to leave the hole, but opened it anyway. Inside was a bright yellow, hand-held detector. He recognised the symbol on the gauge.

It was the Trefoil, the international radiation symbol. He was staring at a Geiger counter. Why would these people need to measure radiation? Why was it hidden down here, on a nondescript boat on the coast of Morocco? Nick switched it on and it gave the familiar, clicking sound. It went into self-test mode, and then registered a small amount of radiation. He pointed it slowly around the tiny stowage hold. When he pointed it inboard, towards the saloon area on the other side of the bulk head, it clicked loudly. Something was radio-active there, or had been on board.

Nick's heart was racing. He couldn't think straight. Time to get out of there, get back to the safety of his boat. Taking more skin off his armpits making good his exit from the hold, he replaced the lid and took the handle back to the engine room. He hung the handle back on its hook and came up the steps.

As he was leaving the hatch, he heard the scrape of keys moving in the padlock to the boathouse.

# 7

As the key turned in the padlock, Nick took two steps towards the port side, vaulted the guard rail and moved his back against the wall near the door. There was no time to ensure silence. The keys no longer jangled in the lock. Both parties were silent and still, neither knowing what lay the other side.

The door creaked open under its own momentum until it came to rest, clanking against an empty paint tin. Through the opening and along with the light from the jetty came the smell of decaying fish basting in the humid night. There was no shadow of a man in the doorway. Nick tried not to breathe. A bead of sweat trickled down his forehead and into his eye.

The silent stand-off continued.

Suddenly there was a noise and a searing pain shot across Nick's back and kidney. Whoever was outside had swung at the indentation Nick had made by backing against the tarpaulin wall. He dropped to his knees as much from the shock of it as the sharp pain in his back. He looked up, then saw the swish of long white robes as his adversary showed himself.

Bayonet looked round the corner, saw Nick on the floor and moved in for the kill. He had a piece of wood about four inches square and four foot long. He swung it like a golf club in a wide arc at Nick's head. Nick moved backwards and to the right and tried to protect himself with his left arm. The club hit him a glancing blow on the elbow and forearm, taking with it a long piece of jagged skin.

Bayonet's midriff was now unprotected with the momentum of the wild swing, and the heavy weapon had taken his arms high into the air. Nick, already crouched, moved onto the balls of his feet and seized his moment. He drove forwards and up at the man's sternum with all the bunched-up power in his thighs. Nick's head was down and his arms wide as he found his target.

Bayonet's feet left the ground as Nick's shoulder smashed into him. The wind was driven out of his lungs and Nick momentarily got the smell of halitosis, a mixture of sweet liquor and strong tobacco. The wooden club bounced off the jetty behind them. He pumped his legs and carried Bayonet backwards, over his shoulder, until they both crashed into a sturdy work bench. Nick's legs stopped him as he slumped forward across the bench, and Bayonet flew off his shoulder and into the shadows. There was the sound of splintering wood, and tools landing on the jetty. Something splashed into the water. Nick paused to take stock of his injuries. He was alive and able to fight, that would do. He looked over the bench to where Bayonet had landed. It was dark back there and he couldn't see him.

Nick heard a movement to his right and caught a glimpse of white as a doubled-up figure scurried around behind the launch. He now had a choice. Either, jump into the water and make good his escape, or... or what? There was really no other choice.

If he left his man here, the chances were that he would follow. If he went to sea, they would run him down. And if he went into the marina aboard *Orelia*, they would surely pay him a visit by morning. Nick wasn't even officially in the country so he couldn't go asking for help. Anyway, he had to question his new friend. There was also the small matter that the man had nearly killed him, twice. The night before it had been pure luck he had caught Nick with the flat, wooden part of the rifle butt and not the brass end-plate. That would have depressed his skull and it would have all been over in an instant.

With his anger renewed, he turned and calmly walked out of the door.

He shut it behind him, snapped the padlock on the hasp, then walked to the end of the floating finger and sat with his feet in the dark water. Bayonet was now locked in. Nick took a deep breath, dropped into the harbour and came to the surface back inside. Now the dull lights of the wheel-house illuminated the launch.

*So, scared of the dark are we?*

Revived by the cold of the sea, Nick dragged himself out of the water. With the salt water stinging the new wound on his arm, he stood in a wide stance, ready.

"Come out, come out wherever you are!" he called. Perversely, Nick was beginning to enjoy himself, and went in search of his quarry.

\*

This English was going to die. How did he get here? How did he find us? Never mind; he, Aghilas - The Leopard - was going to kill him. He would slit his throat like he had the Germanic one who had tried to stop them robbing his boat. Then, oh what fun they had with his woman. It was a shame this one had been alone.

The English was big and strong, so The Leopard would have to be careful, but to listen to his squeals as he bled him would be fun. This... Nik could not be allowed to ruin their sideline. If the Captain found out he had been on board and Aghilas had let him live, he would face a terrible death. So, he would not find out. It would end here.

He made his way to the galley. Taped to the back of the door in a low cupboard, was his father's Turkish Jambiya. His favourite knife. The curved blade was exquisite in its craftsmanship, made from the finest Persian wootz steel. He felt the cold blade and thought how the English was bare-chested; that would mean watching the blade sink in. Even more exciting. The handle fitted snugly into his fist. He felt the familiar warmth of the walrus ivory. The knife would taste blood again tonight. The English was saying something in his repulsive jabber. It meant nothing to Aghilas. What loss was a westerner? He would offer this man to Allah as a sacrifice. He crept up the forward steps anticipating a quick and bloody one-sided knife fight.

*

Still dripping wet, Nick inched below, searching, listening. He saw Bayonet's feet going up the forward access steps. He turned and went back up through the wheel-house and onto the deck to face him. They both reached the deck at the same time. Nick wanted to beat this man to a pulp. Then he saw the flash of the blade.

"Shit, that's not fair!" he said.

Bayonet no longer looked a foregone conclusion. Nick reached inside the wheel-house and took a smock that hung just inside the door. Without taking his eyes off his opponent, he wrapped it tightly around his left hand and forearm and walked towards the bow. Bayonet was grinning, but focused.

*He's done this before*, thought Nick.

He would use the longer reach of his feet to keep Bayonet at bay. Years before, Nick had been a follower of the Korean art of Taekwondo. He and Smudge would spar regularly. Smudge was a student of Karate, which meant they could each glean something from the other's discipline. Hours of sparring teaches you to move, to anticipate, and to get used to fighting. If you rarely fight, the adrenaline coursing through your veins can make you do stupid or rash things.

As both men started to circle the large hatch, Nick focused on the blade. And on not panicking.

Bayonet was flashing the blade around; he was skittish, sweating, and then Nick remembered he had smelled alcohol on his breath. He carried the self-confidence of a drunk.

"Come on then, piss head," he said, beckoning with his fingers.

Bayonet moved up onto the hatch and made a diagonal slash at him. Nick stepped back, which encouraged Bayonet on. He was getting excited, and moved in again. With a shout, he made an exaggerated swipe across Nick's belly. Nick parried with his padded left arm and went for a straight front push-kick to the solar plexus. He made good contact with the sole of his bare foot, and Bayonet staggered backwards with a look of shock. He tripped over the fish hatch and landed on his back. Now Nick was smiling, and Aghilas was angry.

Their arena was the confines of an old fishing boat, and it could be the place of death for either of them. Aghilas leapt to his feet and slashed the knife around in a flurry of exaggerated hacking and chopping motions. He was suffering from an adrenalin rush and had lost temper and control. None of the swishing blade movements came close to their target.

The adversaries continued to move around each other. Nick was attuning to the rhythm of his opponent. He'd had more than one or two dust-ups in his life, and in his experience it wasn't until you squared-up with an opponent that you really knew how it was going to turn out. Unfortunately, by then it was usually too late. Too late to then notice how broad he was, how thick his forearms were, or how his fists looked like huge hammers. Those were times when you thought, 'I've made a mistake here; this is going to hurt!'

*

Aghilas made his mind up. He was going to gut the westerner. He saw him relax and went for his favourite underhand feint. The knife flashed in towards the flesh of his belly. Just when he thought he had stuck the English like a pig, his head exploded in pain.

*

Nick had seen the clumsy move, pushed the blade to one side with his protected arm and hit Aghilas with a straight palm strike. He rammed the heel of his hand up into the base of Bayonet's nose. He hit him so hard that the cartilage in the end of his nose hurt Nick's palm. The shock of the blow and the sheer trauma of the strike turned his nose to mush. He didn't fall over as Nick had expected, and still had the knife in his hand. So Nick leaned backwards then lunged forwards with all the strength of his neck and arched back. He drove his shaved head into the same place that his nose had once been.

Something gave way under his forehead, and it wasn't the already-broken nose.

It was not strictly a Taekwondo move, as he'd learnt the Glasgow-kiss in its birthplace, Scotland.

Aghilas took a pace backwards, stood for a split-second longer, then crumpled to the deck like a knocked-out boxer. He fell at an odd angle and lay still. His eyes rolled up into his head, then closed. Nick stood over him and saw that there was an unnatural hollow to the middle of his face, and it was filling with blood. He kicked the knife to one side, and leaned down to feel the carotid pulse in the man's neck. There was one, but it was erratic.

"I thought I'd killed you then, mate."

He took the smock from around his arm and placed it under his head to catch any blood and laid Bayonet's face to one side to stop him from choking on his blood or tongue.

Then he took stock. He had a vague idea of leaving the fallen man somewhere to be found in the morning, and maybe try to make it look like a mugging. Bayonet would not be overly keen to tell many people that he had lost to a man he had robbed the night before. Most importantly, he wanted it to look like nobody had been on board, and that would be impossible if Bayonet was running around looking for him. He moved about, tidying up and putting things back where they had been. He also checked the finger jetties and cleaned up as best he could.

Then all work was halted by a hollow, thumping sound coming from the boat.

Nick cautiously moved over and looked towards the prone figure. His right foot was jerking, moving as if he were being electrocuted. Then Bayonet made a sort of gurgling grunt and let out a loud exhale of air.

Nick jumped back on board just as Aghilas took his last breath. He knelt beside him and felt for a pulse. It kicked once under his fingers, then once more... then nothing. His foot twitched again, and went still.

Nick stared down at the body for a long time. The blood had stopped coming from its nose, and that was because there was no longer a working pump within to force it out.

"Shit, shit, shit!"

Nick moved about aimlessly, in a daze-like state. Then he realised what had to be done, he ditched the man's curved knife over the side and turned out the lights on board. Then he gathered his fins, mask and headlamp and went back again. *He's still dead*, he thought wryly.

He spoke aloud: "Think man, think. Right, get yourself and your man out of here, ASAP."

Nick tied a rag, then the smock over the body's head and with an old carrier bag he found in the wheel house secured it round the neck with string. He dragged the corpse aft, behind the wheel-house, checking he was not leaving a trail of blood. Scouting around inside the boat-house, he found a short piece of heavy chain and tied it around Bayonet's waist. Whilst securing the chain, he felt something under the body's garments; it was some sort of leather money belt with two zips and a larger, buckled pouch. Nick undid it and put it around his own waist.

He found a coil of unused thin line and opened it, then took the end and tied it to Bayonet's ankles. Manoeuvring the body up onto the gunwale, he hung it over the side by one arm then let it slip. It hit the water with a noisy splash, but with the help of its chain belt, it sank near the curtain, which conveniently hid all the grisly proceedings. Nick's last view of Bayonet as he paid out the line was of a plastic bag and one hand reaching up as if in desperation as the dead man disappeared from view.

Scouting once more around the deck, Nick saw some blood on the fish hatch. He went in search of an open paint tin, and found one by the door. He wiped the evidence of wrong-doing as best he could with a rag, and smeared the black paint over the stain. Then he picked up the coil of rope and climbed onto the jetty. Putting his swimming gear back on, he lowered himself into the water.

Ducking under the boathouse curtain, Nick came up outside and could just see the outline of his boat some eighty metres away. He looked around the vessels, walls and jetties and checked there was no one about. In no state to sit and calmly hyper-ventilate, he took a bearing of his mast and left surface.

The reel of line was over his right arm, and as he made off across the small harbour it spun and unreeled behind him. Nick couldn't give the compass his undivided attention and felt sure he was getting pulled off-course by the resistance of the unravelling reel. About a minute into the swim he glided to a halt and slowly headed up. The top of his head and mask broke the surface. He was indeed too far right, and had about thirty metres to go. Nick aimed at *Orelia's* stern, stood to attention and sank again. This time, his hull came into view and he worked his way aft until he saw the unmistakable twin rudders.

He pulled himself up and onto his bathing platform like a swimmer exiting a pool. The relief of being back home was short-lived. Looking back across the harbour he thought: *you are by no means out of the shit yet, my son.*

Fish-breath was nowhere to be seen. Moving to the seaward side, Nick passed the line outside the shrouds and put a turn round the jib sheet winch. After looking around the harbour to be sure no boats were moving, he heaved in on the line that led back towards the boat house. With the remainder of the coil on the cockpit floor, the line eventually came up taut. Nick then put more turns around the chrome winch and heaved. The clicking of the winch seemed way too loud for his heightened senses. The line then came up to the surface of the water, but didn't go straight back to the launch. *It had better not be snagged; please tell me it's not snagged.* He put the winch handle in the recess and wound it until the thin line was bar taught and straight. He then wound slowly, praying for movement.

Suddenly, the line went slack. The body must have moved. Nick wound like the winch-man on an America's cup racing team. The line came aboard smoothly and coiled down in a bunch at his feet looking like a snake's honeymoon. He was allowing himself the luxury of relief, when, about ten metres away from *Orelia's* bow, the line went tight and refused to move. He thought about just keeping going, but the winch could easily snap the line. The body would then maybe get stuck under whatever it was in the middle of the harbour. Worse, it might well pop upright in the middle of the harbour, in broad daylight and just as Nick was leaving harbour; then who would they want to speak to? With a sigh, Nick resigned himself to having to pay Bayonet one further visit.

Jumping down below he lowered the lifting keel, came up with a half-empty bottle of water and tied a length of line to the neck. He walked forward with the bottle in his hand and jumped over the side landing as upright as possible to minimise the noise. The time for silence was over; speed was of essence. He turned, found the blue line and pulled himself down it. On reaching the bottom a few metres further on, he swam straight into a pair of handlebars. The line went under the front wheel of a moped. Nick still hadn't seen Bayonet and was waiting for the shock when it happened. He pulled the line but it still didn't give, so pulling himself a little further on he came to a coil of thick rusty wire. *Fuckin' fishermen*, he thought.

Bayonet's feet were under the bite. He looked back up past the body's now uncovered knees and in the glow of his headlight he saw Bayonet, with his ghostly white djellaba gown floating up around his neck. Some air had become trapped in the plastic bag around his head which made him sit up. His arms were moving freely in the disturbed water, like a grisly Mexican wave.

Nick had seen lots of dead bodies in his life and job, many of them in the water, but he would never get used to it. It wasn't right to see the human form under there; it was always shocking, even when expected. Nick grabbed the body's wrists and tied them together with the line that led to the bottle floating on the surface. Then he moved the wire off the trapped feet.

Back on board, he wound the winch-handle; it went tight, then gave as the body began to move across the seabed again. He wound quickly until the bottle was just level with his bows. He then went forward with the boat hook, grabbed the bottle, moved it round to his port side and tied it off to a guard rail stanchion. Nick now brought the thicker line from the winch drum forward and came up on it until, shockingly, a pair of sandalled feet broke surface. He then adjusted the stiff until it was under the keel. Nick pulled up and aft, tight on both lines and hoped Bayonet would behave and stay under the midships, forward of the fin keel.

With the body secured and hidden, he went below. He had just killed a man, it was not a feeling he was overly familiar with. Nick's stomach lurched and his head hurt as he rubbed his temples. He took off his weight-belt, shorts and mask and dropped Bayonet's leather belt into the shower tray.

He drank a litre of orange squash straight down, then picked up the still-wet belt and carried it to the table. On the back of the belt was stamped: Aghilas Lehri.

*Was that your name?*

Nick then envisaged the body strapped to his hull. It was a realistic visualisation and summed up his predicament.

He sat and opened the first zip on the dead man's belt. Inside the pouch was a set of keys on a ring with a bird of prey feather attached to it, an ancient-looking BMW fob, and some change.

In the next zipped compartment he found a roll of wet money. Some Moroccan, and some Libyan. *Libya, what are you doing here?* Then he undid the two buckles on the large pouch and looked inside. There was a new-ish mobile phone and some Euros. He wondered if that was maybe his money. Nick took out the phone and held it between two fingers as water came out of the key pad.

"That's buggered that."

He sat back, alone and silent in his saloon. *Now what?* Alternative scenarios raced around his head. In the end, it was simple. He knew what he had to do.

"Shift the body, and call Smudge, that's what."

It was 03:50. Arguably the best time to dispose of a body. He untied all his ropes, brought in his fenders except for two up front, one port, one starboard, which coincided exactly with the ropes to his passenger beneath the hull. Nick pushed one of the start buttons on *Orelia*. The engine seemed to splutter into life twice as loudly as normal in the deathly quiet of the night. His two fuel gauges teetered just under a quarter full.

He waited. No one stirred - no lights came on. He put his starboard engine astern at minimum revs and reversed out of the fish port of Al-Hoceima. Then he had a horrible thought. *What if Aghilas were washed forwards now he was going astern?* He was tied to go ahead, so the water moving over the hull would force the body onto the ship's long drop keel. He put *Orelia* ahead and spun her nose round to face the Mediterranean. As soon as she was moving dead slow ahead, Nick went forward and checked the two Bayonet ropes: both were tight. He left his steaming lights off.

A quick look at the chart told him to head North East for the nearest, deepest hole. Setting the auto-pilot to zero four zero and still on dead slow, Nick headed out to sea, and not without a nervous glance over his shoulder.

As Al-Hoceima's lights faded astern of *Orelia,* he began to feel slightly better. He went below and found his ancient mobile phone. He had kept it for a reason: it had Mariyah's last text saved on it and he could not yet bear to upgrade it. Switching on, it found a signal and eleven text messages scrolled down his screen. He ignored them and dialled Smudge's flat in Notting Hill, London.

It rang six times before the recorded message came on. He hung up, and tried the mobile number. That went to his personal message which was abrupt and very professional.

He accepted the invitation and left a message:

"Smudge, it's Nick. I don't care if it's gone four in the morning there. Wake up and call me or I'm gonna keep ringing you every five minutes. I've stumbled on something out here - something I need to speak to you about *urgently.* Does Twitching Tug still do the security at Westminster? Oh, and can you do an internet search for me and see what the prisons are like in Morocco, and how long do you get for murder? Cheers. Call me. NOW!"

He hung up and did the same on Smudge's home number.

"That ought to get the lazy bastard out of his scratcher."

Half an hour out, *Orelia/Reliant* sat silently drifting, engines off. The echo-sounder read a depth of 1,650 feet. With a strange butterflying in his stomach, he walked forward and cut the port rope, bringing the water bottle inboard. Then he did the same on the starboard side and sat in the pitch black with his feet hanging over the side. He had a mental picture of Aghilas, bound hand and foot, hanging upside down directly under him, with a bag over his head. With a sigh, Nick cut the second rope and estimated how long it would take Bayonet to sink the half mile to the seabed. As he did so, he wondered about the man's mother, his wife - if he had one - and kids.

He stared down into the black water and thought about what he had done, then realised his phone was ringing.

# 8

Fumbling to press the right button, Nick finally blurted out, "Smudge?"

"No-it's fucking Santa Claus. Who else is going to call you at three in the morning? And don't forget the fucking time difference. Didn't you get my texts? No, you can't have, 'cos your phone is never on. If it is, you switch it on and use it at 4 am, which for you nocturnally-minded types, may be normal, but for those of us who like to sleep when it's dark is a total pain in the arse..."

Nick waited until the storm abated, then said: "Shut up, will you. Did you get my message?"

"No. What message? I just called on the off chance you may be up. Just to shoot the shit, see how you were really. Course I got your message, you numbskull. Not that I gleaned anything useful from it. Have you been on that weed out there? I hear the stuff from the mountains is..."

"Smudge, shut up and pin your ears back. I'm in the shit... big style."

"Too right you are! I was tucked up in bed with a dancer young enough to be my daughter when all my phones start ringing. I get this message from an ex-friend, asking me to check out the D.Qs in Morocco. Nothing odd about that if you hang out with African drug-lords maybe. You're not top of my Christmas card list at the moment, I can tell you."

"Will you shut up and listen?"

"No, you listen...!"

"Smudge!... Shut up! I've killed someone."

"You've *what*?"

"Jesus mate, I told you to pin your ears back. I think I've... I've killed someone."

"You *think*?"

"Well, to be precise, I have definitely killed someone."

"Where is he, who was he?"

"It doesn't matter who he was. He's underneath me."

"What! You're sitting on him?"

"No. You're not getting this, are you? He's under the boat. I've just dumped him in 500 metres of water wearing a big chain belt."

"Jesus Christ man! I've got this horrible feeling you're not kidding are you? What happened?"

"I haven't got time for all that now, I need your help."

"YOU haven't got time for that now? You called me, remember? Oh no... you've done something else haven't you? You'd better start telling me what you've been up to. I thought you were meant to be diving around Alboran, not slotting the locals. It *was* a local, I'm guessing."

"I can't tell you it all now, it would take too long. Yes it was a local, and I *was* diving around the island. I was robbed Smudge, mugged on board *Orelia*, they took... well, whatever they wanted. The short of it is, I followed a boat back into Al-Hoceima."

"Jesus, that's where you said goodbye to Mariyah, isn't it?"

"I know, I know. They stole the pendant Mick. I couldn't let them get away with it, so I followed them. I was so angry mate. You know what that pendant means to me."

Just hearing her name, and talking about her and the pendant, Nick's voice broke. His body was so weary he could barely sit upright in the saloon. Smudge could hear the stress in his buddy's voice, so lowered his tone and said, "I can guess how angry you were but... did you have to kill him?"

"It wasn't like that. Honest it wasn't. I boarded this old launch that they were on and had a look around. I found guns Mick. Armalite AR10s, and hand grenades.

"Shit! You've rumbled a bunch of local guerrillas I expect. Can't you tell the local law?"

"Oh yeah. I can see me walking into the local guardhouse with that story, and telling them I've already taken care of one them. No, that wouldn't be a good idea. Anyway, I hate to say it but you're right. That isn't the whole story. I also found a Geiger-counter on board!"

There was a long silence then: "What the fuck would they want with one of those? It wasn't a hospital one, was it?"

"I don't know, mate. And there's something else. There was a reading of radioactivity on board. You know when we used to use the Mine Radiographic gear in the navy? Well it was like one of those. Something hot had either been on board, or was still there, but I didn't see it. On its own, I wouldn't be so worried, but with the weapons... I don't know. I don't like it."

Smudge just whistled as he thought about the implications. Then asked, "Did anyone see you - kill this bloke, I mean?"

"No."

"What do you want me to do, Nick?"

"I want you to call Twitching Tug. Please tell me he's still the security officer at Westminster?"

"Yeah he is, but what can he do?"

"Well, last time I spoke to him, he said he was always out on the lash with the MI6 boys. They check out the foreign nationals that go round the House of Commons. He could speak to them, maybe, I don't know. I'm clutching at straws here. What do you think?"

"I'll call him now and give him the same shake you just gave me. He'll know someone."

"Smudge, my phones beeping. The battery is on the way out."

"Jesus H Christ man, haven't you charged it? Hang up, turn it off and I'll text you at say... 7am."

"How can I charge it, I haven't been alongside for weeks?"

Smudge sighed theatrically. "Nick, there are 12volt chargers, solar chargers, you can even purchase spare batteries you know. You really have got to catch up with the twentieth century if you're gonna spend as much time at sea as a - as a fucking dolphin! Right, turn it off, and don't go getting yourself in any more shit in the next hour and a half. Okay?"

Nick said okay, but the line was already dead. He looked at his battered, varnish-stained phone, it had one flashing battery bar on it. So he turned it off.

# 9

Smudge called ex-Lt Commander, Richard (Tug) Wilson. It was just after 3 a.m. in the UK, and he got no response on the home number. Not knowing his mobile number, he worked his way though a list of divers who had worked with Tug since leaving the Navy.

"What a surprise. Nobody wants to answer the phone at this hour."

He tried another number and got an answer.

"Jim? It's Smudge - no! Don't hang up, I need a favour. Yes it's urgent and yes, someone has died."

He got Tug's mobile number and tried twice, hanging up just as the answering service came on. The third time he recognised the gruff voice; it was even hoarser than usual.

All the closely knit team of divers knew Tug as a likeable officer who was heavy-drinking, hard-nosed and hard living. He was a bloke to have on your side in any stressful situation. He'd been everywhere, and done everything in the diving and bomb disposal world, both in the Navy and since leaving.

After apologising for his timing, Smudge explained the situation, receiving only periodic grunts to confirm he was paying attention. "Uh-huh," at intervals appeared to mean carry on, so he did. Smudge heard no grunts when he got to the bit about the Geiger-counter, but he did hear Tug lighting a cigarette. *This man is hard core*, he thought. Eventually Smudge had explained everything, except the bit about the dead man.

"That's it – that's the lot?" Tug asked as he blew smoke into the phone's receiver. Smudge had a vision of the man, head in hands, sitting on the edge of a bed, thinking and drawing on the first coffin nail of the day.

"Leave it with me and I'll get someone to call you. You say Al-Hoceima is his nearest port? Okay, okay, seeing as the daft sod's phone is dying I'll get someone to call you. I know how it feels. Don't move, Smudge. Stay by your phone."

Smudge padded bare-foot into the flat's kitchen and switched the kettle on. Then a voice came from the bedroom: "Mick... come to bed will you?"

"In a minute love, in a minute. You go back to sleep."

Shutting the door to the bedroom he sat amongst the debris of his bachelor pad, and drank one strong coffee after another.

Nick never asked for help. He was self-sufficient almost to a fault; he must be worried. Poking out from under a copy of Exchange and Mart was a photo with Mariyah's laughing face. Smudge dragged it out and looked at it. The three of them were sitting aboard *Orelia* just before Christmas dinner in Malta. Smudge smiled, and thought about the time they'd all had. Diving, drinking, eating, the blue water, the perfect sailing. They'd even had a good two weeks as a foursome, which was about the limit of most of Smudge's relationships, but the holiday-maker had gone home and they were soon back to three.

They were his two closest friends, but that changed in March '04. He had last spoken to her early that month about the wreck on Alboran. She was a godsend to Nick: she could work a PC, keep a mobile charged, and handily, ensure it was switched on. This was a revelation to Smudge as he usually couldn't reach his partner from one week to the next. Mari had playfully argued again with Smudge just after she had supposedly found a bronze cannon from the wreck. She was buzzing and highly excited on the phone. In that week, she had swum with a baby dolphin, found a bronze cannon, and was coming back to the UK to get her degree.

"I will see you soon at Waterloo station, Mickey Smith, and I may have some more gossip for you." She had then given that infectious giggle, and hung up. Those were the last words he had heard her speak.

# 10

*Spain 2004*

Nick and Mariyah had planned to leave Alboran with plenty of time for Nick to pick up a lucrative charter booked to leave Malaga on the 11th of March. He also wanted to drop Mari off in Gibraltar, so that she could catch her train to Alcala De Hanares. The town was north-east of Madrid and she was going to spend the night with her Spanish University friend, Emiliana. After that, it would be into Madrid, then Paris and then onto London via the Channel tunnel. Unfortunately the weather was horrendous and the forecast so bad he had insisted she catch the ferry from Al-Hoceima to Gib or else she might miss her connections. Nick could then push on alone across the Mediterranean without having to worry about her. She would not admit it but he'd heard her being sick twice that week and she was definitely under the weather.

Mariyah had to be in England by the 14th of March for the graduation and Nick had been telling her forever how flying was the safest form of transport in the world, but she would have none of it. After much ear-bashing she was finally coming round to his way of thinking and at least considering flying from Gibraltar. That was until Emiliana called her to finalise their meeting at the station. When she told Emiliana she might not be visiting, and could be flying to the UK, Emilia burst into tears over the phone.

"Mariyah, please, please don't do it," she implored. "I told you what happened to my younger brother, Edgardo. My mother had to listen to him say goodbye as those vile people took over the plane on the 11th of September. She has never been the same since."

That was it, Mariyah's mind was made up. She would spend the extra time required to go by train, and would see her friend. Nick kissed her goodbye as she boarded the ferry and she had cried. *You silly emotional cow*, she thought. Sitting on the ferry, she tried to put her finger on why she was such a sentimental wreck.

Nicholas was her man, she had not been married a month yet, and she was loving every minute of it. The days they'd had in Gibraltar were hilarious and such fun. The Royal Navy divers had treated her like a queen, although some of the wives had not taken so kindly to her.

They had stayed at Rex and Mo's house, a chief Navy diver Nick had served with. It had been perfect. When they weren't being entertained by someone, they would lock themselves in the bedroom. Mo had given them their huge comfortable bed at the top of the house that overlooked the bay and all the ships that anchored there. The big four-poster was a novelty to them both; they usually had to be content with the hard bed on their floating home.

She had still found new scars on Nick's body and hadn't tired of him one bit, as she had with both her other lovers, and he didn't seem to tire of her either. But then, he was her husband, lover and best friend. She had never been so happy, so utterly content.

She was smiling at these thoughts and looked up to see a young Arab man smiling back at her. She stood up and went down below to the ship's heads and was sick again. The ferry was crashing alarmingly through some steep seas, but she had never been seasick before in her life.

She enjoyed the six-hour train journey to Alcala De Hanares and Emiliana had been there to meet her. It was not the same as their University days though. The laughter had left the once bubbly innocent girl. The over-hanging sadness in the house since the death of her brother almost suffocated Mariyah's happiness and enthusiasm for life. Emiliana's mother was a devout Catholic and still wearing black for her lost son. When she found that Mariyah was not Catholic the atmosphere turned almost hostile.

The girls walked the ancient university campus near the house and Mari went into a farmacia. Without Emiliana seeing, she bought a draft for her sickness, and a pregnancy-testing kit. She declined to drink all night.

That night in Emilia's house, she didn't do the test, telling herself, you're a fool, Mariyah Carter; you're sick, not pregnant, you probably have a virus, but she slept not a wink. She even went as far as taking the tiny test strip to the loo, but bought it back unused and just lay staring at the ceiling all night. She was up at 5am and couldn't get out of the tiny house fast enough.

Mariyah said her goodbyes and knew she would never come back or hear from Emiliana again. She boarded the train with all the commuters making their way to Madrid. The packed compartment was making her feel queasy again and she made her way to the cramped toilet.

So, it was in a dirty train toilet and attempting the almost impossible that Mariyah saw the blue stripe that leapt out at her from the little pen's window. She went back to her seat but a man had taken it. He tried his hardest not to look up so as not to give her the seat, but when he did he saw the positively beaming face of the pretty, slim girl, he stood and apologised.

She sat staring out of the window in a daze.

*Mrs Carter, Mummy Carter, Mrs and a Mum. Mummy... How would that sound? Last month I was single, and now I have a husband and am with child,* she thought. There was another life growing in her and she wanted to cry again with overwhelming happiness.

Mari reached into her bag and texted: *thrs 3 of us now, I luv u. Mummy Carter. XXX.*

She was shaken out of her daze when the train started to slow as it came into Atocha station in Madrid.

There was a commotion half-way along the carriage, a lot of shouting in Spanish and one voice in another language. Mari stood to see what was happening. There was a young, dark-skinned man wearing a red jacket with the hood up, which seemed odd in the heat. He was wearing a rucksack and had a suitcase held between his knees. Sweat ran down his face and he had a wild, far-away stare in his eyes. He opened his jacket, took out a mobile phone and held it up for all to see. She instinctively put her hand to her heart, and found the pendant. It had become her good luck charm since Nicholas had given it to her.

The man then looked up at the heavens... his arms outstretched.

*

Mariyah never knew what happened. Half-an-hour after the explosions, she came round lying outside of the train. She could not feel any part of her body; it was an odd experience. She felt no pain. There were two men above her, one covered in blood and torn clothes, the other in white. The blooded one was crying and speaking to her. She could see his lips moving but there was no sound, only utter peace and calm. She focused past them to a helicopter high in the sky as it flew through a pall of rising black smoke. She was feeling so weak she just wanted to sleep. She noticed her sickness was gone, and with it her baby. She closed her eyes, and gave in to the all-consuming veil of tiredness.

911 days after 9/11, it was Spain's turn to feel the wrath of international terrorism. With ten bombs going off within minutes of each other in packed, commuter trains, one hundred and ninety-one people from fifteen different countries lost their lives and over two thousand were injured on that one day in Madrid.

*

Three days later, having barely spoken a word, Nick stood in the cold, white, featureless mortuary in Madrid. After queuing for an age, the man with the clipboard finally asked him for the name of the deceased and he wrote it down on the form. They walked swiftly past the body-bags on the floor. The smell of burnt flesh and embalming fluid was enough to make anyone retch. Nick could only look ahead where the man was leading.

One bag was on a trolley, and tied to the end was a white label with a red cross through it that read: Hembra/Female. There were two men in masks wearing long blue robes and white Wellington boots; they stood a respectable distance away. As the identifiers of the various bodies were allowed in, the men would lift the bodies up onto one of the few available trolleys.

The man unzipped the bag just to show her face, but Nick motioned him to unzip further. He had to see what had happened to her. He nearly lost consciousness; not at the sight and extent of her injuries, but at what felt like the loss of half of his soul. He rested his hands on the trolley to steady himself, then leaned down to kiss her forehead. He spoke her pet name in a whisper close to her ear and was about to leave, when he noticed her left hand was balled up in a tight fist. He took her hand and tried to pry her fingers apart.

The mortuary attendant stepped forward shaking his head and said something. He put his hand onto Nick's forearm, as if to stop him. Nick's head whipped round and through tear-filled eyes, gave him a glare that was the warning of a man who had lost all reason. The attendant bowed his head and stepped back.

Nick forced back the blackened and cold, cut fingers. Her wedding ring was gone, along with most of her flesh, but in her fist was the pendant. He put it across his chest to his heart, said "Goodbye my love," and left.

# 11

The old boys' network moved into top gear for Smudge and Nick.

Lt. Commander Tug Wilson started the sequence with a call to his drinking buddy at MI6. His contact was a former Royal Naval Captain. Acutely aware of the time, Tug dialled his friend's bleeper.

Smudge's phone rang within ten minutes and he was given a series of security checks. Even then, he was put on hold five times before reaching the senior Ops controller (OC) for the Western Med and North Africa, or area 22 in official terms. The OC22 left little unexplored in grilling Smudge, and was particularly interested in the weapons Nick had found, the fact they were AR10s, and particularly that there had been a Geiger-counter with them. The OC thanked Smudge and said he would call back if he required anything else.

Fifteen minutes later the phone rang again; this time Smudge sat bolt upright, spilling his coffee into his lap. The woman introduced herself as the deputy head of the Secret Intelligence Service. There was no thought of doubting her; she seemed to know everything about his past. She spoke with a natural air of authority, giving him a long list of instructions.

The first was that he would be going for assessment training.

Silent, engine-less and sail-less, *Orelia* was drifting where the wind or tide took her. Nick had slept, but woke sporadically. Every time he looked up, he searched the horizon from his seated position in the cockpit. Although there was nothing to see, he was convinced that he was being followed. In rational moments, he understood that it was probably his conscience at work. He had killed a man, so there would and should be retribution.

Finally he awoke, sweating and holding his breath. He tried to escape the vision of swimming down to a body lying on the deep seabed, bound hand and foot and with a bag over its head. The body was covered in weed and sand and looked like it had been there for years. In an underwater slow motion, he tore at the bag to try and save the man, but when he got it off it was his own dead face staring back at him.

It was nearly full daylight. He realised he must have had at least an hour's rest, if not sleep, in his sitting position. There was not much on the radar, and no vessels in sight. So maybe Bayonet hadn't been missed.

Nick looked at his watch. It was 07:05. He went below and picked up his mobile. With a resigned sigh he switched it on. Two new texts came through immediately, and both were from Smudge. Nick opened the first:

*Spoke 2 tug, help on way. Go in2 Al Hocma. Charge ur F\*ing fone! S.*

Nick spoke to his phone: "Go to Al-Hoceima? Jesus, I can't go back in there."

He texted back.

*Cant go back there cos of trouble n I'm in2deep already.*

Then he read the second message.

*som1 will meet u in marina @12. S*

"12 when, what day?" Nick growled at the phone, "and why the hell Al-Hoceima again?"

He mused on the problem for half an hour, before starting one engine and plotting a reciprocal course.

"This is the last time I'm going there, the very last time."

Nick had no idea if he would be arrested, kidnapped, shot or suffer an even more grisly ending. He just had a feeling it was unlikely to be a happy event awaiting him.

Motoring past the outer fishing harbour, he glanced to port at the covered boat-shed that had concealed the ugly proceedings of the previous night.

In the marina, a man in shorts with a hand-held radio indicated for him to berth in one of the end fingers. As he had no money, Nick tied up as quickly as possible and tried to disappear below deck, but the man asked for payment, speaking in Spanish. Nick played dumb and motioned to pay by card, to which he received a shrug and shake of the head. Cash was king in these parts. Then he remembered, went below and took the roll of still-damp money from Bayonet's money belt. The berthing man was not keen on the damp notes but put them straight in his pocket, offering Nick no receipt.

A French family opposite seemed to be watching his every move, or was he just being over-sensitive? The woman wore what looked like three serviettes, held precariously together by dental floss. Could she really have had a child? In any other situation Nick would have paid her the attention she seemed to be paying him. But he wanted - needed - to go and look at the boathouse, to see who was there, and what were they doing.

Picking up his more powerful binoculars and putting them in a rucksack along with some chocolate bars and water, Nick put on a floppy hat and his biggest shades to cover his face then made his way along the quay. When he reached the old sea wall that led to the natural tall rock in the centre of the harbour, he paused. He was tempted to walk straight past the scene of the night's events just to have a quick look. Instead, he turned and went to the tall rock where he had first sat looking for the launch.

"Christ! Time flies when you're having fun," he muttered as he tried to walk nonchalantly up the rough steps to his vantage point. Taking off his rucksack, he sat in the same place as before. He kicked off his deck shoes and scrunched up his feet in the warm, red, volcanic sand. The water was cool and he managed to drink a litre in one go; the rest he poured over his still-aching head. He felt for the injury and found the large crusty scab that reminded him why he was there. Picking up the binoculars, he focused on the makeshift boathouse. Everything looked the same and it was quiet, which had to be good. At least it wasn't teeming with police or bad guys. Nick scoured the rest of the fish docks through the binoculars, then looked at his yacht and the marina. Finally he took in the central square of Al-Hoceima town itself. All seemed quiet and normal on this hot, still morning.

Nick let the binoculars hang around his neck while he poured some water over his ridiculous floppy sun hat and placed it back on his sore, shaved head. The sensation of rest and the coolness was spectacular. He let his head loll back to rest on the wet hat and the rock behind, and closed his eyes.

Pure nervous exhaustion had him lose himself more than once. He woke as his head fell sideways, so he moved, lay the hat over his face and gave in. He awoke again after about an hour. The sweat had pooled on his face. He snapped his head up and looked down at his boat.

"Shit! I still haven't charged my phone. Smudge is going to kill me."

He knew he should go straight back to the boat and plug in the mains supply and get his phone charging. Whoever was supposedly coming to see him would probably call first.

"Sod it," he said aloud.

He relieved the muzzy tiredness with the cooling effect of some more water on his damp hat. This, combined with his distended belly-full of fresh water, was having a magical effect on his psyche. It was only late-morning but the sun was already burning his shins and tops of his feet.

Something out of the corner of his eye made him look towards the boathouse. Someone had appeared from the hidden side and was walking away. Nick snatched up his binoculars and zoomed in. The figure stopped, his back to Nick; he was on the phone. He was sure it was the boy he had seen before. Then, the boy turned towards him. He was talking excitedly on the phone and looking round the harbour. Nick zoomed in on his face, only to realise, it wasn't a boy at all. It was a young woman.

She seemed to look directly up at him. He immediately moved the binoculars up and out to sea. He waited a few seconds, before dropping them and looking as casually as he could back to her. She'd gone. He lifted the bins again and searched the area. She appeared out of the cover of the boat house with the keys. It looked as if she had just locked the door and was heading off; searching for someone, maybe?

He thought about following her, but knew he would attract her attention by running down from his vantage point. He would have to be content with following her with the binoculars. She was undoubtedly not trying to announce the fact she was a woman. She was small, slim and wearing men's scruffy dark clothing. *Unusual in this part of the world*, thought Nick.

She moved slowly towards the harbour wall, looked out to sea then walked back past the boathouse as far as the perimeter fence of the marina compound, gesticulating as she talked into the phone. She was presumably wondering where Aghilas was. She put the phone away, looked around again, then walked purposefully off towards the town. Nick watched her. She swung her hips a bit too seductively for an Arab woman, and in her man's guise, it gave her an odd, almost gay appearance.

She could be no more than 5ft tall, young, and either dark skinned or she had been at sea a lot and was a healthy colour. Her hair was not visible hidden under her baseball cap. She went into the nearest bar to the marina, then another, she came out looking perplexed. Nick saw a man follow her out of the café-bar and harass her. She ignored him turned on her heel, saying something to him which stopped him in his tracks, then disappeared down an alleyway.

Nick waited for forty minutes, watching the town. She didn't appear. But a Caucasian man in a light blue tropical safari suit did catch his eye. *Where does anyone pick up threads like that nowadays*, thought Nick? *He looks like an extra from Casablanca.* Carrying a black rucksack, the man strode across the square and headed for the marina.

Nick studied the bars and tiny alleys, but the woman had gone. He decided to go back to the boat and put his phone on charge. He stood and stretched out his aching limbs, and as he did so, saw that the western man was studying his boat. Nick squatted down out of sight again and reached for the binoculars. The man crouched and was obviously looking at the name of Nick's boat. The name change was a decent enough job, but it wouldn't bear close scrutiny. The man stood up, looked around, then boarded the yacht.

# 12

"Mr Carter?" There was no reply to his call. The only person paying any attention was a pretty woman on a French-flagged yacht moored nearby. Nodding to her and smiling confidently, he stepped aboard. His eye was drawn to the jury-rigged mizzen-mast and he raised an eyebrow; most people who knew him would say this was a display of some emotion.

Miles had been a field operative for nearly ten years. They kept offering him what they called promotion, but he just saw it as a desk job. He was too good to be wasted in a desk jockey's position; I.D2 had told him so herself. And last night, she had spoken to him personally again. She wanted him to take charge of this case.

Officially, I.D2 stood for Deputy Intelligence Director. Inevitably and because of her resemblance to Iron Lady Margaret Thatcher, his deputy boss had been tagged Iron Drawers. Her age was indeterminable, she was unmarried, and was certainly a more formidable figure than any man Miles had met or commanded.

Everyone knew that one day she was going to be in The Chair. She would then be able to sign documents with a green 'C', a system initiated by MI6's first director, Sir George Smith-Cumming. It had become a tradition observed by all who had held the coveted post since. The first woman of such senior rank in the service, she had manoeuvred herself brilliantly into a position where most MI6 insiders wanted her in the chair. When she got the job it would be very useful to know and be known to her.

Miles surveyed the cockpit, and apart from the mizzen, saw nothing to interest him. Along with his rucksack, something he always carried with him was confidence in his own ability to do his job. He was always self-assured in his actions. He went below as if he owned the boat and his trained eye was instantly looking for clues or potential problems. Consequently, he wasted no time giving the saloon the once-over.

*

Nick arrived breathless and a little dizzy and climbed aboard. He stood at the top of the companionway and looked down at the blond stranger rooting through his cupboards.

"Can I help you?" asked Nick, in his most sardonic voice.

"Yes, yes please. I expect you can," responded the intruder, speaking in impeccable English.

"Can you tell me how to get the gas on? I'm absolutely parched and in dire need of a cup of tea."

"I'll tell you what. You tell me what you're doing on my boat, before I have to come down there and chuck you off!"

The man looked him in the eye and said flatly, "I would advise you not to try that, Nicholas."

"How do you know my name?" Nick stepped onto the top rung of the ladder and blocked out the sunlight.

"I didn't, or wasn't sure until you spoke. But I can assure you I know a lot more about you than just your name. Where is the gas cock? And please tell me you have some milk, Nicholas."

"It's Nick. What exactly do you want, Mr...?"

"Just call me Miles," the stranger said, standing up and dusting off his knees.

Nick took another step down into the saloon, studying his uninvited guest carefully.

Miles got a closer look at Nick: "My, we have been in the wars, haven't we? I'd say you've lost a lot of blood, and could do with some rest. My God, you look absolutely awful. Please come down and take a seat before you fall down."

"It's nice to be invited aboard your own boat," said Nick, resignedly. "What makes you think I've lost some blood then, Sherlock?"

"It's Miles," the man said, looking puzzled. "There's blood all over the place down here. I can see you've tried to clear up but all you've managed do is spread it around a bit. Look...it's everywhere. Ahh." He winced as he looked closer at Nick's wound. "I see. You've got a rather nasty cut on the back of your head, and another on your arm.

Nick bent and turned on the gas under the cooker. As he stood up he saw stars again and had to stand very still for a few seconds. Then he filled the kettle and put it on the stove.

"Please sit down, Nicholas," said Miles as though talking to a child. Nick was in no shape or mood to argue, for now anyway, so dropped heavily onto the seat opposite the galley.

"Who the hell are you?" he asked. He was sure the man was English, but couldn't possibly be the one Smudge had organised. There hadn't been enough time.

"I'm on your side, Nicholas, and I'm going to help you, and in return, you will help us."

Nick sat with his head in his hands. He might as well see what his visitor had to say. After all, he didn't really know where to go from here.

"When was the last time you had a proper meal?" Without waiting for an answer, Miles began sorting through the cupboards. He poured half the contents of the kettle into a saucepan and lit the gas ring, found a packet of *fussili* pasta and emptied the contents into the pan.

Miles turned to look at Nick and sighed. Nick had laid back and was massaging his eyes.

"Are you going to tell me what happened before you pass out, or when you wake up, Nicholas?"

"I'm not going to tell you anything until you tell me who you are, what you want and who sent you. And... my name is Nick!"

*

Miles could see the state Nick was in: exhausted, anaemic, touchy and a little out of his depth. But, he had what it took to become a good FA. He had recruited fifty-one freelance agents over the years, and considered his early judgement of their suitability impeccable. So far, Nicholas fitted the bill almost perfectly. He was ex-military and a Clearance Diver, a course that had the same level of fail rate as the SAS. CDs were perhaps a little harder to come by, and this one had just landed smack into his hands. He was certainly not going to let him go, or at least not without a fight.

Miles had been recruited whilst still a junior officer in the parachute regiment. MI6 had come after him in Northern Ireland. From that moment he knew his destiny lay with intelligence. He was flattered to be wanted by his country's finest minds, which was why of course they were jointly known as *Intelligence*. They were the real deal, and they wanted him. He'd had to prove himself of course, and for a long two years. They had him on intelligence, survival, escape and evasion courses and, ultimately, the 14 Intelligence Detachment or 'The Det' as it was known in Int circles.

He was a good organiser and had a sixth sense for diagnosing and acting on people's nature and so was posted out to the western Med in 1997. He knew he had not been expected to stay the course, but had successfully grown a network of freelance agents and also almost as many Numbers.

Numbers came in many guises. There was the traditional informer, but he also had men and women on his payroll who were simply in the right job or situation. Of one thing he was sure: nobody else could recruit and run a team as well as he. And no other team could rival his team.

And this in spite of the fact that most governments found it too expensive to have hundreds of fully-paid-up agents these days. Since the British Secret Intelligence Service had had its budget cut by 25% in the mid-Nineties, it had been increasingly inventive in its use of freelancers. Things had improved since 9/11, but expenses were still battened down.

It was also known in the business that, regardless of budgets, Miles ran a tight ship. Nobody was allowed to ruin his team. That was why he had a clear-out every now and then. He liked to keep his team on a short leash.

Most importantly to the government, the premium value of the freelance agent system was that if any were taken by some hostile unit, they were virtually clean. They could deny ever training him or her; there was no paper trail to link agent and employer. The money was always cash or paid from bank accounts set up in false names. That was the dirty, underhand world of Int; Miles knew it, I.D2 knew it. That's why they needed the best minds running the show on the ground, and that's why they had chosen him.

"Nicholas, I work for the British government. I know all about you."

Then, while opening a tin of tuna he recited Nick's military and civilian history.

"Nicholas Paul Carter. Born, Hillingdon on 20th of April, 1963 to English parents. Nothing to shout about at school; in fact, this part of your life is best forgotten. Joined the RN as a Seaman Diver in November 1980. Qualified as Bomb and Mine Disposal Diver at just eighteen?"

"I know what I've done. I don't need to hear it from you, thank you," said Nick.

Miles carried on as if Nick had not spoken:

"Northern Ireland. Served with distinction. Qualified as Clearance Diver 2nd Class in only 2 years, top of the class. 1982, Falklands Campaign with Fleet Clearance

Diving Team, received a Commendation from the SBS, and the Conspicuous Gallantry Medal for work on UXBs."

Nick sat back, let out a heavy sigh, and closed his eyes.

"You worked 'Cross Service' with the SBS, performing in many theatres of operation and receiving the Queen's Gallantry Medal. The scrip didn't say what for. What *was* it for?"

Nick just shrugged.

Miles continued: "In 1988 you qualified as a Saturation Diver and undertook some deep experimental and shall we say... sensitive dives for Her Majesty's Government. Served in the first Gulf war and received the George Medal for Explosive Ordnance Disposal work. Recommended for your commission but turned it down and left the Navy in 1993. Since then you have been hard to pin down. You were awarded the civilian SGM, the Sea Gallantry Medal for a diver recovery for Oceaneering but failed to collect it. Why was that?"

"I was pissed."

"Oh" Miles turned to look at Nick to see if he were serious, but could not tell.

"I know about your friend, Michael Smith, although I've not spoken to him directly, and I know about the tragic loss of your wife. You either have some friends in high places or you've just been lucky to wind up with me. Whatever it is, we can make a good team. I can help you, but you must help me first."

Miles drained the water from the pasta, tipped in the tin of tuna, poured in some olive oil, and added salt, pepper and sweet chilli sauce from the cupboards. He mixed it and put it onto two plastic plates. Without speaking further, they devoured the carbohydrate-filled food, sizing each other up over the meal.

Eventually, Nick pushed his plate away: "Thanks. It's good." Miles just raised his eyebrows as if to say, of course it is, and nodded at the litre bottle of water. His signal meant drink more, you need it.

The carb-filled meal had the desired effect on Nick's weary bones. He lay back again and closed his eyes as

Miles took to quietly washing up and clearing away. Miles knew Nick was running on empty, and he also knew he had accepted him on board and now didn't feel so alone. He was more relaxed, and would sleep.

As Nick slept, Miles cleaned the boat of blood. He put the bloody towels in bin bags and took them to the huge marina bins. He then went round again and cleaned all the edges and corners with hot, soapy water. He also cleaned the shower and the cockpit. Whilst working, he searched with an expert, inquisitive eye.

When content with his work, he sat opposite the curled-up figure at the saloon table and opened his rucksack. From it he took a laptop computer that looked like it had been used as a work bench. It was scratched, chipped, and had a large dent on one corner. It even had a 'Windows 95' sticker on it; hopefully, no one would bother to steal it.

Miles took out a large, old fashioned mobile phone and slid a small memory stick out of the back of the case. He plugged it into the USB port, then took a long metal strip from around his neck and slid it into a small recess at the front of the notebook. Then, holding his finger over the fingerprint pad, he pushed and held down the space bar and number 9. The computer came to life. As he watched, it logged into the MoD satellite and immediately flashed up four messages. Three were updates on Nick, including a photo.

Also there was a long piece about one of Miles's and MI6's most highly sought-after men. On file, the terrorist was known simply as T, but the security services and media knew him as 'The Tunisian.' They also knew he had repeatedly been in and out of Iraq, Iran and Libya. The Americans had had a source close to him for a while, but he had suddenly disappeared. Then the Tunisian had gone to ground.

Until now, that was. He had recently been spotted in Libya and Morocco and nearly been picked up, but managed to buy his way out of trouble. This was one of the main reasons Miles had been in Melilla the previous night and had been able to make the uncomfortable journey over to Al-Hoceima so quickly. Everyone was convinced T was in the upper echelons of Al-Qaeda. So if he could be reached and taken, there was always the possibility of getting closer to the world's number one terrorist, MOBIL, or Mr Osama Bin Laden. The game was to find him and retire. Not that Miles could see the day he would ever want to retire.

Nick jumped in his sleep and grunted. Miles gave him a minute to return to that deep restful place, then got up. He went into the heads and lifted the heavy leather belt that hung from one of the shower hooks. He'd seen it on his earlier reconnaissance and thought it unlikely to be Nick's. The name on the back was unusual; he would put it in his next message to England, just to see what came back.

Next, he took out the mobile phone. Unlike Nick, who saw nothing of value in a water-logged phone, Miles saw a possible world of information. He took the back off and removed the SIM card, then, after looking through his rucksack he pulled out a tiny card reader and plugged it into a USB port. Next he opened what looked like a small ladies make-up kit, removed a hand-pump spray that said 'Fresh Breath', and sprayed a fine mist onto the gold surface of the SIM card. In the kit was a gauze cloth, and he used it to gently dry the card. The reader took all sizes of cards, and Miles's fast and expert fingers moved swiftly across the key pad. He created a file called 'Lehri Aghilas', selected: *Copy files to*, and within seconds had transferred every number in Aghilas's phone to his computer. Clicking: *Save,* he then opened the phone's address book on his computer and scanned down a list of about twenty names and numbers. One leapt out at him. He had seen it before. With a stirring of anticipation and even excitement, he opened his address book for targets and there it was; the same number.

Forgetting himself, he spoke aloud: "I knew he was here somewhere." To alert the boffins in the core of the Comms department that he wanted everything on that number, he placed an * next to it. He then added all the numbers to the list and pressed: *Send*. The encrypted message with all its details would be in London and Cheltenham's GCHQ immediately, and he couldn't wait to see what came back. Then he paused for thought, and copied the file to I.D2. *Best to keep the old girl in the know.*

While he was in telephone mode, he turned around and saw Nick's 'phone on the worktop next to the galley. Now that was a good idea. Miles repeated the whole process, and within two minutes Nick's phone was back in the galley having, in essence, been cloned.

# 13

Nick woke swiftly at the mention of his name. There was no gradual dawning of who and where he was, and he was instantly alert.

His hand went to the back of his head and felt the crusty scab, then he rubbed the pain gnawing at his temples. In front of him were two painkillers and a mug of water. He looked at Miles, who was tapping away on his laptop. Downing the tablets with the water and plonking the plastic mug down with a thump, he enquired, "Now what, Einstein?"

"It's Miles," said his visitor, continuing to work.

"Okay Miles. I think it's time to stop fannying about with your act, and tell me what the fuck is going on?"

Miles stopped typing and looked across at his puffy-eyed companion.

"It's not complicated. One of your friends contacted some of my friends, and here we are. Look... I work for the British government - your government - as a sort of... well, a sort of problem solver. We're on the same side. If we work together I'm sure I can get you out of this mess."

"What sort of a mess do you think I'm in?"

"Well... your friend Michael Smith said you'd stumbled upon some sinister circumstance on a boat at sea, which may have security implications for British interests. It would also appear that an altercation has taken place, and someone has been seriously hurt, or even... killed?" Miles looked at Nick with one eyebrow raised, waiting to be enlightened. Nick shook his head.

"Nicholas..."

"It's Nick. Which bit about that don't you understand? Call me Nick!"

"Okay, okay. I can help you. I want to help you, but before I can do anything, you need to tell me everything. I will however, tell you this…"

Nick looked up, straight into steely blue eyes. They held each other's gaze across the saloon table.

"If I get the slightest inkling you are lying to me or have left anything out, even if you think it's unimportant, I'll drop you. As quickly as I arrived, I'll leave. Not only will I leave, but I may be forced to tell our Moroccan friends what I have already learned. We have a good working relationship with the Moroccans, the Algerians, the Spanish and Tunisians all along this coast. Part of my job is to keep it a good relationship. I don't need some kind of military maverick sailing in here and upsetting a delicate balance. Something like this can set relations back years, and I'm not about to let that happen. You must be very sure about that fact, Nicholas. I will know if you are lying. I've spent years working with some of the best liars in the world."

Nick noticed a sinister look in his eyes. It wasn't the physical side of Miles that sparked an alarm; it was something else, a macabre and cold hardness. He was a complete son-of-a-bitch.

"First of all, Nicholas, I would like you to outline how you came into contact with these not-so-gentlemen."

It seemed Nick would have to put up with this man being one of the few people in the world who addressed him as Nicholas; the last one was Mariyah. He took in an exaggerated breath, and begun by recounting the dive. He considered not telling him about the wreck and finding the bronze cannon, then, knowing that the only charts of its whereabouts were in his head, he told him anyway.

"So, you are, in effect, a thief?" asked Miles, tapping away on the laptop.

"I'm not a thief. It's been there since the early 16th century, and, even then, it had already been stolen by a pirate. Show me the rightful owner and I'll gladly tell him where to find it."

Nick then went on to recount being boarded by the three supposed Moroccan customs officials. As he spoke, he was aware of Miles looking deep into his eyes and scrutinising his every word.

"So... they would have known you had been diving in a restricted area?"

"No. I don't think they'd any idea. Anyway, I don't think they were interested."

Nick then explained about coming to the surface, with no gear on, and leaving all of the evidence in an area he would be able to find again. Miles didn't ask stupid questions about the diving side of it; he just nodded as if he knew exactly what Nick was talking about. That was the first time Nick had inkling that Miles may have had some special service training.

"I'd like to believe they were nothing more than thieves who came aboard this boat, my home, in the dead of night with the sole purpose of stealing whatever they fancied."

"What did they take that was so valuable to make you risk your life and go after them?" Nick, dropped his gaze to his hands, shook his head and was about to tell Miles it had no bearing on the story, when he was interrupted.

"Don't even think about it, Nicholas, don't even consider lying to me, please."

Nick paused for a moment before continuing. He told Miles about them searching his yacht and finally ransacking his safe. He told him about his valuable Rolex and for a split-second, thought about turning that into his reason for giving chase. Miles noticed the hesitation and was studying his every word.

"There was 1500 Euros and also... a *very* valuable antique pendant. Valuable in both senses of the word. It's gold for one. And I would guess it's more than... two thousand years old? It also holds a little secret. We never had it valued, but its worth is considerable. I would be surprised if there was another one like it anywhere in the world. Also, I'd given it to my wife. She loved it, cherished it. She saw it as her good luck charm although, on that day, it obviously wasn't. She was wearing it the day she died in Madrid. In the mortuary, I had to prise it from her... from her fist."

There was a period of silence. Miles allowed Nick the time to reflect, to gather himself.

Nick had been talking while staring mostly at his hands, but every now and then he would engage Miles's eye and hold it. Nick left Miles in no doubt about his determination when he looked up.

"I want it back Miles - I want it back real bad."

Miles nodded. "I see. What did he look like, the one you call the Admiral?"

Nick gave him as detailed a description as he could. Then, dragging his finger over his own head, he explained, "He had a scar over his eye. A diagonal scar, that went up from his eyebrow and across his forehead. It looked perfectly straight. I thought at the time it was maybe a knife wound, but, it could be anything. He was a right thieving git. Not only was he on here with the sole purpose of seeing what he could half-inch, he nicked stuff in full view of me. Then he left me for dead."

"What else did he take?" Miles was tapping away as he asked the questions. Nick felt like a mugging victim giving evidence to the duty police sergeant.

"He had my deep diving watch, a Bremont, which I now have back, a pair of brass dividers, some cigarettes..." Miles kept looking up from his typing as he quizzed Nick. After noting the descriptions of all three men, he asked about the boat and the unseen helmsman.

"I never saw him until this morning - well, I did but I thought it was a boy not a woman."

"Pardon? You thought *he* was a boy, not a *woman*? Explain please."

"I think, but don't know for sure, that the boat driver was a woman. I saw her this morning going to the boat shed."

"What boat shed?"

"The one just over there," said an exasperated Nick, pointing vaguely towards the fish docks. "You haven't heard about my little fracas over there, have you?"

Miles shook his head, "No, it would appear not. Maybe, your friend, Michael, has been trying to protect you and not told our people everything. This is what happens if you lie to us, Nicholas. I don't have all the facts, so consequently, I can't present you with the best course to take, and as a problem solver, that in itself presents *me* with a problem. Do you understand?"

"Well I don't know what Smudge told you."

"Who... who is Smudge?"

"Mick Smith, sorry, Michael, as you will no doubt insist on calling him. Look, I couldn't tell him everything, my phone was on the blink, and I was... shall we say, a little distracted. After I watched them ransack my safe, one of them smacked me on the back of the head with the butt of his Lee-Enfield. I woke up an hour or so later, lying there, tied under the chart table. One thing I haven't been able to figure out yet is, when I came round I found someone had tied a tea towel around my head. To stop the bleeding, you know? Without it I would probably have bled to death."

Miles had now stopped writing and was listening. "So... all the blood that was on the floor in here. That was all yours?"

"Yeah, of course it was."

"I've just spent the best part of an hour cleaning up your blood?"

Nick smiled a big beaming smile, and just said, "Thanks, Miles, you will make someone a good mother one day." Miles wasn't happy.

"Why didn't you tell me it was your blood?"

"You never asked!"

Miles shook his head. Nick continued: "When I finally managed to untie myself and make it up to the cockpit, there was no sign of them, until I switched on my radar. One small craft was heading away from me. So I followed, and it rendezvoused with either a bulk carrier or tanker not far from here."

Miles opened his mouth to interrupt, but Nick was on a roll and continued.

"The launch was alongside the bigger ship for maybe fifteen minutes before it took off towards Morocco. I didn't follow closely as I didn't want to arouse suspicion. The launch disappeared for a few hours. I don't know where she went. Anyway, I came into Al-Hoceima and when I saw the launch wasn't here I was convinced I'd either lost it or followed the wrong boat. Then, late last night, it came in and sailed straight past my mooring without seeing me. She disappeared into a boathouse, over there. It was dark, so I waited for them all to leave and swam under the curtained doors that hang at one end of the boathouse." He tapped the black non-magnetic Bremont on his wrist. "That's where I found my watch, the weapons, grenades and Geiger counter."

"What type of grenades were they?"

"There were Russian RGD-5s. And some others, I didn't look in all of the boxes, I didn't have time. There were some with NFDD stencilled on the box. I've seen them before but I can't remember the acronym."

Without looking up from his computer, Miles said, "Flash Bangs!"

"Jesus! That's it, I knew I'd seen it somewhere before. They were American, or at least the box was American, M84s, and I have no reason to believe the contents weren't as well. What does it stand for?" But before Miles could speak up, it came to Nick. "Noise & Flash Diversionary Devices - Flash Bangs."

Without a break from his typing, Miles reeled off some facts about the grenades. "They were originally designed for the SAS. Fabricated specifically to stun, confuse and disorientate any potential threat for up to a minute. They will seriously degrade the combat effectiveness of any personnel within the immediate vicinity not wearing protective clothing."

Miles asked more questions about the radiation on board, the weapons and his consternation was visibly growing. He typed everything into his computer, then said, "So then you just left?"

"No. Bayonet-the one who had the bayonet on his rifle-came back and caught me in the boat shed."

"Ahh! So that must've been our, er, Mr Lehri, Aghilas Lehri?"

"How do you know his name?"

Instead of answering, Miles made his way to the heads and shower and came back with the heavy leather belt, and put it on the table with the name facing upwards.

"I see. So you know?"

"I don't know what happened to him. I was hoping you would enlighten me."

Nick started pacing up and down behind Miles. Up to the forward cabins, then back to the cockpit stairs, backwards and forwards. He wrestled with his conscience, deciding how he was going to explain himself, then stopped at the stairs and looked out of the boat and said bleakly: "He's dead."

*

Miles sat back. That explained a lot. He reflected on how he had felt the first time he had to kill an IRA player. He had relieved an SAS man and had orders to only observe the targets house. He had been laid up for fifteen minutes in a dilapidated shed when the man showed up, but not in the expected place. O'Shea was a big, naturally aggressive street fighter, and surprised Miles by smashing through the rotten wall of the shed. Someone had obviously tipped him off.

As they engaged, all training immediately became irrelevant. It was the will to live that would decide survival. For what seemed a long time, the pair rolled around on the muddy earth in the rain in the back garden of the murderer's Armagh house. Both ended up with their hands on the only weapon within reach, which was a large screwdriver. Miles had used all his body weight to force the tool into O'Shea throat, but somehow missed all the arteries and larynx. In spite of his wound, O'Shea had fought back until Miles drove the blade further into the nerves at the back of the man's neck. The animal wail O'Shea had made and the desperate fight for life had stayed with Miles ever since. He had gone through the same range of emotions that Nicholas was clearly suffering now. But telling him that it would get easier would certainly not help get him on the case.

Instead he asked in a crisp, businesslike manner: "Where's the body?"

"Out there, in 500 metres of water. I don't think anyone saw me, or knows who did it. They may not even know he is missing-yet."

"Is there anything else, any little detail you've either forgotten to tell me or held back for some other reason?"

Nick shook his head, then remembered: "Yeah, there is one other thing. I checked their GPS to see where they'd been, as you do. The launch had been to Gib, and here obviously, and there was also the liaison point for the large ship. But there was another way-point for Tripoli; you know, in Libya."

"I know where Tripoli is, thank you very much." This news both disturbed and excited Miles, and he again began furiously typing away. "Why didn't you tell me this earlier?"

"I forgot. Sorry - *sir*."

"Right!" Miles tapped the *Enter* key for emphasis. "I feel it's time now that I said my piece." He cleared his throat, sat back and folded his arms before beginning:

"I don't know if I can help you get your pendant back, but I will try. But I can certainly be of some assistance where you need immediate help, and that is with the financial muddle you're in."

Nick turned to interrupt but Miles just carried on regardless.

"I can also help you with names, and I'm getting our people to look into the possible ship with which our illustrious Admiral may have had his illicit liaison in the dead of night. If indeed, that is, he is on a boat at all. Seeing as you lost the launch for several hours and the rest of the crew are here, it seems to me he may be in Morocco. I also have people looking into that."

"You've done all that while you've been on board, on that heap of junk?" said Nick, indicating the battered laptop, resigned to the fact he would never catch up with modern technology.

"Of course."

Miles's computer kept bleeping and Nick had assumed it was the battery going, but this time he noticed his expert fingers flying over the key-pad and realised he was online. Nick wandered over to his phone in the galley area to find it plugged into the three-pin mains system. He snuck a quick look at Miles's computer screen as he was behind him. It was just dark blue with yellow text and as soon as he got to the end of a line, it disappeared.

He said nothing, then walked as nonchalantly as he could to the companionway, where he could just make out the blue lead that snaked off the yacht and connected him to the shore-side mains electricity. He looked up at the main electric circuit board and noticed the three red lights that indicated that Miles had also figured out how to get the main yacht's batteries onto charge mode. *How long was I asleep*, wondered Nick. And what else had he been up to?

Miles inadvertently answered with his next question, "How much do you owe on *Orelia*, Nick; really-how much?" Nick was looking out towards the marina again and didn't answer. So he continued, "We estimate it to be around the £110,000 mark, including interest, of course."

Nick was astounded at the accuracy of the prediction. Could these people find out that much in a day?

"We can help you with that. Already I have the go-ahead to pay off this year's interest. You would have nothing to pay for a whole year."

He got no response, "I can also give you a bit of working capital, to keep you going, so to speak – expenses, you know? Say... £30,000."

"What?" Nick said, turning on his heel to face Miles again. "Are you serious? And I have to do what? Kill someone. Sorry, should I say *Take them out*, or is it *slot them*?"

"No, no, no," said Miles, holding up his hands, "You have to do nothing of the sort. We would simply ask you to follow up any leads we give you."

"I'm no copper. I don't follow up leads. I'm off out of here tonight and I am never coming back. Nobody is looking for me, and I don't owe you anything. So don't you come here and ask me to do your fuckin' dirty work. Jesus! You people. What are you like? I think you had best leave, before I really go off you. You can't buy me, Miles, or whatever your real name is. I'm a free agent, I do what I like, when I like. I go where I like, I'm my own boss and answer to no one, and that's how I like it."

"That's how it would stay, within reason. Alright, what about £40,000? I can't really go any higher"

"*Hellooo.* Can you hear me? I don't want your money, I don't work for anyone. All I'm interested in is *me*." Nick bent close to Miles and tapped himself on the chest. "Me – callous and shallow as that may seem. There are two virtues right there that I'm sure you're familiar with. I suggest you leave, now. I think you have outstayed your welcome, don't you?"

Nick went up the saloon stairs into the cockpit. He stared out of the marina towards the expanse of the Mediterranean. The attractive French woman was still sitting in her cockpit and couldn't seem to take her eyes off him. Nick barely looked at her. He was too angry. Who did this bloke think he was, coming on board his boat and offering him money? *Cheeky bastard. Forty-odd grand to follow a few leads - likely story*. He heard Miles still tapping away on his keyboard and the computer bleeped a few more times.

He walked back to the top of the stairs and said, "You're a stubborn bastard aren't you? Shall I assist you onto the jetty?"

Nick was aware of a breeze picking up and its cool touch was welcome on his back. He looked up at the halyards banging against the collection of aluminium masts in the marina. It was the sound of protesting yachts wanting to be out there in the wind, at sea, not tied up and used once or twice a year - as was the case with most marina boats. His father had always referred to the masts and sounds they made as money trees.

"Come down here, Nicholas, and stop being so stupid." Nick just sat down on the cockpit deck, with his feet on the top rung leading below. "I have some more information for you."

"Start packing, Miles. You're leaving."

Miles read from his screen, "Three ships were travelling near Alboran between oh-five-hundred and oh-seven-hundred. Two were cargo ships and one was an oil tanker. We think the cargo ships passed through the straits of Gibraltar into the Atlantic. The tanker was scheduled to stop at the Spanish CEPSA oil terminal near Gibraltar, whether to on-load or offload we're unsure. If our man was on one of the outward bound ships, he may be gone. If he was on the tanker, there's a chance we can still catch up with him. If he's here in Morocco... well, we'll see what turns up."

Nick, trying to remain uninterested, said: "So you've got nothing?" then, after a short pause, asked: "Why are you so keen to help me, anyway? Why is there so much money on the table? What have these guys supposedly been involved in?"

Miles let out a sigh, "We think... we think they may have already been involved in terrorist bombings; one or two of them certainly have. We also believe they're up to something now, but we don't know what. That sort of information is worth a lot of money, Nicholas."

"And you want me to get involved with professional terrorists? I've no training for this sort of thing. I would be out of my depth. I'm sorry, I'm not interested and that's my last word. Can you please pack up and leave... now!" Nick stood, as if to make way for Miles to pass him on the stairs.

Miles received another bleep on his laptop. He read or saw something which stopped him in his tracks. He typed *Wait*, then jabbed the *Enter* key. The message disappeared off to some distant satellite miles above the Earth, and before he spoke it was being received in the Government Communication HQ (GCHQ) in Cheltenham.

Nick was still waving an imaginary gangway up the stairs, when Miles said: "At least one of them was involved in the Madrid train bombings."

Nick was speechless. He sat on the top rung of the ladder and said in a low tone, "There's nothing I can do about that now. It's over, it's past, gone. That was a different life. Please leave."

Miles didn't move. Like a skilled director, he knew it was time to reveal part of the plot to his audience.

"The leader was a man called Hachim Hadda. He was the Operational Commander of the cell that planned and carried out the bombings. They were known as the MICG, the Moroccan Islamic Combatant Group. When the police raided their bomb factory only two weeks after the bombings on the 4th of April 2004, he blew himself up in the flat. Or that was what they thought..."

Then Miles laid his trump card on the table. He slowly turned his laptop towards the companionway.

On the screen was a photograph of a man.

Just visible under his hairline was a long thin scar...

# 14

In the calm waters just off of Gibraltar, Hachim Hadda stood on the bridge of the 27,000 tonne *Yamm-Amira* as she crept into her anchorage. He had a thin cigar in his mouth which he was desperate to light. He could not light it because of the NO SMOKING sign in ten foot high red writing along the front of the bridge. Even he had to be seen to obey the rules.

He congratulated himself as he sucked at the unlit cigar. If - or more than likely - *when* his operation came to fruition, he would be more famous than the 9/11 flight crews. He would be a martyr. Again. Not many of his brothers got to be a martyr twice. But Hachim preferred to be a martyr without actually dying. He loved the adulation that came with a successful mission, and in certain circles he was already a hero.

His first wife thought he was dead. His second wife, who was only seventeen, thought he had died in the dingy flat in Madrid in 2004. He rarely thought about them now. It was as if parts of his life had happened to someone else.

It had been so easy to give some fake IDs to one of his soldiers and tell him to sacrifice himself in the name of Allah. The stupid man had cried for the honour Hachim had bestowed on him. The Spanish police had been easily duped. Until recently he was convinced he had fooled the world. But lately he was sure someone was watching him, which was why it was good to get away to sea. Nobody could follow him out here without him knowing.

The plan, his plan, would make the glorious 9/11 and the 11M (Madrid) seem like, how would the Americans say, like a picnic, or was it a walk in the park? He smiled as the Spanish ship's pilot gave the order to drop anchor. The rumble of the huge cable tearing through the hawsepipe shook the ship all the way back to where he stood, hundreds of feet away.

As he had predicted, it had been so easy to sail in here, within spitting distance of the British Rock of Gibraltar, and because he was not taking his ship into anyone's harbour, there were no questions and no paperwork.

Turning to his right, he studied the magnificent Rock of Tariq. *What arrogance, calling it Gibraltar*, he thought. *How could they ever claim it to be British?* The very name Gibraltar came from the Arabic phrase *jabal Tariq*. And every Muslim knew that meant, The Mountain of Tariq. It was named after the Moorish general Tariq ibn-Ziyad, who led the first force of Muslims to invade Spain in 711. Gibraltar was obviously derived from *gibr al-Tariq,* the rock of Tariq. Either way, it was neither English, nor Spanish. The Spanish were as bad as the British *kafirs*. What was the English translation for *kafir* again? Infidel, that was it. The English denied Allah and Mohammed, but they would learn when the Holy war of *Jihad as-sayf* (Jihad of the sword) was waged on them.

The Spanish pilot wanted to say something to Hadda, maybe about the cigar, but he was an old man and had lost his nerve. It did not help his resolve that Hachim struck such an imposing figure on the bridge. He had his finest uniform on, including medal ribbons, peaked hat, four gold rings on his lapels and mirrored sun glasses. He took to the Captain's chair and remained aloof. Every now and then he would get up and wander nonchalantly over to the bridge wings and lift his brand new 7x50 Steiner Commander Electronic Marine Binoculars. His budget for this operation had allowed for some essential luxuries.

The permanent ships crew had accepted him as their temporary Captain, but he knew little about the sea. He had hired a captain who had been recommended as a reluctant sympathiser. He was no *mujahid* though. To be a true *mujahideen*, you needed commitment to the cause. You needed fire in your belly for the fight, striving in the way of Allah, as it said in the Qur'an. Hachim looked across at the officer and could see him sweating and worrying about coming into anchor. He was no warrior, and Hachim may have to take care of him when the time came.

With the ship settled in her anchorage, the pilot said something and wanted to shake hands before leaving, but Hachim-the-captain just nodded. He couldn't wait to have his ship back. He looked down at his recently acquired Rolex. Its sword hands read: 17:10.

His only worry now was where that idiot Aghilas had got to. Everyone knew he was a drunk, a liability. He had been kept on board because he would do anything he was told. Kill him, cut his head from his body with this blunt knife, steal this or that; he would do it with no questions. They had all watched him castrate one man on board this very ship. Now he'd gone missing again. Hachim had a horrible feeling it might be down to him. He had given the two monkeys ⬚100 each from the money he had taken from the Englishman's yacht. He had done it to buy their silence. *You must be getting soft in your old age*, he thought. The fear of what he would do to them had they spoken out should have been enough to ensure they kept their peace. The money was too much, he could see that now. Aghilas would probably have gone out and done his utmost to drink his in one night.

Hadda knew that all the trouble had been caused by his own lust, his *need* to steal. And not for the first time. As a boy he had stolen food and money out of necessity, to eat and clothe himself. As a young man his skills had been recognised and at first, he was ordered to steal weapons and explosives for the holy warriors. Even now, the rush from a successful job took him back to his youth. He stroked the smooth dome glass of the Rolex - *his* Rolex.

Soon though, his most indulgent luxury would be back. Hachim had taken to Najia instantly. She had come along with the launch; she seemed to be part of the package. Being one of Gadaffi's girls, she was along to keep an eye on the Colonel's investments. Hadda was under no illusion she would be reporting back to Libya at the first opportunity, but that didn't mean they couldn't have fun together. While she was away with the launch he'd told her to watch Aghilas, but she had failed as he had disappeared. It had been a perfect excuse to question her, to start a fight. He loved feisty women, and she was certainly one of those; she'd fought back alright. Hachim felt the familiar glow in his loins, anticipating the engagement, and then there was always the making-up to be done.

Hadda had realised early on that Najia was money orientated. She wanted to better herself, as she put it. She knew he held a large purse for the job, so when she thought she would be rewarded, she was extraordinarily kind to him.

She wanted what he had plenty of, so he would take what he wished from her. That was the way of the world. He was still squirming in his seat as he played the image of Najia in his shower, when a seaman came up to the bridge.

"Captain. The pilot has left the ship."

Hadda nodded. He could continue his preparations.

# 15

On board the newly christened *Reliant*, Nick nearly fell down the stairs in his eagerness to get closer to Miles's laptop. It was not the clearest of shots. It had been taken covertly, using a long lens. Nick recognised the profile, though.

"When was this taken?"

"About six weeks ago, near a tanker undergoing some sort of re-fit in the docks... in Tripoli."

"Tripoli? That's where the launch had been, so maybe the tanker heading to Gib had been there. Maybe it's Libyan registered?"

Seeing Nick's renewed interest, Miles went for the kill. Using his mobile again, he scrolled down his photos to a better image of the man. He gave the phone to Nick. The photo looked like it may have been taken on an old mobile phone. It was outside in a dingy, narrow street, it was grainy and too dark, but there was no mistaking who it was.

"This one was taken more recently. His name is Hachim Hadda. He was the brains behind the Madrid operation. It was all his idea. He picked the trains to be hit, recruited the soldiers, raised the money, stole the explosives, set up the safe flat, the lot. Of course, he had no intention of killing himself; he's not that brave or committed. Mr Hadda just wanted to kill a lot of innocent civilians to make a name for himself in the appropriate quarters. We've been sure for a couple of years now that he didn't die in the flat in Madrid. These photos prove it."

Miles let his words register, then continued, "We think he started out on his road to murder by chance, more than via a strict religious ideology. He's attended bomb-making camps on the Pakistan Afghan border, and he has certainly murdered before. After Madrid he disappeared, presumed dead for a while. But he's got the taste for fame and the adulation of his superiors. He sees himself as a doer. Someone who can make things happen. A general, if you like."

Miles paused, then continued: "We think his father and mother were killed by a smart bomb in 1991. That wouldn't exactly foster love of the West. His father was not much better. He revelled in torture, by all accounts. It's unclear if they were after Hadda, his father, or the company they kept."

Nick looked up and interrupted, "And, you know all this because you are a government, what did you say - problem solver, and you want me to be truthful with you? You come out with all this bullshit - *don't lie to me, Nick*, then you come on board here and lie through your back teeth!"

"I am not lying to you. Look, these people, Hachim Hadda and his team, are up to something and we need to find out what. What do they need cases of Armalites, hand grenades and Geiger counters for? That's scary enough. Put all that together with maybe an oil tanker and there's the possibility of, dare I say it, a dirty bomb. If they manage to put together some kind of nasty device like that on board an oil tanker. Well... it would make Madrid look like a tea party."

Nick was now leaning across the table. He was becoming angrier and angrier.

"Now I see where you're coming from. Oh, yes - yes, I'm getting it. You come on here with a vague idea of getting some nutter like me, perhaps with bomb disposal experience, to go on board a tanker crewed by suicide bombers and Al-Qaeda henchman. Let me guess what's meant to happen next. I kill the baddies and stop the bomb going off in the nick of time. But - but I'm your get out of jail free card. If I fuck it up, it's nothing to do with you or the bloody government!"

Miles was shaking his head and waiting for a chance to interject, but Nick barely stopped for breath.

"You poke around in my private life, decide the minimum amount you could buy me for, or is it blackmail me? I'm not quite sure which it is, yet. And if I don't go for your plan, well, you can always fall back on emotional blackmail. How did the conversation with your superiors go, Miles? Let me guess, *Luckily, Nicholas lost his wife in the train bombings, he's bound to come on board. If we lose him, what's it going to cost us? Only a little money?* When I phoned my mate for help, that's what I wanted. Not a job, not the offer of getting down and dirty with international terrorism. I didn't ask for money. But I've now made up my mind. I think I'm better off without your kind of help."

With that, Nick reached over and slammed Miles's laptop shut, picked it up together with Miles's rucksack, put them under one arm and went up the stairs to the now positively breezy African twilight. At the top of the hatchway, seeing Miles was still seated, Nick said, "You have ten seconds to leave, then I'm going to throw your laptop one of two ways: to port, it goes in the drink; to starboard, it bounces off the jetty."

Miles, stood and raised his hands to buy himself time, but before he could speak, Nick started counting: "One... two..."

*

Fifteen minutes later, Nick was at the helm motoring out of Al-Hoceima bay. The sun was sinking lower towards the sea behind the red Rif mountains to the west, bathing the Mediterranean in a rich, deep glow. It would be another two hours before *Orelia* was safely shrouded in darkness. Nick was decidedly uneasy until he passed the fairway buoy marking the entrance. Now alone and at sea, he could think. Engines were off, his main sail was up, the drop keel was down and about three-quarters of the jib was set.

Earlier, as he let go his ropes, started his engines and left the marina, Miles had still been pleading. He had even threatened to jump on board to come with him, until he saw the look on Nick's face. With his binoculars raised, and in between de-rigging the ridiculous mizzen-mast, Nick's constant scanning to the south had revealed nothing untoward. He doubted Miles would follow through his threat of telling the Moroccans what had taken place, but he couldn't stop himself from looking astern. He would be in no hurry to switch on his sailing lights when darkness arrived.

With the false mizzen now struck, his yacht looked and behaved as she should. The prevailing warm easterly Levante was now blowing and *Orelia* was scudding along in a steady force 4. Nick now had to make a choice: alter course into the wind to starboard and head further in to the Mediterranean or turn to port, to the west, and Gibraltar.

For some while, Nick had been nursing the idea of making his way to the Canary Islands. The plan was to provision there, then do a solo transatlantic trip to the Caribbean. There was a choice of wreck sites there. One was in a decidedly dodgy part of Cuba that, to Smudge's knowledge, had never been dived before. Smudge had told him it wouldn't be easy but was certainly worthy of investigation. Two others, he said, could be interesting and were also in the Caribbean.

To do that he would of course have to trust himself to sail straight past Gibraltar and a possible liaison with the Admiral. He couldn't kid himself; the draw of the pendant and revenge was strong, but so was his will for self-preservation. He tried to put all thoughts of the ship into a deep recess in his brain. That was not for him, not for now.

Nick looked to starboard. In that direction lay the land-locked Mediterranean. He always had his other secret dive sites, one being where he had found the pendant. He had been back there twice since that magnificent find but, the wreck had been re-buried in a storm. That was one possibility, or he could resume his dive on the cannon at the Isla De Alboran and get that lifted and sold. He sailed on directly north towards Spain as he turned the options over in his mind.

*Orelia* was heeling well over to port in the now rising breeze. Nick glanced to port and starboard and said, "To port we have, Operation Certain Death or Caribbean cruise. To starboard, there is, Operation Can't Find The Wreck or Alboran cannon."

The beam reach was a comfortable and fast point of sail. *Orelia* was making 7-8 knots as she skipped across the short breakers. Nick unfurled the rest of the jib, adjusted the main and felt the seas through the wheel and up through his legs. She was now driving herself through nature alone, utilising that free and awesome power, the wind. The first bigger wave slapped into the yacht's starboard bow and threw up spume and white spray. It hit Nick in the face; he was back at sea, alone.

Barefooted and still only wearing shorts and a T-shirt, Nick wiped the salt from his face with his hand and let out a satisfied sigh. The goose bumps appeared on his forearms but the coolness was invigorating. The radar repeater showed no-one on his tail.

Isolated from other people, at sea and thrashing along, it was the first time in two days he felt human again. Holding onto the wheel, he rode the motion of the yacht, anticipating every rise and fall as she ploughed headlong to the north. That was the problem: north meant only Spain. Nick looked up to the clear reddening sky as if waiting for some guidance, a sign. Which way to turn, east... or west. East or west?

He was feeling better, much better, so why ruin it? With his mind made up, he pressed Auto on George the autopilot, and the wheel whirred as it tried to maintain the course. He let go and the course stayed the same: a steady three five five degrees.

"You have the ship, George." Nick swung his legs down the hatchway and landed crouched inside the dark saloon. He reached into the well of the saloon table and pulled out the already open bottle of Scotch and poured himself a generous measure. "Hands to bathe," he muttered to himself after the whisky burned down his throat. Picking up his headlamp and a foulie jacket, he made his way back up top. Nick put the drink in the little recess by the compass. He then sheeted in the jib as hard as it would go, and did the same on the main sail. *Orelia's* rigging groaned and complained as she lay over on her rails. He then jabbed the Auto button again, and George went silent.

He stood with a wide stance, the salt water running down his foul-weather clothing onto his bare feet; both hands on the wheel ready to make his move. All he had to do was put some starboard wheel on, to turn to the east. It had to be to starboard; in that direction lay an end to this mess. On that bearing lay the peace and tranquillity of the life he knew only a few days ago. A life where he had almost managed to carry on without Mariyah: a new life which he had tried to rebuild on his own. Two days ago, he would have considered the job almost done. The demons of the past had been laid to rest. Yet now, fate had dealt him a rum hand he found difficulty playing: he literally didn't know which way to turn. East or west? He was now ready to turn east. His mind was ready, *Orelia* was sheeted-in ready to go head to wind, but still he punched on to the North as he wrestled with his conscience.

Finally, with the wheel in both hands and out loud in his finest officer's voice, he said: "*Starboard 10 please, Coxswain...* Starboard 10, sir... *BELAY that! Sheet out and bear off to port, onto a course of 295°. Steer 295°...* 295 it is, Sir!

Still speaking aloud, Nick said: "So bargaining is out. Begging it will be. We're going into Gib to restock, plead forgiveness, then leave. Nothing else, none of Miles's dirty work. Just in and out, my son. That's it."

As he paid out the jib and mainsail, he turned the yacht to port. She picked up speed and began to surf downwind. The noise of the wind instantly reduced as the vessel now went with the prevailing elements instead of across them. The strain on the starboard shrouds relaxed as the weight began to shift to the back stays. It was almost the perfect sailing angle. The wind was just off the starboard quarter and *Orelia* responded with a kick in her speed. She was now surfing along, touching 8-9 and occasionally 10 knots whenever the stern was picked up by a wave.

The seas and the wind were building steadily. It was now a force 5 occasionally 6. Nick's full attention had to be on the course he steered. The faint glow of his compass and dull lights of his instruments were at the forefront of his attention.

There was no real need to rush; there were no deadlines, nobody to meet, but something was pushing him on. The almost frivolous attitude of when he first escaped Miles and the murder scene was, just like the weather, slowly deteriorating. A few storm clouds were scudding low overhead across the dusky sky, and Nick's mood was beginning to reflect it. Something was making him angry. *It's no good punishing yourself. You fucked up, you lost it. Get over it.* But still he drove hard for his destination.

Throughout the night he pushed on despite the steadily worsening weather, never shortening sail or easing up. By midnight, he was wearing full foul-weather gear as the temperature dropped and the wind increased. He saw one distant ferry, but apart from that he was the only yacht or pleasure craft out there.

It was around 85 nautical miles to Gibraltar, so at eight knots it would take eleven hours, but that was an impossible speed to maintain. He had slipped into his single-handed automatic mode. There was no time for tiredness, and little time for food or refreshment; he wanted to make miles westward. Nick was at one with his craft. All lone sailors have to become a part of their yacht. They know every sound, every feeling, and every inch of their vessel; not necessarily because they want to, but because they have to be in touch with the boat. That thin, fibreglass hull is what separates them from certain death. The rigging, the sails, the ropes, the engines, the navigation equipment, all become essential aids to staying alive. If one part of that loop breaks down, you can find yourself in a world of trouble in an instant. Nick was in tune with *Orelia/Reliant* so when a sound he definitely didn't recognize interrupted his thoughts, he immediately went to investigate.

Having handed the ship to George, something he never liked doing whilst running downwind, Nick jumped below and looked around for the offending sound. It had gone. He had definitely heard it when - he stopped as he heard it again, then moved to the chart table and opened the top drawer. Lying face up was a phone, and it wasn't his. He looked to the back of the chart table, and his phone was in its usual stowage and switched off. He picked up the strange phone and looked at it. At first he thought it was Miles's, but it was smaller and newer. It felt unusually heavy, and it bore no maker's name. It was black, had the normal keys, the same as any phone, and what looked like an old-fashioned, somewhat mottled screen. The screen and the green Dial, key were flashing.

As he held it in his hand, it beeped loudly again. The screen lit up, and Nick read the words: *Urgent. Call me. Press Green. Miles.*

# 16

"*A*h! Nicholas... at last, I was wondering when you'd call, in fact, I was beginning to wonder whether you'd ever call."

"You said it was urgent, Miles. What do you want?" Nick was at the helm, steering into the darkness one-handed.

Something he rarely did was speak to anyone in the outside world while sailing. It was an unwritten rule whilst at sea; he had to be alone. It was partly superstition and a simple matter of just wanting his own space. That privacy and solace always felt invaded if he spoke to anyone on a phone, no matter where they were.

"*The er... vessel on which you had your, little disagreement has gone. I went poking around the boat shed after we parted company. I cut a hole in the tarpaulin and said vessel is not there. We, or should I say, the authorities, would very much like to know of its whereabouts. I don't suppose you've seen it on your travels?*"

"No. I've not seen anyone. Goodbye Miles."

"*Wait, wait, don't go. I have more information. Your friend Michael Smith is coming out to Gibraltar to meet you. Oh, and another thing. I took the liberty whilst on board your fine vessel of checking your fuel status. It was very limited. I have taken steps to organise re-supplies at first light. Also, in light of your financial situation I have left you some cash. You will find it in the chart-table drawer where you found the phone.*"

"Smudge is coming to Gib? What on earth for? And anyway, how did you know I was heading that way?"

*"I think I have a fair measure of what makes you tick, Nicholas. Let's just say that your course of action was an educated guess."*

There was a pause between each break in the conversation, and Nick wondered if their exchange was being scrambled.

*"The ship, the large ship we are all interested in? We are now pretty sure it was a tanker, and it was heading towards Gibraltar. Also the phone you are using is a little out of the ordinary, please treat it with respect. I have left a charger, but if you leave the unit face up in the sun the solar panels will provide a charge. I will speak to you again soon, Nicholas. Please don't hesitate to call me on this phone any time. Just press the green button. I must dash, I have an important appointment. Good day."* The line went dead.

Nick studied the phone and tried to make sense of what Miles had said. Surely Smudge wouldn't be coming. What about his day job? What was he on about? The man was off his rocker. How was he meant to be re-fuelled at first light? *I'm in the middle of the sodding Mediterranean.* There were also a few other questions he would like answered.

All these were put on the back-burner as he noticed a marked drop in wind speed. It was backing round to north and easing off considerably. Nick made the adjustments to the sails and realised his journey time was going to be increased if the wind continued to die.

Within an hour the swell was dropping off and Nick didn't need to keep such a sharp hold of the wheel. The yacht would keep a course steadily now without George eating up the precious batteries. He considered running an engine to increase speed and charge the banks, but one look at the fuel gauge was enough.

Nick continued to run silent, on course for Gibraltar.

# 17

Having spoken to Nick, Miles was in the back of a taxi on the way to Tangiers. He had also spoken to I.D2 again. She was worried, so Miles was worried. Everything had been going perfectly and he could do without a catastrophe slap bang in the middle of his area, Area 22. Until recently he'd considered most security measures under control, but that was before three days ago. Then Hachim Hadda had popped up under his nose, and Miles was making it his primary objective to figure out what the man was about.

Miles was not angry with his potential raw recruit Nicholas Carter for causing this uproar. Far from it. He might end up owing his career to Nicholas.

The Information Director had agreed with Miles that decisive action was needed. A Hercules C-130 transport was already winging its way to the Mediterranean, and once the necessary personnel could be rounded up, another would follow. On board the first flight would be one of the most specialised, varied and downright odd teams that had ever been put together by the British security services.

Miles was anxious, largely because all this was taking place as a direct consequence of what Nicholas had told him. He had no proof, not a shred of evidence to back up what Nicholas said he'd seen, or what had gone on. He was running on instinct.

The first photograph he'd shown Nicholas of Hachim Hadda or The Tunisian, was many months old, but the more recent one had come into Miles's hands only days earlier. He'd received it from one of his DPs (Double-Players). It was a man Miles didn't care for, or trust, but he was well connected and had a stall in Fes near an area where T had been spotted more than once. The consensus was that there was a recruiting/safe house in the city, but finding it would be almost impossible, at least for a European. This player, known as Yusef, was a poisonous individual who had been given to Miles by his opposite number in the MSS (Moroccan Secret Service) in Casablanca.

Miles distrusted Yusef because he was on the take from both sides, hence his DP tag. He seemed to have his fingers in everything. This, in Miles's considerable experience, always tended to cloud a player's judgement. But this time he had come good. He'd sent Miles the picture of Hadda on his mobile. The text with the picture had said that he would not inform Moroccan Security if Miles could pay him 4000 Dirham, about $500, before the week was out. Miles suspected the same text and demand had gone to the Moroccans, but had thought it best to pay and have a word with him at the same time.

Miles was pleased that contact with Carter's boat had been restored, if only briefly. He was now convinced the treasure-hunting loner was on side, even if he didn't know it yet. The few details he'd divulged of the impending operation would do the trick.

Miles caught the first available train to the ancient city of Fes to settle with Yusef. The train journey was no quick run, but there was no easy way to Fes. The first fifty or so miles were straight south and offered an uninterrupted view of the Atlantic surf crashing onto white empty beaches. Here, Miles was on the edge of the continent of Africa; the beach he was looking at went on, unbroken, for a further seven thousand miles to the tip of South Africa and Table Mountain. The rhythmic clanking of the ancient carriages coupled with the hypnotic rocking sent Miles into a semi-conscious state. Then the track turned inland and left the temperate coastal area, and the train began its climb. Almost imperceptibly at times, it slowed on its arduous winding trawl uphill. There never seemed to be a straight stretch to let the automotive run. It weaved its way through towns, villages and hills, one corner after another, followed by a short descent, then another steep, slow climb. From his vantage point high in North Africa, and through heavy eyes, Miles witnessed the most perfect sunset.

His fellow passengers were a typical African assemblage. Some seemed to carry their life's possessions with them. Miles walked through two guards' carriages, both full of men and their push-bikes. Some were so loaded down it was impossible to imagine them being ridden.

There were goats and brightly coloured exotic birds, as well as dogs barking and chickens squawking. He stepped gingerly over prostrate bodies on the floor of the never-ending, rattling train. He even came across a group of old mullahs brewing tea and smoking a hubble-bubble pipe.

Three and a half hours into the five hour, 180-mile journey and they had wound their way up the mountains until they were some 1900 feet above sea level.

It was time to change.

Miles would now play his caterpillar-moth card. He would pupate not from one insect to another, but from one human to another. He didn't need a cocoon of silk to make the change; the toilets would do. He inspected three until one met his requirements. A young Arab-looking girl of about twelve whose mother was asleep next to her was the only one who witnessed the stranger, enter the toilet. Her huge, almost black eyes appeared to be drawn to him. Miles looked straight back at her, but got no reaction.

It was not, however, cleanliness this supposed tourist was seeking from the tiny space, but a mirror. He entered the toilet a westerner, in a blue safari suit, locked the door and made his preparations. Out of his rucksack appeared a small roll of cloth about the size of a newspaper with two elastic bands around it. Shaking it free of its bindings Miles smoothed out a long gown, not unlike a kaftan. It was a drab grey colour, grubby and creased. He threw it over his head and looked in the dirty broken mirror. He then reached up under his hem to undo the zips just above the knees that turned his trousers into shorts.

Dress attended to, he turned to those parts of his body that would be exposed. After using his mobile shaver, he sprayed liquid from an aerosol labelled Suntan Oil, Factor 10 onto his face, hands, forearms and feet, rubbing it in thoroughly. The colour of his skin responded in minutes. The desired effect was rough, but in keeping with his fellow travellers. Into his rucksack went his shoes; out came a pair of sturdy sandals. He then went to work on his eyebrows and eyelashes, using a dark tint to tone down his natural fair colour. Next he brought out a scraggy black wig. It had unusually long hair with hints of grey. The transformation was nearing completion. All that was now required was a steady platform.

Miles stayed in the cubicle making fussy but effective changes to his new look until the train pulled into Sabaa Aioun station. He had only just managed to put his brown contact lenses in before the train got shakily under-way again. He put on his round, slightly tinted glasses, and liked what faced him in the mirror. Finally he pulled out a screwed-up Hessian sack and put his rucksack inside before tying up the top with string. All he now had to change was his posture and attitude.

The little girl looked astonished when the toilet door finally re-opened. The man who had entered the cubicle half an hour earlier had yet to come out. She jabbed her sleeping mother as the hunched-up Arab man walked past them. The mother looked disinterestedly at him, then went back to sleep.

Miles had been learning the Arabic language since his first week on the job and now could get by. More convincing, perhaps, was his manner. The combination of his dress, attitude, and head-bowed walk enabled him to mingle in a city such as Fes without attracting attention.

Stepping off the train, Miles clutched his sack and made for the exit. It was 22:15, dark and quiet as Miles told the taxi driver to take him to Bab El-Gougna, the gate nearest Yusef's shop.

One thousand five hundred feet above sea level, Fes-al-Bali sits in a low dusty basin in the foothills of the Rif Mountains. Miles had been there on more than a dozen occasions over the past ten years but it was not the kind of city someone could get to know easily. As a westerner, he was sure you could never get used to it. He knew people who had lived there all their lives and could still get lost. The city was built in the ninth century, so the streets had only needed to be wide enough to accommodate people, donkeys and hand-drawn carts. The broadest street was about fifteen feet wide, the narrowest being no more than two. There were no vehicles.

The ancient, castellated, walled city is a unique medieval metropolis. Miles knew you had to prepare yourself mentally to enter one of the few gates. It was a touch intimidating, and often exhausting just to walk around.

The taxi pulled up at the archaic pointed-arch gate. The night was already sultry and muggy as the hot easterly *shergui* wind blew in from the Sahara. He knew the temperature would rise another couple of degrees when he stepped into the enclosed cauldron of humanity that was Fes. So it was important to remain true to his dress, to the custom: not to rush, but to amble with purpose and dignity.

He maintained his Arabic approach to life and tried to walk as if he'd done it, not a dozen, but hundreds of times before. His senses were already being assaulted by the smells of the tanneries on the other side of the walls. As he entered the city, his first job was to blank the army of hustlers intent on giving him a guided tour.

"Sir, sir, are you familiar with Fes? Don't go in alone, very dangerous, I will show you the way, very cheap." They tried in English, French, Arabic and German, anything to get the fare. Miles trudged on staring at the ground until the hustlers picked on a more likely, gullible looking group of tourists.

Crossing the thresholds of the city walls, was to be instantly transported from the 20th century back in time to the Middle Ages. Miles knew the first part of his journey from memory, but one false move and he knew he would be lost.

There are over nine thousand tiny alleys and streets in the ancient walled quarter known as the Medina. Many of the confusing lanes are simply dead-ends. Around 200,000 people live there, each working in or owning one of the 150,000 small businesses. A 700-year-old house was the norm. It was a city like no other and Miles was again smacked full on with the excitement and frenetic energy of the place. Making his way past the tanneries, the stench nearly made him gag. There were freshly skinned bulls heads hanging on the outside of the tanning buildings and hides so recently stripped that they were still covered in sinew and blood. A dark swarm of flies fought with maggots to feed on the scraps of putrid flesh.

The men who worked the leather being dyed must have no sense of smell, he thought. The hides were treated with guano and urine to soften it, and then dyed to every colour in the rainbow and more. There was not a machine in sight. The huge vats of toxic coloured dye were made of thick clay and looked as if they had been there for centuries. The men, clad solely in what looked like large brown nappies, trod the leather into the dye with bare feet, smoking, bartering and arguing as they toiled, apparently unaware of the offensive acrid smell of death, excrement and decaying flesh.

Miles looked below street level through an opening and saw a man under a public bathing house shovelling wood into a furnace to heat the baths above. He was coated in ash, grime and sweat. Their gaze met for a second; the man had no life left in his eyes.

As he made his way deeper into the labyrinth of tiny cobbled paths, he kept looking at his watch's digital compass. At every turn he checked he was heading as west as it was possible to go. He walked down a street no more than five feet wide with tiny shops on either side, its keepers calling to tourists, "Come this way, sir. Try this beautiful dress, madam." They would sell anything and everything. Miles had been in this part of the world for years but still had no idea what half the things were.

At every turn he had to make way for the taxis of Fes, the donkeys, some seemingly over-burdened with top-heavy loads. One passed him with several large gas canisters on its back and a boy balancing on one side to stop the whole load toppling over and spilling onto the street. If the donkeys were the taxis, thought Miles, their jockeys fitted the bill as the drivers. Ever skilful, they drove the poor beasts on with a stick and shouts of, "*Balak, balak* - watch out, watch out!"

On Miles trudged, deeper and deeper into the dizzying maze of streets and alleys. Seeing a set of steps, he took them. They led onto a shop roof and he was able to look across the myriad of flat roofs and square courtyards to the minaret of the Mosque which he knew was close to Yusef's place. With no one about, Miles used the time to magic the 4000 Dirham from his blue shorts underneath and stuff the roll of notes into the folds of his kaftan pockets. Come the moment, it would have to be handed over in the usual underhand way.

Coming down again from his vantage point, Miles was swept along in a throng of tourists, donkeys and a large party of local women. The ladies were all covered head to foot in fantastically coloured gowns and holding hands while chatting excitedly. One wore a purple and gold turban that covered her face, and she had a child strapped to her back who was wearing a black, deep red and gold suit. You could either do battle with the place and lose to exhaustion, Miles reflected, or be swept along on the strangely hypnotic human tide.

Eventually, the alley opened out to a generous twelve foot width. The party of women turned left through two colossal carved-oak doors. Miles looked up and could just see the top of the mosque's minaret. On the outside, all that could be seen was a beautifully tiled entrance to the place of worship, but inside those doors he knew there was room for thousands of people.

As Miles approached Yusef's stall, he could see his man talking to a pretty young girl in a short skirt and flip-flops. She was backing away with her hands raised, refusing to touch the brightly coloured silk turban he was proffering, even at his keenest price. His shop at street level was no more than a stall in a doorway, surrounded by beautiful silks and dresses and carpets lit with a multitude of dull yellow lights. Outside, the building was a blank, high-sided wall with no windows; it was indistinguishable from its neighbours.

Miles drew nearer until their eyes met. He had made some subtle changes since his last visit and Yusef was at first wary. Yusef said in Arabic, "Can it be? In the name of Allah surely not... my friend is it you? It is, it is. My, my, how you look like my uncle Dumak. Well done, my friend, well done. If I didn't know better I would think you were born and bred in Morocco. Please, please come through to my humble home and we shall talk." Yusef was obviously doing his utmost to smile, but the result was little more than a grimace.

Miles's DP barked an order, and a girl who was weaving a rug just behind him immediately stood and came forward to run the stall. The counter was cleared and lifted, allowing Yusef to step out. He looked up and down the narrow bustling street, then ushered Miles inside to a larger porch. Every inch was packed to the rafters, covered in goods and cloth of the highest quality. A few feet further back, hidden behind a silk curtain, Yusef opened a door and stepped through, holding it open for Miles.

They entered a sizeable, well lit courtyard. Suddenly, the outside hustle and bustle of Fes el-Bali was forgotten.

Inside the walls, all was tranquil. The courtyard was about five metres square. It had a trickling water fountain, lemon, orange and palm trees, and sitting areas outside the rooms whose doors were all open. The second storey housed the bedrooms and had open double doors leading on to ornate wooden carved balconies.

Yusef placed his arm around Miles as if he were a long lost friend. Miles, uncomfortable though it made him feel, didn't complain and reciprocated. *If that's the way he wants it, so be it,* he thought.

Miles was ushered to a bench covered in decorated cushions. Yusef whistled through his teeth and a boy stuck his head out of one of the rooms. Yusef just indicated the seats, then waved the boy away.

He said, in heavily-accented English, "My friend, you should have told me you were coming tonight, I could have offered you a room, something to eat. You stretch my ability to provide you with the customary welcome when you arrive, as you say, out of the blue." Again he was trying to smile, but wasn't quite pulling it off. Miles just kept staring at his large bent nose, wondering what had happened to it.

"Please do not concern yourself, Yusef. Alas I cannot stay; it is just a flying visit. I must leave this very evening."

Yusef tried to look upset, but his true feelings shone through. The boy appeared from the shadows with a tray. He lowered it onto the tiled table and offered Miles a choice of drinks: Sahari Moroccan wine, lemonade or Casablanca beer. Also included were some boiled eggs dipped in cumin and a selection of pastries. Miles took a long drink of lemonade and nibbled on the pastries filled with meat and rice.

As he ate he said, "Our man... where did you see him? Where did you take the picture?"

Yusef leaned closer. Speaking excitedly but in a hushed voice, he said: "That is just it, Mr M, that is the strange thing about this one. I have had many of my... *associates* looking out for him as I don't do this thing myself, nowadays. You understand, this very dangerous man, yes? But, luck be on my side. A man I don't see before, he stop him and talk to him, right outside my shop! Can you believe? Everyone wants him, and he stop here, right outside, just here! Amazing no? I pretend to be on the 'phone and 'snap', I have him recorded for ever on my memory."

Yusef waited for a reaction from Miles, but getting none he carried on. "So, I send picture to you. I hear also something else. I hear he has a boat. I don't hear where or how big. Maybe this information will help you too, eh?" Then, leaning even closer and whispering, he added, "This man, Mr M, he is Mujahideen, you know, a holy fighter."

Miles nodded, "You have done well, Yusef, very well indeed. You are helping your country by telling me these things. This man will only damage Morocco's reputation throughout the world. I trust this... information has not been made available to anyone else? That would, of course, considerably reduce its value."

Yusef tried to look hurt, but only managed to exude guilt. Laughing, he said: "Mr M, Mr M, you are my friend, and I am a man of my word. I told you if you came I would keep, as you would say, 'for your eyes only', eh, eh?" He appeared proud of his joke, but was wasting his time on Miles.

Miles looked at his watch and said, "I am sorry, Yusef, but I must run. I have another important appointment and I fear I'm already late."

Yusef, hardly able to conceal his eagerness to see the back of Miles, guided him to the door. Just as he was about to open it, he said: "Mr M, I must ask you, Sir, there is the question of... my fee?"

Miles said, "It is in your pocket." Yusef was at first alarmed, then his hand went to his pocket, he smiled and nodded as if that was just what he had expected. As Yusef turned to open the door, something caught Miles's eye. It was a sudden movement, a flash of white on the flat roof of the house. Someone, or something, had quickly moved back from the edge of the courtyard. Miles continued to look, his eyes searching the spot. Yusef, on seeing the direction of Miles's gaze, guided him gently out of the door back through the shop.

Now Miles was eager to leave. He put up his kaftan hood and said, "Goodbye Yusef, and thank you."

# 18

Miles slipped quietly away from Yusef's stall and joined the throng of shoppers, traders, worshippers and locals.

If anything, the market area was even more jammed with humanity than before. He turned right, looking for the Tala Kebira, which was one of the relatively wide lanes that traversed the Medina from east to west. He became increasingly uneasy as he dodged running children and ducked under enormous baskets of goods carried on bobbing heads. What concerned him was Yusef's even shiftier than usual behaviour, and what he did or didn't see on the flat roof. Consequently, Miles kept stopping and looking back while pretending to be inspecting one of the many herbalist-come-healer stalls. In the sea of people, he could see nothing untoward.

He moved on through the crowds until he found himself in a metal-working souk. The market was packed with smiths, hammering away at brass bowls, tin and pewter pots and pans and delicately engraving metal-work. Heads bowed, they worked by candle light or one dull light bulb, oblivious to the cacophony of noise.

It would be difficult to spot anyone attempting to follow him inside the city walls; some parts of the city were pitch black, perfect for a would-be pursuer. He would have to lure his follower outside the confined spaces, and into the open.

The quickest way out of his predicament was straight north, but there was no such thing as straight in this rabbit warren of lanes. Looking at his compass watch, he stole sly looks behind him. Picking one of the many unnamed turnings, he took a right to head north. One minute he would move quickly and duck into an alley to see who would pass, the next he would stop and stare back the way he'd come. He saw nothing.

The relentless wave of people carried him upwards until he was high on a hill and could look back over the dark valley with its mass of flat green roofs, undulating like a river in flood. The only thing that revealed Fes-el-Bali to be a 20th century city were the thousands of uniformly-aligned satellite dishes and the leaching of electric light skywards. Miles moved on north and took at least three wrong turns that gave no clue that they were just dead ends. Each time he had to retrace his steps.

Pausing to let pass another train of donkeys carrying loads of sweet smelling mint, he continued to look surreptitiously behind him. Perhaps he was imagining it and maybe there was nobody there? Perhaps his acute sixth sense had let him down. After waiting and watching for five minutes, he turned abruptly to carry on toward the exit.

That was when he saw him.

A man in a white shirt and jeans. The figure ducked into an opening ahead, and Miles realised he was not being followed. The man was in fact 'front tailing' him. And he had nearly got away with it. But nearly was not good enough. Miles realised he'd had a fleeting glimpse of him before. The man had overtaken him just as he'd made one of his first wrong turns.

Miles had learned the art of following someone from in front on his nine-month course for The Det. Of course, it only worked if you had a rough idea where the target was heading, and was perfect if you had a nervous individual who was always looking over his shoulder. After weeks of training, Miles and three of his Det trainees were let loose in London to follow various targets. Sometimes their controller would pick a target at random, say a businessman or a jogger. At other times it would be an MI5 agent or special service soldier. The followers would all be in radio contact and be furnished with reversible jackets and a selection of hats and glasses. They would also be taught to adopt different gaits. His controller's words now echoed in his ears: "The way someone moves or walks marks them out as surely as if they were wearing a fluorescent jacket or a pink hat."

One operative would tail the target and another might follow on the other side of the road; others would be in a vehicle or on a bike, and then there'd be one in front. The front man would rarely get spotted. Untrained people never thought to be suspicious of the people in *front* of them. But Miles was trained, and berated himself for not thinking of it earlier.

If his front man had guessed he was heading for the nearest exit and knew his way around Fes, then he could remain ahead and let Miles take all the wrong turns. He'd be safe in the knowledge that he had to come down a certain road that led to a gate, and out of the walled city.

Miles decided to carry on out and not let his adversary know he'd been spotted. He felt his shirt sticking to his back under the kaftan, hands wet with sweat. It had begun, the game was on.

Heading more or less north down one of the infinite alleyways, he was careful to give the impression of calmness with fewer and fewer glances behind. He seemed to be fooling his adversary and spotted him several times. Miles became increasingly confident the man was working alone.

He was of North African appearance, but dressed in western clothes, fit-looking, with an immaculate short haircut. His only attempt at disguise was the prodigious use of a map of Fes, which he seemed convinced made him invisible. Down one such dead end, Miles decided to test the man's patience. As he realised he'd taken yet another alley that led to a cul-de-sac lined with cafés, Miles ordered a cup of Fes's famous sweet mint tea from a hand-drawn cart. He leaned against a wall where he could see the only entrance, but could not easily be marked himself. The tea tasted good and the sugar would help give him the energy he'd need before the night was out.

Evidently his stalker was not a patient man. It was no more than a minute before he peered down the dead end over the top of his map. In the reflection of a large tin plate Miles was able to see the man searching the café area until he spotted his quarry. Immediately, he turned on his heel, backed out of the dead end and went left towards the north gate to wait for Miles's arrival.

Miles considered his options whilst watching a scruffy urchin try his utmost to sell fruit to the café customers. He beckoned him over. Miles spoke to him in Arabic. "Which way is the nearest gate from Fes?"

The boy said, "Sir, there are two about the same distance from here, one that way," he pointed roughly north. "And the beautiful Bab Boujloud, (the blue gate) which is that way," he said, pointing west. Miles rummaged in his kaftan pocket and bought out some well-worn Dirham notes. He gave the boy a fifty and said, "Guide me to the blue gate, and I'll give you another one of these." The boy's face lit up with a wide grin. The note disappeared as if by magic, and off they went. As Miles paused at the alley's only exit, he looked to his left. There was his man, about twenty metres further on, attempting to look lost. The boy grabbed a piece of Miles's long flowing kaftan and gave it a sharp tug, "*Hni hni*, (here, here) he said. They went right, so now his white-shirted man would have to follow.

The boy took off at a pace, eager to get his second fifty. They passed through a bottleneck. It was just gone midnight, but there was a human traffic jam in the well-lit meat souk. Miles was pushed hard up against a camel meat butcher's store as yet another train of donkeys threaded their way through the mob. It was led by a skittish horse wearing a blinkered hood. He couldn't help thinking that if the horse bolted with seven donkeys in a train behind it there would be utter carnage.

The back of his kaftan's hood was touching something that smelled somewhat less than fresh. He turned to see his head was touching the stiff lips of a huge camel's face. The forlorn, dead head was hung on a meat hook and its long eyelashes seemed to stare out at the crowd. Its hairy, still wet thick tongue was also dangling out, as if making a rude gesture at the passing hordes. Stuck for that instant where he was, he tried to pick out the smells that permeated his nostrils: blood, cumin, mint, cigarette smoke and - cats piss?

Miles looked back, and for the first time, made eye contact with his follower. The man looked to the ground to avoid his target's gaze. He noticed the man in the white shirt also had dark wet stains around his armpits. Under his left armpit through his wet and now slightly see-through shirt, was a slightly darker protrusion. Is that a weapon you carry with you my friend, Miles wondered. Just as worryingly, the man was speaking on a phone. Calling for help?

Feeling another pull on his robe, Miles looked down to see the boy encouraging him on through a gap in the crowd. Off they went again and the alley slowly opened out, wider and wider. Miles then saw a sign for Bab Boujloud, and an arrow. He put his hand in his pocket and pulled out a hundred Dirham note; that would do. He caught the boy by the shoulder and pushed the money into his hand, then strode purposely towards the gate. As they parted, the boy shouted "*Shukran, shukran, tisbah ala-kheir!*" (Thank-you thank-you, goodnight).

The boy was so pleased with this unexpected bonus to the night that he barely noticed a fraught-looking man wearing jeans shove past him, almost running after the Arab with the funny accent.

# 19

Nick stayed awake all night. The wind had died again to a typical Mediterranean breeze. He had every scrap of sail up and was still only making 4 or 5 knots. *Orelia* was now lolling and rolling heavily. The steep short waves built up by the night's gale had yet to drop. It was an uncomfortable and tiring motion. Nick was constantly fighting the wheel, adjusting sails or checking his course. After a while the physical things that have to be done by a lone yachtsman happen almost automatically, without thought. As he went about his many tasks on a sort of autopilot, his mind raced. Why would Smudge be coming to Gibraltar? It had to be something to do with the Geiger counter and weapons, if indeed it were true. Nick dismissed the idea. Smudge had a full-time job; *it'll never happen.*

Miles's odd phone was now in the cockpit with him. It had started bleeping again in the morning watch, this time with a request for information. The text simply read:

*Orelia. What is your position please?*

Nick ignored it. After all, Miles had no need to know Nick's position. He already knew he was going to Gibraltar. *Interfering bastard*, he thought. The same message then came up again and again, on the button, every fifteen minutes. Nick tried to turn the phone off but could not. Eventually the noise wore him down. He texted his latitude and longitude from his GPS and pressed the green button. The phone stopped its infernal noise.

Nick occupied himself with the jobs that take up a single-hander's time at sea. He pumped his bilges, noting the pink tinge from his loss of blood. He took his GPS position again and compared it with his dead reckoning position. Close. He checked his water and worked out his fuel, trying to fathom out how far he could get if he pushed *Orelia* hard on his remaining dregs. Not far enough, he reckoned.

His next job took him down on his hands and knees with his head beneath the deck boards just for'ard of the starboard engine's flywheel. He was sponging out the last of the bloody, oily, foul-smelling bilge water when he felt an odd vibration through the fibreglass hull; it resonated up through his knees. A faint, foreign noise grabbed his attention. This time it was definitely not Miles's phone. This time its origins were outside the boat.

Only five minutes earlier Nick had scanned his radar and the slowly lightening horizon and found there was nothing within miles of his position. He dropped the disgusting sponge in the bilges, and pulled himself up the companionway stairs. The sun was not yet up; it was twilight, in between daylight and night-time. The time when a yachtsman is at his lowest ebb after a long night.

He could still hear it, a deep, low, throbbing tone, receding quickly. But when he stood still and scanned 360°, the noise had gone.

"What the... bloody hell was that?" he asked George his autopilot. Receiving no answer, he began to wonder if he'd imagined it. He took the wheel away from George and stood looking and straining to hear the strange sound again. There was nothing.

"I said, what was that, George? You were on watch. Didn't you see anything?"

\*

Two thousand feet above *Orelia*, the Royal Air Force C130 Hercules transport was flying a long, slow thirty mile arc. The navigator, Flight Lieutenant Paul Morris, had picked up the yacht on the aircraft's radar. He knew the yacht's approximate position after receiving a reply to his computerised text message requesting its location. That had been an hour ago, so taking that position and giving the yacht a rough sailing speed of 5 knots, heading west towards Gibraltar, the area of sea they had to search was considerably reduced.

The aircraft started a search pattern about 30 miles to the east of the anticipated position. A lazy creeping-line ahead confirmed what the radar had initially indicated. Nothing, apart from a huge bulk carrier. As the Navigating officer reduced the range of the E190 radar, a return 20 miles ahead of the aircraft briefly blinked, then vanished, but the hint was there.

A couple of runs along the creeping-line, and the radar return flickered intermittently and then steadied. It had to be what they were looking for. But Paul had learned always to be cautious when reporting a target. If it wasn't the yacht they were after, the grief he would get from the rest of the crew could go on for days. There was only one way to find out.

*"Skipper... Nav... Radar contact. 50 degrees left of the nose, 16 miles."*

Everyone on board wearing a headset was listening in to the cockpit's conversation. *"Roger Nav. Turning on, any idea of its size?"*

Paul looked at the radar return, now on the nose of the aircraft and at 15 miles. *"It's small, there's no doubt about it... come left 5 degrees".*

*"Coming left. Range?"* The captain was peering anxiously through the aircraft's lower windshield.

*"12 miles, now on the nose and moving slightly right to left."* Paul glanced at the two pilots and wished one of them would spot the yacht soon.

*"Come further left 4 degrees, range 2 miles, you should be visual any moment."*

*"Contact!"* the co-pilot exclaimed as he pointed slightly right of the nose. The yacht passed below. It had to be their target.

*"Skipper... Nav 'O' here. The vessel we've just flown over stands a good chance of being our target yacht, seeing as it's the only one out here. Sun up in sixteen minutes. Suggest we come in from the east, we will have the sun directly behind us, he'll never know what hit him."*

*"Roger that. I agree; we will surprise this bubblehead. Sgt Willis... lower the tailgate and get loads one and two ready for despatch"*

*"Lowering the ramp now, skipper. Bombs one and two ready for your mark."*

*"I never expected anything less,"* said the skipper, wearing a proud smile as he started to drop the Herc down to 300ft.

\*

Nick wanted to stay on deck and watch sun-up; something all true mariners never tired of watching. Sun-up in the city means nothing but time to go to work. Sun-up on a clear day at sea is a thing of beauty that reminds you what a small cog in the universe you are. A reminder of how insignificant you are compared to the wonders of nature and the vastness of the sea. Unfortunately, Nick needed to finish the bilges and had to check both oil levels in his two powerful diesel engines. He also toyed with the idea of using the slowly calming weather to change one of the fan belts on the port engine. When that was done, he promised himself a decent hot breakfast.

With that in mind, he was back on his knees in the bilges with a dipstick in his hand, when again he stopped and strained his ears. This time the noise was growing louder. Nick jumped up, smashing the back of his head against the engine compartment lid. It reopened his wound.

"FUCK!" he shouted as he slipped and skidded with wet feet up the companionway stairs to look around the horizon. With one hand on the back of his head, he squinted and peered aft to the east. "It sounds like a..."

Whatever was making the noise was closing at an alarming rate.

There! A huge four-engined Hercules revealed itself and flashed by, barely metres above his mast. Nick nearly fell over as he craned his neck to follow the ungainly aircraft from east to west. Staring open-mouthed ahead, Nick watched aghast as the aircraft dipped its wings in the internationally recognized signal for, *Don't worry, we've spotted you.*

Its flat rear-loading ramp was wide open. Two men were standing by the ramp. One, obviously the loadmaster, was wearing green and seemed to be gesticulating and speaking into a mouthpiece attached to his headset. The other figure was wearing all black overalls and paratroop-type boots with a black lifejacket. He was also wearing a headset and a baseball cap on back-to-front. Then the plane banked hard to port and Nick couldn't help wondering why the figure in black was waving furiously at him.

His deck VHF radio speaker then spat out some squelched feedback: *"Orelia-Orelia-Orelia... this is flight H6957 Channel 09... please respond!"*

Nick watched the Hercules's changing profile as he moved towards the deck VHF. He picked up the hand-held microphone and tuned the set to Channel 9. In a slight state of shock, Nick pressed the transmit key and said, "This is *Orelia,* over."

*"Orelia this is flight H6957, can you please continue on your course to steer and not deviate for the next ten minutes. We have a delivery of EFBs for you. Suggest you take in all sail and start your engine. Over."*

Nicks reply was simply, "EFB delivery?"

*"Roger, stand by!"*

As Nick watched, the Hercules banked and climbed to around a thousand feet. It slowly got smaller and smaller. Still stunned at this unexpected turn of events, Nick didn't know whether to ask questions of the Hercules crew or to do as he was told and take in sail. He took in sail. With his port engine running, he furled up the large jib and his mainsail. By the time he'd done that and looked astern, the aircraft was looming in on his position. He handed the wheel to George. That way, he could give whatever happened next his undivided attention.

*

*"Okay, listen up everybody, we're going to come in at 250 feet directly down his starboard beam. I want both loads dropped about 100 feet in front of the target vessel. Let's get them away as close together as possible, okay? I want this done quickly and safely. Any questions?"*

The man in black who had been standing watching at the tailgate was now wearing a headset and grinning from ear to ear. He pressed the transmit button on his headset and said: *"I have a question, captain. Do we have permission to throw missiles at the yacht, and possibly the contents of the aircraft's toilets? I owe him that, at the very least!"*

There was a long delay as the captain could be heard through the on board communication system asking who the devil that was. Eventually he said *"Smudge, I'm sorry, not this time, maybe another day. There are influential people on this flight, and you know the important cargo we are carrying. We need to offload in Gibraltar as quickly as possible. The last thing I need is complaints from any of the crew, or a rather pissed off sailor who's had blue loo dumped all over his gleaming white yacht from a great height."*

Smudge just smiled. *"Roger, no problem skipper!"* But he still held an egg in his hand.

*"Two Minutes."* Paul had worked out the range of the yacht and at an airspeed of 140 knots they would be over him in no time. The loadmaster readied himself at the ramp.

The Navigator then gave the commentary, *"Slow down, slow down... easy... Go!"* The captain pulled back the throttles and reduced the aircraft's speed to 125 knots, which was the ideal speed for dropping the two loads.

Paul warned the crew, *"right 5 degrees, 15 seconds!"*

*"Roger,"* answered the Captain, *"Action Stations"*

Paul pushed his intercom switch to on: *"Red on... Green on!"*

*"Both loads gone!"* shouted the Loadmaster

*"Red on... Lights Out."* Paul flicked his intercom switch to standby, *"That'll be within 100 feet of the yacht. 50 feet if I've got my calculations right."*

# 20

At last Miles was outside the walled city of Fes. There were taxis, buses, horses and donkeys milling about the beautifully tiled Blue Gate. Without running, he headed as fast as he could for a group of tourists boarding a bus. No matter how much he would have liked, he had no intention of joining them, and barged through the middle.

One taxi in the square looked as though it would suit. It was just the other side of the coach. As he approached the black Mercedes with 'TAX' on the roof, his hopes faded. There was no driver to be seen. It was the newest and best-kept taxi available, but would be no good without anyone to drive it. Whilst scanning the area for another, he noticed a pair of feet clad in one red and one blue flip-flop on the steering wheel. Smoke drifted from the driver's window.

Without another thought, he strode towards the car, opened the back door and got in. In doing so, he achieved two goals. He would be out of sight of his persistent tail, and he could begin negotiations for the long journey ahead. The driver sat up in a cloud of smoke and swung round, somewhat alarmed at the speed with which he had picked up his new fare. There was no time for pleasantries.

"How much to Casablanca?" Miles blurted out in English.

The driver, who appeared so small he could barely see over the steering wheel, replied, "*lo tismah?*" (pardon?)

Miles switched to his modern Arabic and said again, "How much to Casablanca?"

"Casablanca! At this time of night? You crazy, or desperate. Do you know it is 350 kilometres from here?"

"280," said Miles. "I will pay you two thousand Dirham." Miles looked back towards the gate for his man.

"But-no sir, I have wife who is expecting me home. I would die," he said as he turned down the hypnotic Arab music on the car radio.

"And a further thousand if you can get me there by Azaan." (*Azaan* - the call for morning prayers at sunrise.) As he spoke, Miles became aware of a dusty Jeep tearing into the square and skidding to a halt close to the ancient gates.

He showed the man a bundle of notes. The driver's eyes lit up. He paused, then stubbed out his joint.

"If you would please give me the two thousand now, so that we know we can trust each other like brothers."

Miles quickly counted, then handed over the money. The driver then started to count the money again and Miles reminded him, "By Azaan for the bonus!"

The man smiled a smile that carried an equal number of black and gold teeth. Looking back at his passenger in the rear-view mirror he said: "Would Sir please fasten seat belt?"

Miles looked around, but there were no seat belts in the front or back.

"My name is Mohammed. You have picked the right man and the fastest car. Now we shall be away to the coast." He slipped off his flip-flops and gunned the engine. As he did so, Miles conveniently dropped some small change in the back of the cab and bent low to find it. Mohammed reversed out of his space and the back of his car was facing the triple-gated entrance to Fes. He selected automatic and the German car's tyres spun in the dusty square. Miles sat slowly up and peered over the back seat to see two men at the Jeep. One was White Shirt, the other he couldn't see as he was still at the wheel. White Shirt was watching the departure of the Merc, open-mouthed.

Mohammed kept to his word. The tyres of the old Mercedes didn't stop spinning until it hit proper tarmac just outside the city walls. Then they turned left to head west towards the Atlantic coast, and Mohammed kept chatting away.

"My wife, she is going to kill me... until I give her some money. I may die before I can spend it, but, *Inshallah*, if it is Allah's wish, so be it." Improbably, the small man was chuckling and seemed happy about his possible demise.

Miles was barely listening; he was busy studying the road behind him. As he did so, he was thinking: *Yusef, Yusef, Yusef... you have sold me, haven't you? You have sold me to the Tunisian's henchmen, but not until you got paid by me. This is a dangerous game to play, Yusef, and if I survive this night I will teach you that.*

By now, he had convinced himself that the flash of white he'd seen on the roof as he left Yusef's house was the same armed man in the white shirt who had been following him for the last hour. The problem was, there were now two of them, and they might be summoning more help. But Miles's hope that they had lost him as Mohammed sped out of the square and shot round the outskirts of Fes was soon shattered. The car that had been a steady distance behind them was overtaken and cut up by a dusty Jeep.

The Jeep then roared up close behind them and the inside of Mohammed's taxi was lit up by the full beam headlights. There was no point in Miles crouching any longer. He sat normally in the seat, listening to Mohammed's incessant ramblings.

"As Satan is my witness, will you look at this madman? He is trying to drive *inside* my car."

Mohammed stuck his hand out of the speeding taxi and waved the Jeep past. It pulled out of the slipstream and came alongside as if to overtake. Miles pulled his hood up and forwards to cast a shadow over his face.

Mohammed kept gesticulating out of the open window, encouraging the Jeep past him, but it stayed level. As the two cars sped along side by side, Mohammed slowly became quieter, then wound up his window. His bravery had deserted him. Miles tried to look round the material of his hood. He could make out his white-shirted adversary sitting in the passenger seat, but now he was wearing mirrored aviator sunglasses and staring into the back seat at Miles's shadowy figure. Watching with peripheral vision, Miles was preparing to dive flat down on the floor at the first sign of movement or a possible gunshot.

But it didn't happen. The Jeep slowed and took its place behind the taxi, seemingly content for now to follow. It dropped back until the distance was quite normal for the 60-70 m.p.h. they were travelling. The convoy sped through a relatively built-up area with road lighting and roadside shops and stores, but he knew this would not always be the case. There were barren mountainous areas of nothingness along their route.

Miles had to think, to seize the initiative. Mohammed now couldn't keep his eyes off of his rear-view mirror, but had thankfully shut up. The bravado had left his driver and he was paying Miles as much attention as he was the following car, no doubt now wishing he was in bed with his wife.

"Seize the initiative" is what Miles's controller kept saying during those long training days. "*Carpe diem*, gentleman. Seize the day. If you are being followed, or you find yourself in a situation where you are not in control, your first thought must be to seize the initiative, to turn it around, get yourself back in control. To bumble on or sit idly by while your follower or captor is in charge will only get you killed."

Known as C1, the controller would end every day's lesson with that same comment. He was a wily old soul and it was rumoured he had had some 50 years in the field, which was why MI6 now had him teaching. With those words in mind, Miles sought to alter things.

He picked his sack off of the floor and undid the old piece of string. Reaching inside one of the side pockets of his rucksack, he pulled out two black wrist sweatbands. Keeping his arm out of sight in the sack, Miles undid the button on the blue shirt he still wore beneath his Kaftan. He slid a sweatband up under his baggy sleeve until it was around his left forearm, near the crook of his elbow. He placed the second band on the same arm, but around his wrist. Miles then felt for an opening near the bottom of one of his rucksack's shoulder straps. Pulling a small Velcro tab, he pushed down on the hard metal-like object hidden within the strap. Out came a long, thin and very sharp stiletto. The blade and handle were made of a compressed ceramic material which rendered it undetectable by metal detectors. It was housed in a thin plastic sheath. The sheath had a thick piece of elastic around its centre. Sticking out of one end was the knife's short handle and the two quillions.

Miles drew the knife, placing his fingers around the quillions; the short handle fitted perfectly into the heel of his hand. He then placed the blade back in its sheath and looped the elastic around his forearm, tucking both ends under the sweatbands. The knife now rested snugly along the inside of his arm. He pulled down both shirt and kaftan sleeves and looked up to the rear-view mirror. Mohammed had been craning his neck to see what was going on.

Miles sat forward between the two front seats.

"You need some fuel."

It came out as a statement, not an inquiry. The taxi driver looked down at his instruments and nodded.

"There is a place not far from here, but... am I expected to...?"

"I will pay. You will stop there and fill up. I need to freshen up as well."

Just as the houses and shops dwindled and thinned, the garage appeared, like a last trading post before the long and lonely mountainous drive to the coast. Starkly lit in bright white light, there would be no hiding for friend or foe. Miles studied the layout of the place as they arrived. He bundled some Dirhams into Mohammed's hand and was out of the car almost before it had stopped. As he approached the garage front, a man in a turban who seemed to have been asleep looked out at him from behind thick plate glass and bars. Miles asked him for the bathroom, and the man pointed to the right. As he turned the corner, he sneaked a look back at the Jeep. It had pulled up just outside the garage in a dark spot, and the lights turned off.

As soon at he was out of sight, Miles ran.

He sprinted down the side, along the rear, then back to the front of the garage at the opposite end of the building. Approaching slowly and in the shadows, he could now see the Jeep and its two occupants.

His adversary in the passenger seat was sitting, looking towards the garage. As Miles watched them, he removed his wig and glasses, pulled the robe over his head and rolled it up. He then backed away from his vantage point and ran back towards the toilets at the rear. He opened the door to the stinking bucket toilet and looked for a light switch. He turned it on, shut the door, and walked away.

Miles searched around behind the garage. There was nothing but dusty brush and desert, no perimeter walls, no boundary fencing. Moving gingerly away from the building, he noticed a trail of rubbish leading to some rough dusty steps down a ravine. He took a rock and threw it into the dark hole. Judging by the sound of the 'plop,' the smell and the flies, it was some sort of combined open sewer and rubbish tip.

Miles crept back through the dusty yard towards the toilet. He stopped, crouched down then froze as he picked up movement, away to his right. It was a white shirt.

The man was tiptoeing along the back wall of the garage, his eyes fixed on the slivers of light escaping the toilet door. As he approached, he drew a pistol. Arriving at the door, he stood with his back to the wall, screwed on a silencer, and listened.

After a minute he said in Arabic, "Excuse me, sir, is everything all right?... Sir, are you okay? Please come out... there is a problem with your driver."

White Shirt moved to face the toilet door, legs apart. With the silenced weapon in his right hand, he snatched open the door with his left, pointing the gun inside. The bright light and empty room momentarily confused him. There was a small bundle of what looked like clothes on the toilet seat. Reaching in to pick them up, he heard a sound behind him.

He spun round, his weapon pointing level. There was a blonde European, who momentarily stopped and raised his hands when he saw the gun. He dropped his gun to his side and was about to tell him to get away when the man did a very strange thing. He hugged him.

Miles had showed the man both of his palms as if to say "Look, I am no threat, I am not armed. Please don't shoot."

When White Shirt dropped the weapon to his side, Miles pinioned him in a bear hug, which was probably the last thing he expected. It also trapped his arms by his sides. With his arms wrapped around the man's back, Miles drew the stiletto from his sleeve, placed his left hand around the nape of the man's neck and parted his knuckles. In the gap between his fingers, he felt the soft hollow depression, behind which lay the *medulla oblongata*, the point that joins the brain stem to the spinal cord.

He placed the tip of the stiletto there and rammed home the heel of his hand with a quick and lethal up-thrust.

After the initial 'pop' of breaking skin, there was little resistance. The two quillions came to rest on Miles's parted knuckles.

The man froze in his standing position. No sound passed his lips. There was no movement or last gasp. His life did not flash before him. He just died, instantly. The trauma to his body was such that it was shocked into a ramrod straight pose. The cardiac centre is located in the *medulla oblongata* and the knife stopped his heart, in a beat.

Miles felt nothing more than hot fluid seep onto his thumb. Slowly, the body slumped onto his chest. He walked it backwards and sat it on the toilet seat. He pulled off some toilet tissue and twisted it into a long pen shape, holding the slippery handle of the knife in one hand and the tissue in the other. As he removed the knife from the man's cranium, he pushed the end of the tissue into the hole, twisting it in with his thumb. He noticed it was mainly clear, cerebral fluid, with tiny spots of deep red blood in it. The already small discharge stopped, so would hopefully not drip over him.

He bent low and put the man's waist onto his shoulder, then pulled himself up with the toilet door-frame. With something approaching a fireman's lift, he walked White Shirt out into the desert, slowly making towards the pit.

\*

With two thousand Dirham and a full tank of gas to the good, Mohammed was considering whether to cut and run back home to his warm bed when his strange passenger walked briskly from behind the garage.

Miles was pulling down his dishevelled kaftan and got into the car.

"I was wondering where you were. Did you have to take a sh..."

"Drive please, if you want your bonus."

"Okay, okay, I drive, I drive." With a loud tutting, Mohammed started up the Merc's big engine and pulled out onto the road. Miles turned to look at the Jeep. The driver was standing by the car door, looking first towards the garage and then after the disappearing taxi. He was clearly unsure of what to do.

After watching his passenger adjust his glasses in the rear-view mirror, Mohammed risked a question. "Who are your friends... behind... in the truck?"

Miles said, "It's none of your business. Just drive." Then thinking he still may have some work to do that night, Miles added, "If you must know, between you and me, you understand, it is a jealous husband."

Mohammed thought this was very funny and slapped the steering wheel and laughed as they negotiated a roundabout and rejoined the carriageway leading to the mountain roads.

Miles was unsure as to what he should do next. He had emptied the first man's pockets of anything interesting, including his phone, but he still had a list of unanswered questions. Questions like: had he used his phone again to tell anyone the direction they were heading? Was the driver simply a driver, and if so would he now be high-tailing it home, or was he another one of T's hired thugs? Having lost his pal, was it likely he would follow on alone?

There was one thing Miles was sure of. He now had a battered-looking silenced Walther P22 hand gun.

# 21

Nick felt tiny as the lumbering aircraft with its distinctive massive tail fin slowed almost to stalling speed. It settled on its course directly astern of the yacht and seemed as though it was about to pass directly overhead. But at the last minute, it dropped its starboard wing and moved slightly to the right of *Orelia*. When it was directly on Nick's beam again he could see the loadmaster and some of the crew stood on the edge of the open tailgate.

As Nick lifted the binoculars to look inside the huge rear door, he noticed a container being pushed out the back, closely followed by a second. As soon as they left the hold, a trailing parachute opened, slowing the forward motion of the container, and it began to swing under the chute.

Nick had no idea what was being dropped, apart from the fact it was called an EFB. It was an acronym that rang no bells. The containers were black plasticised bags with a cone-shaped bottom. The only distinguishing marks on them was a white label with a box attached to one side. As the Hercules disappeared ahead, the first container made a gentle splashdown. Nick put his binoculars away and without further thought spun the wheel to starboard and opened the throttle.

"What is going on George? What is going on?"

Nick came alongside the first container and noticed a floating line leading to the second one. The large white waterproof label had written on it, "READ ME."

He lay on the deck, reached out and tore it off. What he could now see was a flexible rubberised bag, and judging by the way it was moving on the surface of the sea, it appeared to be full of liquid. There was also a carton of long life milk taped to the top of the first bag. Nick said aloud, "Miles."

He then read the idiot's guide, written in typical MoD speak:

### Emergency Fuel Bags. Marine Diesel (EFB/D)

Turn off all the engines and all sources of ignition.

Unravel flexible hose from reel, insert into fuel receptacle.

Open quarter turn valve. Decant fuel.

When empty, transfer of liquids will cease.

Ensure escape route is clear. SAFETY OF PERSONNEL ESSENTIAL!

Set countdown timer to 5 - 10 - or 30 mins.

Stand clear. Extreme fire and burn hazard. White Phosphorus charge. (WP)

Nick killed the engine and secured the fuel bags now bumping gently alongside. He took the hoses and placed one into each of the fuel tanks. Then, looking at the idiot's guide, he opened both quarter-turn valves. A battery in the boxes began pumping the fuel. The speed of the transfer astonished him. His starboard tank had more in it than the port, so he turned off the quarter-turn valve when his fuel indicator was approaching full. The humming of the pump stopped instantly. Satisfied both tanks were brimful, he chucked the now limp, flat hoses back onto the part-full bags.

Looking at the two control boxes on each bag, he noticed a see-through protective cover over the control box, with four hand-tightened screws holding it in place. A large pin went through the centre of the box with a red tag on it that said, "PULL FOR LIVE." Nick pulled the pin from both boxes. Underneath the covers were four buttons.

On-Off. 5 - 10 - 30 mins.

Nick started both his main engines, had a good look round at the horizon to make sure he was alone, undid the line to the fuel bags, pulled them close and pressed On.

Two digital clocks flashed up with 0.00. He pressed: 5 on both bags, and tossed the line far away from his propellers. The timers began to count down with a quiet if somewhat sinister *beep* with each passing second. The bags began to drift astern and Nick cautiously put his port engine slow ahead. When he was sure he was clear, he opened both throttles. *Orelia* surged forward. He looked around for the elusive Hercules, but there was no sign of it. At about 500 metres away he put both engines to idle, picked up his binoculars and studied the two black marks on the sea.

Exactly five minutes later, there were two simultaneous *whumps*. Not explosions, but the bright white phosphorus and diesel stood out in the sea as white fireballs. The bags and fuel burned fiercely. Nick thought the environmental impact would be minimal in a thousand-plus metres of water. One bag sank below the surface and the second soon followed. There was now nothing on the surface except white smoke and bubbles as the white phosphorous grenades continued to burn on their long descent.

Nick weighed up his situation and checked the weather. "Almost perfect," he announced. Jumping down below he lifted the retractable keel and replaced his deck boards. The fan belt would have to wait. "I hope it lasts!"

Checking his radar, Gibraltar and the entrance and exit to the Med was still beyond his 30 mile sweep. He grabbed a chocolate bar from an emergency ration pack, hopped back up top and prepared *Orelia* for take off.

Back on board the Herc, the captain had a change of heart.

*"Okay, listen in all. This is our last bombing run. We're going to pay our friend another close visit. We will come down on him from about 3000 feet. One chance, Smudge, that's all you get. Then it'll be the flypast, then we are off. Our reason for revisiting the area, of course, is to make sure our man is motoring happily, and the fuel bags are no more. No other reason. All clear...? Right, stand by..."*

*

Nick was leaning over the transom checking the cooling water from both engines, munching on a Snickers bar when he heard a deep rumbling sound. It sounded completely different to the Hercules, but before he could lay his eyes on it, it was on him. Again it came straight out of the sun and he couldn't look at it until it was directly low overhead. As it buzzed him and swept round, he noticed there was more than just the one figure in black now. Many men, in various patterns of camouflage, were packed onto the rear cargo door. That's when he first recognised the tall figure in black wearing the headset:

"Smudge?"

He then realised he was under air attack. There were splashes around his port side and something hit the coach roof. Nick was splattered by some wet and gooey slime. He wiped his cheek and picked off a tiny piece of eggshell. "Smudge."

As the warm exhaust smell of spent aviation fuel wafted down onto *Orelia's* solitary crew, Nick decided to put on a show of his own for the final fly past he knew would follow. As the Hercules lined up for its last run, Nick shouted, "Full ahead, both, Coxswain! *Understood, full ahead both. Both engines full ahead, Sir.* Understood, steady as she goes!"

Nick pushed the two throttles forward and *Orelia's* tail dug in. The engines were noisy and complained. Their revolutions gradually increased as they tried to shift the bulk of what was, after all, a sailing vessel, from a standing start. He opened the large ballast dump valves and the deluge of sea water from within the hull mixed with the huge boiling mound of salty sea behind her. At that moment, it would have looked anything but impressive from the sky above. The Herc was still some way off; she had out full flaps and was crawling along at no more than 125 knots, four tails of dark smoke bellowing from her powerful Allison engines.

*Orelia* strained to break free of the shackles that bound her to the surface of the sea. The deck shook, the rigging vibrated and Nick's binoculars took a tumble from their stowage.

Black exhaust spewed out of the churning white water as slowly, the weight decreased and the speed increased.

"Come on, girl... come on my beauty, you can do it."

It was not ideal to attempt to get up on the plane with two full tanks of diesel and half a tank-full of fresh water. The extra weight was phenomenal. A yacht's shape was designed to sail through water, not plane on top, but *Orelia* continued to shoulder aside the heavy sea, relentlessly gathering momentum.

White water was now crashing over the bows and rolling astern, adding still more weight. The last of the ballast water trickled out of the stern as she reached 12, and then 15 knots. *Orelia's* tail was picked up by one of the last bigger swells from the previous night's storm. The stern kicked ahead, and as the wave rolled forwards, the nose lifted on the crest. That was it. She shook off enough water to climb laboriously onto the surface of the sea, just as the huge lumbering Hercules drew close astern. Nick tweaked the helm over to port and as she keeled over, the last of the deck water ran out through the scuppers. The course change had the other desired effect of taking him out of egg bombing range. She was off, 19... 20... then 21 knots.

The Herc drew level and there were dozens of men vying for position to see the yacht doing a seemingly impossible speed. *Orelia* now tore along the surface of the sea with a scraggy white mane of water pouring from her decks and being whipped aft by sheer speed. Only one on board the transport knew why such a speed was possible. Smudge cheered him on, applauding, and roared, "Go on, my son, give it some!"

The Hercules drew ahead dipped its wings for the last time, then climbed and shaped course for Gibraltar.

# 22

Mohammed the taxi driver seemed relaxed. They had left the garage some ten minutes ago and Miles was beginning to get a lid on his adrenalin.

There was a wind blowing, and the red hill's dust was everywhere, making visibility poor. Consequently they were driving at a more sedate pace up a long hill and Mohammed was his old chatty self. Miles ignored him. The noise suppressor made the handgun rather long, but he tucked it between his legs and begun his search of the dead man's possessions. A wallet, some rolled up notes, a spare magazine clip, and the mobile phone he'd seen the man using back in Fes.

As he picked up the phone, it vibrated. It was ringing, but on silent mode. On the screen it had the caller's number and the name: Rass. It also had six missed calls, from the same caller. It must have been vibrating silently in the bag. Pressing the Ignore button, Miles tried to find his way around the menu. Hurtling down the increasingly bumpy road in the back of a cab was no place to break out his laptop and copy another SIM card. That would have to wait. He pressed: Calls Made, and found one that was recent, 38 minutes ago.

Miles thought. *That's the one you made in the meat souk, isn't it? Did you tell the caller who you were following?*

As he searched through the phone his driver spoke. He looked up to see Mohammed's eyes in the mirror.

"Sir - sir, I think your angry husband is upon us again," he said somewhat gleefully. "Is he going to follow us all

161

the way to Casablanca? Maybe it was his daughter, not his wife? He is angry man."

Miles became aware of the inside of the cab being lit up by some headlights behind. He looked over his shoulder and could just make out the Jeep's outline. Not just a driver then, he reasoned. He would have to put plan B into action. The thing was he had no plan B. One would have to be developed, and quickly.

He sat staring ahead through the windscreen. It was now desolate out there. There were no houses, no buildings, no street-lights, just a dark, dusty mountain road with steep banks of rock climbing up each side. The phone vibrated again. It was Rass.

"Mohammed, can you do something for me, can you slow down? I would like to see who it is."

He tutted loudly, shaking his head. "You ask me to get you to Casablanca before sunrise, and then you ask me to slow down. You take for ever in garage. I cannot do both." Then as Mohammed slowed the car and looked into his rear-view mirror he said, "You don't know who it is? How many women have you pookered?" and he giggled again.

The Jeep also slowed behind the Mercedes. One headlight was brighter than the other and both were covered in a thick film of mountain dust. Miles could not see the driver's face, but he could make out his silhouette.

He took the phone, and dialled the number that had desperately been calling.

Miles dialled Rass.

Turning and resting his chin on the back seat, he stared at his follower's shadowy outline. As the first ring sounded in his ear, the man grabbed something from the dashboard and the Jeep wobbled across the road as he put something to his ear.

"*Sonny... Sonny, is that you... where are you? Sonny, Sonny!*"

Miles hung up. The line went dead, and he whispered towards the Jeep, "Good evening, Rass."

Miles mulled over the situation for a while. How many more aliases did Hachim Hadda have? He was also known as the Tunisian, shortened in intelligence circles to T. What did his henchmen call him? Miles planned to find out, maybe from the phone he now held, a phone that had once belonged to a man called Sonny.

For one of the first times in his life, he was unsure what to do. Stroking his chin as they bumped down the road, he thought long and hard about his next move. He could not lead this man all the way to Casablanca, to the headquarters of the Moroccan secret service, or Hadda would find out that the British were working with the Moroccans.

The Jeep had now dropped back a good distance. The road worsened, with pot holes that could jar your teeth if you didn't see them in time to skirt them. Some holes would be better described as craters. One took up the whole width of the road. Mohammed had to slow to a crawl, drive down into it, and gun the engine to get out the other side. There were parts of the journey where the road narrowed to a single lane. In places it would round a rocky outcrop and appear to hang precariously on the side of the mountain by what appeared to be more luck than engineering design. In some high parts there were crash barriers, in others you could clearly see where some poor soul had driven straight through, or the cliff had merely eroded away and the barrier itself had tumbled into the abyss.

They passed one vehicle coming in the other direction. It was a heavy truck, trundling its way round the mountains.

"At least we know the road is strong from here," Mohammed muttered with not quite so much of his usual humour.

Mohammed had stopped his chattering. He was so short, in some places he had to pull himself up on the steering wheel to see down potholes or drive round fallen boulders.

A semblance of a plan was building in Mile's mind and with a hint on an American accent, he confessed.

"Mohammed, I am not really Moroccan, or an Arab. All this I'm wearing is a disguise. I am an American. I have a wife in Casablanca." Then with a heavy sigh he continued, "I have just ended an affair. She was very upset and I think has told her husband, who is the man behind us." Mohammed was listening intently, his gold teeth glinting in the rear-view mirror, he was smiling and gloating at Miles's sordid confession.

"I cannot let him follow me all the way to Casablanca or I will have another woman in tears, my wife. Do you understand?"

He nodded and said, "But... there were two men, before, in the Jeep. There were two men?"

"The other man I think was the husband's friend. Perhaps he didn't want to be driven on a wild chase in the middle of the night. I think he got out at the garage."

"I too wish I had not undertaken this journey tonight. At least I know you are not sleeping with my wife, because you are here." He giggled again at his own joke.

Miles tried to smile along with him. He needed Mohammed on side.

"If you do as I ask I will double your fee when we reach our destination." A heavier gust of wind rocked the car and threw a dust devil up in front of them. The wind was increasing as they climbed.

"Six thousand! You will give me six thousand when we reach Casablanca? What about the time? I doubt we can arrive before Azaan?"

Miles turned and looked again behind. "Never mind the time, just get me there, and I will pay." Mohammed lit another cigarette and hummed a tune to himself.

Miles checked his stiletto was still in place against the skin of his arm. Then, hiding his handy-work behind the drivers seat, he ejected the clip from the pistol's hand grip and replaced it with the full one. He knew the Walther P22 pistol held ten .22 rounds. Not exactly what he would choose, but one round, in the right place... He studied the weapon, it seemed serviceable. There was a stamp on the right-hand-side behind the grip, a crescent moon and pole. It was vaguely familiar but, from where?

They were winding their way up a steep part of the climb and soon, they would have to start downwards towards the coast. The road was tight, snaking turns, as it wove its way through a high peak on one side and a dark drop on the other. The moon would periodically show its face as they took a sharp turn one way, then the road would disappear into darkness as they turned back the other.

"Mohammed... can you go as fast as you can for a while, when I tell you? Show me what a good driver you are."

Mohammed shook his head and muttered under his breath, "Faster... slower... faster... Americans... Americans, money, but no sense." Then a little louder he said, "When it's good, long straight road, you want I slow down. When it's twisty turn, you want I go fast." Then maybe thinking about the fare he said, "Sure thing, you boss."

The Jeep was a good distance behind. Maybe Rass, the driver, was getting tired, or maybe he was content to sit behind them all the way to Casablanca. Perhaps his orders were just to follow? As the Jeep went out of sight behind a double bend, Miles said, "Now! As fast as you can around these bends." Mohammed put his foot down and gunned the Mercedes engine.

As the car lurched forward Miles spoke again to his driver. "When I tell you, I want you to stop and let me out. Then drive on around the next bend and wait for me. I don't care how far on it is, go round the next bend and stop. Have another cigarette if you must. I'm going to talk to this man, I hope I can talk some sense into him but it may take a while. You understand you must wait for me to get the money?" He nodded, looking a little concerned as he swerved around a huge rock fall.

"Don't worry, Mohammed, I am a diplomat, you understand, a politician?"

Mohammed then broke into his gold and black-toothed grin, as if this was exactly the sort of behaviour he would expect from a politician.

"What your name?"

Miles was staring behind, he turned to see a sharp bend coming up in the Mercedes headlights, "George Bush," mumbled Miles. "I want you to stop just round this corner, let me out then go to the next corner, go around it and wait, understand?"

Miles pulled the Kaftan off over his head, removed his little round glasses and his wig and stuffed the lot into the old hessian sack that had held his rucksack.

"I understand, I understand," said Mohammed as he slowed the car. He chuckled again, "George Bush."

Miles went into field operative mode. He checked the safety on the Walther and pushed it down his waistband, pulled out a small Maglite pen-torch from the rucksack pocket and checked it. As the car slowed to a halt on the sharp bend, he noticed there was another broken crash barrier off to the right and a large fallen rock in the middle of the road. He grabbed his rucksack, got out and was about to repeat his instructions when Mohammed said, "I know, I know, go to next bend and wait, I know. Don't get into fight." He turned to see Miles in his new guise and said. "No, not George Bush." The rear door slammed, the wheels kicked up more dust and the Mercedes was off round the next corner.

The milky moonlight was all consuming, and it was cold and crisp so high up. Miles slung the rucksack onto his back, took out the gun and cocked it. He placed it into his waist band in the small of his back and tested the speed he could reach it. Satisfied, he switched on his torch. He could hear the Jeep's engine approaching from one direction and his cab disappearing in the other.

Looking at the barrier he could see that it had been repaired some time ago with wood. One piece was hanging off. He grabbed one end, wrenched it free and stepped backwards. With it came a second longer section. *Block one side*, he thought. He dragged the two entwined pieces of wood to the rock face. They now closed the side of road the Jeep would normally take between the rock and the high vertical mountain. Miles surveyed his work in the half moonlight and scurried to the large rock. He pulled out his gun and crouched down behind. It wasn't quite big enough to hide him. He heard the Jeep approaching, it began to slow having seen the partially blocked road. On his haunches and making himself as small as possible, Miles realised there was a smaller bolder close behind him, the size of a basketball. Changing his plan in that split second, he put the gun back into his waistband and pulled the bolder towards him.

Crouched on the flats of his feet he pulled the rock against his knees then up onto his thighs. The Jeep's lights began to light up the barrier and road all around him. It was now at crawling speed, picking its way through the only narrow route left. As it drew near to the large boulder, Miles stood, straining with the rock. The driver was concentrating on the edge of the broken barrier. Miles rolled the rock up his chest then, bending his knees to squat, he straightened and heaved the rock above his head like a weight-lifter. The man in the car suddenly spotted him. But he didn't stop, he kept coming. Miles heard the engine rev up. As the Jeep drew level Miles stepped forward and launched the boulder at the windscreen.

Partially blinded by the headlights, he couldn't see where it struck as he jumped backwards out of the way of the Jeep. The sound of smashing safety glass and wrenching metal shattered the night. The rock did not come back off the car. It was in the cab. The engine revved high, and the jeep leapt forward out of control. It swerved to the right and smashed into the metal part of the barrier. There was a loud screech of metal on metal as the Jeep dragged itself, sparking along the crash barrier. Miles drew his weapon and ran after it. The engine revs dropped as the car tried to lurch forward, still in gear and with nowhere to go, the engine stalled.

With his weapon aimed towards the driver, Miles stooped to look inside. No movement. With his senses buzzing, heart pounding in his chest, Miles yanked at the passenger door and it sprang open. The strong smell of French tobacco invaded his nostrils. Still aiming his weapon he looked at the driver. He was sitting perfectly still, eyes wide and staring out of the windscreen. His mouth hung open at an odd angle. Miles cautiously leaned inside the passenger seat and peered into Rass's eyes. There were tiny squares of broken glass embedded in his cheek, the rest was spread all over the seats and his legs. The rock had rolled forward under the impact, bent the gear lever and was now jammed under the dashboard.

The driver didn't move, "Rass... Rass... can you hear me?"

Looking at him more closely, Miles could see a small tear of blood coming from his left eye. Underneath the embedded glass in his cheek, was a large area of missing skin on his jaw line. His left arm hung limply at his side, his right arm still gripped the steering wheel.

Miles made his appraisal, "Broken jaw and a dislocated shoulder I would say. You *are* in a bit of a state, aren't you?"

Rass answered by coughing. A large dark red splatter of blood shot out of his gaping mouth onto the dashboard. Rass made a gurgling sound as he sucked in his breath in short sharp gulps.

"Oh dear, internal bleeding as well. Maybe a pneumothorax, collapsed lung. What you need is a hospital my friend. Unfortunately..." his voice tailed off.

He shone his pen torch around the drivers foot-well. There was the man's phone, some *Gitanes* cigarettes and a spilt can of coke. On the passengers side was an open packet of pistachio nuts. Miles picked up the packet, shed one of its shell and popped it into his mouth. Chewing, he shone the light up at Rass's face. Looking into his eyes he said in Arabic, "Who sent you? Tell me who sent you and I shall get you to a doctor. You were meant to kill me, weren't you?" Rass's eyes shifted to look at Miles. He took a deeper breath, which made him wince, so much so that he scrunched up his eyes. He tried to speak but his jaw was shattered and the forming of words was impossible.

"Was it Hachim Hadda? Did he send you? Nod your head if that's true." Rass's eyes flicked open and a look of horror shot across his face. "It was Hadda, wasn't it?" There was a barely detectable movement of the head. "No! You are saying no, Hadda didn't send you. Then who did?"

At that moment, Miles heard a noise.

Coming up the mountain was another vehicle, it sounded like a high-revving small car. Miles immediately ran over to the boulder and dragged the two long pieces of wood out of the road. He then ran back to the Jeep and got in, sitting on glass in the process, and shut the door. He leaned across Rass, who let out a pitiful high pitch noise through his nose.

"Sorry," he said as he turned out the lights. He pulled down the sun visor and adjusted the small vanity mirror so he could see back down the road behind them. "Friends of yours?" He pulled the gun from his waist band, lay it across his groin and waited.

Rass coughed again and dribbled a mixture of bile, spit and blood down his broken chin. Miles said, "Shhh." He wound down his window an inch and listened to the engine tone. It didn't falter, there was no slowing from this driver. A small, mustard coloured Fiat went tearing by in too high a gear, the engine working overtime to keep up the momentum. Its driver never gave the crashed car a glance. Miles caught a fleeting glimpse of the driver, a man with a long dark beard, hunched forward over the steering wheel, almost urging the tiny engine up the mountain.

As the lights disappeared around the bend ahead, Miles turned to look at Rass. He now had a gun.

His only good hand had the weapon laying across his lap. Miles didn't flinch, "You haven't got the energy, have you. Let's have a look?" Reaching across he took the weapon from Rass's limp hand. "Look," he tutted, "You haven't even cocked it."

The smell of bile was strong in the cab and Miles opened his door to allow the cold fresh air into the car. Dust and exhaust fumes from the speeding Fiat whirled and danced past.

Miles looked across at his dying combatant and reverting back to English said, "How many have you killed, roughly, how many? I'm into dozens now, I don't count, although I could probably remember them all." He grabbed the bent gear stick, wrenched it backwards into neutral and said, "The difference is, all mine have been for the greater good. You just kill innocent civilians, don't you? What god... tells you to do that? Allah certainly does not. I have read the Koran and I can't find the bits you chaps quote all the time. No, you are a little mixed up, my friend. I don't suppose this is how you envisaged your end is it, cold, on a mountain top, slowly drowning in your own blood? Still..." He never finished.

Getting out of the Jeep, he went round to the front and put his backside on to the warm grill and used his legs and bottom to push the Jeep away from the crash barrier. It moved a lot easier than he thought, the slope down the hill helped. It started to roll under its own momentum, and he ran back to jump in the rolling car. He reached across and grabbed the wheel to steer slightly round the corner as they moved backwards down the hill. Just level with the broken barrier, he wrenched up the handbrake. The Jeep stopped.

Miles looked again at Rass, "Are you... are you blind in your left eye?" He shone his torch into the pupil, it did not dilate. "You are, aren't you? You look awful, absolutely awful. Now, where were we?" Rass coughed again and this time vomited up some blood. "Oh dear, you are very very pale. That will be the internal bleeding, I suspect." Rass's breathing audibly got quicker and quicker.

Miles got out of the car and looked down the road for the long barrier wood. Spotting it he walked back and dragged the two pieces behind him and dumped them behind the car, kicking one up against the back wheels. Walking calmly back to the passenger door he reached across and released the handbrake. He rummaged through his rucksack and found Sonny's possessions and dropped them onto the passenger seat. He took out the dead man's SIM card and threw the battery and phone onto the floor, thinking, no one will ever know. He placed one of the two identical handguns in Rass's lap, the other he placed in the glove compartment.

Rass had his eyes closed and was still clinging to life, breathing in short rhythmic gasps.

Miles turned the steering wheel full lock over to the right, picked up the pistachio nuts, wound down the window and shut the door.

He then leaned back through the window and said, "I don't want to gloat, but... I doubt there are any virgins where you are going," and walked to the back of the car.

He tried to push the Jeep forward up the hill, but with the sharp lock on the steering, his feet just slipped. So Miles picked up the longer of the two pieces of wood and used it as a long lever. He put it in under the back end by the exhaust pipe, put the other end on his shoulder and lifted. The Jeep moved easily toward the precipice.

# 23

Thrashing along, and there was really no other word for it, at twenty plus knots all morning, Nick and his charge *Orelia* passed more and more shipping as they converged on the bottleneck that is the entrance to the Mediterranean. He studied every ship from his bumping, bouncing platform. What he was looking for, he wasn't quite sure, a suspicious crewman in a black balaclava, or someone carrying a Kalashnikov. Maybe even Hachim Hadda himself?

It was a perfect July morning, the sea was flat, the sun was out but he was pleasantly cool because of the wind in his face. *Orelia* picked up even more speed as the heavy fuel load was devoured by the two engines.

At midday, with more than half of the fuel gone, he had just touched his world record. Spotting a wash approaching from the stern from some distant fast-moving ferry or possibly even a warship, Nick aligned himself slightly to the North to try and surf the wake. He knew one mistake on the wheel could have him lying on his side with a multitude of broken equipment and possibly limbs, but he did it nonetheless. The wake caught up with *Orelia's* stern, picked her up and helped her to just touch the 23 knot mark. It had not been for long, but it had happened.

As the wake left him and with the sun burning his back, he slowed down to a still outstanding 21 knots. Steering with his knees and elbows while eating a bowl of instant ration pack porridge, the first hazy glimpse of the top of The Rock appeared as if by magic out of the blue sky. It was dead on the bow, exactly two nine zero degrees. "You haven't lost it, mate, you haven't lost it."

The moisture-laden easterly breeze often strikes the flat eastern face of the rock to be driven upwards until it condenses to form an annoying cold pall over the city and bay. The famous Levanter cloud was missing that day and there was nothing but a blue and perfect sky. Even through the binoculars there appeared to be no base to the Rock of Gibraltar. It gave the illusion of just floating above the sea, as if suspended by an invisible thread.

Slightly to the left of the rock, he glimpsed another slow-moving tanker. The waters in the entrance were policed like a busy road, complete with a two-mile-wide separation zone in the middle to act as a crash barrier. Ships passing close to the rock could only do so if they were going out. Ships coming into the Mediterranean had to stay on the African side. He tweaked the wheel to port; well...what harm could it do to have a closer look? As he did, he heard a splash. A dolphin jumped and sent a light film of spray up across the deck. Steering with one hand he leaned over the guard rail and peered ahead. There was another one, and another. Eventually a pod of six or seven were leaping and playing around the bow. They startled a shoal of flying fish, which left the sanctuary of the sea and flew, darting off to port, with the dolphins in pursuit.

Nick took his phone from his shorts and dialled a friend and fellow Falklands veteran. Rex was chief of the Navy clearance diving team based in Gibraltar and was not always as pleased to see Nick as he tried to make out. Nick would usually be after some piece of kit or other and Rex usually ended up providing it, and more often than not didn't get it back, like the re-breather set Nick knew was lying a hundred and forty miles away on the seabed off the Isle of Alboran. The phone rang half a dozen times before it was picked up. He heard the familiar sound of a diver breathing noisily through a communications system, a compressor running in the background and someone hammering something metallic.

Without any pleasantries exchanged, Rex shouted down the phone, "Wait one, will you?" He could then be heard talking to the diver, "If it won't come off, just leave it, mate. You've got five minutes left and I want you out of there, okay?" Then he said down the phone, "Hello, hello."

"Hello Rex, It's Nick. Nick Carter. Don't panic, I don't want anything. I just want you to ask your mate at QHM if I can berth in Rosia Bay again, like last time. Could you call him for me?"

"Nutty, I-don't-want-anything Carter is it? That'll be the fuckin' day? You do know I'm trying to run a dive here don't you?" Then he broke off and Nick heard him say, "Roger Davey, left bottom. Come up on his slack, Ash. He's coming out." Then back to Nick he said, "I'll call him, mate. What's your ETA?"

"Err... 30 minutes?"

"Fuckin' hell, mate. Give a man some warning why don't you? Gotta go."

The line went dead and Nick had to hope he could swing it.

Having studied a dilapidated looking cargo ship called the *Java Moon,* and finding nothing suspicious to keep his interest, Nick altered course and headed directly for the southern tip of the rock, marked by a small red and white lighthouse on Europa Point. Within a mile of the rock itself his echo-sounder still showed the seabed to be more than 300 metres. As he crashed through the disturbed races, an up-welling of water around the headland, he cut back on *Orelia's* speed. The Mediterranean's seabed had risen sharply up to meet him and was now just 17 metres.

Nick put up his mainsail, cut one engine and broke out his blue British ensign. He now had a collection of ensigns to appease fussy officials around the Med. For today he selected the Royal Gibraltar yacht club. He then tried a ruse he had used on previous occasions with surprisingly successful results. Picking up his VHF mike and tuning to channel 08 he called the Queen's harbourmaster. *"QHM QHM this is yacht..."* he paused and thought for a second, *"English yacht, Reliant. Request permission to berth in Rosia Bay. I have urgent spares for the Clearance Divers. Over."*

The almost immediate response was, *"Reliant. Wait one."* Nick waited, and waited. Then came the answer. *"Reliant, what duration, over?"*

Nick said. *"One night only, over."* Another long pause then came, *"Reliant approved, out."*

*"Thank you sir, Reliant out."* Then Nick smiled and said: "It's not what you know, but who."

There were a couple of enormous oil tankers anchored just off Europa point, and Nick studied them through his binoculars as he rounded the southernmost tip of the rock. Then, as the full panorama of Gibraltar Bay opened up before him, he realised the futility of studying each and every one of these multi-million pound ungainly, floating hulks. He stopped counting after 22. They were everywhere. All waiting their turn to enter Algeciras, or to off-load their highly valued and volatile cargo via the buoy at the head of the Bay, linked to the ugly petro-chemical plant of CESPA, the Company Espanol Petrol.

Studying them all was pointless, what was he looking for? Putting his binoculars in their stowage, he turned to starboard and motored close in to the historic rock. There were gun emplacements everywhere, some dating back to the early 1700s. Every available headland had a fort or castle walls with cannons or World War II defences. If there were no obvious places to mount a weapon, some poor soul had dug deep caves directly into the rock, and in many the barrel of a weapon was still pointing out. Motoring past the swimming pools towards Rosia Bay, he tried to pick out Rex and Mo's married quarters just above.

As the famous Bay opened to his starboard side, Nick made his turn in, pondering on the history of the place. In October 1805, a barely recognisable and ruined HMS *Victory*, with scarcely a spar left standing, had made exactly the same turn and entered this bay. It was unlikely she did it under her own sail, though. She had been battered and smashed during the valiant, heroic fight on that glorious day, October the 21st. But that wasn't the end of her fight. That very evening, cruel storm-force winds drove the already battle-weary and depleted crew to the very edge of exhaustion.

Not only did the Victory carry hundreds of horrifically disfigured and fatally injured men from the Battle of Trafalgar, it also carried Nelson's body. Just above the entrance and to the left he could see the colossal grey barrel of one of the 100 ton guns left over from the late 1800s. What damage could Nelson have done with a rifled weapon, even a tenth of that size? Nick dropped his mainsail and motored as slowly as possible into the historic mooring, expecting all the while to get a radio challenge from either the MoD or the Gibraltar police. It never came. Rex must have kept his promise.

Tying up under the twenty-foot-thick stone walls, it was not difficult to imagine the scenes on that day as Nelson's body was swung ashore. The cries from the injured, the 21-gun-salute, the mourning of the garrisons in shock at the demise of 'Our Nel'.

Nick made his yacht fast to the stone jetty, trying not to look up at the listening post he knew overlooked the bay. Look innocent, look uninterested, he kept telling himself. The impervious glass of the listening station stared out like a blind man's mirrored glasses. It was bristling with aerials and odd shaped antennas, giving it a sinister, forbidding look. Someone would be asking: "How come this yacht can moor here and no one else is allowed?"

Nick didn't want to announce his arrival to the whole world, hence he'd used the yacht name *Reliant*. He liked to do things his way, the quiet way, no fuss. He was sure that had he gone into the main marina, Miles and his MI6 cronies would have been there, cajoling, making their thinly-veiled threats and asking awkward questions. Smudge might have been there too, but he could contact him without letting the rest of the world know. No, this was the way to do it, stealthily.

With the engines finally off, the silence was deafening. Whilst setting his fenders, switching off the cooling water and the range of other tasks he had to do, he mulled over his next move.

Call someone, anyone who might be in the know as to what was really going on. Or, go up and see Rex's wife Mo. He hadn't seen her since just after his wedding with Mariyah, so it might be a bit difficult, but there was no point in putting it off any longer. It had been three years already. Decision made, he shut up shop and walked out past Parson's Lodge and started up the rock of Gibraltar to the naval married quarters.

Sweating from the brisk steep climb up through Gibraltar's narrow-stepped passages, he pushed the doorbell. This was one of the few houses he and Mariyah had ever stayed in, and he felt his heart pounding in his chest. He could hear Mo on the telephone to one of her friends. She opened the door wearing a white dressing gown, a towel around her head and no make-up.

She looked at Nick and simply said, "Sorry Marianne, I have to go," and hung up. She put her hand to her mouth, then launched herself at him. They embraced. She sobbed and sobbed. He held her tightly.

They stayed like that for some minutes, on the doorstep, in the sunshine. One sobbing and one with his eyes tightly closed, hanging on.

Eventually she sniffed, wiped her wet eyes and said, "I'm so sorry, Nick. It was just seeing you again. If you'd warned me you were coming - it was just a bit of a shock that's all." Then she forced a laugh and said, "Not much of a welcome is it? I'm sorry, come in, come in."

Without asking, she poured two large Bombay Sapphires, Gibraltar-sized gin and tonics. As she chopped the lemon and sought ice from the freezer, she told him about Rex, about their children, about her next draft to Cyprus, anything but Mariyah. She turned, looked him in the eye and said, "Will you be staying the night? I mean, would you like the four-poster, the one you had with...the one you had last time?" She realised what she'd said, and that started her off again.

Most of her crying over, they sat on the balcony and talked for hours. The view was spectacular. Ships of every description came and went constantly. The house was perched high on the rock. Nothing moved in the bay without them seeing it, which was why the British hung on to the outpost. Nothing, but nothing, could enter or leave without passing the Rock. The small outpost was in the unique position of being the last, or the first stop, in or out of the Mediterranean.

One oil tanker dropped its anchor below, no more than half a mile from them. The sun was past its zenith, it was early evening and around 30°C. Two beautifully coloured parrots were squawking in the palm tree a few feet away, having a battle with the domineering seagulls. The nurse came out in Mo as she enquired, "What happened to you anyway? Your head, your arm? You are a mess, Nick." She stood and went round behind his seat and had a good look at the cut.

"Oh, I was mugged in Morocco. It's okay, I'm on the mend."

"Mugged... you! It's a brave or stupid man that mugs you, Nick. More than likely a stupid man. Has a Doctor had a look at this, I mean, you should've had stitches here? You are lucky you didn't lose a lot of blood."

Her phone went and she wandered inside talking. She came back out and said "Rex is delayed down at the airport. I don't know what they are doing down there but the whole diving team's had to go down. He told me to leave you alone, which is exactly what I will have to do." Looking at her watch she took a sharp intake of breath and said. "Christ! I'm on shift at 19:30, and I'm not even dressed." With that she ran to her bedroom at the top of the house. She shouted as she changed, "So-will you stay the night?"

"I don't know, I'm not sure Mo. I'll have to speak to Rex first. I might just shoot off though."

She shouted back down, "Where are you off to? Are you going to disappear again for a couple of years?"

He sat at the bottom of the stairs. "I might do an Atlantic crossing. There's a site in the Caribbean I want to have a look at, but I don't know for sure. It all depends what happens here."

"Not a lot happens here, Nick, you should know that!"

"That might be about to change," he half-mumbled.

Mo came down the stairs in her midwife's uniform, "What did you say?"

"Oh nothing. I expect I'll be here, for tomorrow at least."

She then looked him in the eye and said, "So will you stay tonight? You could sleep in the back room. I would take it as a personal insult if you were to sleep on-board and not here."

"Okay-okay, I'll stay tonight."

"Fantastic, Rex will be made up." Then looking at her watch she said, "I'm sorry but I have to dash." She kissed him on the cheek and hugged him again. "Two of my girls are about to drop, one probably will tonight. Help yourself to anything. You know where it all is, and I'll see you in the morning."

Nick heard her car pull out of the port. He wandered across the lounge to the balcony, sipping his G & T and staring out at the ships. He could hear the rhythmic clanking sound as one of the big ships hauled in her anchor, and briefly wondered where she was bound.

Leaning on the railing, he had a thought and carried his drink up the stairs. Nick stood at the door of Mo and Rex's bedroom, took a deep breath and pushed it open. The white linen, the four poster, the sea breeze blowing in, the white net curtains gently fluttering. It was all exactly the same as before, and he struggled to keep his emotions in check. He walked slowly past the bed and looked down at the indentations in the pillows. He could hear her voice, the sound of their lovemaking, the things they had tried, and achieved, in that bed. Things they could never manage on the small bed on-board. He had a vision of her lying there, naked, sleeping. He tore himself away, forcing his mind not to dwell.

Rex kept his brass telescope on the bedroom's balcony. It was an antique that sat on a stable oak tripod with polished brass fittings. Nick put down his drink and swung the long telescope to point out at the cranes on the far side of the bay in Algeciras. He twisted the focus and they got clearer and nearer. He moved to the farthest ship and that swam into the view-finder. After studying the ship for a while he moved to the next nearest, then the next. He looked up from the view-finder as the house telephone rang, he ignored it.

He noticed the large tanker that had been hauling in her anchor was now turning in a slow ponderous arc to point her nose out toward the vast Atlantic. From his high vantage point he had to point the telescope downwards to study the vessel as she churned up white water behind her. The phone stopped its noise, "Good, leave me alone," he said.

He could clearly see the crew in the bows with the fire hose jetting water out through the hawsepipe to wash the colossal heavy anchor clean of mud and silt. As she headed out, she passed a smaller tanker, still at anchor and Nick found his attention moving to that. He focused on the bridge and could see a figure just move out of view behind the starboard bridge wing. He looked up to find his drink and something caught his eye on the tanker. He bent down again and moved the telescope to look at the funnel. He froze, stood and looked again with the naked eye. The phone started again and it made him jump. He'd seen that symbol before, the crest on the tanker. He focused again on the funnel and zoomed the lens to make it as big as possible. His heart picked up a beat. Nick peered one-eyed through the powerful lens and wracked his brains.

"Where the fuck have I seen that before?" Then he stood upright, eyes wide, turned and ran across the bedroom, nearly falling over in the process. He leapt three stairs at a time, past the ringing phone in the hall and out the front door, slamming it behind. He took off down the steep steps through the Gibraltarian houses, crossing roads, and nearly getting himself run over by a girl on a scooter. Her pathetic horn sounded behind him, but Nick didn't look round. He dived into an alleyway that led down the steep hill to the sea.

Running flat out around the edge of the cobbled stone jetty Nick could see a middle-aged couple with a yapping dog looking at his yacht. He ran up to them and hopped on-board, sending the dog into an even more frenzied barking session. Jumping below he went straight for the galley and opened the top drawer. Where was it? He pulled out the cutlery drawer, and the roll of money left by Miles and a few other things fell on the deck in the process. Not seeing it, he went to the next drawer and pulled it right out of the unit and tipped it upside down on the decking. Dropping to his knees amongst the can openers, scissors, matches, plasters and cutlery, he found it, lying the wrong way up.

The Zippo Hadda had left. He turned it over in his hand. On the other side was the same yellow crest he'd spotted on the tanker's funnel. He looked at it and for some reason opened it, and lit it.

*"Gotcha!"*

# 24

Mohammed still seemed determined to get Miles to Casablanca by Azaan. The road straightened and improved considerably as they closed on the coast. He'd been fast asleep when Miles returned to the car and had been very quiet since, which suited Miles's mood. He had just killed two men in one night; this was an unusual experience, even for him.

It was unlikely anyone would find the car with Rass's body in it for some time. When they did, it would look as though he had been hit by a rock fall. It would probably be assumed that Sonny had been in the car with him - after all, his personal belongings were there. When the Jeep had finally toppled off of the edge of the cliff, Miles stood waiting in the dark for the noise of impact. There was one sound almost immediately after it went over the side, then, nothing. It must have been a long way down.

As for Sonny, it was anyone's guess whether he'd ever be found. If he was, would anyone want to pull out a dead body from a garage cesspit? Would they do an autopsy on a man who had little chance of being reported missing? Hadda would want to find out what happened to his two henchmen, but it would be unwise to ask too many questions. No, he was happy with the loose ends, but something was niggling him.

Just outside the coastal town of Rabat, Miles became convinced his driver was periodically nodding off at the wheel. Miles offered to take over, but Mohammed refused. Then he did fall asleep, and Miles insisted.

Mohammed curled up on the passenger seat and fell asleep. As he drove, Miles examined the past few hours again, trying to track down what it was that troubled him. It was not the actual killing, he was over that. Something wasn't right; something didn't fit into the puzzle, or... there was a missing piece. The disposal of the two bodies was relatively okay, though one could never make it perfect.

By the time he had his first glimpse of the city, he was fairly sure where his anxieties lay. It was the weapons, the handguns of the two men; they were identical.

He drove down the hill between the tall, skinny palm trees as the famous ancient city of Casablanca slept. Miles stopped and was the only car at the first set of traffic lights on the outskirts of town. He woke his snoring driver and had him drive the final few miles to the docks.

Mohammed became more and more excited as they approached the magnificent Grand Mosque Hassan II. The great Mosque's minaret is the tallest in the world, taller than the tallest pyramid. It was still just dark and they instinctively slowed down to view the laser that shone from the top of the tower towards the east and Mecca. To, "Point the way to God," as Mohammed kept saying. Even at this early hour the worshippers flocked toward the place of worship. The mosque seemed to hover out over the sea as if on an invisible platform; it appeared to rise up from the ocean.

Inside, it can accommodate 25,000 kneeling worshippers on its highly polished marble floor. Outside is a courtyard for a further 80,000. The tall square tower is decorated in millions of turquoise, blue and green tiles which contrast perfectly with the cream stonework. A thing of beauty which would call anyone to their knees to wonder at the building of it.

The sun came up as they passed, and they were both inspired by the mosque's majesty. The car's windows were wound down as the muezzin started to sing his haunting call to the believers, his chant echoing around the mosque's many walls and pointed arches.

They drove along the beach-front road until nearing Casablanca's port. Ever cautious, Miles didn't want Mohammed to know his final destination.

"Here. This will do."

Mohammed's eyes were drawn to the great mosque's tower. As Miles got out of the Mercedes, the sun was just beginning to throw some light over the old city and the mosque's minaret cast a long shimmering shadow over the Atlantic.

Before he paid, Miles did what he would do with any of his players; he drilled him.

"So...where have you been this long night, Mohammed?"

"What? What sort of question you ask? I have been with you, I have..." Then, pausing, he pondered, looked down at his odd flip-flops, and began nodding. "I... pick up English lady. Yes, an English lady, very wealthy, quiet. She pay me, six thousand..." Then a grin appeared as he seemed to rehearse his story in his head. "Not six... four thousand Dirham. No, it was three, three thousand Dirham to take her to the... the Hotel Balima in Rabat. What could I say? Three is a good fare, I took her. She slept all the way."

"Excellent, excellent, we understand each other." Miles pulled a roll of notes from his pocket and handed them over. Mohammed's gold and black toothy grin spread from ear to ear. He then handed Miles what he at first thought was a receipt, but it was a telephone number written on a cigarette paper.

"If you ever need driver again, call Mohammed. Now, I go pray for another customer like you," he said.

Miles strode across the manicured grass and crossed the road towards the sumptuous triple-arched entrance to Le Royal Mansour Meridien Hotel. He checked behind him to make sure Mohammed was not watching, but he was walking away, eyes fixed on the mosque.

It was early, and Miles felt awkward having to call his opposite number in Morocco. But Ikbal had promised him the use of one of the country's military helicopters. Miles considered Ikbal to be one of the few men in the world he could call a friend. He had worked with many men from intelligence units of many countries, but Ikbal was one he actually trusted. Miles had even lived with his family, which was how he picked up all sorts of Arabic slang, habits and traits he could never have learned from a book.

Still in his creased safari suit, he entered the resplendent lobby of the hotel and was greeted by a porter sporting a gold-inlaid waistcoat and a deep red fez with gold tassels. The porter looked him up and down and gave a half-hearted bow.

"I have an appointment to see the interior security minister." The porter's mood changed in an instant. He stood almost to attention and said, "Yes, Sir. If sir would like to take a seat in the lounge, I shall tell him you are here."

Miles followed him through the elegant marble, gold and black reception area past two more porters attending two gold lift doors. As they entered the lounge Miles said, "I have been travelling all night and would like to freshen up. Do you have a shower I could use, and tell me, would you have a clean white shirt I could purchase?"

"Yes sir, you may use the shower by the pool over there. I shall have some shirts bought to you right away. We also have a selection of tropical suits if you would like to inspect them? Would sir also like some refreshment, perhaps something to eat?"

"Please, that would be most welcome. A pitcher of iced water, and a sandwich, whatever you recommend." Miles offered the man a platinum card and said, "Tell the minister I'll be here at... 08:15, would you? I don't wish to keep him waiting."

Half an hour later, clean and refreshed, Miles was sitting in the lounge in a new beige lightweight suit and pristine open-necked shirt, drinking iced sparkling water. After five shampoos and much scrubbing to remove the tan off his face and body, he felt ready to greet the

Minister. Ikbal stepped from the lift and his face reflected his delight when he saw his friend. They embraced and kissed cheeks in the Moroccan way.

"Miles, my brother, peace be unto you. It has been too long, too long by far. You are well I trust?" he offered in his best Arabic, no doubt testing Miles's accent. Miles replied in the same language, "*Oo-alleh koom salam*, (and unto you be peace). I am well, brother, thank you, very well. Your beautiful wife and son, they are both in good health?"

Switching to English, Ikbal said, "They are very well and happy. Amina would love for you to come and stay again soon. You promised you would, and a woman never forgets a promise. She has been learning English and has come a long way since you started her off. But now, how was your journey? Did you come straight from Tangiers?"

So, Ikbal also distrusted Yusef. He was fishing to see if he had sent the picture to both of them. With that one question, Miles knew that Yusef had lied to him and wondered how many other people had received his picture of The Tunisian.

"Yes, I had a pleasant journey. I caught a train from Tangiers, but I have just had word, I am required in Gibraltar... now. Is the offer of the helicopter still on?"

"Of course, of course it is. There's a helipad beyond the tennis courts, I shall have it here... Wait, would you, and I shall find out how long." Ikbal moved to the hotel phone and dialled just four digits. Miles watched and waited, eating a huge and beautiful goats' cheese sandwich and drinking the iced water. Ikbal knew nothing of his visit to Yusef's; he knew him well enough and would have known if he'd had even an inkling. He had just checked, to be sure, by asking his route. Had Miles said he'd arrived from Fes, he would have been suspicious. Ikbal looked at his watch, nodded and hung up. He then took out his mobile and checked it, shaking his head. "It is on its way from our base. Should be ten minutes at the most, or so they tell me. Come, I will walk you to the pad and we can catch up."

Miles wiped his mouth with the serviette and followed him out through the enormous glass doors which overlooked a pool surrounded in exotic plants and palm trees.

They passed six tanned and giggling Lufthansa air stewardesses, each pulling their flight bags behind them.

As he allowed the glass door to shut behind them, Ikbal said: "It is not ideal having our office here, Miles. Yesterday these ladies were lying around the pool in barely adequate bikinis. I could not get my men out of the office. They of course can look. Most of them are young and not married. Me... I just pray to Allah for strength." He laughed his infectious laugh.

As they walked, they exchanged a few pieces of information. Ikbal told Miles about new arrests of a group of suspicious students who were showing signs of getting too fundamentalist in their views. Miles had spent time earlier in the year with him studying the group from afar. The leader and most radical was an English passport holder and had been arrested by Ikbal's men, and not seen since.

Ikbal had carte blanche to do what he wished to rid the country of terrorism. There were no human rights issues for suicide bombers in Morocco. No law to protect them and Ikbal had found it impossible to understand the lenient position countries like Britain took. Morocco, and especially Casablanca, had suffered a spate of suicide bombings in 2003. Fourteen young men had walked into various public places - restaurants, hotels and Jewish centres - and blown themselves up. Calling themselves 'Salafia Jihadia,' they were an offshoot of the Madrid train bombers terrorist group, the MICC (Moroccan Islamic Combatant Group).

As they walked and talked, the noise of the helicopter's engines could be heard as the machine approached the Royal Meridien. Being by their nature suspicious, both men used the noise to speak of more delicate issues.

Ikbal begun by taking Miles's arm, pulling him close and gabbling excitedly, "We have a good lead, I think anyway, of T's whereabouts."

Miles interest grew. "Where? Please Ike, share this information with me. I fear Hadda is up to his old tricks again. I don't know for sure, but our hunch is his next attack will not be on Moroccan shores but in Europe."

The noise of the landing helicopter was now deafening, and Ikbal turned Miles away from the flying dust. Behind the tennis court shower block he cupped his hand, and shouted into Miles's ear. "Yes, my information is the same! I had a tip off, from our mutual friend, who you know as Yusef. I don't trust him, so I had two men on a round-the-clock surveillance. I wanted no mistakes, so I sent my brother who is new to this game, and another good man. It had been a week and cost us a fortune, then, Mecca! One of Hadda's men turned up for a drop-off. They were following him from Fes last night - only..." he took out his mobile and checked again for messages or missed calls. After a pause, he carried on, "Only they should've been in touch by now." Shrugging his shoulders he continued, "But, I really feel this time the net is closing in on our friend, Mr Hadda. I feel it in my bones."

Struggling to hide his concern, Miles managed to stammer above the noise, "But - how... but how do you know it was one of Hadda's men?" The noise from the army-camouflaged Bell 206 Jet Ranger chopper was reduced to a whine as it touched down and slowed its engine.

Ikbal looked around the building and seeing it safely on the ground, put his arm around Miles's shoulder and walked him to the waiting aircraft.

"They say he was in disguise, wearing a kaftan of sorts, his hood was up and he was behaving suspiciously. Never you fear, Miles, my baby brother will follow him. You will be the first to know when we have him." With that, he patted Miles warmly on the back.

Miles turned and looked at Ikbal. He couldn't speak, he just hugged him, kissed his cheek, turned and ran, hunched down beneath the rotors. As he did up the seat belt and put on the headset, he thought of the guns, the P22's. They were standard Moroccan army issue. He had seen Ikbal's, just the once, when his wife was out with her mother; Ikbal had hung it up in the kitchen.

It, too, had had the crescent and pole stamped into the grip. He felt the sickening guilt rise in his throat as the chopper's revolutions rose and it jerked and bumped its way into the air.

# 25

Nick motored out of Rosia Bay and headed towards the suspect tanker. Keeping a safe distance, he drifted and tried to make out her name. It was painted on the stern as is traditional but underneath he could make out the raised letters of an old name. He wrote:

*Yamm-Amira, Monrovia, yellow crescent moon funnel crest?*

He placed the post-it note on the saloon table with the lighter on top of it.

Studying the ship through binoculars, he realised there was nothing to be learned just by looking at it. He picked a spot between the closest ship and Rosia Bay. The one nearest the shore was a smaller bulk cargo carrier being re-fuelled by one of the oilers, and would conveniently hide him from his target vessel. Nick tied a 50 metre length of rope to his anchor cable in order to be able to reach the deep seabed. He paid out the cable and line, all the time waiting for a challenge from someone on the Rock.

As *Orelia* bit and held steady on her anchor, Nick wasted the final half an hour until sunset with a show of pretend fishing. He was still under the watchful gaze of the navy's listening station, but nothing happened. There was no awkward challenge on the radio, so he abandoned the fishing rod and went below to make up his inflatable canoe.

Whilst below, he heard the sound of a fast-approaching engine. He went on deck to the stern and noticed a craft heading straight for him from Gibraltar harbour. She was powerful and parting a white bow wave as she surged headlong towards his location. The boat already had her lights on, ready for the impending sunset.

The bright orange pilot boat was bearing down on him. Nick took up his rod again and concentrated hard on his fishing, convinced this would be a, "You can't anchor here, sir." But the pilot raced straight by, its wash sending *Orelia* into a series of steep uncomfortable rolls

*That's it then*, he thought; *let's get this show on the road.* He rolled out the canoe on the decking. It was a dark green ocean-going kayak. Deflated, it rolled up and easily fitted into a normal size rucksack. No kiddie's toy, it had cost him the best part of £1200. He had got it made via one of his friends still in the SBS. J.D was short for Jon Dog. He'd been a Clearance Diver, then joined the SAS, but when they disbanded their Boat Squadron he had transferred across to the SBS in order to continue his love of diving.

Whilst rolling out the canoe, he tried to remember what J.D's real surname was; what did the D stand for? The Dog part was easy: once he got his teeth into something he was like a dog with a bone. It didn't matter what it was. It might be weightlifting, sniping, running, cards, a certain woman, anything he wanted to do or obtain, he generally got. More recently, since he had been in the two finest regiments in the world, it was because of his relentless pursuit of any fleeing enemy. He wouldn't let any sleeping dog lie. If he was on a trail, he would worry it, harass it and pursue it until he caught it. He was one man, but like a pack of dogs when in pursuit of an objective or result.

J.D had given Nick the name of the man who made the canoes for the regiment. They were made of an incredibly strong double-skinned material, by request only. He plugged in the 12 volt pump, and inflated it. He fitted a hinged keel that gave the canoe rigidity for punching through waves at sea. There were four separate compartments in the hull, so even a rip in three wouldn't stop you paddling it home. It had a double skinned bottom, an inflatable seat, a spray sheet to keep out any heavy weather, and could even be turned upside down and used as a shelter in emergencies.

Old habits die hard, and Nick found himself checking through his waterproof emergency container. He checked everything: mini flares, a waterproof VHF radio, torch and spare batteries, quick-drying repair kit, signalling mirror, four emergency ration packs, Kendal cake, dextrose tablets, a space blanket and more besides. He didn't plan to be gone for more than a couple of hours, but his training took over. "Hope for the best, plan for the worst" his chief diver used to say before they went on a mission. With that in mind, he chucked in two litres of water as well.

He switched on his phone to find a message from Smudge.

*In Gib. Wots ur ETA?*

"I'm already here, sunshine," he said with a grin.

Nick typed into his battered phone: *ETA Rosia Bay about midnite, meet me. Alone!*

Then he looked out of the companionway, stepped up a couple of steps and looked to port. The tanker's mast and superstructure were visible behind the smaller container ship, her deck lights now on in the fading light. He looked down at the phone, and thought, *not yet, I'll send it when I get back; there might be a reception committee.* Miles and his cronies, maybe the police would be asking some difficult questions. *Sod that for a game of soldiers.*

He watched the sun going down whilst partaking in another bout of pretend fishing and ate four tins of sardines straight from the can. As he did so, he leaned against the push-pit rail and stared across the water at the tanker. He was quite convinced that the killer of his wife was on-board.

Nick set his all-round white anchor light, took his fixes again, switched off every other electrical item and waited for real darkness, then changed into his last remaining shorty wetsuit. The lights from the shores of

Gibraltar and around the Bay now lit up the coast, and the tankers did their best to put on their own illuminations.

*Orelia* was lying beam-on to Gibraltar and he could almost feel the binoculars trained on his yacht from the listening post. He lowered the canoe into the water on the port side, hidden from the shore.

It was dark, at last, and Nick put his single paddle together and was just about to climb aboard when he had another thought. He went below, lifted the pilot berth seating and took out a long thin coil of black parachute cord. He had resisted putting it in up until that moment, as he had no intention of going alongside the tanker, even if there was a way on board. "Just in case," he said, then put the red night-light head lamp on and hung the small monocle around his neck. Laying down on *Orelia's* deck he tied the loose end to the sturdy bow-ring on the canoe, climbed aboard his green goddess, pulled the line taught and tucked the coil between his knees.

He paddled away from *Orelia*, leaving her between him and the shore for as long as possible. At about half distance, Nick turned the nose of the goddess out towards the straights of Gibraltar. He quickly found his silent paddling rhythm, his muscles and body remembering the easiest and most effective stroke. The smaller container ship was about fifty metres off to starboard, and he was convinced he was virtually impossible to spot. He paddled on to the West, his target tanker appearing out of the night like a massive solid black pier as he rounded the stern of the smaller ship. As she came into full view, he took a deep breath. The dark-hulled tanker loomed over him, menacing and hostile.

The slight ebbing tide meant he had to paddle harder as he turned the pointed bow in towards the tanker's stern. He fought his feeling of foreboding. Moving in pitch darkness, the rhythmic soaring motion of the paddle, the gentle splash of the sea - it took him back to happy and not so happy exercises and operations in Scotland, Ireland - and even Iraq.

As the tanker drew nearer, he looked up and froze. There was a faint red glow on the stern, just under the flagpole. It vanished. *Maybe not*, he thought, then again... there it was. Someone was drawing on a cigarette. The canoe drifted to a halt, and Nick felt under his wetsuit for his monocle. He lifted it and focused on the figure. It was a man leaning on the guard rails, trying to hide his highly illegal smoking activities by going astern in the darkness. He appeared to be looking straight at Nick. He lowered his eye piece slowly and sat still. The man then flicked the butt over the side, straightened and wandered off. Nick lifted the tiny telescope and thought he saw him carrying something. Was it a broom, or a weapon? Then he disappeared. Nick waited, then picked up his paddle and eased his way nearer the target.

He headed towards the darker, farthest side of the tanker, her port side was away from the prying eyes of Gibraltar. Level with the stern, about fifty metres out from the ship's side he became aware of voices.

Sound travels extraordinarily well across water, a fact drummed into him on many occasions in the Navy. "You can hear a fish fart at a hundred metres!" one chief would say. Someone called out in a foreign language, but it seemed too near. Then he saw a hint of a torch light, close to the water; it was enough to focus his attention on that spot. His eyes strained to see into the tanker's dark hull. There was another sound, another voice. He paddled, ten short hard strokes, then long slow silent ones. He stopped. As he drifted closer he saw it.

There was a boat alongside.

The Jacob's ladder had been lowered and someone was climbing up the vertical ship's side from the boat. Nick's night vision was now as good as it was going to get. As he drifted in, he could see two men on the deck of the tanker silhouetted against her deck lighting. They appeared to be handling ropes, perhaps tying up the boat, perhaps letting her go? As the climbing figure reached the deck, he was embraced by one of the crew. Then the three of them looked over the tanker's side down to the boat. He heard them talking, then all three walked off toward the bridge.

Nick paddled gently towards the ship's side. He let his gaze drop to the boat alongside.

Thirty metres away he was sure it was the launch; the thieves from Morocco.

*Shit-shit-shit, now what? I have to have a closer look.* This was the boat that had got him into this mess in the first place. He recognized the wheelhouse, the dark wooden hull. He hung back, listening, watching, and thinking about what to do next. Without reaching a clear decision, he began paddling towards the launch.

There was a light above the chart table in the wheelhouse: a faint 12volt glow, almost like a candle light, shining out from the square windows. Nick, edged his way towards the stern of the launch. He put the nose of the Green Goddess in between the launch and the tanker so that she was sandwiched like a fender.

He put his ear to the launch's hull and held his breath, listening. He found he had to hold on to the launch tightly, out in the deep anchorage; the tide was a lot stronger than he'd expected. With his ear on the launch he looked down at the dark water below and estimated it to be moving at about half a knot, maybe a bit more.

The cold waters of the Atlantic flow eastward in through the straits of Gibraltar and some of that surface water inevitably finds its way north into the Bay. It then follows the natural contours and profiles, past Algeciras, then round the natural horse-shoe shape at the head of the Bay and out beyond Gibraltar. It was like a constant, gentle whirlpool.

Hearing nothing from the launch, he gently pushed the boat away from the tanker's side and edged forward in the canoe until he could just reach the Jacob's ladder. He lifted up the bottom rung, took the coil of black rope from between his legs, tied the end onto the bottom rung with a bowline, and dropped the coil into the sea.

Nick didn't give himself too much time to think; he tucked up his knees, leaned backward and rolled quietly out of the canoe, touching the tanker's cold steel hull as he did. The salty clear water was a welcome distraction. When he bobbed back to the surface, he said to himself, "What... are... you doing, Carter?"

He put his back against the launch and shoved the canoe's bows away with his feet as hard as he could. The canoe moved off under the momentum, helped by the southerly flowing tide. Nick lost sight of it when it was no more than five metres away. He then turned and swam forward to the ladder. His bare feet felt the thin black cord, streaming out to his refuge.

He climbed the ladder and stopped with his head just over the launches railing as he strained every sense. He heard nothing, but why the light if the launch was unmanned? As he looked across the deck of the boat he could make out the familiar fish hatch. Then just to the right... the old hatch with the metal lid.

It was off, the lid lay discarded on the deck. Beside it he thought he could make out the special key to undo it. Nick climbed aboard. He was aware of the launch's gentle roll to starboard as it took his weight. He crouched down and crept towards the wheel-house for some cover and shadow. Listening again by the outside ship's wheel, he heard nothing, so he peered in toward the dull light. It was empty. He looked up as the moon lit up the deck for a moment, but there was nobody high above on the tanker. As quick as the moon's light came, it went. It did light up the deck enough for him to see the hatch was off, and to see his own wet footprints across the deck. *Wanker*, he thought. *Should have bought a towel*. Nick moved over to the hatch and lay down, putting his head in the hole. He switched his headlamp to red. The Armalite boxes were gone. On the shelves were some of the grenade boxes, the lids all off. On the floor, just poking out from under the lowest shelf, was the biscuit tin that had held the Geiger counter.

Did it hold it now? *No - go, get out of here now!* Nick did a sort of press up to go, then lowered himself down again. *Maybe it's still in there*. He swung his feet over the hatch and lowered himself, searching for the shelf to rest his bare foot on. He found it and took some of the weight off of his arms. He felt the boat rock, *was that me, or a passing boat*, he wondered?

He lowered himself down to the deck and looked in all the boxes. The moon came out and cast its creamy-white light into the secret stowage. The weapons were gone; the grenades were all gone. He then picked up the biscuit tin. There was no need to touch the lid. It was too light. It was empty.

The moon went in. It went in a little too quickly. Nick looked up. There was a silhouette of a woman. A woman carrying a... fire extinguisher? In the combined dull lights of his headlamp and the moonlight, Nick wondered if she had a swollen eye. She shone a bright white torch into the hold and he had to look away.

A metallic click followed. It sounded like a weapon. He put his hand up to try and block some of the light, to look up.

He had time to call, "Don't shoot!" before something hit the tip of his fingers as it dropped into the hold. There was a thump on the wooden deck, then the object rolled away. It was black, about the size of a cricket ball. There was the metallic scraping noise of the hatch going over the hole and he was plunged into his slightly red world. The black thing rolled out again. It stopped by his knee and had a hint of smoke coming out of it. Written on it was M84, in white; the smell of cordite hit his senses.

"FUCK... NO!"

He grabbed one of the wooden boxes on the shelf and threw it over the Flash-Bang, then shoved it under the low shelf with his foot, as far as it would go. He curled into a ball with his back towards the impending explosion, put his fingers in his ears, screwed up his eyes and breathed out.

The first thing he registered was heat, closely followed by the sound and an incredible light. The light was so intense his eyes seemed to fuse closed. It was a flash heat, an instant burn. The water trapped in his thin wetsuit felt like it was boiling. The remaining air in his lungs was driven out by the blast.

The awesome sound bypassed his eardrums. It penetrated through bone and flesh, through muscle and skull. It drove deep into his core, dislocating all senses.

He lay, useless, at the bottom of the hold, in the foetal position, and as helpless as a baby.

# 26

Hachim Hadda was in the day cabin below the bridge of his command. He liked the sound of, *his command*. Captain Hadda had a ring to it. He had to remind himself this post was temporary. If it was Allah's will, he would be moving on very soon.

The men were coming along well, and were ready. *If all goes as planned*, he thought, *I won't even need them. If all goes to plan, not a shot will be fired. The Spanish, the Portuguese the English in Gibraltar, most of southern Europe won't know what hit them.*

The cavernous empty hold amidships was invisible to the outside world. The Americans could fly their satellites and spy planes but would never spot his men. If they did get a hint someone was looking, or suspicious, they could simply sail away to more friendly waters. And, the best bit was that it had been his idea. It had quickly been approved by the top men, maybe even by Osama himself? The money to start had arrived within days, and the project had grown at such a speed, it had almost taken on a life of its own. It was a shame it would all have to end after this mission, but, *if I survive again*, he smiled, *I will think of something bigger, something better*. The beginning of a plan was already formulating within.

Tank 4, which used to hold two thousand cubic metres of oil or fuel, had been re-tasked. First, every tank on board had been emptied and thoroughly cleaned. A tubular passageway had been installed low down in the ship by the brilliant dockyard workers of Mr Gadaffi in Tripoli. To most of the fitters, welders, painters and electricians it was just more pipe-work on a tanker, even if a little larger than they were used to. They, of course, had no idea what they were doing. One team would clean the tank, another would install the water-tight doors, and no one had the slightest idea what the final purpose was.

Gadaffi helped by gifting them the old tanker and launch, and had even contributed to the expensive refit. Hachim had the impression, from Najia that the Colonel had been quiet for too long, and was desperate to get back into the fight.

Tank 4 was lined in six-inch-thick hardwood. The lining meant groups could train with new weapons; they could fire to their heart's content without fear of piercing the ship's hull. The tank had not carried any oil for years and Libya had lent the tanker to many like-minded groups. The most prolific of users was rumoured to have been the IRA.

Hachim had been eager to test the wooden walls. While they were still alongside in Tripoli at one o'clock in the morning, had taken one of the newly delivered Armalites and fired a full magazine at the far wall; then another; then another. One of his men had been stationed on the quay and reported that hardly anything could be heard above the noise of the ship's generators. With the ship fully laden at sea, nothing would be heard; he would put his reputation on it.

His men had fired some 5,000 rounds testing the new weapons since embarking, and nobody in the outside world was any the wiser. Perfect.

A sharp knock on the door wiped the smile off his face. *Please let it be Najia*, he thought. He wasn't ready to forgive her yet for losing that idiot, Aghilas. He had shouted at her and typically she had faced up to him, to the point where he had been forced to subdue her. She was sulking because of their fight, but it would be fun when she came crawling back. She had shown a fascination for the trinket he'd taken from the Englishman's yacht. That's how he would win her over;

he would offer it in return for her favours. He straightened his crisp white shirt, picked up the brass dividers and with the parallel rule in the other, leaned over the chart of Gibraltar bay.

"Enter." The door opened and his hopes were dashed. It was one of the somewhat reluctant ship's crew. What was he called? The bosun, whatever that meant. Hachim's anger and disdain for the man showed in his voice:

"I thought I told you I was not to be disturbed. What is it?"

The bosun's voice was so excited and nervous he had trouble getting his words out. "I'm sorry, sir, Captain, sir, but it's the lieutenant, the girl, sir!"

"What is her problem now?"

"Sir, she has just called up from the boat and said she's captured someone, a swimmer... sir!"

When Hachim arrived on the port side, it was utter bedlam. The larger steps were over the side, and the crew were lowering the ship's small crane hook with a bright orange evacuation stretcher on the end. Despite his order for the absolute minimum of deck lighting and restricted upper deck movement, five of his men were already down on the launch. As the crane's boom lowered over the side, its idiot driver put the light on and bathed the boat's deck in white light. One of his men immediately shouted to the driver to turn it out, but the glimpse of the scene below revealed one of confusion. Before it was lost in darkness, Hachim saw a man lying face down on the deck, hands tied behind his back, legs bound and a man was sitting across him, tying a sack over his head. Najia was kneeling over him with the medical bag.

Who was it? The British special services? They were the ones he feared most. They didn't seem to bother with laws like the rest of the pathetic western world. Maybe it was the Americans. It can't all go wrong now. He paced up and down the deck until one of his men came running up the stairs.

"Who is it? Where did he come from?" he shouted at the man.

"I don't know Sir, he..."

"You don't know. What use are you? Didn't you question him?"

"He can't speak, sir. The lieutenant, she shut him in the hold with a stun grenade. There was a small fire but she put it out before we got there."

Hachim was worried. How many more were there? Was this an attack? A shiver went down his spine. He looked around the dark bay expecting to see fast boats, a warship closing in, something. "Is he alone?" he said to no one in particular.

He could contain himself no longer and rushed down the dark stairs to the launch.

The man was lying face down and strapped in. The back of his wetsuit was scorched, he had a red neck and a large cut on the back of his head. Hadda's attention was immediately drawn to something else. There was the pungent smell of burning wood smoke.

He looked around the launch's deck. "There's been a fire?"

A raging fire on board a wooden launch alongside his tanker would soon scupper his plans. The rest of his men seemed preoccupied with making sure the prisoner was lashed onto his stretcher. Not one of them met his eye.

Najia stood beside the prostrate prisoner. She had an empty syringe in her hand and the familiar fight in her eyes, the air of defiance. She met his accusing gaze. "It is the Englishman, you know. The one from the yacht."

She was defying him again. She knew full well she was not to mention their covert sideline, especially in front of the men.

"How did he get here?" Hachim looked around the dark waters of the Bay again. If it was just the English, then hopefully, he was alone.

"I don't know," she said "I was down in the engine room, checking the oil levels ready for tomorrow. I felt her move so I came up on deck and saw him as he was going into the hold. He knows something. He picked up the tin that had..." She looked around at the men who were unaware of all the details. "...had some of your special equipment in it. How would he know that, unless he's been on board? I was wondering - he may know something about Aghilas?"

Hachim whipped his head round and looked her in the eye. She was hard to figure out, this one. Maybe that was what fascinated him. Her black eye and the other bruises he'd inflicted during their altercation seemed to have had little effect. He had tried humiliation in the bedroom, and violence upon her body; neither seemed to bring him a reward. Hachim found this confusing, and exciting. Here was a woman, the likes of which he had seldom come across before. She was hard to break.

Hachim turned to his men. "Get him on board now, and do it quietly, no lights. Take him into the accommodation, then use the lift. Get him into number four and into the tank. Go... go now!"

Hachim followed the stretcher up. On the tanker's upper deck he again peered into the darkness, searching for moving lights, for any unusual activity.

Was it possible the English had come aboard alone? Was he that mad, desperate, or just stupid? Or had he, Hachim, taken more from him than he realised? Had he missed something? Carter, that was his name. How had he found them? He would need to be thoroughly interrogated before he was disposed of. An idea came to him. Maybe he would let Najia do it. She said she had interrogation training; not the same thing as experience, but her English was excellent. That would test her mental toughness. Not everyone had the stomach for it. She had a point though, maybe this English had killed Aghilas? Maybe he had forced the drunken monkey to talk?

Najia arrived on deck, the medical bag slung over her shoulder. She was sweating but still managed to look elegant, if a little smug. Hachim decided he could do something about that.

He looked away as she said, "I gave him 30mg of Morphine. I don't know how he got here. I can see no boat. Maybe he swam out. He had a wetsuit on."

Hadda watched as the stretcher was negotiated into the accommodation level under the bridge, then he turned back, grabbed her chin and pulled her close.

"You nearly ruined the whole operation. What if the fire had taken hold? Don't you realise you are alongside a floating bomb? We are carrying thousands of tons of fuel and oil, and you let a man come aboard. Then you let off a stun grenade, on a wooden boat. Are you trying to finish us before we've even started? I have a mind to send you back to your beloved Colonel... with a recommendation for court martial."

He pushed her face away and her hair flew up and stuck to her cheek. Immediately his words hit home and he saw the hurt and fear in her eyes. It seemed the only way to scare her was to threaten to send her back to mundane duties, or was it the fear of what Gadaffi would do? Before she could utter a word, he headed for the bridge. His anger surprised even him; she had actually done well. But he was worried.

He looked up beyond the bridge, into black starry heavens. "Allah, Allah, grant me two days... two more days, and I shall have a great many more unbelievers for you."

# 27

Mick Smith - known to all as Smudge - was again texting his buddy, Nick. He was used to getting no response for weeks on end, but this time he was worried. "Where is the useless...?" he said under his breath and pressed send for the umpteenth time. He pressed the dial button only to be greeted with:

*The mobile you are calling may be switched off - please try later.*

"It's never fucking switched on."

He looked around the boat shed in Gibraltar dockyard as dozens of men went about their business of checking and re-checking the boat. The clatter of the compressor outside the building was just loud enough to make it annoying, but the buzz of being around diving and more importantly, the vehicle, was definitely there.

He had volunteered to drive the Swimmer Delivery Vehicle for the SBS. Usually it would've been a flat *no* as he was no longer a serving member of Her Majesty's forces. But, they knew he had done five and half years piloting for the Special Boat Service all over the world. It was now out of his hands. Every time Smudge looked up he could see the Sergeant, Jon Dog, and an officer, looking over the data from his exercises on a laptop.

Before they had left England he'd spent twelve hours in the simulators at their headquarters in Poole, Dorset. He knew he'd done well, but they still hadn't said yes, but, to look on the bright side, they hadn't said no either.

In Smudge's favour was the fact that the usual Royal Naval clearance diver pilot had managed to get himself a bend only three days earlier whilst diving off the Isle of Wight. He hadn't been allowed to fly. Another suitable CD was on an operation. Smudge knew J.D himself was a formidable pilot of the submersible, but he also knew J.D would not want to stay on board the sub if there was a chance of action. He would want to lead his men, if it ever came to that. Smudge still had his doubts if anything would kick off at all.

Going against him was the fact the submersible had undergone a mid-life overhaul since Smudge had done his many hundreds of hours. The vehicle now had a lot more sneaky gizmos on board. They had shown him around some so that he could do his runs on the simulator, but they were reluctant to tell all. Coincidentally, the first dummy run involved leaving Gibraltar at night and approaching an unknown ship. They had put all the co-ordinates into the on-board computer for him. He just had to follow the way-points to the target, so kept telling them: "I don't know what the fuss is about. It's a darn sight easier to pilot than in my day. We had to do it all on dead reckoning."

He was trying his utmost not to get caught staring in the direction of the sergeant and his boss. *Don't look too keen*, he thought, but it was no good. He was definitely twitchy and noticed J.D shaking his head. J.D then shut the laptop and looked around for Smudge.

"Shit!" He muttered, and looked down at his mobile phone. "They've said no. I knew it - they've said no."

Smudge and J.D had had a long discussion on the flight over from England. The sergeant was aware of the history between the two clearance divers, and he knew how much Smudge wanted to be involved in anything that might concern his friend and partner, Nick.

As J.D made his way across the boat shed, one of his men stopped him. Smudge tried not to watch or let his impatience show as the two chatted. Jon Dog was a thickset, gentle-speaking man. He had a slight Bristolian accent, but had the reputation in the Special Forces as a ruthless soldier. With his West Country twang, he appeared more like a fit farmer than a man with more than 25 years of fighting and diving experience all over the world.

Smudge decided not to wait for him. Convinced he was not on-board anyway, he wandered over to the mini-submarine where Special Boat Service troopers and two technical men were working. The craft's characteristics came flooding back.

It looked like a cross between a baby sperm whale and a miniature submarine. It was just over six metres long, under two metres wide and a little more than two metres in height. That was without any extra equipment strapped to it. The genius was the simple design and the fact it was a wet submarine, not, as everyone who saw it thought, a dry one. That meant it was always occupied by divers and was fully flooded when underway. It carried its own on-board compressed air and pure oxygen so the team could breathe the boat's supply, or through their own bubble-less re-breather diving sets.

His thoughts were interrupted when the compressor outside was shut down and the boat shed returned to its relative peace. The reduction in noise also caused J.D to look up and round for the ex-Clearance Diver.

Smudge looked into the pilot's side of the cockpit and checked the gauge. The on-board air was charged to 5000psi. *Crikey*, he thought, *they've upgraded the working pressure of the bottles as well.*

"Smudger!" He looked round to see a stern J.D. "Smudger. Do you want the good news, or the bad?"

"The good, and it better be good."

"Well, it is good. I think you'll think it's good anyway. Whether you'll think that in a couple of hour's time... well, we'll have to wait and see, won't we?" He broke into a grin. "You're in mate. You're on board. Last resort if you like because we can't get anyone else at such short notice. You're our pilot."

The surge of emotions almost overwhelmed him. There was relief that he was not in Gibraltar as a spectator. That was quickly followed by a healthy dose of

207

fear. Not fear for the job so much, more as to whether he could still pilot one of these miniature subs as he used to. The overwhelming sensation, though, was excitement. He was back on an operational job.

J.D nodded his head towards the man in combats that Smudge took to be the Special Boat Squadron officer, "The boss has left it up to me, so I'm gonna trust you. We'll both get shot if this all goes tits up. You know that, don't you? So... I'm gonna give you to Atkins here. He's our senior tech. He knows these boats inside out. He'll update you on everything that's changed since your day."

"Atkins!" The man looked up from his clip board and gauged his pupil through thick furrowed eyebrows. "Atkins, this IS Smudge, he will be pilot this evening. Run him through would you, just the essentials, alright?"

Smudge stared back at a wiry man in a white coat. Atkins looked him up and down, then stuck out his small hand. Smudge gripped it until the man winced.

J.D turned to leave with a smile on his face. Smudge called to him, "Hey, J.D! You said there was bad news. What's the bad news?"

"Looks like we'll be leaving surface in about two hours. You'd better switch on Popeye."

"Jesus! Two hours?"

As Smudge watched J.D retreat, Atkins cleared his throat and asked, "Are you SBS?"

"No. Are you?"

"Of course I'm not. You must be Navy then, are you a CD?"

"No."

"Then I don't think you are qualified for this."

"Unfortunately mate, I think you'll find it's not your decision. You're just a number cruncher then, are you?"

"I am not. I am a scientist, I virtually designed these boats, I keep them running..."

Smudge cut him off, "Designed them? That's funny, I've never seen you before; where have you been hiding?"

"Never mind that; have you any idea how much one of these costs? It's not a toy, you know."

"Really? The sergeant there said I could come and play with it..."

J.D, who had been listening in, interrupted. "Children, children, can we save this for another day? Smudge here is teasing you; he has many, many hours on the Mk6 boats. Now if you gentlemen could just remember that we leave surface in two hours, we might fuckin' get somewhere!"

Atkins looked accusingly at Smudge, "You said you weren't a CD."

Smudge stepped forward and towered over the man, "I'm not, I was thrown out for decking a pedantic commanding officer."

Atkins looked up, "Oh. You should've said you used to be a CD, and a pilot."

"You never asked."

"What boats were you on, and when?"

"It was the Mk6, about nine years ago, maybe ten."

Atkins jotted something down on his clipboard. "I see, I see. It would've been more like twelve years ago, but anyway, let's start with everything that has changed since you were a pilot."

"I was *the* pilot, there was only one, back then."

Atkins nodded. "Follow me, will you?"

Smudge, didn't move. He watched the man go around the front of the sub's bulbous nose. One of the men in the rear of the boat, who Smudge had not taken much notice of, stuck his head out, and in an American southern drawl said: "Welcome aboard, buddy. Don't worry about Atkins there. He's fuckin' brilliant at his job. The name's Texas, I'm a US Navy Seal. I'm over here to teach these guys how to do it deep and do it right."

Another trooper rolled out from under the boat on a mechanic's wheeled trolley. Looking up and offering his hand, he said, "Don't take any notice of Texas, he's BHNC that one... big hat, no cock, thick as shit; we just use him as ballast." Texas tipped a plastic bottle of water down onto his face and a frank exchange of views ensued.

Atkins looked around the bows of the boat and called: "Mr Smith, please, we don't have long. We should do pre-dive-checks together and you can fire questions at me."

Texas whispered, "He's not as bad as all that, just up his own ass a bit that's all. Typical Brit, ya know?"

Smudge followed Atkins around the outside, then the inside of the boat. Together they traced every valve on board. They ended up in the cockpit, sitting side-by-side in the tiny compartment, Atkins ensured his trainee was armed with all the knowledge he might need. He passed Smudge the laminated CDC's (Cockpit Dive Checks) and had him read it out.

"No 1. Ballast blow, spring-loaded. Closed."

He looked up, put his hand on it and checked it was closed.

"No 2. Slow ballast, needle valve. Closed. No 3. Main $O^2$ to on-board re-breather. Closed. No 4. On-board breathing air, bank one. Open. 5000 PSI."

With the 56 internal valves checked, they moved on to the new computer instrument panel. This was unfamiliar ground, and Smudge was a little concerned.

Atkins was now enjoying himself, as though extolling its virtues to a potential buyer.

"The Mk 6 you piloted was largely mechanical and used the bulk of its available power for propulsion. They were limited by the battery technology of the day. You, I believe, would've had the old silver zinc power units." He tapped the floor. "But these Mk8 boats are furnished with the latest 'Li-on' units, that's lithium ion, as I expect you know? They're still kept under the deck plates." Smudge just nodded as if to say, of course I know.

"That means we can now have a lot more electronic aids. When you dive, you will plug in this short umbilical. That will be dominant. By that I mean, when it's plugged in, you will be breathing on-board gas. If you leave the boat, you twist and unplug... thus. And you're on your own breathing set. The through water communications will also work automatically."

"How long can I run then, say at a depth of six meters, no tide and fully laden, at four knots?"

"I would say... six hours, and even then you would still have emergency power for a further four. You could also cruise at 5 to 6 knots now. The new batteries give you more speed as well as longer duration. As you would expect, most of the power still goes to the motor. The rest goes to your onboard systems." Atkins then leant slightly forward in the navigator's seat and punched in a four-digit pin code. With a theatrical sweep of his hand, the thick Perspex screens lit up.

"These Mk 8 boats now take out a lot of the human error we used to see."

As the screen loaded, Smudge just grunted. "Not in my day, mate."

"I didn't mean you, I meant... oh never mind. All your gas is obviously still mechanical, that's breathing gas and all ballast. Also, your controls are still mechanical: planes and rudder are virtually unchanged from the first boats. The pilot's and navigator's joysticks are between your legs there. They are smaller and more sensitive than before. They are identical, so if either of you are injured or ill for any reason, you can both fly the boat from either seat. The computer screen in front of you is identical on my side. You can move around the screen with your thumb-operated mouse, try it. You just click or double-click as you would on any PC. It's the same as the simulator you used in Poole. Tell me... did you use the in-water one, or the dry?"

"I did about six hours on each."

"Excellent, so I don't need to talk you through everything. This is your homepage, if you like, your everyday cruising screen. Top dead centre you have your compass with the boat's heading in the middle, your cross track error, then clockwise you have depth, speed over the seabed, ETA to your next way-point, battery power..."

"How does the GPS update while we're underwater?" asked Smudge, moving the thumb mouse around the screen.

"J.D, who I assume will be sitting here, can release a small buoy to get a fix any time. He may ask you to slow down. When it breaks the surface, it receives a burst signal, and then it's automatically wound back in. There is also a receiver on the top of the periscope if you are shallow enough or in no immediate danger of being spotted. It also transmits everything that's been said in the boat at the same time, so be careful who you bitch about. In this smaller screen you have a combined sonar/magnetometer. They tell me it works brilliantly, I designed it. So if you are heading towards say, a ship, it gives an excellent 3-D colour picture of the hull. The computer will record everything that goes on, so we can analyse it when you get back."

"Great! Fuck-ups for all to enjoy," said Smudge.

Atkins carried on as if he had not spoken. "This is your gruesomely-named dead man's key, DMK. This isn't on the simulators yet. If you punch in your pin code, then pull this key, the boat will completely shut down. That is so you can park up on the bottom somewhere, and send your six or more operatives ashore. We've tested it and the boat keeps virtually all its power for at least six months, although I don't think you'll be using that feature on this mission."

"As a matter of interest, what exactly is this mission?"

"All I know is what I've managed to glean from listening to the grown-ups. They don't tell us anything. It's all a bit secret-squirrel around here." He looked out into the boat shed, and then said in a hushed voice: "I have heard it's a reconnaissance mission, though."

They went through everything on board, quickly and thoroughly, Smudge asking probing questions and Atkins always having a technical answer. As for the actual handling of the boat, Smudge would have to find out whilst U/U, underwater and underway. They were going through the navigator's menus when he heard his name shouted out.

"Mick Smith! What the fuck are you doing in there? And in the pilot's seat. Jesus! They must be desperate."

"Rex! Blimey, I forgot you were out here." They shook hands, and Smudge turned to Atkins and said, "Thanks for all that, mate. I'm happy I've got all I need up here." He tapped his temple. "Anyway, J.D will be next to me."

Atkins let out an exaggerated sigh and shook his head. Smudge got out of the sub and joined Rex, who asked: "Have you got a suit and a re-breather yet. You are going along for the ride?"

"Nope. I've got bugger all. How are you anyway? How's Mo?"

"Fine - brilliant. Listen, Smudge... come into the drying room will you? I want a word." He grabbed Smudge's elbow and led him to a large army-green container. An SBS trooper came out of the 'sweat box' carrying a lightweight dry suit. He had a camouflaged face.

Before they even looked at the array of diving suits hung up, Rex turned round and looked Smudge in the eye.

"Have you heard from Nick Carter yet? Tonight I mean?"

"No. But then, I hardly ever do, he's about as hard to reach as..."

"He called me, about midday and said he was only thirty minutes away!"

"So - where is he?"

"Well, I've spoken to Mo, and she's seen him. He went up to the house, so he has been to Gib."

"What do you mean, he's *been* to Gib? Isn't he still here?"

"He got me to get him permission to go into Rosia Bay. I've just called the sneaky bastards up on windy hill. That's the MoD lookout post at the top of the Rock. They said he sailed again just before dark. Mo's confirmed that - *Orelia's* gone."

"Have you told anyone else?"

"No, why? What's up?"

"I think he's caught up in something big. That's what this is all about. Why didn't he call me, or you? When I catch up with him I'm gonna knock his fucking stupid head off."

Rex frowned. "He must've had a good reason for not contacting us."

Smudge looked around the boat shed. There were now ten SBS men checking their weapons and diving gear. Two were fitting small rubber tyres to the top of the mini-sub. *So*, he thought, *we are planning to come up under something, and round here. It can only be a ship.* Apart from that, the boat was charged, gassed up and looked ready to go.

"RIGHT! Listen up! Texas, shut up will you? Gather round, gents, we've got our brief from the powers-that-be."

They all stopped what they were doing and moved over to join the sergeant, Jon Dog. Finally, they would find out what was afoot.

# 28

In the bowels of the *Yamm-Amira* and crudely erected in one corner of the tanker's cavernous innards was a small metal room.

Nick came round slowly. His level of confusion and disorientation was extreme. Semi-conscious, he couldn't make sense of anything. His eyes didn't seem to open on demand, his limbs would not function at all and his mind was playing tricks. There had been dreams. Strange, incomprehensible dreams. Swirling, bizarre and psychedelic thoughts and images. There were feelings and visions of floating-flying weightless-carefree and almost enjoyable out-of-body experiences.

That had ended, though. Shivering violently, he still felt weightless. Was this, too, part of a dream? He shuddered again. No such luck. He mustered himself to move his head and registered the sound of water but the sound was... wrong. Maybe there was water in his ears? There was hardly any feeling anywhere. All his senses seemed uncertain, numb.

He was sure his eyes were open, but, if they were, he was in total darkness, or... blind?

Nick struggled once more to move, to gain some semblance of control over his body. There was the sound of running water; he was sure of that now, but it was a blank, hollow sound.

He opened his mouth and found it filled with liquid; his natural instinct was to breathe in through his nose. He coughed, spluttered and retched all in one go, but the sound was muffled. He gagged, and mucus came from his

215

nose. His mouth tasted foul, and there was an acrid bite of petrol and oil. There was the strange empty echo of his heaving and spitting. This was not sleep, this was something far more sinister.

Unable to figure out where he was, or what had happened, he tried again to move, to stand up, to turn around, anything, but all he could move was his head. The panic began to increase inside. Was this... death... a stroke... had he drowned?

Forcing himself to calm down, he racked his brain and tried to retrace the last memories. The paddle out to a tanker; then, slowly, he remembered boarding the launch - and the stun grenade. That had done exactly what it was meant to - so he was stunned - but there was something else going on.

There was a somewhat faded recollection of being hauled roughly out of the hold. Then there was a faint memory, a feeling, whilst lying face down on the deck of the launch, of a needle. Was there an injection? That might explain the lack of feeling in his skin, and the strange dreams. He lifted his chin as high as it would go and opened his mouth. There was no water, so he was not drowning, thank God.

He wiggled his toes. They were touching something solid and he was sure he had nothing on his feet. He tried his fingers. They moved but there was no feeling in them. Was that the cold, or drugs? It felt like his hands were tied to something; his wrists were touching underwater. He could feel his left ankle was tied tightly to something cold and hard, something... steel maybe? As he tried to move his throbbing foot, something dug deep into his ankle bone and the pain welled up inside. *Maybe the drugs are wearing off*, he thought. In the darkness he looked down towards his feet and yanked up hard with his thigh and back muscles. He yelled out, but all he could hear was an underwater gurgling sound and he choked again. More of the foul-tasting water went down his throat. His stomach convulsed violently until he vomited it back up.

As he spat and dribbled the sick out of his mouth, there was a loud echoing clang, and Nick stopped his struggle. There were voices and the sound of hollow footsteps. A fear gripped him. He felt sure, whoever appeared, it was not going to turn out well. He tried to calm himself and thought about his first reaction. The classic conduct after capture doctrine was that the quiet, unnoticed individual is the last person a captor might think of executing. *Play dead*, he thought, *well dozy at least*.

The footsteps drew nearer until they stopped somewhere behind him. A door opened and his blindness fears were wiped out. Light filtered through the thin shroud of his closed eyelids.

Someone walked close by him. There was a click and brighter light shone onto his face. The voice said something and the door closed.

There was movement nearby, and his head snapped to one side as he was slapped hard across the face.

"Don't play with me, I know you are awake."

The voice was familiar and Nick tried to open his eyes. He had to screw them tight shut again immediately as the lamp was only inches from his face. After the total darkness the pain was excruciating and tears welled up. The heat from the light was hot on his cheek.

"Mr. Nick," the voice said, "you are a resourceful man. What brings you all the way to Gibraltar? Surely not a watch and a paltry amount of money? More importantly, how did you find us?"

Nick didn't know what to say, or even if he could form recognisable words, so he stayed silent.

"I have a feeling we may have some fun getting the information out of you. We will see if you are as tough as you look, or as tough as you think you are."

Nick tried to move his head to the right, to try and see something but there was only darkness aside from the spotlight in his face. He felt he was slowly coming to his senses but still couldn't quite figure out what was happening.

"We have you right where we want you, Mr. Nick. You cannot escape, as I'm sure you have figured out. It's pointless to struggle. Your bath isn't quite full yet, but when it is, you will find it very uncomfortable. We have used it to great effect before and it has proved to be a worthy tool. You see, when it is full you will only just be able to breathe. Soon, you will not be able to rest or sleep. Relax and you will drown. I've found sleep deprivation brings reliable results. Did you know the CIA use it all the time?"

The voice then switched to Arabic and said something he couldn't understand. Nick blinked and tried to make sense of his surroundings. The area was bathed in a dull light. There was a filthy plastic hose not far from his face that was trickling water into the cold metal container.

Hadda came into view. He moved the spotlight away from Nick's face and leaned close.

"You are a strange one, Mr. Nick, I can't figure you out. Why have you come all this way? What did I take of yours that you would risk your life for? Surely it was not just anger that drove you here. What made you board my vessel, on your own? No - there is something else I'm missing here, isn't there?"

Nick looked up and was sure it was Hachim Hadda himself, the Madrid train bomb mastermind; the killer of his wife and unborn child. He wanted nothing more in the world than to kill him, right here, right now, with his bare hands, to strangle the life out of him, beat him to death. He yanked up on his wrists but the pathetic attempt achieved nothing but a ripple of water around his shoulders.

Hadda studied him and continued, "Maybe I am wrong. Maybe it was just anger at being robbed. I was robbed once and I know I would have killed the man had I ever caught him." Then Hadda looked past Nick and spoke to someone else, in English. "So, you gave him 30mg of Morphine. How long will he be like this?"

A woman's voice replied. "Another hour, maybe."

"Question him. You know the information I want. Keep him awake, do you understand? Fill his tank to the top. He's not to have a moment's rest. Keep a close eye on him, he's shaking already and I don't want him dead by morning. I want him talking. And how is the other one?" Hadda moved to an area behind a partition, and the woman joined him.

"He is fine, he sleeps, I gave him Rohypnol. He will remember nothing."

Hadda said guardedly, "Get rid of him, his time for being useful is over. I will teach him not to question me. I should have shot him there and then."

She shook her head to protest but he cut her off, "DO IT! What you achieve here will determine if you are to be... rewarded, or punished. I know what you want. This is how to earn it. Understand?"

He wandered back and stood in front of Nick. Hadda held his chin and shook his head as he said, "You, Mr. Nick, you and I are going to get to know each other better. You *will* tell me everything I want to know. Now I am a little tired and shall take to my bed. I have a big day tomorrow."

An almost imperceptible grin spread across his face. "In fact, I may let you get involved, as an observer, you understand?" Hadda turned to leave, but seemed to have another thought. He came back and grabbed the back of the swivel spotlight, moved it closer into Nick's face and said, "Does anyone, anyone at all know you are here?" Nick could not look at Hadda. The light was too bright. He was still playing the drugged victim, so he bowed his shaved head to look at the water.

Hadda swivelled the light away from Nick's head, then asked again, a little louder, "This is important. Does anyone know where you are? I know you sailed alone, but did you tell anyone, anyone at all?" Nick was silent and hung his head in submission. Hadda bent down and picked up what looked like half a broom handle. Crudely attached to one end were two long rusty nails. Hadda gently lowered the pronged end into the water and lifted

Nick's chin with it. "Look at me when I ask you a question!"

The two men locked gazes. Hadda was wearing a pristine short-sleeved shirt with four, gold, merchant Navy rings on his lapels. He looked immaculate, and the thin scar above his eye was hardly noticeable. Nick allowed his eyes to drop and noticed Hadda was wearing *his* Navy Rolex.

"I am not known for my patience, Mr. Nick - I am waiting."

Nick looked directly into the man's eyes. That may have been the first mistake he'd made. He must have shown defiance, insolence, or the hatred he felt for the man, because Hadda removed the pronged stick from under his chin and his mouth dropped back into the water. Hadda then rested the wooden stick on top of the spotlight, shook his head and pushed the bulb down below the surface.

As the bulb sparked and sank, Nick's crude bath of putrid water was immediately electrified.

His naked body tensed and arched. The current passed through the fillings in his teeth as he bit his tongue. His eyeballs felt like they would burst. Every muscle in his body contracted and froze solid, like an all-over body cramp. Nick heard someone cry out, but did not recognize the sound of his own primal scream. Jaws clamped closed, the noise was inhuman. The bulb blew but the current continued around his makeshift torture chamber.

Eventually the shock ended, but Nick's body was set solid, still tensed up; all the veins, tendons and sinews in his neck were stretched bow-taut.

Slowly, oh so slowly, he managed to move his head from side to side to release the tension. On opening his eyes, he saw a woman, the one from the launch he had seen through the binoculars, and now, he realised, the one who'd thrown the stun grenade into the hold. She bent close to his face and was smiling. It was not a warm smile but a cruel one, totally without affection. She was enjoying herself.

He lifted his head to look into her eyes; they seemed huge and very dark. She was... striking; her teeth gleaming white. The black eye she carried was turning blue and yellow and still puffy. An immaculately plucked eyebrow was swollen.

She was studying Nick, looking him over as she might inspect a caged animal, or a trapped insect: maybe judging the degree of hurt he was suffering. She cocked her head and said, in perfect English, "At last... we are alone."

The salty taste of blood from his bitten tongue filled his mouth. He took a deep breath and spat it out. A large globule of blood and spit landed mostly on her dark overalls but a spot landed on her chin. Her hand shot up to wipe it off with her palm. The transformation in personality was astonishing and instant. One moment, beaming and beautiful, she gritted her teeth, almost snarled, her dark eyes narrowed and he glimpsed an entirely different persona. She spun around and walked briskly away from his tank. She had her back to him and appeared to wipe her face clean, then she put on a pair of long, black gauntlets and flipped a circuit-breaker switch on the wall. As she walked towards Nick's tank of water, he realised she had lost it; she was not all there. She picked up the pronged pole Hadda had used. This time, he realised it had wires running off towards the floor.

Nick wanted to say something, to plead, to apologise. His mouth moved, but nothing recognisable came out. She was no longer beautiful; she was... seething. She lifted the pole with the long rusty nails and moved them towards his face, stopping an inch from his eyeballs. He focused on them; they were the same width as his eyes, and, there were thin wires taped to them. He looked at the points, then up at his captor and tried to look apologetic, beaten and non-threatening. He managed to shake his head, pleading, as if to say, please... no.

She stared back with a hate-filled expression. Right then, he knew she was hard, and crazy. The seconds ticked by, Nick pleading without making a sound. Then she seemed to calm herself, to relax just a bit, and the devilish half-smile returned. She moved the prongs to one side, so he could see them, then touched the nails to the metal container's side.

She said, "You shouldn't spit. Mind your tongue. They always bite their tongue." Then she pressed a button on the handle.

# 29

Departing in convoy from RAF Gibraltar were two cars and a minibus. Complete with blue flashing lights, the MoD police Land Rover led the dark green Royal Air Force convoy through the narrow streets and high bastion walls of Gibraltar town. I.D2 and the First Sea Lord sat in the rear of the first car. On their way to the Royal Naval dockyard, they sped past an innocuous looking BP petrol station.

"That may be appropriate," said Sir Michael Clapp. "Do you remember the ITV documentary, *Death on the Rock?*" He indicated the garage on their left. "That's where the SAS shot those three IRA terrorists."

I.D2 looked across and said matter-of-factly, "Yes. One of them works for us now." Sir Michael opened his mouth to enquire further, but then just nodded.

The stone city walls jutted out of the earth like an impenetrable fortress, which was exactly what Gibraltar had proved to be for hundreds of years. At speed, they negotiated a roundabout with a huge anchor set into it. They were now close to the stone-arched gates of the walled city. The words 'Ragged Staff' was painted above the gateway. They turned right off the main street and down a small road with 'NO ENTRY MoD PROPERTY' written above it. As the convoy slowed down at the red and white barrier, two armed Royal Marines approached the leading Land Rover. They stepped back and saluted smartly as the barrier was raised.

"That's why I brought you, Michael," said I.D2. "It would've taken me a month of Sundays to convince them who I was, and, do you know, I have no Identity card? Me, I.D2, with no I.D."

The small convoy sped through the dimly lit dockyard, bumping over the old railway lines and manhole covers. They passed a stone boat shed where dark-clad men were supervising the lifting of a large heavy-looking object.

Sir Michael craned his neck as they were passing, then ordered: "Stop! Stop the car!" The car screeched to a halt and he was out in a flash. He ran over to a man he seemed to recognise, who immediately shouted, "ATTENN-SHUN!" The crane stopped in mid swing; all the men stood still when they saw the gold flashes of a First Sea Lord standing almost beneath the mini-submarine.

From the car, I.D2 was looking at her watch and about to wind down her window and complain, when the First Sea Lord slapped the man on the back, laughed and ran back to the car. They drove off just as the Land Rover that had been escorting them returned to retrieve their lost VIPs. They drove on, the FSL saying, "Drive on, man. I know where we're going!" He turned to his cohort, lowered his voice and said, "That was the SBS sergeant, a good man. The sub will be in the water in fifteen minutes." Then, rubbing his hands together and whispering he added, "They're going to have a look about the anchorage. Perfect, perfect... they may well find something out soonest."

They bumped further along the dockyard until he said, "Left here. That's it, those big blue doors. Stop there." They waited for the next car and minibus to disembark. The MoD Land Rover then caught up at last and a cross-looking MoD policeman strode toward them. "Sir... Ma'am... I must protest. How am I to guarantee your safety if..."

Under his breath, the FSL said to I.D2, "Bloody Mod Plod. They're all frustrated coppers," then more loudly, "Oh stop fussing man. We are, after all, in the Navy dockyard are we not? Now what is today's code? Well? I've just landed, so I don't know." While they all looked at each other for the entry code, a small hatch in the larger blue door opened and out stepped a three-ringed naval officer.

He chopped a smart salute off to his Commander-in-Chief. "Evening, Sir, Ma'am. Commander Briggs, at your service. I'm JFC on the Rock. My, you have got a large contingent haven't you? Welcome to Gibraltar. I've just been made aware of your requirements but I've made the JOC ready for your good selves and..."

I.D2 stopped him in mid flow and asked, "JFC? The Jock, did you say?"

"Sorry, Ma'am. I'm the JFC, Joint Forces Commander, and JOC is the Joint Operations Centre. It's in the centre of the..."

"Yes, yes, I know where it is. I do wish you military types could remember that not everyone is in or was in the forces. My God, you have an initial for everything. There are a few civilians here. Try and speak English to them, would you? Now, if you would please lead the way, I'm eager to get started."

Briggs was a little taken aback at the authoritative response of the woman, but said nothing and led the way.

They were in effect walking into and under the huge natural edifice that is the Rock of Gibraltar. They soon came to another door, only this was the real one that made the oak door on the outside look like a garden gate. Briggs nodded to a small camera set high up in one corner and the excited chatter from the following group was stilled. There was a loud clunk, then the sound of powerful hydraulics as the white metal wall began to move up and towards them. The party moved back in unison as the two-metre-thick metal door swung up into a recess in the solid rock. It was wide enough to take two lorries and as high as a double-decker bus. As it stopped, snug into its recess above, they could see that beyond the door was another, already open.

Briggs walked over to a sentry post and announced to no one in particular, "Double blast-doors, built to withstand a nuclear strike. We've never had to shut them

225

both." The security camera had tracked his movements over to the wall. He stuck his thumb up and instantly the tunnel was lit up. Strip fluorescent lighting flickered on and threw light on a row of blue golfing buggies. The lights kept blinking on down the tunnel, further and further into the distance.

Walking to the electric cars, Sir Michael asked, "Are these golf carts for us? Last time I was here we had to walk. Churchill and Eisenhower used to take a jeep, you know, right through these very doors. Eisenhower was quoted as saying his quarters inside the Rock were the most dismal setting we occupied during World War II!"

Briggs said to his two most important guests, "This tunnel cuts right through the Rock, but we won't be going that far." Then he announced to the whole group:

"Ladies and gentlemen! Please… thank you. One volunteer driver for each buggy. Each has an ON, an OFF, a FORWARD AND BACKWARD. That's your safety brief, oh, and don't drive down any holes as it punctures the tyres. If you follow me closely, please, you won't come to any harm."

With that there was another buzz of chatter as they boarded the carts. Briggs drove the first with Sir Michael and I.D2 facing backwards and an older man with round glasses in the passenger seat next to him. The man introduced himself to Briggs.

"Professor James C. Fleming, Director of the Dalton Nuclear Institute, from Manchester University." Briggs took one hand off the wheel and shook the proffered hand.

Small cameras monitored their progress as they headed off. When the last cart moved away, the blast door started to come down, and those not driving looked back at the entrance. Then, the second blast door started to move. There were raised eyebrows and exchanged glances. The Professor said, "Nuclear threat… one wonders?"

Briggs replied, "We don't yet know what the threat is."

There was a pause, before the Professor asked Briggs: "Where exactly are we going?" Briggs kept his eyes on the dusty track, driving round small rock-falls and holes in the road.

"It's called the Joint Operations Centre. It's the safest operations room, possibly in the world. The Yanks might disagree but that's my view. It's kept in a state of semi-readiness and can support a large contingent of... shall we say VIPs for about a year. It has air scrubbers, desalination units, and every type of communication, old and new."

They drove on for five minutes, perfectly straight, deeper and deeper into the rock. The empty tunnel disappeared into the distance. They passed turnings, huge storage areas and mysterious closed doors, one showing a tantalizing hint of light from within. There were thick power cables attached to the walls: pipes and telephone lines carrying Gibraltar's essential services.

Constant drips and the cold, dark, damp atmosphere made for an eerie ambience. At one point they drove into the edge of darkness, Briggs stopped the lead car, got out and pushed a large red button with A1-East-Peterborough, written above it. The switch lit up another seemingly never-ending line of fluorescent lights, leading into the distance. The professor asked, "The sign, it says we're going to Peterborough?"

Briggs answered as he put his foot down again. "During the war, convoys of supplies would come through here. They could get all around the Rock without the Germans seeing where they were going or what they were carrying. The Germans had spies permanently located in Spain watching naval and troop movements. Only, drivers would get in here and occasionally get lost. So, they called this the A1, after the road in England. They could just say to a driver, 'Drop this load off at Durham, it's up the A1, past Peterborough, past Doncaster, stay on this road; you can't miss it!'"

The Professor seemed excited, pointing out turnings and more sign posts. He chatted away, barely taking time to breathe.

"They told me I was coming, they didn't really ask me, I think that is because I once signed the NPT, the Nuclear Proliferation Treaty and the man on the phone said it was like the Official Secrets Act. Of course, I can't remember everything that was in it, although I do remember most of it. In fact I'm sure I have a copy somewhere, but I'd never find it, my apartment is in such a mess, you know how it is? Fifteen years ago I signed it. Anyway they said it was urgent, so here I am." Then taking his first, short sharp breath he carried on, "I've never been to Gibraltar. I hope we get a chance to study the apes. You know what they say. As long as the apes are in Gibraltar, the Rock will be British. Do you think they'll organise a tour. I do hope so. This is fascinating, not to you, I don't suppose. You're in here every day I expect…"

Briggs looked across at him, convinced the professor's brain was so full, everything had to come tumbling out. Doncaster rescued him from his ear-bashing. They stopped and Briggs shouted back to all. "Alight here, Ladies and Gentlemen. Please mind the gap!" He swiped a card through a slot in a box on what looked like a prison door, then covered his hand as he punched in a code. The door was old, rusty and impenetrable.

"There are 121 steps here so please take care and use the banister to your right."

They all filed down a spiral staircase, deeper into the earth. The nervous chatter had abated and all that could be heard was the echo of the dozens of feet vibrating around the claustrophobic pothole blasted out of solid rock.

After a dizzying descent, they saw light: bright, white light and a modern door with bolts protruding from every corner. They filed through into a different world. It was a dazzling, modern, long corridor and there was the sound of voices, modern machinery, air conditioning, and the alluring smell of coffee.

A Wren, waiting for them, said. "Could you all follow me, please?" They trudged down the corridor, all sense of direction, time and whereabouts having left them long ago. She eventually turned right and opened a pair of large doors. Inside was an airport-type security port. They passed through into an operations room that was a curious mix of old and new. Around the outside were a dozen or so navy and army personnel, glued to computers and wearing headsets they murmured into microphones and tapped at keyboards.

Some seats were laid out facing a huge wartime chart of the Mediterranean and North Africa. To one side of the chart was a table, on which sat two large bronze busts, one of Dwight. D. Eisenhower, the other of Winston Churchill.

The chorus of introductions and hushed chatter merged with the ops room personnel to form a buzz of excitement. The Information Director stepped from a side room, followed by a few new faces. She looked concerned and was staring down at a piece of paper in her hand. She stepped up to the group.

"Now, gentlemen, I have already heard a few mutterings about the ridiculous nature of our surroundings, and our journey to get here. These rooms are as secure as you will find anywhere in the world, and that's no exaggeration. Eisenhower spent months down here during the Second World War, planning and directing the North African and Mediterranean campaigns. What made it good enough and safe enough for him then, holds perfectly true for us now. Above you, you have half a mile of solid rock. To your left, right, front and back, you have a rock wall many hundreds of metres thick. In the unlikely event of there being an explosion on the Rock or tanker now, I doubt we would even know about it. We know little if anything about our enemy, but we have no doubt of his resolve and determination to bring about his view of the world."

She took a deep breath and continued. "That is why we are here, to protect what we know and hold dear. The very life we all lead, everything we take for granted is at threat this day. So, please, I would not like to hear any more moaning about the journey here, the tripping hazards or lack of refreshments or anything else. Please focus on what you're here to specialise in. Rest assured, each and every one of you is a leader in his own field. The best. I want you all to have your thinking caps on. I want to hear your ideas. If you hold back now for fear of being ridiculed, it may be too late by this time tomorrow. By that I mean... if the worst comes to the worst, there may only be us left on this rock if we get it wrong. That may seem over-dramatic... but we don't yet know what these people hold."

She let her words sink in, then simply said, "Thank you."

# 30

It was just after 03:00 in Gibraltar and no one paid any attention to the buff and black buoy-laying and recovery ship, *MV Torrid*. It was pitch black, still and tranquil as she left Gibraltar harbour. The ship was running dead slow, and for good reason. She was towing a large, open and heavy-looking barge. The *Torrid* was showing all the correct towing lights, including her red-over-white-over-red, denoting 'Restricted in my ability to manoeuvre.' The lights and the towing served two purposes. One, it would make sure everyone gave the ungainly tow a wide berth. Two, she could go as slowly as she wished.

Outwardly, no one was paying her much regard, but, covertly, many eyes were glued to the long, disjointed silhouette.

One scruffy-looking vessel was close and paying her particular consideration. She was just one of a half-dozen brightly-lit fishing boats. Many open boats in the Mediterranean cover the gunwales in bright lights facing the surface of the water to attract the small fish, which in turn attract the bigger predators like sea bass, tuna, and dorado. As well as having fishing rods over the side, the boat was also deploying a long torpedo-shaped object that gave a similar side-scan sonar image to the Swimmer Delivery Vehicle. The four anglers were decidedly uncomfortable. Armed to the teeth and dressed as fishermen, they were unaccustomed to being lit up like a London play-house. The Special Boat Service had found that sometimes, to sneak about would arouse suspicion. Act like you belonged and blend in with the locals, and no-one gave a damn. If trouble did flare or the SDV needed assistance, the boat could shock a few of the real anglers with its speed. She went by the call sign of *Gemini Three* and one of the men had on a head-set attached to a small box which led to a powerful microphone dangling ten metres below them.

Half under and half in the towed barge was its secret cargo. The SBS had used the barge to get close to many a target. To all intents and purposes, it looked, like a rusty heap full of stinking black mud dredged from the harbour.

The skipper of the *Torrid* had been given strict instructions where to tow. He was to take the inshore route as usual, not to pass between the anchored tankers.

Tucked underneath and inside the belly of the barge, lay the SDV. There was a heavily-built protective cage around the front end of the recess in which the mini sub sat, protecting the vehicle which just protruded from the barge's flat hull.

Smudge was not yet piloting the miniature craft but his heart was racing with a combination of excitement and nervousness. All six of the swimmers on board were in effect being towed by the barge above, which was being towed by the *Torrid*. Over many years of operational and training exercises, they had learnt it was always best to tow as near to your target as possible. Having to tell the government they had lost one of the multi-million pound submarines because the batteries had run out, was not an option they relished.

The chat in the sub was kept to an absolute minimum. Smudge was content to check that he could put his hand on every valve he might need. During the tow he intended to familiarise himself with every menu on the navigational computer screen in front of him. All that could be heard inside the vehicle was the rhythmic breathing of the on-board divers, the hypnotic throb of the tugs powerful engines, and the passing of the sea around the boat.

When they had left surface they were still not one hundred-per-cent certain which tanker they were going to look at. The powers that be inside the ops room had narrowed it down to two. Two of the twenty tankers in the Bay had suspicious backgrounds and recent docking history. The team was hoping to get updated on route and go direct to the correct vessel.

Only twenty minutes into the tow, the familiar click of the communications to the *Torrid* warned the submarine crew to stop breathing and pay attention.

One of the SBS men was on the through-water communication system next to the skipper on the *Torrid's* bridge.

"Moby... topside," said the echoing voice.

Inside the sub, Jon Dog answered, "*Go ahead, Flaky.*"

"Moby. We are coming up on a yacht anchored in deep water on our port side. It is unusual for one to be out this far. It shouldn't be in this deep channel. Also... it matches the description of the yacht Smudge mentioned... you are about 100 meters north west from it... may be nothing, but while we are here, do you want to have a look?"

There was a pause. Smudge took a deep breath and looked to his right at J.D alongside him in the cockpit. Smudge was tempted to break protocol and say 'yes'. Instead he looked at J.D's screen and could see he had maximised the colour sonar picture of the water in front of them. It was covered in back-scatter from the churning water caused by the *Torrid's* engines and the metal echo from the huge barge they had wrapped around them.

J.D muttered under his breath, "*This picture's a cluster fuck*" Eventually he said, "*Understood... affirmative, we will investigate, then go west to T2. Give me two when we are, fifty metres north of the yacht. What's our ETA to that point?*"

"Moby. Topside, ETA... two minutes errr... now! Over."

Smudge's heart-rate leapt as he went through his controls. He didn't have as long as he thought.

"*Roger. Two minutes to release. Slow to one,*" answered J.D.

"Moby. Topside... engines neutral, slowing to one knot. Coast is clear, no local traffic."

Smudge turned the main engine batteries to ON, checked his neutral buoyancy indicator, then his pilot screen, and was as ready as he'd ever be. He looked over to J.D, who was just visible in the dull glow of the instrument lighting and intent on doing his own checks. He turned round and offered the 'thumbs up'. They were ready.

In the rear were four more of the covert swimmers: Stanley, so called because of his penchant for knives; then there were Texas, Jock and Harvey. They were all listening in on the conversation with the surface. The doors to the sub had been closed in transit and all passengers were breathing the craft's on-board air supply. J.D opened his door by pushing it outwards and back. The dark, cool water outside wafted into the front compartment, creating small whirlpools, lifting and shifting the laminated drawings and emergency charts between the two men.

"Moby. Topside. Will lose through-water comms to you soon as we move ahead." There was a click then a long pause and the voice said. "Moby. On site, dead slow, in neutral... Slip - slip - slip."

*"Loud and clear, Flaky. Slipping now!"* said J.D.

J.D nudged Smudge to open his door and pull the large stainless steel handle that released the port side. As he did, J.D released his. The sub edged and bumped along as the momentum of the moving barge above pushed the boat backwards. J.D said, through the on-board comms system, *"Slow astern, Smudger."*

*"Slow astern."* The whirr of the electric motor spun the propeller and the boat moved out of its protective cage. The lumbering barge continued on her ponderous journey south, as it ghosted overhead. They were free, on their own, and Smudge was piloting again.

J.D looked at his rapidly clearing sonar image and said, *"Contact. One seven zero degrees, seventy metres, non-ferrous. Come ahead, four knots, give me a depth of 5 metres. Close all doors, boys."*

Smudge engaged his motor and the boat picked up speed. He was at a depth of six metres and a little heavy so he opened his slow-releasing needle valve to put air in the for'ard ballast tanks. The nose came up and he counteracted the rise with his bow-planes. J.D said, *"Easy, easy with those bow planes, Smudge. Smaller movements, and trim the boat."*

Smudge nodded. He could see he was a little heavy-handed. J.D put the sonar picture onto Smudge's lower right-hand navigation screen. Most of the picture was dark blue but off to starboard was the huge metallic yellow shadow of the barge slowly moving off into the distance. Also ahead, on his port bow about 65 metres away, was the image of a yacht's hull in deep red. Right in the middle was a longer yellow impression of a metal keel. J.D leaned over to Smudge and just pointed to the yacht's echo, meaning, 'Take me there.'

Free of the barge, on the move and at a steady depth, J.D said to all on board, *"Clear and running. Changing to $O^2$ on-board re-breather."* There came five almost simultaneous replies of *"Roger."* The transformation was instant and dramatic. Gone was the noise of the air breathing; gone were all the annoying bubbles. The boat now ran silent, on her own, invisible from the surface and independent of the outside world. A more distant, delayed voice said, *"Moby. Handing you over to Gemini Three. Be careful down there, boys. Flaky out!"*

There was a short crackly businesslike retort from an eavesdropper, *"Gemini Three, copy and listening. Out."*

Smudge made a bee-line for the echo, now dead ahead. At twenty metres distant and eyes glued to his colour sonar picture, he put the sub's engine into neutral. He then slid open his door and startled a large sucker fish which had come along for the ride. The gentle quarter-knot tide eased the boat nearer and nearer the sonar echo. He and J.D could make out the boat's anchor line on their screens. J.D reached across and tapped it on

Smudge's screen; he'd already had the same idea. Checking his depth and believing his instruments utterly, Smudge put the motor to dead slow astern. It took the way off and the torque of the propeller kicked the nose slightly round to port.

J.D opened his door and with his knee wedged inside the boat, leaned out. He took off his diver recovery strap and grabbed the yacht's anchor line in the crook of his elbow. He then put the strap around the rope, and secured it to a ring on the boat. Then he leaned back inside, set his screen to 'Sleep' and switched on a dull red overhead light.

J.D tested his own re-breather, removed his short umbilical connecting him to the sub's on-board gas and pulled himself out of his door. He moved aft and, pulling open the rear door, pointed to Stanley and Harvey and gave some hand signals.

Smudge trimmed the boat as the four armed men disembarked by gently filling the stern ballast tanks with sea water.

J.D swam back to Smudge's side, reached inside the cockpit and grabbed a scratch-board on a tether and wrote *DROP DOWN 2M. BACK IN 10*. Smudge offered him the thumbs up and J.D pulled himself on top of the craft to join his men.

With the submarine now that little bit deeper and the assault team moving off, Smudge could contain his curiosity no longer. He switched to his re-breather, disconnected his own umbilical and edged out of his door, aiming to stand on top of the craft. As he did, he could see a figure and a pair of fins moving up and then along a dark hull in the faint back-light of a moonlit sky on the surface. Then, one figure disappeared from the water as he climbed up and onto a yacht's stern. Smudge jumped as someone grabbed his ankle. He looked down at the huge frame of Texas, the American Navy Seal. Texas ushered Smudge back to the cockpit and motioned up and down with the flat of his hand, meaning. 'Your job is in there, keep her neutral and trim.' He was right, but

Smudge was now happy, certain that the yacht was Nick's. There couldn't be many yachts with those long, twin rudders. He got back in the boat as she settled and rode the tether that now held her to the sea bed and the yacht above. His elation was short-lived. *I hope he's okay,* he thought.

Jon Dog removed his fins in the water and clipped them to a 'D' ring at the side of his belt, pulled himself to the stern and climbed slowly and as quietly as he could onto the yacht's rear bathing platform. He opened a short waterproof screw-top container and took out his stubby black HK MP7. The tiny Heckler and Koch sub-machine gun was one of the smallest, most modern self-defence weapons in the world. It was already cocked. Harvey had drifted off some five metres and made himself buoyant by inflating his dry suit. He aimed his silent H.K P11 underwater pistol at the rear of the yacht. Only then did J.D steal his first look over the transom. Stanley was right behind him. He took off his mask and spat out the mouth piece, only he didn't aim his weapon. He preferred the quiet way. He had a commando-type knife in his hand as he moved swiftly over the back deck, protected by the arc of J.D's barrel. They covered each other as they took it in turns to move to a place giving protection, whether it be the companion way or the mast tree. Between them they searched above and below decks. They explored every large space that might conceal a man, every cupboard and bunk.

Satisfied that the boat was clear, Stanley moved forward as J.D searched the saloon and galley. Harvey stood on the bathing platform, mask off, searching for any movement on the dark horizon.

J.D was confident the yacht was English, and that it was Nick's. There was the chart work, the logbook, the pictures on the bulkheads, the food, the Johnnie Walker bottle. Then he found a passport in the galley drawer. He put it under the flexible chart light close to the table to dull its glow and switched it on. Nicholas Carter stared back at him.

237

"Where are you, mate? Where are you?" He muttered.

Stan moved aft and shook his head at J.D. He showed Stan the passport, then moved over to the large saloon table. As he moved, he kicked an empty dark green bag he knew once carried an inflatable canoe that he, Jon Derrick, had recommended to him.

In the middle of the table was a Zippo. He picked it up and looked at the crest stamped into the lighter. There was a post-it note stuck to the back. It read:

*"Yamm-Amira, Monrovia, yellow crescent moon funnel crest?*

# 31

As the woman touched the metal surface of the crude bath with the improvised cattle prod, the nails initially just sparked.

She pushed harder to get a better contact, and the agony this time was altogether different. The electricity was not dissipated by the water, but followed the path of least resistance and flowed around the metal container.

First, it bit the soles of his bare feet. The pain was so intense his instinct was to lift them from the base of the bath. On doing so, his remaining weight transferred onto his buttocks. Nick didn't know it, but he was sitting on a metal girder that now made contact with all his weight on his bare cheeks. The shock travelled through his rump and scrotum. Those seconds were spent jumping and twitching from one excruciating position to another. In desperation, he leaned forward and grabbed the girder with both hands between his knees and the volts swept up his arms. The current latched onto his fingers and forced his body to grip the girder with a series of involuntarily muscle contractions.

Nick couldn't have let go if his life depended on it. His jaw locked into a skeletal, bared-teethed grimace. The excruciating, intolerable convulsions froze his contracted muscles. He lost control of his bowels and blood came from his mouth and gums.

Time had no meaning, he just wanted it to end. At that moment, he would have told anyone anything they wanted to know to make it stop.

Nick had no idea he'd been unconscious. He was confused, exhausted and limp. There was a voice, the woman's voice, but it was drowned out by the noise from inside his head. His ears were buzzing and screaming a high pitch constant whine.

For some reason, whenever his head dropped forward, he was no longer drinking in the sickly water. There was something under his chin. Something was supporting his head. With his head resting, he tried again to muster himself, to think, to find a way out of this impossible, intolerable situation. Maybe this woman had a sense of compassion. If she did, could he find it, could he reach it? Nick rested his now unresponsive head and tried to gather himself, to concentrate. He tried to force open his dry eyes. She was near - he could smell her. She was talking, and Nick tried to focus on her words, to listen, to find something to latch onto. She was very close, her breath touched his face.

*

"We need to get to the bottom of your story, Nick. Oh... hello! You are back with us. Good... good, I was beginning to think I was talking to myself. That just makes me angry and then - well, you know what happens then. That's it, open your eyes."

She reached over and lifted his eyelids. He recoiled; there was no moisture left. She flicked water from the tank into his face as he blinked, and some of it ran into his eyes. The oil in the water irritated them further and they began to well tears.

She stared at the figure in the filthy water. He was coming round, and his eyes were streaming. His face was a mixture of exhausted contortion, blood, sick, and oil. He would be dead soon anyway, and there was nothing she could do about it. Nothing she wanted to do about it. He was English, so at least they could understand each other. He would talk. She could always make men talk.

Najia had not wanted this tanker job. She had been chosen, presumably because of her experience on Gadaffi's private yacht. It was a good sign, it could be seen as trust, even promotion. But she wanted more, so much more. She was already missing her son, Jamil. The pay in the Libyan army was pathetic, although she was assured she would be well rewarded for this job. *First I have to survive*, she thought, and that was by no means certain. This plan of Hachim's could go either way. She wasn't sure of the details but, she had built up a picture in her head and wanted nothing to do with it. Terrorists made her sick; they were not Muslims. They were cowards. She wanted to be away to see her baby again, *before* the fireworks started.

First she needed money and lots of it if she was going to make a life outside the army for herself and her son. She already had a country in mind. She had the false passport, and now just needed money and a way out. Hachim seemed to have taken a fancy to her, as most men did, but he was a sadistic bastard. He was not short of money for this project, though; she was sure of that. He also had a piece of jewellery in his cabin that she found... intriguing. On scratching it with her nail she had seen a glimpse of gold underneath, and it was heavy. She had an inkling, an idea that it was not all that it seemed, and it was going to be hers. She usually got what she wanted, especially where men were concerned.

She'd had her share of luck with the Libyan army. There'd been the three years in London where she'd taken her degree in English. She had also entrapped the intelligence officer. He was low-ranking, but her superiors had been delighted. At first it was just work, it was her job to get information on Britain. But Adam was nice enough and he worshipped her. She had just sort of got used to him.

Najia embellished every detail she got from Adam. She made out she had searched his brief case, been through his office in the dead of night, listened to phone calls, when all she had to do was ask whilst in his bed. He would deliver, time and time again.

Then she became pregnant and had to keep the baby quiet from her bosses. They would not have allowed her to keep him. She would probably be executed if they found out, and where would that leave her son? She had glimpsed the good life, the parties, clothes, the money, some of which she'd siphoned away. Adam had provided everything, the house, jewellery, the cars. She could only guess at how it must have broken his heart when she disappeared with Jamil, but what could he do? He couldn't search for them. Their relationship would have been just as forbidden by his work. The western world was for her. She'd got used to it. Then, she was unexpectedly summoned home and slung back into Gadaffi's all-female close protection unit.

Now, somehow, this was her work. She had to concentrate on keeping Hachim happy and that meant dealing with this. Why had she opened her mouth about the interrogation training?

She looked at her prisoner and asked: "Are you listening?" Nick nodded.

"The Captain wants to know what you are doing on board, in fact, so do I. Do you know, I've saved your life once already? You were bleeding to death on that yacht after that animal put the hole in your head. I put that towel round you, otherwise... you were gone. They wanted to leave you but I thought you were just a sailor, on holiday. At least if we kept you alive, someone might find you. Then you make me regret it by jumping on my boat and sneaking about in the hold. My fault again. That makes the Captain blame me. Now you are here and I have to get you to talk. Do you understand?"

Nick still didn't speak. She reached forward and he saw her small hand with painted nails grab the pole supporting his chin. His head lolled forwards like a drunk. She shook her head, pushed the chair back and moved away. With her back to him she opened a bottle of water and drank. A voice made her look round. At first it sounded alien for such a big man. It was almost a whisper.

"Please, ma'am... may I, may I... have a drink?"

She walked over to look at the man in the tub. He looked beaten and blue with cold, but he was tough enough. He would survive the night. His eyes were open and he could speak again. With that cursory glance over, she drank the rest of the bottle in front of him.

Wiping her mouth on her blue combat sleeve she asked, "Nick... we have to earn our treats, don't we? And what have you done to earn a treat? Nothing, apart from getting me in trouble. See this eye? I know this was your fault. I was meant to keep a watch on that ape, Aghilas. I don't know how it became my job. Just because he was on my boat, I guess. He disappears and I get this. How is that fair? You go out for a sail and look where you end up. As my ex used to say, life's a bitch and then you die. "

\*

Nick had been concentrating, trying his utmost to listen to every word. But it was not easy. He suffered cramp in his right thigh and had tried to massage it with his elbow under the water. He spat out a filling the electric shock had ejected, and was fighting off the worst bout of shivering and shaking he could remember.

She squatted down close to him, looked into his eyes and tilted her head to one side as if actually seeing him for the first time. Nick shuddered so violently his head dropped forward into the filthy water again. She put her hand on his shaved head and pushed it backwards, then put the pole back across the sides of his bath and lowered his chin onto the makeshift rest. Walking away, she said "You are freezing," and went to the work bench to turn on a tap.

The filthy hose that had been trickling cold water constantly into the bath spluttered and spat out hot then warm water. He tried to lean forward to get nearer to the hose. As he did, the metal girder he was manacled to moved. It rocked to one side. Until then, he'd been sure it was part of the tank.

She sat back down, her face only a foot from his. She wore no make-up that he could see, and he realised she was not just striking, but beautiful. Her skin was perfect, unblemished. Her huge dark eyes did have humanity in them, he was sure of it. Her dark hair shone in the gloomy light, and for some reason, he formed the impression she was not as tough as she thought. In her hand was a bottle of water. She held it for him to see.

"So... question one, for a sip of fresh cold water. How did you find us here?"

Nick tried to think; he had to tell her something, to get her on side. She didn't seem like Hadda's sort at all, and she spoke English with hardly any accent.

"I - I followed you, using radar."

"What? Impossible. We did 15 knots leaving your yacht. You were out cold, *and* tied up. Try again." She sipped from the bottle while looking at him. Nick was about to answer when he heard another voice, a moan from nearby. So there was someone else down here with him. She ignored the noise and waited for Nick's reply.

"I can - could - do 20 knots. The yacht is t-twin-engined, very f-fast," he stuttered through a bout of shivering.

"Hmmm. Unlikely, but let's press on. Let's just say you followed the tanker using your radar, here to Gibraltar. How could you be sure which one it was, and how did you get out here? The truth please."

She moved even closer and stared into his eyes, searching for the lie.

"Your b-boss, he left his Zippo on board the yacht. It has this tanker's funnel crest on it."

"He is *not* my boss. So... it was his fault. That will please him. How did you get out here?"

"I had a blow-up canoe on board. I paddled out, just for a look, then I saw the launch. I recognized it as the one... the one from that night."

244

She studied him, then: "Hmmm! Now then, for the big question. Why? Any normal person would be happy they had survived an act of piracy. They would call the police, the coastguard, transmit a mayday even. Not you; you give chase and come on board, alone. Why?"

Nick hesitated. He broke eye contact with her and looked away. She reached up, grabbed his chin and yanked his face back.

"Why? Tell me, and you can drink."

He thought, *fuck it, give it to her*. He stared back, unblinking, and with every shred of hatred he felt, replied. "Because - because he murdered, he murdered my wife. She was pregnant when H-Hadda and his fucking cronies blew her to bits."

She was visibly taken aback by the revelation. She squinted and he could see her thinking.

"What happened to her, and how do you know it was him?" she said.

He struggled to speak, his bitten tongue seeming too large for his mouth. "I knew that face," Nick lied. "He was in the papers. They thought he was dead. Did you ever hear of the Madrid train bombings?"

Nick's failing voice broke, but he continued. She nodded and listened intently. He told her the story, and as he spoke, he tried to tilt one side of the underwater beam. It moved, but he knew he would struggle to lift it at the best of times. In his weakened state, it would be impossible. He could feel his wrists were tied together and the binding went under the large beam. Nick noticed she was still listening. He kept using Mariyah's name, to make her a person. He described her and said how much alike they were.

"My wife, Mariyah... looked a lot like you. She was mixed race and religion, English-Saudi... she was a Muslim." He then told her about identifying Mariyah's body in the mortuary. He was after a shred of sympathy from this woman; it was his only hope. Unless - unless he could move the wire forward enough, and there was a gap at the end to lift it over. "She was kind, caring. She

245

was mine, and she was murdered by someone who never even knew her. A lunatic with a bomb on his back who didn't give a shit about the innocents, the sons, brothers, mothers, daughters. Each one of them was somebody's child. None of them went home that night. And for what? Can you explain that to me?"

She held his eye, "I'm not one of them, you know. Don't you lump me in with these..."

"But... you are with them, aren't you?" said Nick as he moved the beam the other way and the wire strop moved another centimetre forwards.

His endeavours were halted by an echoing sound of metal on metal, loud, hollow clangs. She moved rapidly, flipping the circuit-breaker on the wall, turning the tap to cold and moving over to him. She whipped the rod from beneath his chin and put the live end in the water. She tilted her head and listened. There were voices approaching.

"Sorry," she muttered, with little compassion.

Nick yelled out in agony again.

# 32

The briefings in the deepest depths of the Rock of Gibraltar continued into the night and everyone was learning something. Next to speak was introduced by a naval chief as, "Jeremy, a Mediterranean Field Operative."

The expressionless Field Op stepped up to the podium carrying a clipboard and pen. He had an instantly forgettable face, one that would melt into any crowd. He looked tired, verging on exhaustion. Jeremy cleared his throat, looked at his notes and began in perfect, Queen's English.

"Good evening, ladies and gentleman. I have to be brief. Pressing time restraints have been put on this impromptu lecture. I don't know how much you know as I'm told some of you have been in the air from the UK. Things on the ground, and at sea, are changing fast. I will outline what we know."

"A group of guerrillas, terrorists, religious fanatics, call them what you will, have taken control of a tanker, not a mile from this very spot. When I say taken control, they sailed in here on the vessel. As far as we know they didn't take it by force. One or more of the men on board are known Al Qaeda activists. There may also be a Brit involved. That hasn't yet been confirmed."

Glances were exchanged around the room. Until that point, a lot that had been happening had been subject to supposition and typical military guesswork. Now, because of the word, Al Qaeda, everyone's worst nightmare had been realised and they paid attention to

Jeremy's next words. The same Wren who had shown them into the operations room, pulled a screen down and handed the Field Op a laser pen.

"Suspect number one is a gentleman known by many names, his real one being Hachim Hadda. Some of you may know him as the Tunisian, or the initial, 'T', or any number of other aliases. Others may think you have never heard of him, but you will all, believe me, be familiar with his work." He then nodded towards the Wren. A picture of Hadda flashed up on the screen.

"I don't think I need brief you on his previous record. It has no bearing on this operation. Suffice to say, his actions and leadership have been directly responsible for the death of two hundred and fifty innocent civilians." He let the significance of his words sink in.

"He's not the bravest of souls but he makes up for that by surrounding himself with willing fighters and martyrs, whom he keeps in line with a combination of fear, violence and money. He seems to have no shortage of the latter. At this moment we are not sure of their intentions. That, I hope, will become clearer in the next few hours. So - that is all I can tell you, for now. I hand you over to - sorry, I don't recall your name?"

A slim, tanned and lived-in looking man stepped up. He had on a well-fitting pair of black overalls covered in pockets. The tip of the index finger of his right hand was missing and he was sporting an angry-looking, purple, and very recent scar on one side of his top lip. He unconsciously touched the disfigurement before he began and his tongue darted out to moisten the wound.

He didn't introduce himself, but nodded a thank you to the Field Op and the Wren handed him a wireless presenter. Before speaking, he tapped its button and started walking around the room. The first slide on the screen simply read M.A.T.A. When he begun, he was very matter-of-fact, self confident; there was a definite London accent.

"I have already been warned - informed may be a better way of putting it, that I have to explain all

248

military jargon and initials." He then nodded to I.D2, who inclined her head in approval.

"MATA stands for Maritime Anti Terrorism Assault. These are ideally preceded with weeks, or at least days of detailed preparation." His tongue shot out to moisten his wounded lip. He continued:

"What we have here is what we would call an ER, not a DR. That is an Emergency Reaction, not a Direct Response. What I mean by that is, we have to react quickly to what is already happening. The men on the tanker hold all the cards. They can decide to explode what ever it is they have on board. They can bring it forward, or abort.

We have no idea what they intend to do, or when. So we are going to act first, not react. We are going to take over the ship. Ideally I, or we, would like two complete units, which would constitute some 60 men on this. But, because of the speed of developments and the number of men in action around the globe, enough highly trained troops could not be bought into theatre in time. We are going to do what the British have always been good at and that is making do. We would like more time but that is the one element we are not going to get. We have to take the initiative away from the men out there who have their own agenda. The big question here is, what are their plans? Despite our best efforts we still don't know. That may change soon. Before you gentlemen arrived here we thrashed out what we envisage to be the best plan for taking the ship, with a minimum of casualties."

His tongue swept his lip again, then he looked up at the onlookers and said. "I shall re-phrase that. They would not be casualties, they would be dead friends of mine, many of whom I have served with all over the world. The SBS, that is myself, the captain of the SAS squadron, and around 30 or so Special Forces personnel, will be half of what we would like. We will make up the largest part of the assault group assisted by some of 42-Commando we have stolen from nearby warships. We will be ably assisted by Fleet Diving Unit One, the Royal Engineers Search Teams, snipers from the Weapons Support School in Warminster, and the Special Reconnaissance Regiment, among others."

The sergeant then nodded to a marine in the corner. The ancient Ops room was plunged into darkness and all eyes were drawn towards the large drop-down screen where a PowerPoint presentation was about to be shown.

The SBS officer carried on, "Please excuse the crude nature of these drawings, photographs and aids. For one thing we are not used to sharing our plans with anyone. Also, we knew nothing about this operation until the day before yesterday. My drawings, I realise, may resemble an eight-year-old's. The matchstick figures are meant to represent no one individual. I'm aware they barely resemble any human form."

The moment of light relief was acknowledged by the tightly packed and nervous audience. He moved forward and clicked the wireless presenter in his hand and the first slide appeared.

"This, gentlemen, is the tanker we are going to board. This picture was taken as she anchored, by our friends up on windy hill listening station, so this is where she is and how she looks at this moment. Now - despite all our efforts it has been impossible to hazard a guess at how many terrorist there are... in fact, we will call them players from now on. We don't know how many players are on board. Therefore it is impossible to gauge the level of their response. We have a vague idea of their weapons, and hardly any idea of their plans. This is going to be a 'suck it and see' operation. Not the sort we like." He turned his back to the audience and studied the ship along with everyone else in the room, in complete silence.

They were looking at a tired old lady; you didn't have to be a shipping expert to see that. The deep red underwater anti-fouling paint blended perfectly with the long rivers of reddy-brown rust that streamed down the ship's sides like filthy stalactites. She looked like it was her last voyage. She looked worn out and was due her well-deserved destiny with the great ship-breakers of India. Her once cream superstructure and bridge was pockmarked with large spots of rust that had been chipped and repainted in a slightly different shade. The only thing in the photo that looked new was the Muslim symbol on the red funnel. A large crescent moon stood out in bright yellow.

Breaking the silence, the SBS man said: "As far as we can gather she was built in 1973, in Japan. We can find no other identical or even similar ship afloat. Our normal modus operandi, given plenty of time, would be to practise and practise and practise boarding an identical ship. That's a luxury, therefore, we don't have. We have, however, found a reluctant BP tanker nearby that has an increasingly irate English captain, because he is being attacked and boarded approximately every hour, day and night, as I speak.

Now, sources close to the ship have just given us its new name, written on the stern. It wasn't the name she carried previously, according to Lloyds of London anyway. The name is the *Yamm-Amira*, registered in *Monrovia*." The name means *Sea-Princess*, in Arabic.

A voice from the back spoke out in a strong Spanish accent, "Senyor, senyor. Can you spell, please?"

While the name of the ship was being spelt out, Sir Michael beckoned to the Mediterranean agent. The First Sea Lord whispered to Jeremy, "Who is the Spaniard?"

"He is a Spanish naval officer, sir. We know him as Naldo. In reality we all know he is an agent, but it is the price we pay to keep the peace here. He got wind of this affair a few days ago. We were tempted to send him back across the border but... he has sworn not to inform his superiors until this is over. Anyway, he may come in handy. His background was bomb disposal. Apparently he is, or was, the best in the country."

Sir Michael then asked, "And the one next to him, to his left, in the suit?"

The agent became cagey. "He... he is one of ours, Sir."

251

The SBS man touched his lip as he continued, the wound obviously causing him discomfort.

"Ideally, we will initiate the attack in the early hours of tomorrow morning, but our players on the tanker may change that timing by the nature of their actions. If zero hour is of our choosing we aim to overwhelm them by sheer weight of numbers, speed and aggression. We will attack all angles at once."

On the screen, he flicked through the crude drawings he had warned the audience about, actual photographs of previous exercises, and written sequences of events. One drawing had the whereabouts of all the operational ships at the time of the planned attack.

"HMS *Exeter* will be on station here. HM submarine *Triumph* will be around this area, in the deep water. But in all honesty she will be - well - she will be wherever she is at her most effective. We, the SBS will have smaller fast craft in the water standing by here - at Rosia Bay, and one or two will already be out there trying to blend in with the local fishing boats. There is also, I can tell you, a smaller sub-surface craft already approaching the target vessel. She will, for this operation, be designated the code name, *Moby*."

He looked at his watch. "I hope she will soon update us on what she has found out. She - that is *Moby*, I hope will also be able to attack from beneath, to add one further element of surprise."

Pointing to the drawing with his red laser, he then said, "This tanker here - is closest to the target and is a friendly. She is the *Mersk Defender* from Copenhagen. The Danish government have given us free access to the ship for as long as we require. She has already offloaded and is empty which, of course, is important if any fire-fight ensues. The Weapons Support School should have four of their top snipers and spotters from various regiments on board any time now. So, we are hoping our intelligence will be increasing throughout the night."

He clicked up a photograph of a twin-rotored Chinook with gas-masked, heavily-armed men hanging from ropes underneath.

"Two Chinooks will come in from behind the Bridge at the same time as Lynx helicopters to give covering fire with snipers. At least one, maybe two Sea Kings will stand by with Royal Marines. They will come straight down from a high altitude after the initial assault. This should all happen at the same time as the SBS swimmers are coming over the side from underneath the tanker. All clear so far?"

There were technical questions from the highly trained audience about timing, weapons, rules of engagement, prisoners, friendlies on board and much more. Eventually the information director stood up and called a halt to the proceedings.

"Gentlemen - gentlemen please, we could discuss this all night, and I'm sure some of you probably will, but we need to move on. If the Divers, Special Forces and military involved in the taking of the ship would like to move on, to do what you have to do. Please do so now."

The noise level rose rapidly as everyone moved at once. As dozens of chairs were pushed back, the echo in the large room became a babble of excited chatter. Everyone at last had a chance to speak to their neighbour or boss or partner, to new working acquaintances, to pass on vital information.

I.D2 shouted above the din, "We will re-convene in - six hours, which will be midday here. None of us will get much, if any sleep these next few days but you understand the importance of our work here. Understood?"

There was a unified, "Ma'am."

# 33

On board *Orelia,* Jon Dog spelled out the name of the tanker and her home port, Monrovia. As he spoke into the hand-held radio, he also requested an updated weather report and an immediate response as to the whereabouts of the vessel in question. He mentioned there was no sign of Nick Carter, and that his canoe was missing.

The request was recorded on the handset's internal memory, then, when he pressed transmit, it was spat out in a burst of less than a second of garbled static.

*Gemini Three,* acting as the mini sub's mother-ship, heard the micro burst on her own handset but had to wait for it to be deciphered. The listening station at the top of the Rock also picked up the signal. Within seconds the request was being printed out in the war rooms in the core of the Rock.

J.D. sat on the rear bathing platform of the yacht and was about to put his state-of-the-art MP7 back into its watertight container when the radio vibrated on his ear. Within three minutes he had been given the coordinates for his new waypoint, and the approximate distance, 360 metres, west. Before going on gas and lowering himself back into the water, he stood and looked around. There it was... the nearest big ship to him. A smaller coastal container ship was in the way, but the target was the closest tanker to the Rock. The only thing between the ships and the beach was *Orelia.* The tanker was just an outline in the dark, back-lit by the dock lights of

Algeciras. She had a few deck and bridge lights on and he could clearly see her anchor light.

Stan, who was patiently floating with just his head showing above the water, slapped the surface of the sea to get his attention, and waved a 'come on' gesture. J.D signalled wait, then pointed two fingers to his eyes and indicated the ship. Without having to look, his thumb searched out the night-sight switch on his weapon. He aimed the barrel at the ship's bridge and stared down the bright green luminescent night-scope. Sweeping the decks, he saw nothing. Moving to the funnel he saw the crest of a crescent moon with what looked like a mushroom in the middle, or was it... a tree? Panning the target cross-hairs up to the bridge, he saw nothing. "I hope it's the right one. It looks mighty quiet on board - mighty quiet."

J.D and Stan left the surface of the sea as quietly as they'd arrived; *Orelia* was once again empty and crew-less. Back inside the Swimmer Delivery Vehicle, he connected his short umbilical and was back on ship's gas. He then clicked his *Press to Talk* button.

*"Listen up, gents, there's nobody on board. It is Nick's yacht. His canoe has gone."* He then took a deep breath of the submarine's pure oxygen. *"There was no sign of a struggle, so your guess is as good as mine. We found the name of a ship on board. She is less than 400 meters directly west from here. We have permission for an LDT..."* (SBS talk for Look Don't Touch). Then, tapping out the new coordinates on his nav screen, he said, *"Weather's coming up so we will go back to air for the crossing. Depth 8 metres. Smudge, course... two six zero. Close all doors, standby to get underway."*

Smudge got the boat trimmed with his three swimmers back on board, and quickly got underway, westwards towards their new target. He tried his utmost to concentrate on the job in hand, to get her trim and running steady. *Moby* cruised along slightly north of west, to allow for the tide. He set her eight metres deep, and slowly increasing her speed. Three hundred plus metres was too far for a good sonar echo, so he followed the waypoint J.D had entered. The speed rose to five knots and the cross-track error was calculated on the computer screen in front of him.

The hum of the electric engine, the sound of the men breathing over the communications, all merged with the tranquil sound of the passing sea. The distance to the target ticked down quickly. *Estimated Time of Arrival, 12 minutes*, it said. With that ETA in mind, Smudge had a minute to reflect on his close friend and confidant, Nick Carter. He didn't want to admit it, but he had a bad feeling.

If he *is* alive, *"I'm gonna fuckin' kill him - I swear I'll wring his fuckin' neck."*

*"Say again?"* someone said from the rear.

*"Sorry - nothing,"* said Smudge.

Lost in his own fears, he was brought back to reality when J.D changed his screen and the navigation display was replaced with the dark blue sonar image. The tanker stood out as a bright yellow flat-bottomed hull. The bulbous nose made famous by oil tankers around the world leapt out at him. The distance was 50 metres. Everyone's earpiece clicked, and J.D announced, *"Listen up. Target approaching, three minutes, large tanker. Check each others re-breathers. Jock, check the wheels as soon as you get red. Texas, listening gear. Harvey, free swimmer, take a swim line and magnet. Any questions?"*

*"Bollocks!"* said Texas as he dropped the long coil of wire attached to the microphone.

*"Wanker,"* said Jock.

*"Alright, alright, wise up, everyone. Smudge take me - here."* He leaned across the dark cockpit and pointed to the hull on the tanker's echo just forward of where the enormous propeller shaft disappeared into the hull. *"Watch out for engine inlets everyone. I don't want to go through that shit again. Back on re-breathers lads. Silent running as of... Now!"*

He switched them all to on-board $O^2$ again and the silence of the craft resumed. J.D switched the ambient sound onto everyone's earpiece. A hydrophone in the bow listened to the sound of the sea ahead. The slightly spooky noise of the ocean was only broken by the alien sound of the tanker. Her engines were not running, but a smaller, higher revving generator was.

As they approached under the unseen propeller, they slowed and headed up the centre line of the massive, flat-bottomed hull. J.D opened his door which gave a red light in the rear of the sub, and Texas pulled open his door. A few bubbles left over from the air breathing escaped to the surface. Texas watched them travel and burst as they expanded on their upward journey. He stuck his hand out into the darkness guessing their speed. He didn't want to have his face mask ripped off if they were still doing five knots. They weren't. J.D was too good for that. He looked up and behind towards the bubbles and the surface, but there was only darkness... then, above him, he spotted the bubbles shatter as they struck silver. It was the tanker's huge propeller shaft, the size of a large tree trunk. As they ghosted underneath, he noticed there was a length of blue, part-melted plastic rope hanging off it.

Smudge ignored his instruments and switched to Mark One eyeball. He put the sub into neutral and peered upward as the sub glided along and gently rose towards the massive hull.

Jock leaned out of the rear doors and clicked the soft pneumatic tyres on the top of the sub and looked for a suitable place to land. J.D was also hanging out and he motioned Smudge to edge her forwards. The electric engine whirred and the propeller turned slowly. The sub edged up and ahead, until J.D signalled to stop. Smudge put her back into neutral, got the thumbs up, and opened the needle air valve to *All Trim Ballast*. The sub rose, slowly, oh so slowly, until she touched, 'Up' level and made a soft landing. The tyres on the roof made sure there was no noise.

There were now five heads hanging out of the sub, all looking for hazards. In particular, they looked for things like the gaping, main engine cooling water intake. They had once been sucked up hard against the grilled inlet of a similar-sized ship and nobody had forgotten the experience. J.D clicked the *Press to Talk,* and everyone heard the click and looked his way. He gave a circular motion with his forefinger, meaning, first stop here.

Texas took out a plastic scraper and cleaned the considerable marine growth away to make a smooth surface. He then held up a cone that looked like a miniature satellite dish until its magnetic pull sucked onto the ship's hull. Jock held onto a reel of black swim line as Harvey swam out and away, searching the perfectly flat bottom of the vessel above him.

J.D re-tuned the sub's hydrophone, from the one in the bows, to the one now attached to the tanker. The only thing they could hear was the high-pitch whirr of the ship's generator. He adjusted the gain and tone to reduce the noise of the engine, but there was nothing else recognisable, which was not unusual for a tanker.

Harvey swam back and indicated he was happy and wanted to move ahead. J.D gave two clicks meaning 'we will move forward'. Smudge joined everyone else by hanging out of the door as he put the electric engine ahead slow. The sub, pressed upward by the buoyancy in her ballast tanks, moved onward again. The soft rubber wheels turned as the reconnaissance force edged their way ahead.

On the third stop Harvey went off to the ship's port side and was gone a long time. Jock gave him a pull on the black line and he answered, then he gave a signal for, 'I have found something.' Jock tapped the comms system so everyone heard, then pointed to port. Texas removed his listening phone from the hull and began turning the wheels on the roof. He rotated them so they moved across the ship, pointing port and starboard. Then they all pushed on the metal hull above them. The boat moved effortlessly to port. Smudge was impressed. This was a new design feature: left and right as well as back and forth.

Near Harvey's swim line, where the hull started to turn up towards the surface, they stopped. J.D swam out and gently followed the thin black line. Flushing his re-breather through with fresh $O^2$, he made his way towards the surface and could soon see what had caught his buddy's attention. There was a boat alongside. As he approached the bottom of the smaller craft he could see Harvey had his head by the keel, listening for movement. As they neared each other, Harvey looked down at his boss and gave the thumbs up. Nobody on board then. He then took out his P11 pistol and indicated upwards. J.D shook his head. It was tempting but his orders were look don't touch.

It was still dark on the surface but the light from the tanker's deck lights gave a clear outline of the vessel above. Not long until dawn. J.D looked at his watch; it was 06:30. They had to be away. The chances of them being compromised were quadrupled in seas with good visibility. Chuck in daylight and they might as well surface and start shooting! He turned to Harvey to give him the finger across the throat, but he was not under the keel. He looked around and saw his black swim line heading to the surface between the boat and tanker. Harvey then swam back into view carrying two lines. He offered J.D the second line, it headed off astern. It was identical to their swim line. MoD issue. They looked at each other and Harvey, still with his pistol in one hand, made the canoeing motion.

Back at the mini-sub, J.D was anxious to be away to find out if it was the canoe and to beat the impending daylight, but Tex could not be moved from the headset of the underwater stethoscope. J.D swam over and tapped him on the shoulder. He didn't move. He shook him and Tex looked round. Through his full-face mask, J.D could see his brow was furrowed: a look of concentration, mixed with one of complete mystification.

J.D felt a tug on his leg and Stan handed him a scratchboard. Written on it was the message, *The Yank says he can hear automatic gunfire.*

# 34

Barely conscious again, Nick began experiencing violent muscle convulsions. It wasn't the barbed spasms of electric shock treatment; this was something new. It was the agonising torture of his body adapting to an unfamiliar position. Having been hunched up and leaning forward in freezing cold water for around twelve hours, the muscles and bones in his body had frozen as if he were a statue. His spine had developed a curved memory. It had forgotten how to straighten out.

The men were not gentle when pulling him out. They tried to stand him up. It brought him round with a shriek of agony.

That didn't stop the two guards who dragged him out of the room. He became aware of many men's voices as he was hauled, face down, out of his tiny torture cell into a brightly lit area. They tried their utmost to make him stand tall so that they could hang his wrist bindings onto a hook. Nick was dripping wet, freezing and naked as the day he was born. His white puckered skin bore the hallmarks of his harsh treatment and hours of submersion. As he forced his eyes open, his head hung and he looked down at his feet. He saw blood drip from his bottom lip onto his chest. He was bleeding from both his ankles and covered in a collage of oil, rust, bruises and angry red burns.

One deep voice stood out above all the others. Nick noticed that whenever this voice barked orders, everyone moved. Whilst looking down, he also noticed that what he thought was wire lashing his ankles was in fact rope inside plastic tubing. As the voice cracked a seemingly hilarious joke to the assembled men, Nick lifted his head to see what was binding his wrists together. His hopes were dashed. It was a piece of wire. There was a hook under the wire going to a block and tackle which was being hoisted over his head. Above that, was a tall room, the walls disappearing up into darkness. He realised he was standing as far down in the oil tanker as it was possible to get. This was the base of one of the vast hollow tanks that would normally carry the precious cargo.

The voice was calling his name, "Nik Nik Nik. What a place to die. You like to die here, Nik? Put your hand up if you would."

This caused another bout of hilarity as both hands were tied above his head. The deep baritone belonged to a big black man, older than the rest and balding down the middle of his enormous sweaty head. The head sat on top of no discernible neck, just an impossibly large chest, matched only by a gut hanging over his belt that made his legs seem out of proportion. He wore a different uniform to the rest. The dark-green army dress code made famous by the Iranian military during the Gulf wars.

He was putting on a performance for the younger troops ranged out behind him. They were wearing desert combat gear. It all matched, just a bit too new, as if ready to go on parade.

"You see, my men, he is so keen to die, he has put up both hands." Some of the African contingent found his joke so funny they could barely stand.

"We may be able to help you there, Mr Nik, we could have... what do you call it? A raffle? Yes, that is what we will do, we will have a raffle, to use you as target practice. But I don't think we should see who can shoot to kill. That is an easy game. We could shoot... to keep alive."

His men quietened down and listened to the rules of the game. He walked to where Nick hung from his wrist bindings, his toes just touching the deck.

Stretched out naked, Nick had never felt so vulnerable. Even hung out on tiptoes, he had to look up at the huge bear of a man. He was reminded of the Ugandan dictator, Idi Amin. He had a black wooden pace stick under one arm with the carved head of a roaring lion on the handle. Idi withdrew the pace stick from his armpit and tapped it menacingly into his left hand. His big bloodshot eyes looked Nick's body up and down. He was enjoying himself; revelling in the power he had over his prisoner, and his men.

He spoke loudly as he put his fat fingers into the lion's mouth. "Each man will have just one shot at a time. You will have to hit diss man. If you don't... you will be the next target. If you choose your shot poorly and kill him, or break a bone, you will be next. I have used this exercise before in Rwanda, and a man should live for many hours, a woman... not so long." He put the pace stick between Nick's legs and moved it up sharply until he lifted his genitals. Then turning to face his men, he said. "Some of you, like Chooks there, may be tempted to start firing... here at the hammer, but be aware, the pain, shock and blood loss can kill a man. Isn't that so, Chooks?" The other men looked toward Chooks who sneered and nodded, "Yes, Major Sir!"

Idi turned back, moved his jet black face close to Nick's and hissed. "A lot of men lose control of their bowels and bladder when the shooting starts, Nik. Do not be ashamed. If you were to beg and beg well, I may find it in my lion's heart to shoot you dead. I am a humanitarian as well as an officer, you know?"

Nick thought about telling him to go fuck himself, but remembered his escape and evasion course. The message drummed into him was: never antagonise your interrogator. Try and befriend him. *Fat chance of that so far.*

Suddenly there was a shout of 'Captain on deck!' All the men jumped to attention, grounding their weapons smartly at their side. The round metal door to the tank was opened and a corporal snapped to attention and saluted. Nick looked across and realised the door was directly behind the crude room where his torture chamber was. Hadda made his grand entrance, closely followed by the girl. Nick noticed a momentary look of shock on her face when she saw him strung up naked.

Hadda established his authority and spoke in his best English. "What's going on here? Major! Get these men fallen in immediately." The major nodded to the corporal who barked his orders. Hadda didn't look at Nick. He strode to the major and enquired, "I asked you what is going on here. What do you think I'm paying you and your men for? To stand around joking and gloating? I hired you to get these men into an efficient fighting force. If you cannot do it I will find a man that can. Do I make myself clear?"

*So*, thought Nick, *they are mercenaries*. He looked over at the lines of men dressing themselves into neat rows. There were Pakistanis, Africans, Afghans, among others; a motley rabble. Behind them, there were deep bunkers sectioned off with railway sleepers and sandbags. The walls were clad in thick planks. Around the sandbagged areas the cladding was pockmarked and splintered where thousands of bullets had been fired. What were they preparing for?

He heard Hadda say as they walked away: "Get them to fire these American weapons I've acquired. At least twenty rounds each. They have all been used to Kalashnikovs recently, I understand. I don't want them just blasting away. Short bursts and single shots. They will be killing each other if they open fire inside a ship and it is set to automatic - understood?"

Najia was left alone near Nick. He gained the impression she was there under protest, and within seconds, she walked off, ducked down and out of the door. Hadda heard something, spun round and looked for her. He then looked at Nick and gave an order to the major, who passed it on to the corporal.

Four men came over to Nick, untied the rope that held him, and put a filthy sack over his head, securing it

263

round his neck. It stank of oil and rotting vegetables. Was this it, was this the end?

The men walked him across the tank deck and he heard them knock off more watertight door clips. This must be a door he hadn't seen because the one she went out of had been open already. They dragged him over the sill to the door and he smashed his shins on the metal. He found he couldn't stand in the corridor; it was too low as they dragged him through.

This was it.

Hadda had given the order, and it gave him a surge of adrenalin. A rush of bravado swept through his tired, battered body. All he needed was a glimpse, a hint of a chance, the slimmest opportunity of making a break for it. *Even if I die trying*, he thought, *I'll take some of them with me.* And if it's not now, it will be back to the tank. *Fuck that*, he thought. He'd give it a go.

Nick fell out of the other end of the long tunnel and landed on a metal deck that he noticed had a background stench of crude oil. They laughed as they let him struggle to get up. He made it to his knees, when a boot hit him in the rib cage. It was not a full-on swing, but a hurry-up kick. He grabbed the leg and pulled. The man went over on the oily deck and landed hard. The other guards were on him in a second, raining down blows.

Nick curled up to protect his head and balls as the boots flew. As quickly as it started it stopped. One of the guards yelped out in pain. The major shouted in an African language and swung his lion-headed pace stick around in a series of well-aimed heavy cracks to heads and arms. He was closely followed by the sound of Hadda's voice. Two men quickly grabbed Nick under the arms and stood him up.

He heard Idi trying to explain himself, "Captain, sir. He fell over. My men picked him up. Come, come through, we will go together." Nick heard the shooting start. It was coming, he guessed, from the other tank. As least they were starting without him.

Even through his head sack, he was aware it was dark in the hold, unlike the shooting tank. Coming up behind him, Nick heard Hadda having a hushed talk with the major.

Nick reasoned they had walked for'ard, as Hadda and the crew had come through the open door in the firing range. It was reasonable to assume they had come from the stern accommodation. It seemed to him they had then walked through, or was it under, more oil tanks. The major then said to one of his men, "Jock strap him. Here, use diss ting here."

A piece of rope was tied to Nick's wrist binding, shoved between his legs, up the crack of his cheeks and pulled taut around his neck. He soon found, if he pulled up or forward on his arms, it tightened round his neck. Now he could barely move.

Two men held his arms. Having his vision taken away, his other senses worked overtime. There was the smell of crude, the empty, hollow echo of a metal room, the sound of keys jangling and clanking onto metal plate. Also there was the feeling of more people joining them.

Hadda ordered. "Major, take your men and leave us."

"But Captain, sir. What about the prisoner?"

"My men are here now. I can trust them to not beat him up, or shoot him before I'm finished with him. At least I know they will follow my orders to the letter."

"Yes Sir!" shouted the major, with a hint of defiance.

"And major... close and clip the door when you leave, will you?" The major was last to leave, following his men. Nick was now standing alone, naked, tied up, his head in a sack and shivering. He felt certain he was about to be shot. Maybe questioned first. *What a fucking way to go,* he thought.

He heard what sounded like a metal door being opened; keys were jangling. Then, there was the familiar somewhat sinister click of a Geiger counter. It clicked its rhythmic ticking as it measured nearby radiation. It clicked too quickly for Nick's liking. There was something hot nearby. *I hope they're not going to cook me in that shit!*

His knees shook; whether it was from the cold or the predicament he found himself in, he'd no idea. There was chatter and noise around. The men spoke in Arabic and he understood not a word. He heard the click of a knife, then felt a hand at his throat as the string tying the hood around his neck was cut. Nick blinked as his eyes readjusted to the dull lights at the base of the oil tanker. He was in a low room, deep inside, maybe even under one of the oil tanks.

Hadda was cautiously nosing about behind a thick metal wall. He had a torch in one hand and a Geiger counter in the other. He was flanked by two men. Nick had never seen these guys before. There were two more standing guard outside the screened area. They were all dressed in black overalls with military black webbing. One wore a black bandanna with Arabic writing and was staring at Nick. In his right hand he carried a bag.

So, these were Hadda's men, the ones he trusted. They looked fit, efficient, menacing, and pretty much expressionless. These were more like the brainwashed extremists he had expected to see. These were probably the suicide bombers, murderers, religious fanatics. This was more like the face of terrorism. None of them would look out of place making a suicide video. The two standing outside the container had long black beards. One came out and spoke to the guard carrying the bag. He looked round at Nick. This one was too young to grow any hair on his face. He had a black headband and Nick guessed he was no more than eighteen. Out of the bag he pulled two charges. They both had partially dismantled mobile phones taped to them. It looked like Semtex, or C4. Either way, it wasn't home-made explosive, it was military strength. If just one of those blocks were set off adjacent to one of the massive cargo tanks, the tanker would disintegrate.

The youngest took the charges inside out of sight. Nick heard tape being used and was sure they were being prepared to destroy the contents. He heard the boy talking to Hadda, and a long exchange took place. Eventually, Hadda appeared, seemingly happy with what he had arranged. He turned and shone the torch at his prisoner. Slowly walking over to Nick he put a mobile phone in his breast pocket.

"Mr. Nick...I like you. I don't know why, but I do. I admire your unwavering determination. I think I see a little of me, in you.

Nick couldn't help himself. "If this is what you do to people you like, God help anyone that crosses you." He immediately regretted opening his mouth until Hadda burst out laughing.

"Yes, yes I can see how you may have reached that point of view. We have been none too kind to you but remember, you are on my property, you are the intruder. In my country I would have every right to shoot you dead. Where you come from of course, it would probably go through the courts for years and you would be let off, and I would be in trouble for restricting your human rights."

Nick decided to go for the jugular. He didn't want to make small talk with Hadda. He struggled to talk with his bitten, swollen tongue. "If you're going to shoot me, please do it now and don't hand me over to that... that excuse for a major in there."

Hadda feigned a look of shock. "I am not going to shoot you Mr. Nick, unless you give me reason. Although Ayman here, the young one, has already begged me to let him behead you. I have other plans for you. I want you to live to see my campaign come to its full glory. When it is all over and you live, for a while at least, you will realise the brilliance of it."

Nick responded, with difficulty; he could feel a piece of skin hanging off his tongue. "All you will succeed in doing is to create an environmental disaster and turn the rest of the world against you and your kind. When you blow this thing up, the world will come down on you like a ton of bricks."

Hadda moved in closer to Nick. He had a smug look on his face as he shook his head. "Who said anything about blowing anything up? There will be no explosion here, well, hopefully not."

He pointed to his handiwork. "That, that is merely a precaution, just in case." Hadda tutted and turned away, looking down at his feet, speaking as he walked:

"I don't know your background, Mr. Nick, and I don't really have time to get it out of you, but I think you are an intelligent man. I know you found the Geiger counter, and I think you probably killed Aghilas at the same time. I have never thanked you for that have I? The man was an animal, not a good Muslim, and we are better without him. So... you no doubt thought it was a dirty bomb, yes? A bit crude, don't you think, a bit... obvious? It could, would, undoubtedly cause panic and mass hysteria. In fact I read a piece in The Times that struck a cord. It said an RDD, that's newspaper talk for Radiological Dispersal Device, is not a Weapon of Mass Destruction, or as the Americans like to call it, a WMD. Not in the true sense, until you change the D. The Times said it should better be known as a Weapon of Mass *Disruption*. Clever, no? But what actual, real damage would it do to the West? Would it ever change the views of a bunch of Zionist Jew sympathisers? Would it give the only true religion, Islam, a place on the world stage? No it would not. But something happened at the end of 2006 that changed all that. It gave me a brilliant idea, and here we are. What I have planned for you and your kind is far more... ingenious, far more destructive. It won't just be a disruption. It will make a dirty bomb seem like a child's party. Like a *walk in the park*, as the Americans say."

# 35

Hadda turned on the Geiger counter again. It hummed as it went through its self-test mode and clicked faster as he pointed it behind the metal screen, changing its rhythm every time he swept it left and right, up and down.

The noise of a fresh bout of automatic gunfire reached them through the tunnel between the oil tanks. Hadda muttered, "I told him short bursts! The man is..." He didn't finish his judgement of the major.

Hadda's guards stared at Nick with a mixture of contempt and hatred. Nick watched him lean behind the barrier, and enquired, "So... what do you hope to gain from this... what I assume will be mass destruction of innocent lives?"

Apparently content with his findings, Hadda turned the Geiger counter off and marched towards his naked, shivering captive.

"You all presume you are innocent in the West just because you haven't pulled the trigger. You are no more innocent than the troops in Iraq or Afghanistan. You all have as much blood on your hands as the American President, or your Prime Minister. I have lived and worked in London and Liverpool, Mr. Nick. I've seen people going about their daily business, reading the headlines in the papers and shaking their heads. Some of them say: 'Bloody rag-heads, it serves them right.' A handful will go on anti-war marches and demonstrations, but what do any of them ever really do? Nothing... they do nothing. They go back to work after the weekend, go on holiday twice a year. Some will shed a tear when twenty or fifty British soldiers are killed in a year. While all along, hundreds of thousands of Muslims are being slaughtered. And not just by the Western coalition, but by the Jews. The United States military is run by Jews. That is why they can wage war against the Palestinians, unchecked, year after year. Where do you think Israel gets its war machinery from? Where do you think it gets its intelligence, its equipment? I'll tell you where, from the good old U. S. of A, that's where."

Nick looked to his left as he spoke. The nearest guard had a pistol on his belt. "You haven't answered my question. What do you hope to gain? You'll only succeed in turning people against you. Even your own Muslim councils will denounce your actions."

"Do you think I care who condemns me? I am not in this for the popularity vote. Do you know, we made more headway within two years of the September the 11th bombings than we had since the Second World War? The Americans, especially, were forced to look inwards, to look at their own insular policies. They even thought momentarily, about their foreign policy. Within weeks of the Madrid train bombings, Spain pulled its troops out of Iraq. That's action, Mr. Nick. Those are results."

Nick thought, for a nanosecond, about telling Hadda he knew he'd planned Madrid, but instead nodded in the direction of his nearest guard. "So, are you going to send these brainwashed murderers out across Gibraltar and Spain with your nuclear material? Is that what it is? Lots of small suicide bombers, packed with nails and a bit of radioactivity? Because that won't drive anyone out of Afghanistan. It won't stop the killing on the West Bank. Nothing will change in the Middle East until they stop shooting each other and start talking."

Hadda tossed his head in the direction of his men. "They are not brainwashed murderers. You see, this is what I mean. You people in the West have short memories. In the First World War, your country sent thousands of young men to their deaths. They would step out of the trenches and walk, headlong, into a hail of bullets. Tell me, was that not suicide? They weren't even doing that for their God. They did it for their country, and where did it get them?"

How this man could compare fighting a world war for your country with stepping onto a packed commuter train full of women and children carrying a rucksack full of explosives was beyond Nick's comprehension. If he let slip about Mariyah, or that he knew Hadda's part in it, he felt certain he wouldn't see the next hour through.

Hadda gave an order to his youngest soldier. The one called Ayman stepped forward, looked Nick in the eye and spouted a stream of what he was sure was angry political and religious rhetoric. He was also sure this boy had had his normal life taken away from him, he wasn't thinking for himself. Some religious leader was doing that. When the young Ayman paused, Hadda repeated his words in English.

"First I will ask Allah to purify my soul so I am fit to lay eyes on him. Then I will ask Him to bless my mission with a great many casualties: Jews, Americans, British, it matters not, for they are all enemies of Islam. When my time comes, I will join the knights of freedom and become a holy warrior for jihad and martyrdom." Hadda indicated to Ayman to continue his speech.

"I will march the path to victory and I will carry the Qur'an in my right hand and my weapon in my left. I will have my time with the maidens of paradise, then, I shall sit contented at the right hand of Allah. With me will be Aalam, my mujahedeen brother who already waits for me. I will not become a shahed (martyr) for them, or any idea or people, but for God. I will give up this life, and start a new one with the almighty. Allah is the greatest! Allah be praised!"

Ayman then stepped back and fixed Nick with a distant hate-filled stare.

Hadda nodded his approval and patted the boy on the shoulder. Glowing with pride, he turned to Nick. "You see, we cannot lose. God is on our side. With young brave men like this, we cannot fail."

"You will fail. You will all fail. When these deluded souls go about their ghoulish business, they are killing Muslims, women, children, anyone and everyone. No god, no Allah will let you into heaven for killing his subjects. He made us all and I believe it says in the Koran, to kill one person is to kill all of humanity. And correct me if I'm wrong, does it not say, you should never kill a civilian?"

Perhaps inspired by the dedication of the young man's speech, Hadda's voice rose. "You don't know what life is like for a Muslim, Mr. Nick. These campaigns..." he swept his arm to take in the men and the dark basement of the tanker, "...like my humble operation here for instance, this is just the beginning, the tip of the pyramid. The scale and vastness of the numbers your people face is, I think, beyond your comprehension. Muslim men, and sometimes women, will gladly destroy their bodies for their God. They will always walk amongst you. They will commit self-liquidation wherever the targets present themselves. Among Americans and British convoys, on tube stations in the cities of the world, in desert check points, in markets and shopping streets, police stations, sporting events anywhere and everywhere."

Nick was also getting angry. He was convinced he was going to die anyway. It was time he launched his own version of life, a defence of *his* beliefs. With his last memory of Mariyah's, torn, blackened body in his mind, he engaged Hadda's eye.

"You are kidding yourself. It is not a war about religion or faith. It is a choice of civilised, or primitive, free or oppressed, democracy or dictatorship. A choice of human rights or no rights. I think you and your kind *want* a clash of civilisations. It is *you* and your small, misguided band of extremists that claim to speak for all your kind. I doubt many Muslims share your wishes. You seek to divide all people into Muslims and non-Muslim, believers or non-believers. Then you call anyone who doesn't share your beliefs a dog or pig or Infidel. You urge them to fight, to make everyone believe what you do!"

Hadda enjoyed the outburst. "You, you are a heretic. You will be made to see..."

Nick cut him off and held his gaze. "You are right, I am not a religious man. I am as you find me. I do not believe in anything supernatural until I see it with my own eyes. But... but, unlike you, I respect the rights of others to believe in what they want. Why would you want to force others to believe in what *you* do? It is not your concern. You go on and on about the Jews. How it was all their fault? They survived the hell of the holocaust! And they did it with dignity, and in doing so they forced the world to respect them. Not forced, as you do, with the use of violence and terror, but... but forced with hard work and knowledge, they do not cry vengeance! Have you ever, ever heard of a single Jew blow himself up in a German or Arab restaurant? They don't go about destroying Mosques. It is your kind, your so-called *holy warriors* who disrespect their own religion by using Mosques to hide. It is Muslims who burn each others churches and blow up embassies, killing anyone who doesn't share their beliefs. Your route, your path, will get you nowhere. You should ask yourselves: 'What can I do for my fellow man, for humankind,' before you demand the world respects you and share your beliefs."

Hadda walked away in deep thought. "We will, I think, continue this exchange later."

Nick was so angry he felt light-headed. He wanted to tell Hadda about just one woman he had killed. He wanted to carry on the debate, to try and convince Hadda of the futility of his arguments. But there was no point; their minds were made up. He was so exhausted, beaten, tired and thirsty, it was the best he could do to stay standing. He managed to ask through a resigned sigh, "So... what do you have planned for me, for this ship, these men and women and innocents who will no doubt get caught up in your plan and have to lose their lives for absolutely no gain?"

Hadda wagged a finger at Nick. "Oh there will be huge gain, Mr. Carter. It will be to Allah's gain when the whole world converts to Islam. For a Muslim, life is cheap, but death is cheaper." Then he shook his head and seemed to think for a while, until he smiled. "All this talk of suicide can make a man depressed. Suicide bombers have their place, but if you want big change you need a bigger show. What we will have here is the biggest show on earth."

There was the familiar hollow echo as the clips were knocked off the water tight door and one of the soldiers from the firing range stepped through the tunnel into the tank. He could barely see in the dark and shone a torch around until he picked up Hadda's silhouette.

"What is it?" Hadda shouted.

"Captain, Sir, the major needs you." Hadda waved him away with a dismissive gesture then moved closer to Nick's face.

"This isn't some film set, Mr. Carter, where the villain reveals his whole plan to the hero, enabling the hero to escape in an instant to save the Western world. This is real life. Neither you nor anyone else will stop me, because they don't know what is going to happen to them. You, on the other hand, will find out soon enough because you will be closer to it than you could possibly imagine."

Nick answered, "So... you know... you know that *you* are the villain?" He braced himself, sure Hadda was going to hit him. He could feel his anger. But Hadda didn't. He stepped back and shouted an order in Arabic. The four black-clad fundamentalists grabbed Nick and marched him towards the tunnel, back towards the shooting, to be reunited with either the major or his most undesirable bath.

# 36

Three miles west of Gibraltar, two Chinooks flew in close formation. FRIES is the military acronym for Fast Rope Insertion and Extraction System. Fast-roping onto a ship is usually SBS territory, but this time the SAS and SBS had to work together.

Dave 'Creature' Foot was the senior SBS man on the lead chopper, which held his men. The rivalry between two of the finest regiments in the world was legendary, and plain to see. Creature leaned out of the rear door, the wind buffeting around his face as he searched the sea for the tanker. His ears popped, which told him they had begun their descent. A coil of thick multi-plaited rope lay at his feet. Another team led by his best mate Snowy was only a few feet away on the starboard rear-loading bay.

Creature's plan was to empty the huge twin-engined chopper as quickly as possible. To do this, he had four heavy descent ropes ready; two at the rear and two forward, port and starboard.

This was the sixth drop of the day and would probably be the last as it was rumoured live action would follow that night. *It was a good job*, he thought as he looked at his special thick gloves and noted they were nearly worn through. He checked the rope's quick-release on the roof of the chopper, and checked his weapon. Check and re-check was their way.

Creature looked down at his boys on the seating ranged either side of the Chinook. CD, short for Cot Death, was, as usual, sound asleep. Rumour had it that he had been bitten by a tsetse fly whilst undercover in the Sudan. The fly was said to induce a sleeping sickness in cattle and men.

Moses, their token young officer, was looking worried; a thin film of sweat seemed to permanently cover his brow. This would be his first live job, and Creature was concerned about his state of mind. He had insisted on coming along when really he should've been keeping the grown-ups off their back onshore. He got his nickname after a lot of thought and brow-beating. They finally settled on Moses as he was, to quote the Bible, '...leading his followers into the wilderness.'

Next to him was Boot, one of the regiment's legends. Creature had given him the job of keeping Moses alive, if - and it was still debatable - if he made it onto the live drop, where people might get shot. Next to him was Back-Draught, the demolitions man, then M&M, (Manic Medic), the nervous and most highly-trained medic.

Creature looked down again at the impossibly blue Mediterranean as it got nearer and raced underneath. They were banking round in a long arc, slowing down from 170MPH, towards the BP tanker, *Ocean Wave*. Swinging his size eleven Magnum assault boot at Cot Death's shins, Creature woke him from his slumber. He then waved his finger upwards in a circular motion and indicated three minutes. CD walked down the line getting everybody organized. They were ready. Ready for what, they weren't really sure. Tonight could be a different game of soldiers altogether.

*

Two hundred and twenty-two metres away from the target vessel, the *Yamm-Amira,* were four sniper teams. They'd been aboard the Danish-flagged *Mersk Defender* since the early hours. The camouflage exercise had been interesting, to say the least. Part of their art was not to be seen, and it usually involved hours of preparation. Using the grasses and foliage of the area tucked into their 'ghillie suits' they could virtually disappear in most habitats. They would dress each other in their outfits to ensure that nowhere on their outline was a straight, clean line. They had, on occasion, hidden for days, even weeks in fields, bushes, in derelict buildings and cities such as Baghdad. But they had never had to hide against the background of an oil tanker. The *Mersk Defender* was straight lines, black and white paint. That was it.

Dave Green, the spotter for Team Alpha, had chosen the most highly-prized spot, situated on the bridge roof. After all, one of his T shirts read:

*The moral high ground is a great place to site your artillery.*

At first he was not that happy with his position or camouflage. However, when daylight revealed his target his mind was put at ease. This, he decided, was going to be another waste of time. Dave had a good nose for when there was a kill in the air, and today he could smell no prey. They had set up their LUZ (lay up zone.) He and the taciturn sniper, corporal Jiz Parker, could layup there for days if need be. They were on the starboard side where they had two white sheets of metal to hide behind, one each. The intelligence was there would be no snipers shooting back, but then he'd heard that before. They had rigged white sheets to cover them and their weapons, but it was still baking to be lying on the two mattresses they'd stolen and dragged up from the crew's quarters.

Dave grumbled as he peered through his binoculars. "How long have we been here? Five, maybe six hours? I've seen four people on that fuckin' tub. I thought it was meant to be full of baddies? Methinks we're staring at the wrong fuckin' boat. Either that or they're talking to 'em. Be nice, baddies and we'll let you go. It's not really diplomacy, it's the art of saying *Nice doggy* until your sniper gets the range. What do you reckon, Jiz?"

"No."

"No what? No, we're not staring at the wrong boat, or no, it is full of terrorists?"

"No talking."

"Jesus, lighten up will you? This is a wild goose chase, can't you see that yet? I've been doing this ten years longer than you and I know when it's a wild goose chase and this is a…"

"Shut up and spot something," said Jiz. Dave saw the barrel of Jiz's AS50 sniper rifle inch to the left.

"Bitch on the Bridge. Well, fuck me - guess what - she's wearing combats!" In the top right of Jiz's powerful rifle sight cross-hairs, two red lights winked on, meaning two other teams had pinged her as well. When the time came, and they had permission to fire, those lights would be green. The first shot would be to break the half-inch thick glass, the next one, the target. And he knew from experience you only needed a glancing hit to bring him or her down. The English-built Accuracy International AS50 fired a 12.7mm .50 calibre round that was the same length as a Coke can and travelled at 2700 feet-per-second. The trauma it caused the human body was appalling.

*Bring it on*, he thought, *bring it on. Pity though, she's horny, even with her black eye.*

# 37

The first vessel off Rosia Bay was Nick's lone, empty yacht at anchor. Beyond her was the smaller container ship of about 6,000 tonnes. Further out lay the *Yamm-Amira,* an innocent, if somewhat dejected looking 27,000 tonne petro-chemical tanker. Out deeper still was the much larger 42,000 tonne empty oil tanker, *Mersk Defender.* As well as the four sniper teams, her numbers had been further swollen with the concealment of forty Royal Marines and their fast raiding craft. Beyond her was the really deep water, too deep for even large tankers to drop anchor cables. More tankers could be seen two miles further west, towards Algeciras on the Spanish side of the Bay, going about their business by ploughing on their ponderous journeys around the globe.

So, it was exactly a nautical mile west and slightly south of Rosia Bay's breakwater that Her Majesty's nuclear powered submarine *Triumph* sat submerged and hidden from prying eyes. Thankfully Gibraltar bay lent itself perfectly to submarine operations, and the boat hovered dead still with more than 450 meters of water below her.

The *Triumph's* upper deck was at a depth of only eight metres, the top of her conning tower only just below the surface. The skipper, Captain 'Jolly' Roger Winterbottom, was in the control room and was feeling anything but jolly. He had followed Russian subs under the ice, fired live torpedoes in anger, but this was the worst position he had been in as a captain. The constant threat of an impending explosion above was one thing, but uppermost in his mind was the distinct possibility of being run down by one of the deep-draft tankers that used these waters.

In the surreal red lighting of the control room, he was receiving operational details at a phenomenal rate. His naval ratings fed him snippets of information, all of which he had to formulate in his head like a computer. He had two naval tugs to seaward to ward off tankers coming too near. He had one to the North protecting him from tankers attempting to leave the shelter of the Bay. His radio operators were also in contact with the listening station on top of the Rock, the Joint Operations Centre running the show, GCHQ, the SBS at sea and the shore, and the oil tanker just off to his starboard side.

On top of all this, he had been told to arm and be prepared to fire live Tiger-fish torpedoes in the Bay. The environmental disaster if he hit his target would be phenomenal. The political disaster if he missed would be incalculable, and he was certain it would be an unhappy end to his commission. As he saw it, he was in a lose-lose situation. 'I was just following orders,' would not wash. All this when he only had eleven months to go before escaping Her Majesty's navy with twenty-two years of undetected cock-ups under his belt.

The submarine was closed down to Zulu Alpha: full wartime action stations. His chief radio operator called out through his white anti-flash hood, "Signal from the clearance divers on the hull, Sir. They have visual contact with *Moby*. Approaching from green one six zero, good depth. DDS open and ready to embark."

The sonar desk concurred. "Sonar confirm, sir."

The captain swung his periscope starboard and aft. It was rare to use it underwater, even rarer still to see anything. In the good visibility off Gibraltar, he could see the MCDs (Mine Clearance Divers) out on the sub's hull guiding the miniature sub into position. There was a hint of daylight in the blue of the Mediterranean. "Cutting it fine, boys, cutting it fine!" he muttered into the periscope.

Piggy-backed on the nuclear sub's hull, just astern of the conning tower was a DDS, (Dry Deck Shelter). It was built to house the smaller submarine. They could, and had, delivered it and its crew covertly to many a sensitive area of conflict around the world.

The sub slowly parked on the trolley just astern of the garage. She was made negatively buoyant by her crew and secured. The SBS crew then handed over the operation of docking the SDV inside its protective shelter to the Navy divers, and finned to the transfer lock into the 'Mother' submarine. The hatch was already open as the six members of the covert team crammed themselves into the tiny chamber that also doubled up as an emergency escape hatch. The four-inch-thick metal door was closed above their heads and moments later the water began to drain from the lock.

As the lower door was hydraulically dropped, J.D climbed down with gallons of water into the warmth and safety of the submarine. He dumped his re-breather on the wet deck and the already confined space was further crammed with the extra SBS divers, their weapons and gear. Ready to greet him was the captain.

"Ah, Sergeant Dog, no less." The two men shook hands. He turned to his petty officer steward and said, "Get these men anything they want Michael, will you, within reason, of course. The galley is open for you all. Now then, sergeant, please accompany me to my cabin, I sincerely hope you can fill me in with what the bloody hell is going on up there"

"Shit!" said J.D as Smudge unzipped his dry suit. "I thought you were gonna tell *me*... sir! All I know is we've got to lock out again at twenty-one-hundred tonight."

The skipper did not look pleased as the dripping wet sergeant followed him through the control room. He gave a long list of orders to his crew, the last of which was to his first officer.

"Number One, as soon as the garage door is shut, I want the CDs on board, double quick time. Confirm with me, then dive to... 120 meters, I want some water over our heads. I'll be in my cabin."

# 38

In the tank, Nick had lost all track of time. He'd been unconscious at least twice that he could remember. Stuck inside the hull of the tanker he had no inkling if it was day, night, or whether he'd been on board days or merely hours. He was uncertain of the woman, the major, and more importantly about what Hadda had in mind for him and the tanker. He didn't know if his canoe had been found, and, if it had been, whether it was by the tanker's crew or someone else. If only he'd sent that bloody text to Smudge, at least someone would know roughly where to come and look for him. As it was, there was only his yacht with the wrong name on it for anyone to find... and that was if anyone was even looking for it? His only real hope was that Mo must have told Rex she'd seen him up at the house. He had not confirmed to Miles he would be stopping at Gibraltar. In fact he had told him he wouldn't. Even after receiving the fuel, they may have thought he'd buggered off into the Atlantic.

Having taken him from the for'ard tank, his captors put the revolting sack over his head and stood him in the stress position. They made him lean against a wall with his legs wide apart, so that only his forehead took the weight of his body. He stood for over an hour, knees shaking and his neck periodically giving way. Eventually he was dragged to the dreaded small room. The metal door was slammed shut. Deep inside, his bowels turned somersaults as he heard the running water. He felt cold steel against his neck as his blindfolding hood was cut away to reveal the black-clad fanatics preparing his tank.

Nick listened to the men talk in Arabic, no doubt discussing his future or lack of it.

He kept his head hanging, submissive and non-aggressive, but out of the corner of his eye he could see the back of a man's head. The room was partitioned, and as he stood inside the door he could see there was another tank identical to his. The man was sitting in water and his head periodically lolled forwards, forcing him to wake. Nick couldn't see his face, but he moved and made a slight moaning sound.

Nick looked the other way, concentrating on the guards preparing his tank and trying to see how he had been secured. Two guards lifted a heavy metal beam until it was propped at an angle up against the walls of the bath. A third guard, the youngest, ushered him towards the bath with a pistol. They lifted him into the tank and dragged his feet up and over the end of the beam so that first his ankle restraints, then the wrists, would be underneath. When they lowered the beam, he pushed his hands as near to the end as he could and pretended to choke and panic underwater. They dragged him up and laughed as he coughed and spluttered.

As they continued to fill the tank with what appeared to be bilge-water, they amused themselves at Nick's expense. The boy, Ayman, was a vindictive bastard and had a small and ancient chromed revolver. He continuously spun the magazine, pushing it into Nick's ear, nose or eye and pulling the trigger. Each time the hammer clicked on an empty chamber, his face lit up. "Bang!" he would shout, then mimed the loss of blood and trauma the shot would cause. As the others talked, Ayman found a new game. He would force the barrel into Nick's mouth until he gagged, then they would all laugh and mime lurid suggestions.

Nick looked back at him each time and tried to envisage meeting him when he was not bound hand and foot. It kept him going.

With the tank full up to his chin, they left the room and turned out the lights. He was back to total darkness and cold. If he didn't move, the only sound was the barely audible hum of a distant generator. He wanted desperately to sleep, more than anything he wanted to sleep, but he couldn't. If he relaxed he could drown. *What a shit way to go*, he thought, *either getting shot, dying of hypothermia, drowning or radioactive poisoning. Not much of a choice.*

Remembering his fellow prisoner, he whispered, "Hello... can you hear me? Are you Okay? Hello... do you speak English?" A little louder he tried, "Hey... hey, how long have you been here?" There was a sound, a moan, but nothing recognisable. The man could have been there days longer than him. "No way," he said aloud, "I am not going to die here. I would rather die trying to escape than... than this."

Before he got too cold, he went to work. He worked at rocking the huge beam left and right. Each time, shifting his wrist and ankle restraints forwards. After hours of work he figured he was over half way towards the end of the beam. The cold, coupled with the lack of food and water, was sapping his strength; energy levels were dropping fast. Thirst had him put his face deep beneath the surface, away from the floating oil as he tried to filter the rank water through his teeth. He popped up and nearly vomited, but held it down. It was a mix of stale freshwater and sea water.

With nothing else to do he battled on with the beam, which seemed to be getting heavier. Lost in his thoughts and fears, the time dragged as he struggled in the pitch black. Sometime during the imprisonment, he forgot the cold. His mind wandered off on its own, careering aimlessly away. He thought about when he'd been colder: skin swimming in Scotland on his first diving course, or sleeping in a canoe on exercise with the SBS in Norway. Then there were hot water failures, diving at 600ft in saturation in the North Sea, that was what cold was all about. There was only the water muffled sound of the slight movement of the beam and his grunting and mumblings as he shifted his restraints millimetre by millimetre.

At some point during the prolonged struggle, he heard voices: distant, shouting, maybe arguing voices? One was hers, the girl's, echoing through the cavernous oil tanks and hollow tunnels. They seemed to stop somewhere near the door, in the rifle range. She was shouting at someone in Arabic, and he wished he could understand. The conversation became whispered, more controlled. He heard a man's voice mumbling, then footsteps as someone walked away.

The metal door to the compartment opened and the dull light in the roof illuminated his surroundings. Each time that door opened it was like a knife twisting in his guts. What now?

The desperate wail of a voice came from the prisoner on the other side of the partition. A pathetic cry. The light had woken him from his nightmare. It sounded as if he was gagged or had been hit or wounded in the mouth. He began to snivel and moan.

Nick allowed his own shivering to intensify. If she was coming in, he was seeking sympathy. She walked straight past to the wooden bench opposite him, and turned on the warm tap. She was in her blue combat gear and had a smart leather pouch on her hip, shaped like a small handgun. It was closed, and he had no idea whether it contained the weapon.

She was flushed, fire in her eyes. She was angry. She picked up the broom handle with the prongs, walked across to him and slid it under his chin.

"Thanks," he stumbled.

She marched back to the bench. "Shut up!"

Then she spun round. Sweat glistened from her top lip and she carried a faraway look in her eye. She sucked in a deep breath, drew her pistol and cocked it.

*Shit! She's going to do it*, he thought. *This is it!*

The man close by continued his pitiful cry and sobbed like a child. She strode around the partition to her other tortured guest who was sitting up to his neck in cold water. Najia sounded angry. She shouted in Arabic what he assumed could only be a demand for him to shut up. She kept shouting, building herself up into a seething state. He kept crying. Nick heard water splashing and then the man's voice. There was a slight struggling sound then the voice in Arabic, it sounded like, pleading. The only word he understood was "Najia!"

There was more rustling, and a metallic click, then silence.

Nick jumped as a loud gunshot rang out.

# 39

The discharge reverberated around the four walls. The tortured guest had been silenced. There were running footsteps and the door burst open. A man went to the other side of the partition and spoke to Najia in a calming voice.

They came out together a little later, and Nick recognised him. It was the gap-toothed, gawky looking crewman; the one who'd boarded Orelia that first night. He had his arm round her shoulders and kept his head down; it seemed to Nick as if he wanted to avoid eye contact.

They spoke quietly as they went to the door. The faint smell of cordite hung like a murderous cloud in the room. Gawky didn't want to leave but she eventually closed the door and his footsteps grew quieter. She remained by the door for a while, perhaps composing herself, then she holstered the weapon.

She looked vacant, stunned, as though she couldn't believe what had just happened. Undoing some buttons on her combat shirt, she took out a banana, then undid her trousers to tuck the shirt back in. Nick had a glimpse of her narrow waist and the flattest of stomachs. He saw a feminine pair of white-laced pants, and, tucked in the top, a bottle of water. She placed the blackening banana under her chin and walked over to him, adjusting her clothing.

Nick must have retained a look of shock on his face because she hesitated before putting the fruit in his mouth.

"It's - not my fault. It was an order! It was him or me - anyway, he made it easier with his whining. Now eat, before you join him."

She fed the banana into his mouth and he ate, amazed at how calm she was. *She has done this before*, he thought. She held the bottle of water to his lips and he gulped it down. The natural sugar and water was a shock to his starved system but it was what his body craved.

She walked away and Nick said, "Who was that?"

"You don't need to know who anyone is."

"No, I didn't mean him, I meant, I meant - who was he, the one you..."

"Oh that? He was the *real* Captain." She paused, looking away, then sought to justify herself. "I had to do it. Hadda has something I want. That was the price. There are things... things that have to be done to ensure... ensure certain people's futures, not least of all, mine. This is not just about you or me." Her voice tailed off and it seemed the full force of her actions came home.

Nick tried to move as his back went into spasms again. The long period of lifting and shifting in such an unnatural, bent forward position was starting to tell. If it wasn't for his chin rest he would be fighting the weight of his head as well as it tried to droop forwards.

A sombre atmosphere permeated a long uncomfortable silence.

Najia paced up and down, lost in her world, keeping her head hung low as she reflected. Did she have the same orders for Nick? Was the fruit his last supper? With that thought, he struggled at the unseen beam and tried to distract her, to perhaps change her figure of hate.

"I think I know a lot more about Hadda than you, Najia."

She didn't seem shocked that he knew her name. Perhaps she realised he'd heard the young captain's pleas before he was executed. Nick had nothing to lose. He had no doubt she would murder him in cold blood when the time came, so he said his piece.

"I am certainly going to die, and I don't think you'll be far behind me. Is this the way you want to go on? Think about what you've just done. Will that help you secure the future of people close to you? You are on a path of self-destruction with these people."

*

"Don't lecture me. I am not doing this for me."

Najia walked round the tank. She had just shot a man, an innocent man, but she felt little, if anything. There was no guilt or revulsion at what she had done. It was all for her baby, and one day she would have another one. She didn't need a husband; she would select a suitable man and use him. She could usually take her pick.

She found herself looking at his shoulders and arched back. He was broad; his back wide, well defined and the muscles glistened through the wet oily skin. She could see he was strong and wondered what it would be like to have him. The thought had bothered her since she had seen him stretched out naked. She went back to the bench and looked down at her feet, embarrassed at the vision, glad he couldn't share her thoughts.

She missed her son, and the reliability and physical closeness of Adam - steady, reliable, if slightly boring Adam. This man, Nick, he had never even got to see his child, to know its sex, or to say goodbye to his woman. But, she did not have time for sympathy; this was the time to be strong; to fall back on her training; to do what had to be done and move on.

*

She was quiet, so Nick continued, "Do you know this man's history? He is the one who organised the Madrid train bombings. He was the main man; his men murdered my wife, Mariyah! One of his bombers blew her to pieces. She was pregnant with my child. He murdered her. That's why I followed him here."

289

His voice broke, but he carried on. "Not to mention 191 others who died for the heinous crime of going to work. Over two thousand horrifically injured, blinded, deafened, limbless innocents. They are all out there. They get reminded of that day every day, every morning. He doesn't care if his victims are English, Muslim, male, female, child or baby. He is a murderer, Najia. And... he is turning you into one."

The warm flowing water into the tank, together with the fruit and drink were a godsend; it filled him with hope and a little strength. The rage of talking about his wife drove him on. As he spoke, he continued trying to move his bindings forward. He felt the end of the beam with his fingers and was able to use his hands as a lever. He rocked it to the left and dragged his fingers forwards until the wrist wire was a centimetre nearer the end. He also continued working to reach out to her.

"With your help, we could take the launch. We could be in Gibraltar and safe within minutes of leaving the ship. I could protect you. I mean, I could get you help. But-you have to help me first."

She spun round. "Forget it. I am not going to help you. I have my own problems. I have to get far away from here as soon as possible. Gibraltar is too close. No, I shall be heading back to Morocco. No one is safe around here. That – that man and his poison..."

"Why? What do you know? Do you know what his intentions are?"

She seemed to think about it, shrugged her shoulders, then stepped towards Nick and sat close to him again. She was down. The spark, the fight had gone from her eyes. She looked down at her feet as she answered.

"I think you will survive, for a few days at least. So, like me, you will have your chances. He wants you to see his plan, whatever it is. I think he enjoys your chats, your debates. He said something about letting you see it on TV. Before, before... well you know... I don't know what he plans, well not exactly. As I said, I've nothing to do with him, I should be away really soon. Even his men don't know. At least I don't think they do."

Nick sucked some blood out of his tongue. "If you are convinced I'm going to die, what harm can it do to tell me what you think? If it's not right, so what. If it is right, and I do go down with the ship, no harm done. I just want to know how I'm going to go." He tried to smile at her. "I'd like to know what's coming, that's all."

She looked up, sighed, then shook her head as if deciding; it could do no harm.

"All I know is... I joined the ship in Tripoli when they loaded the fuel into the other tanks. They also brought aboard ten drums of, of something. They were unusual, small, silver and solidly built. They looked like strong, half-size beer barrels."

She paused, they made eye contact, and something passed between them, some understanding, some trust. Was she saying goodbye?

"One of our Libyan scientists was here, on board. He had his own men, army men. They moved them onto the upper deck. He had some sort of air purity gauge and one of those Geiger counters all the time. He was worried every time they were moved. They were very, very careful with them. Hachim, he wanted to pour the drums into the main tanks there and then, alongside, but the scientist, he wouldn't let him. He said it had to be done at sea, for safety. I couldn't wait to get off. I was happy to follow the tanker in the boat. But I saw one of the drums up close. They appeared to be numbered. One I saw I remember had written on it a large P and a number. I think it was two hundred and ten. I gather they were going to pour them into the main fuel tanks."

She looked at him, mystified, as though it meant nothing to her.

"Do you mean, they poured the drums into the ship's fuel tanks, or the main oil cargo tanks?"

"The main cargo tanks. They aren't full of oil, though, I know that. They are full of fuel, diesel or petrol, or both I think. Hachim, he wouldn't let the normal crew, or that paint, made her buoyant, and he watched the lads go about their business. Texas listened again through the hull. Harvey swam off toward the launch carrying the small transponder in a pocket on his drysuit. J.D went with him, paying out the swimline before waiting at the bilge keel.

*

Harvey flushed his bubbleless rebreather through with fresh $O^2$, gave the thumbs up and swam away from J.D. It was dark and it would be choppy near the surface, so he made himself relatively heavy by expelling some gas from the flexible lung on his chest. He approached the underside of the launch slowly, heading for the shaft; something to grab hold of. When there, he took out a piece of adjustable piano wire, moved up and aft to the rudder post and clamped his knees onto it. He measured the length of wire required to keep the transponder just on the surface but hidden under the overhang of the stern, then attached the fish to the wire. It was technology they had borrowed from the International Fund for Animal Welfare. They used it for tracking whales; the SBS employed it for tracking suspicious boats.

He was about to attach it when he felt the impact of rounds hitting the water. Instinctively he let go and dropped down deeper. Did they know he was there? Swimming over to the tanker's hull and at a safe depth of about three metres he looked up. Astern of the launch was something orange. Then it was lit up from above. There was a person, a man. Harvey swam upwards, nearer. It was a white male and he was being shot at. He was ducking under the surface to escape the hail of splashes above his head. Harvey kicked upward and made a grab for a piece of rope tied to the man's ankle, but couldn't hold on. The man kicked out and swum up. The surface again erupted in a spray of rounds. Harvey followed and when the man ducked down again, he got a firm hold of the rope. He made himself heavy, turned

304

bunch of cut throats with the major, he wouldn't let them join the ship until the barrels and box were loaded."

"What box?" She paused, looked at her watch and slid her chair back.

"I don't know. There was a box that came on the same lorry in Tripoli. Six men had to lift it. It is forward of here somewhere. I understand it's full of liquid. It had a radiation symbol on it and warnings in Arabic and English. It had S.N.F. written on it. I don't know what it means. Do you?"

It didn't ring any bells. Nick felt he was winning, she was coming round, she was less threatening. He wanted to keep her talking, but she was becoming restless. She stood as he managed to rock the beam to the right and shift his wrists another centimetre forwards when, suddenly, his left wrist moved higher than before. It was not free yet but it was the most movement he'd ever had. He moved it left, then right and heaved upwards. They moved even more. He was almost there. The wire must be sticking on the rough end of the beam. His ankles were still underneath and his feet stopped him moving any further forwards. He couldn't let her leave; he might not see her again. This was his chance.

Najia gathered herself, perhaps realising she'd said too much. She looked at him oddly and he thought he detected a hint of... was it pity? She checked her watch and was about to speak, when she looked at him again. She was suspicious. Had she spotted the change in his posture? Maybe his head wasn't low enough in the water; he was certainly further forwards than he had been. She stepped towards him and then looked into the tank.

Only inches from his face, she peered down at the water in the bath. She put one hand on her gun and unclipped the holster. With the other she scooped the oily scum from the surface. Then she drew the pistol with alarming speed.

He wrenched his wrists free, his hands shot up, and water flew into her face as he stood. The binding between his wrists hit the weapon and it spun into the air. He grabbed the back of her neck and pulled her towards him. She over-balanced as her hips hit the edge of the tank. Nick forced her head down into the water.

She screeched, "Wait...!"

The final part was a stifled underwater gurgle. He plunged her down and clamped her head with his knees. That freed his bound wrists. He leaned down to grab the belt of her trousers and pulled her off of her feet and dragged her completely into the tank. She weighed next to nothing and was like a rag doll. Her fight was a frenzied, desperate panic.

Her hands searched about the bottom of the tank and latched onto his ankle. The nails dug in, then she pushed up on her hands. Her feet swung up and kicked, flailing about in an obscene upside-down dance. He buried his chin into his chest and tried to dodge the boots as they thrashed about in the air. Bubbles came to the surface, pushing aside the oil. There came a searing pain as she bit the inside of his leg. Nick managed to tuck first one then the other of her swinging legs under his right arm, and clenched hard. He heard another muffled yell; the desperate plea of someone who knew they were drowning. She fought and struggled, scratched and heaved until the bitter end. Her movements became weaker, slower, until, finally, she went limp.

Nick lifted her out of the water by her shirt front and looked into her face. Her eyes were closed and dirty water dribbled from her nose and mouth. He put his fingers to her throat to feel for the pulse. It was there, but she was not breathing. He flopped her over the side of the tank, then flipped her legs over her head. She landed hard on the metal deck.

Nick stood, trying to stretch his hunched, aching back muscles, then he bent down ready to grab the beam with both hands. He had no chance of lifting the whole thing so he moved forwards to the end where he had released his wrists. Crouching down, he grabbed the end of the beam and began to take the strain in his legs. All the muscles in his back, shoulders and thighs strained and ached as the load transferred to his body. His head flushed with blood as it began to move. With the beam end off the bottom, he inched his feet forwards. When he let go, he would have to move his feet up and forwards, or else they would catch the ankle rope and maybe land on his bare foot. Judging the moment, he let the beam go and moved his feet at the same time.

There was a muffled clang as the heavy metal hit the bottom. One side of his ankle restraint was still caught under the corner. He rocked it over again and it fell away completely on its side, releasing his feet.

He scrambled head first out of the container and fell next to Najia's crumpled body. He felt for the carotid pulse in her neck. It was there; her heart was beating, but she was not breathing. Stretching her head back, he lifted her neck, pinched her nose, then covered her mouth with his own. He blew in five large breaths, watching her chest deflate between each one. She still had a pulse, but he needed to get her breathing on her own.

"Come on girl, breathe!"

He blew another five life-giving breaths into her. Nothing, then she spluttered and coughed and he rolled her to one side. Oily water emptied from her stomach and lungs. Nick was puffing, his heart racing with the adrenalin of the moment. He looked around for the pistol. It was under the desk and he felt its weight in his hand.

It was a small Ruger .380 automatic. Six shots maybe? He ejected the magazine and saw there were at least two rounds in the clip, then rammed it back into the grip and cocked it.

She moved, pulled up her knees, scrunched up her closed eyes and retched.

"That's it. We're even. One life save each. You're on your own now, girl."

# 40

Nick moved to the partition and peered round. The body of a man lay slumped in a tank of bloody water. There was a small neat hole just behind the ear. On the man's skin was the imprint of the barrel. The deep red wound was surrounded in black soot. She had held it pressed to his head, and it was the weapon he now held in his hand. The man was dead, but Nick had to check. He moved closer. The bullet had exited his face leaving a ragged hole where his eye and temple would have been.

The familiar sound of the watertight door clips were closely followed by faint footsteps. He shuffled to the door and turned out the light. The door opened and a voice called out. A hand searched inside for the light switch and touched Nick on the chest. He grabbed the arm and wrenched it inwards with all his strength. There was a yelp and both men went to the floor. Nick could see in the light from the door that it was Gawky, and that he was terrified. He straddled the man and held the gun to his face. He babbled, no doubt pleading.

Nick thought for a second, raised the gun above his head and brought down the grip hard onto the man's forehead, just above his nose. Gawky just looked stunned, so he did it again. This time his eyes rolled and he passed out.

Nick felt his pockets and belt. He was not armed. He stood above him in a bit of a daze. Najia moaned from behind the tank and that sound galvanised him to move.

He stepped to the door and looked out into the shooting range. Left was where everyone came from, so that was probably the accommodation and way out. To the right was the container with the nuclear material. Left, then. Left and up.

Nick stepped out of his torture chamber and something caught his eye. Stuck in the top of one of the sand bags was the handle of a knife. It was an old galley bread knife. He sat on the deck and sawed frantically at the rope binding his ankles.

Free of the restriction, he ran naked to the watertight door leading aft. He stepped into a low, perfectly round metal tunnel and scurried barefoot and doubled-up along its length. The tail of the rope left round one ankle whipped the back of his calf with every step. It was a long way and there were only a few dull bulbs along the passageway. The noise of the generators grew steadily louder as he moved, confirming he was going aft. Reaching a closed watertight door, Nick gathered himself and lifted the first handle.

He stepped through into the starkly lit, bright white part of a tanker. To the right, was a heavy-looking metal door that read: Beware Turning Shaft. There was a red light above the door; it would flash if the shaft was spinning. Outside on a hook were ear-defenders, boot covers, and, a pair of oily, engineer's overalls. But, with wrists still bound, overalls would be impossible to get on. He chose a tattered and torn pair of bright orange foul-weather trousers.

He followed a corridor that headed aft and turned towards the midships. Being below the water line, the doors to all compartments were metal. There was a door with a notice reading: Emergency Steering Gear, and another that read: Engine Room Casing. One that did grab his attention was: Work Shop. It was right next to the stairs. It was tempting just to run up the stairs and find the upper deck, to get out of there, but Nick needed to remove the wire strop from his wrists.

He opened the door carefully and peered in. Standing with his back to the door was a man in white overalls, working a lathe and wearing ear-defenders. *Ship's crew,* he thought, *probably nothing to do with Hadda*. Nick looked down at the bread knife in one hand and a pistol in the other, and closed the door again. He went for the stairs.

On the next floor, opposite the stairwell, he found the laundry. Next to that door was a sign and arrow that read: Lift. The small illuminated number above the lift blinked -4. Then it changed to -5. The lift was moving downward, towards him. Before he realised it, the doors opened and out stepped a seaman in a blue shirt, closely followed by four of Hadda's men dressed head-to-foot in black. The first one out spotted him; he was carrying a short silenced machine pistol on a strap around his neck. His manner changed instantly and as Nick turned to run up the stairs, he saw the gun raised and pointed in his direction.

There was a muffled, rapid burst of machine-gun fire behind him as he turned the corner and leapt up the stairwell three steps at a time. The man who had fired at him and possibly the others, were close on his heels. Their boots were making a lot more noise than his bare feet.

Being chased and shot at made him lithe and light on his feet. He ditched the knife and pulled himself up each flight of stairs. Floors -3, -2, flashed past. He pumped his aching legs, leaping upwards, and was opening up valuable ground on his pursuers. At -1 he knocked over a chef in a greasy white apron carrying two hot drinks in china mugs. Among the shouts, he hit the level marked: Upper Deck. Amidships and opposite the galley he slid right. At the end of the corridor was a door with a porthole that read: Deck. He ran, past the dining room and was aware of a noise; it was the lift arriving at the deck level. There was a shout behind as he barged the door open with his shoulder. It was dark outside and Gibraltar's lights ranged out in front of him. Slamming the door, he had a choice to make.

Right astern or left for'ard? Right, it was darker than the tanker's deck. He ran.

Sprinting along the accommodation level into the relative dark of the stern, the door he had just exited banged open. Had they seen which way he'd gone? Darting round the corner and running along the rear of the tall block, he saw a man. A lookout, in front of him. They were both unsure what to do. The man had been keeping out of sight and was in a recess under a huge air intake. He raised something, a weapon. Then he panicked and started to cock it. As the distance closed, Nick lifted the pistol, hesitated, then fired on the run. It hit the man in the stomach. He stopped moving and had a look of complete surprise on his face. Nick raced by and hit him a glancing blow with his shoulder and heard him clatter to the deck.

Heading towards the port side, he could see a huge tanker lit up and high out of the water. He wondered what flag it was. That was maybe a nearer safe haven if he had to swim. A shout from behind. Someone was following. He reached the port side and turned for'ard. A door from the ship flung open five metres in front. Out stepped a man in desert combats. He was standing half behind the metal door. He looked for'ard then aft. Nick was running full speed toward him. He hit the door hard and it smashed into the man, shattering his cheekbone. The man fell back and into the corridor, sprawling across the exit.

*

Dave and Jiz, the watching No 1 sniper team, moved in unison. As if on rails they swung binoculars and rifle to the right. Dave spoke into the mike taped to his cheek before anyone else could claim it.

"T1. Gunshot aft, target vessel." The green world through the night vision lenses was surreal but second nature to them.

"White bald male, running west to us. Handgun is warm. Bare-chested and barefoot, wearing trousers only. Oooo... he's just smashed someone's head in with a door.

He is... hand-cuffed... I think. Awaiting green, over! Three, no... four players giving chase. Armed with suppressed snub-nosed..."

Over the comms they all heard: *"Do not engage... repeat, do not engage. Possible friendly, confirm!"* Jiz moved his cross-hairs to the first of the chasing pack. He had P1 in his sights. He just needed a green light.

"Confirmed, still red, players in black are not friendly, awaiting green, over!"

They instinctively knew the white male was a friendly but couldn't open fire without permission. *"Wait!"* was the only reply.

The leading player stopped and took aim at the fleeing man. Jiz switched to a head shot. He had him, and took up the pressure on the trigger.

# 41

Nick ran full speed down the port side. He was lit up and vulnerable out on the deck. A round hit the guard rail to his left and flew off into the night. More bullets hit the deck behind. The air around his head reverberated as it was ripped apart by the passing of high velocity rounds. Someone was getting the range. He darted left, and saw a hatch close to the ship's side. He took two steps up onto it and vaulted over the side. The trailing rope around his right ankle caught the top rail and dragged at his leg. He fought to stay upright, but running in mid-air and with cuffed arms out in front, he fell. To the right and below he saw the launch.

Sucking in a breath and closing his legs, he hit the dark water almost upright, sinking deep beneath the surface. Kicking and clawing, he made his way up and looked around. He was three metres out from the ship's side and not far from the stern of the launch. Nick had the vague idea of finding his canoe, but realised what a waste of time it had been deliberately coming round to the port side. At least one and more likely two days had passed since he'd been captured, and the canoe would surely be gone. He tucked in close to the hull and kicked out for the launch. Tied together, his arms were useless. There was a splash just in front, then a group of splashes to the left. He took a deep breath and sunk down below the surface. The rounds hit the water above, tiny bubbles tracing their wake.

*Fuck... now what*? Nick kicked out for the launch. At least it would give some cover, but the tide was against him. Heart racing, he could barely muster twenty seconds before he was forced up for air. Desperate to breathe, he broke surface again and heard more rounds glance off the ship's side. Two gulps of air and someone was closing in with their shots. Underwater again, he noticed his kicking legs. They were fluorescent orange. He wrestled the trousers off, then, with burning lungs, ventured up once more, letting go of them when he hit the surface.

There was a wet thwack as the trousers took a direct hit. He gulped another lungful and went under again. He was getting hardly any nearer the launch, and didn't even have the opportunity to give up. *I always knew one day it would be drowning*, he thought. *I just knew it. I can't take much more of this.* The rope on his ankle seemed to weigh heavy, dragging him down. He instinctively recoiled and headed up again.

A light now shone on the water. It was coming from ahead, from the launch. Hanging on, his lungs crying out for replenishment, he saw the surface boil up with shots.

*Fuck! That's that then.* He was almost resigned to drowning. One final deep breath. The panic should come now, but instead he was overcome with a dream-like serenity. The phosphorescence in the water around the bullet bubbles was beautiful. He was sinking. The light got dimmer and dimmer as he was drawn downwards...

\*

Hachim Hadda was on the bridge of his command. Since he'd incarcerated the young captain he'd had to rely heavily on the keen first officer. Hadda promised the bright young man he would put in a word for him to take over as captain when he left the ship.

It was dark and he was almost there. Victory was so close, he could taste it. The radio squelched out and the young officer answered. Hadda didn't move, everyone had to come to him.

"That was the pilot, sir. He will be with us shortly. He requests we shorten anchor by 23:00 and be under way by 23:10.

"Yes, yes, carry on," said Hadda, with a dismissive wave. *Perfect*, he thought... *here we go.*

His self-indulgence was cut short by an abrupt commotion from the stairs below the bridge. One of his men came running up with his weapon, which he had expressly forbade them to do.

He looked wildly around him, knowing he was in trouble and said in Arabic. "Sir, the English... he has... err, escaped. He is on the upper deck!"

"What?"

Hadda grabbed a radio, jumped out of the skipper's chair and ran to where the launch was on the port side bridge wing. Below, he saw Carter running along the deck, then he saw shots being fired at him. They missed and he swerved and leapt over the side. Hadda looked across at the much bigger vessel relatively close by. All was quiet. Had anyone seen? His men followed to the ship's side and one went down the ladder to the launch. Two leaned over the side and fired again with their silenced weapons.

He spoke into his radio. "Deck - bridge, did you get him? Any sign?"

There was a pause, then, *"I think so, sir."* There was the dull, menacing spit of a machine pistol over the radio. *"He keeps going under. He is getting swept astern in the tide."*

Hadda called back into the bridge to the young officer. "Call the engine room. Start main engine NOW! I want to give a quick burst."

The officer was just out of maritime school and didn't even know they had an English who *could* escape. But he risked a comment: "But, but sir, we are still at anchor!"

"Just do it!"

# 42

Jon Dog, Smudge and the team had locked out of the submarine early. They were under way and on route at 20:49. The mini-sub and its crew headed towards the large friendly tanker, dropped under it, then set a course directly east towards the target.

The report J.D had given earlier that Texas had heard shooting through the hull had at first been rejected. The latest news from the powers that be reported that the tanker was scheduled to move up harbour soon to the swing buoy mooring. There she would connect a flexible pipe to the buoy and begin unloading her fuel. That could take all night and so that was when the Special Forces would make their move - subject to change.

Their task was to attach a GPB (Global Position Beacon) to the launch and return to the HM Submarine *Triumph* for passage to the buoy.

They reached the tanker and Smudge eased the same route in under the shaft, along the hull, then as near to the launch as possible. The weather was now not ideal. It was blowing a force 4, occasional 5. They were fine seven metres below the surface, but swimming up to and around the launch could be interesting.

Smudge had been quiet on board the *Triumph*. He feared the worst for his buddy, Nick. He had been unable to eat or get caught up in the excited banter that had preceded the dive. The SBS lads left him to it. They all knew what it was like to lose a mate.

Smudge had brought the sub slowly up under the tanker to the mark they had scratched in the anti-fouling

head down and finned hard. The man came down with him. Harvey stopped, took the emergency demand valve from his chest, grabbed the man by his arm and stuck the valve into his mouth. The man's eyes were open wide but he didn't breathe, so Harvey pushed the purge button and filled his mouth with compressed air. He got the idea and clasped the mouthpiece with both hands and breathed it in.

*

Smudge was day-dreaming, standing on his seat. He watched Texas with the headphones on, listening to the heartbeat of the ship. Small fish scurried around him in the dull glow of the internal red light of the sub.

They were all shaken out of their slumber at once. You didn't need a hydrophone to tell that the tanker above their heads had just started her main engine. The tanker's hull began to vibrate. Smudge dropped down onto his seat and began the sequence for getting under way. He needed the two swimmers back first though and looked to port. There they were: J.D had his red mask light on, so did Harv. Smudge stood again - what the fuck? His head banged into the hull above. There were three of them! The middle one didn't have on a dry bag, or mask, or anything else. The through-water comms silence was shattered by J.D.

*"Jock, Jock, get a survival suit out NOW! Smudge, get us out of here, down to ten metres and head west to Mother."* He sucked in two huge breaths as they dragged Nick's naked frame toward relative safety. *"On air, everyone. Stan, I want an onboard air bib for Nick. We have him. Let's go, GO!"*

Nick was unceremoniously bundled into the rear of the Swimmer Delivery Vehicle. Before everyone was properly in, Smudge ditched some air from the ballast tanks. The sea water rushed in to replace it, and the SDV began, ever so slowly to sink away from her host. Smudge could only guess at the state of Nick in the rear compartment. He gave the electric engine a kick ahead to

305

get some reaction and steerage from the bow planes and rudder. J.D dragged himself into the seat next to him. They began to gather momentum. J.D quickly began hitting buttons, switching valves and helping with the weight that would soon be on the bow planes.

Smudge went full ahead and was just about to put the helm over to port when the sub rocked and tipped violently. The stern lifted high towards the ship's bottom. They were caught in a wash.

Despite still being at anchor, the tanker had put her great propeller astern. The sub rolled heavily and the tail tried to overtake the bow. J.D shouted.

*"Close all doors... close all doors!"*

They both fought the helm but the sub did a complete 360 degree roll to the left. Smudge hadn't had time to close his door and the water was doing its utmost to suck him out. As they came round near to level again, the nose was driven down towards the bottom of the bay. He equalised the pressure in his eardrums and looked at the instruments. Fifteen metres. That couldn't be right. He was nose down 60 degrees, then 70 degrees and still going full ahead. His eardrums stretched and he cleared the pressure by pinching his nose and blowing again, and again. Twenty-one metres. A loose air bottle slammed into the bulkhead behind him. Now well out of the wash of the tanker, he put the engine to stop and they both pulled hard up on the bow planes. The rhythmic click of the electric engine was still fast, too fast. Smudge realised it was the flow of water spinning the propeller, turning the engine over. He put it to slow astern, reached up and opened the large quarter turn valve that read: EMERG BALLAST BLOW. The electric motor tried to move against the onrush of water as they headed deeper. Twenty-five metres. The hissing noise of air rushing into the bow ballast tanks filled the sub as it plunged deeper. The electric engine whined and complained, struggling to get any momentum into the prop. Thirty metres... and the bow began to level out.

"*TRIM! Trim or we bail out!*" was all J.D shouted from the seat beside him. The nose came up high, but they were still descending, albeit at a more sedate pace. Thirty-three metres, tail heavy. Smudge blew some air into the smaller stern DTCs (Depth Control Tanks). She came up almost level and steadied at thirty-eight metres. His door was still open into the black Mediterranean, and Smudge realised they were going backwards. He went to neutral, then ahead, and tried his utmost to do as J.D had demanded, to get the trim right. Thirty-six metres and now he had to slow their ascent. A bunch of so-called expert divers crashing to the surface in a submarine that didn't exist with embolisms and various bends would not be good. Thirty metres and rising, rising a bit too quickly.

J.D pressed the intercom. "*Everyone okay?*" There came five various murmured versions of the affirmative.

"*How's Nick?*" was Smudges call.

"*Fucking cold,*" said Jock. "*If ye could keep this fuckin' tub steady for a minute, I could get his hand-cuffs bolt cropped and get him dressed inte the fuckin' survival suit! And how fuckin' deep are we? My voice has-ne been this fucking high since junior school!*"

"*I'm working on it,*" replied Smudge. "*How is he, Jock?*"

There was a long pause. "*He's breathing, which has te be good. He's given us the thumbs up. Get us shallower. He needs warming, and fast.*"

They eventually made an almost controlled ascent. Almost, but they hit the surface first, before submerging again to periscope depth. It was a lot warmer up there.

J.D said, "*We're nowhere near Mother. We were washed out east.*"

Stan had an idea. "*What about the boat, the yacht. For Nick, I mean. That's our nearest safe haven. We're in dry bags, this guy's gonna shiver him self to death!*"

"*Good idea.*" The GPS was automatically updated when they hit surface. The SBS fishing/safety boat *Gemini Three* also got a fix on them and rushed towards their position.

# 43

The SDV broke surface close to *Orelia*. *Gemini Three*, in her fishing boat guise, was there to meet the bedraggled crew. There had been a slight disagreement during the ascent about who would escort Nick up to his boat.

"He's my oppo, and I know how to start the main engines. I know how to get the hot water running. You can pilot." Smudge took a deep breath. "Look J.D... I want to talk to him. You could pilot back to the Triumph... couldn't you?"

It was 22:40, pitch black, and blowing a steady force 4. The clouds seemed too low as they scudded across the sky. It had been an eventful few hours for all of them but especially for Nick.

Four Special Forces fishermen unceremoniously dragged him, trembling, from the water into their boat then onto Orelia's bathing platform. Smudge had swum from the sub and boarded the yacht to start the port main engine and get a hot shower running.

As his buddy was helped down the companionway ladder, Smudge laughed.

"Alright, shipwreck? Look out it's the fuckin' gimp. Jesus, you look like a beached elephant seal." He was going to shake hands, but then gave him a bear hug.

The survival suit from the sub came in one size: one size fits all. It was tailored to fit the biggest man in complete diving rig. It was built to go over everything. The idea being, if someone holed their drysuit, you shoved the survival suit over the top to keep some of the warmth in. It wasn't meant to be streamlined or look good; it was meant to save life. Nick peered back through the black neoprene hood and shuffled into the shower because the legs of the suit were so full of water.

Smudge undid the watertight zip and peeled the suit off his shoulders.

He and the three SBS lads looked on as a battered and shivering Nick winced and recoiled whenever the suit touched skin.

Smudge was shocked. "Fuck me! What the... what have they been doing to you, Deeps?" Nick's skin exhibited all the evidence of his maltreatment. Oil was ingrained into his mottled, pale skin; there were red marks all over his body. Angry looking circular welts showed where he had been bound.

"How l-long have you g-got?"

One of the SBS men smiled. "They'll get their come-uppance mate, don't you worry." He then stepped back, put his finger to his ear and said. "G3, go ahead," and went out to the upper deck.

Nick got under the warm shower and Smudge went rummaging through the galley. He came back with a Mars bar and bottle of water. He held the bar into the falling water and Nick bit into it with relish.

The SBS trooper came back below. "They're sending a boat out for you two in five. You'd better be ready. Listen, Smudge, we're gonna Foxtrot Oscar and leave you. We're gonna escort the sub back to Mother, okay?"

With just the two friends left on board, Smudge boiled a kettle and poured the water into a mug of powdered soup. He took the steaming mug into the shower and asked. "You okay? I mean... really...are you all right?"

"I think so, mate. I ache like buggery and I'm cold. Not just cold, but cold-cold. My bones, my core feels, feels like it's been in the deep freeze. Ahhhh! I could stay here all night. I haven't slept in... I don't know how long. But, I'll tell you what mate: there's nothing like a trip into the abyss, stark bollock naked, to wake you up." He leaned out of the downpour and sipped the soup as Smudge held the steaming mug.

"Thirty eight metres was our deepest. Jon Dog was panicking a bit. He was talking of bailing out. I had it all under control really. It was just a ploy to get out of the wash."

"Yeah right! What happened? I was out of it, I didn't even have a mask on half the time, I thought I was going to have to *Switch to gills* when I was dragged under by... by whoever it was!"

"It was one of the SB lads... Harvey. The tanker put her engine astern, probably to wash you for'ard, or to try and chop you up. I don't think they even knew we were there, still don't. Anyway, we're all okay. Is that a bite mark? Looks like someone's tried to take a chunk outta your leg there, what *has* been happening to you?"

Nick took a deep breath and sighed. He shook his head, closed his eyes and let the hot water fall on his face. He was mustering himself to tell his story, when Smudge's ears pricked up.

Nick opened his eyes to start, but his mate was gone.

Alongside was a Zodiac with two Clearance Divers and two armed Royal Marines. Smudge knew the diver in the bow as Ash. Above the noise of the wind, *Orelia's* engine and the outboard, Ash shouted up. "You boys are popular. Every man and his dog's after you. We're to take you ashore, and I think they mean now. That's why these Royals are here."

"What, are we under arrest or something? I've got a hypothermic Ex CD 2 in here who's just been to hell and back. They'll have to wait."

"Sorry, mate," said the biggest RM. "They were insistent we take your mate back, sharpish. They're waiting for 'im, so hurry up, otherwise we'll come and get 'im."

"Over my dead body you will."

"That can be arranged, mate. I'm just following orders!"

The second Marine came forward and offered. "Look, two minutes, okay?" Smudge glared at the big marine, then headed back below.

Nick had his face in the corner of the shower, with the water cascading over his head.

"Can you believe... they've sent an armed escort out for you? Seemed more like an armed guard to me. Cheeky bastards. There's two fuckin' Royal Machines out there. Just because he's tooled up he was having a go at me. We have to go, they, whoever *they* are, want you. And right now, apparently."

Nick dressed himself in long johns, combat trousers, thermal long sleeves and even put on a fleece hat to cover his still cold, shaved head. Smudge cut the rope strop from around Nick's ankle, then, still in his drybag, shut down the yacht and went as he was.

The Zodiac sped into Rosia bay in complete darkness, and as they approached the jetty, two green army motor bikes could be seen under a lamp. As they rode over to the boat, one rider shouted. "Carter... Smith? Your rides are here; hop on gents."

Nick flinched as he eased his leg over the pillion seat. There were new bruises to be found with every movement. "You look rough," his rider remarked.

"You should see it from the inside out," replied Nick.

Sarcastically Smudge asked, "Is one permitted to ask where one is being taken?"

"One is going to the best hotel on the rock, if one must know. Hang on and lean with me."

The two bikes roared off up the steep ramparts of the old bay. They turned left to go the wrong way up a one-way street, cut across Rosia Road and headed up Scud Hill. A taxi coming down the rock the correct way blasted its horn and the two skilled riders took evasive action. One mounted the pavement, the other missed the driver's wing mirror by inches. They turned left onto Naval Hospital Road and accelerated up the increasingly steep hill in the dark. On Europa Road, they turned off to go behind the impressively lit Rock Hotel.

Nick's bike tooted and a wire gate opened. Inside was a very pretty naval Wren officer. She stepped forward and helped Nick off the pillion. He still moved gingerly.

"Smudge patted the rider on the shoulder. "That route isn't in any guide book is it? And, you never said you'd be taking me up the tradesman's."

The man grinned back. "You never asked, love." Smudge turned to see the Wren officer giving him a filthy look.

"I presume you are the two divers?" She said while taking Nick's arm and leading him towards the rear of the hotel. "Goodness... you look... awful and... blue. Are you cold?" Nick nodded and shivered. She then asked. "I don't suppose you have any ID at all?"

Smudge answered. "I'm in a dry suit and still sopping wet. What do you think I am... a chef? My buddy and I stand before you having just laughed in the face of death, spat in the eye of fear, escaped the clutches of evil, in the nick-of-time mind you, and you expect us to be carrying ID cards? We are lucky to be alive, Ma'am."

"Hmmm."

"Anyway," he continued, "I don't know if I can tell you our names... for reasons of national security you understand?"

"I have a higher security clearance than you will ever have. Which one of you is Carter? Don't bother, I've worked it out." She said, as she helped Nick through a dark hotel door and down a short flight of steps.

"I'm all right," said Nick smiling across at Smudge and enjoying the attention. "You are right. I'm Carter, Nick Carter. The foul mouth is Smith, unlikely to be his real name if you ask me."

They stopped outside a pair of double doors that read: DANGER SHOCK HAZARD, above it. The officer undid two buttons on her white uniform blouse and pulled out a silver security key. She put it into an unmarked socket in the wall and turned it to the right and then back to the left. She then pulled the key out, tucked it back into her shirt and left the buttons undone. When she looked up she realised she had an audience.

"I bet that key's warm," said Smudge, then "...did I just say that out loud?"

She blanked him and said to Nick: "Nobody and I mean nobody, usually goes this way without high level clearance. But, for some reason you two have managed to bypass years of security. Can you look up into that camera there? Thank you, and you, Mr Smith. Thank you."

She stood by a door in the wall. "Now, this lift is a little rattly and, shall we say, unusual in its direction sometimes, but it is perfectly safe, or so they tell me."

The noise coming from the other side of the door grew louder. Eventually the clattering stopped and she opened a door to reveal an old fashioned lift. She wrenched open the concertina metal cage and they stepped in. The lift was the size of a small wardrobe.

"Jesus, can't we take the stairs?" asked Nick.

"There are no stairs, Mr Carter. It could take you forty minutes to get where you're going, any other way." With that, she dragged the concertina cage and the door shut. She used the key between her breasts again, then tucked it inside her shirt and buttoned herself up. This time she was blushing.

"For goodness sake, how old are you two?"

"Old enough, and I trust you are?" said Smudge. The lift seemed to drop about two metres before bouncing on a stretching wire. It then started downwards.

"That's got your attention, hasn't it? Have either of you been to the Joint Operations Centre before? No, well, you're in for a treat. Whatever you see or hear down there is not for discussion again. Full stop. You are not permitted to repeat anything you see or hear outside the centre. It usually is a long and... shall we say eye-opening course of, well, more than a few days. You two have side-stepped that because of what you have been up to. Others in there seem to have taken the same route as you and not done the course. But, in time, you will all have to study and sign your life away to say you agree to be shot, or worse, if you ever repeat any of what you see or hear."

Nick looked at her as she spoke but was thinking about the lift. It jolted and shifted left and right. He noticed Smudge seemed to be constantly falling against the young officer. The lift then leaned at an angle, like it wasn't going straight down, but at an angle backwards. It bumped round a bit of a corner, then sped up.

"In case you haven't realised it, we are going down into the centre of the Rock. But this wasn't always a lift; it used to be a ventilation shaft, then in 1949 they shoe-horned a lift in. It's been updated in that it now slides on rails. It is slowed down and watched round the worst bends with video cameras. There's only one stop, at the bottom and it takes a few minutes, well, depending on who's controlling it."

"Do any of the public who stay at the hotel have any idea this is here?" asked Nick.

"No. Most forces personnel don't even know it exists. Even the hotel manager thinks it is an entrance to some sort of listening station."

The noise around the lift changed as it shuddered to a stop and the door opened. The three of them stepped out into a long straight corridor. Nick was struck by the brightness. Bright lights were something he hadn't been around for a while.

"This way please." Smudge fell in behind her and only looked down at her behind. After a short appraisal he looked across at Nick and nodded his approval.

Smudge asked. "You haven't given us your name, Lieutenant...?" She stopped, so he bumped into her again. She knocked on a door with C-in-C on it, went in, and held the door open for the two divers.

It had the look of a hastily put-together office. Basic furniture, nothing fancy, and on the far wall opposite the door was a large flat TV screen. It had the live picture of a ship at anchor in the darkness of the bay. Around the edge were smaller pictures transmitting seemingly live feeds. One was an infra-red close up of the bridge of a tanker.

A woman stepped up to the door with her hand out. "Mr Carter. I am the Deputy Director of MI6. This is the First Sea Lord, Sir Michael Clapp, and this is our senior field officer in these parts, Jeremy." They all shook hands.

Smudge stepped forward in his dry suit and said. "I'm Mr Smith, I taught him everything he knows, and have just saved his life."

"Thank you, Mr Smith. You can tell us all about it, but not now," she said, and turned to their escort. "Thank you, Katie. You may leave us."

"Ma'am." She saluted and turned to leave.

As she passed, Smudge whispered: "I know you go down, but do you go up as well? In the lift I mean... bye, Katie."

The door shut and I.D2 continued. "Now... may I call you Nick? I would love a full debriefing from you personally, but I fear time is against us. Things are happening out there in the bay now! So, going with advice, I think you should brief us all at once. Just run through everything that has happened... everything important. I have to ask though, do you know, do you think they have some sort of nuclear device in there?"

"What... do you mean an improvised nuclear bomb? They have some nuclear material, some sort of nuclear waste, I'm sure of that. They have a charge on it as well... but, I don't think it's their intention to blow it up. In fact their boss told me it was not his plan. He could, of course, be lying. What they do intend to do with it... your guess is as good as mine." A wave of cold and tiredness swept over him and his shoulders gave an involuntary shudder.

She looked at his battered, strained face and said. "Are you sure you are feeling okay? You look bloody awful."

Before Nick could answer, she said. "Good, excellent. There is a nuclear physicist, a Professor James Fleming, amongst others, who will no doubt want to quiz you as soon as possible about that."

"Who's... who else is out there then?"

"Well, we have everyone who's anyone. The SAS and SBS and the SRR, that's the Special Reconnaissance Regiment, they have mostly left us for their mission. Your brethren the CDs are here, the Royal Engineers, Nuclear-Biological & Chemical Defence teams, a representative of the Spanish military, and many more besides." She rolled her eyes at the mention of the Spanish getting wind of the affair. "We aim to take over the ship within the next few hours. Whatever they plan we have to try and stop them, don't you agree?" He nodded and was ushered across the office.

The agent called Jeremy handed him a cup of coffee and said. "If you are okay, we would like to start right away... please." He stepped to one side and opened a door.

# 44

The feeling of apprehension was palpable as the small group stepped from the C-in-C's office into the operations room. A Royal Marine stationed at the door snapped to attention as they entered.

A chief petty officer spoke to the Director and the agent in a barely audible whisper: "Ma'am, the target vessel is underway. Weighed anchor at 23:15 on route to the off-loading buoy at the head of the bay. Four sniper teams and the commandos are still on board the Danish tanker, *Mersk Defender*. They will be at the nearest buoy to the target, before she gets there, to ease suspicions. She has jumped the queue and some of the other tanker captains are none too impressed." He looked down at his pad. "Also, *Moby* is back with the *Triumph* and has moved ahead of the target." He then looked at the First Sea Lord. "The *Triumph's* Captain wants to talk to you, Sir, on console... three, if possible. He is not that happy with his rules of engagement."

Sir Michael Clapp barked. "His rules of engagement are simple. If I tell him to fire, he will fire!"

I.D2 whispered in a gentle, but persuasive tone. "Will you talk to him, Michael. Perhaps you could hint at what might be afoot? He is a little out of touch down there." He huffed, then moved off to find the console to talk to his submarine captain.

Most of the console operators were intent and concentrating, their faces reflecting the text or pictures on their computer screens. They all wore headsets and were busy whispering into microphones, tapping away at keyboards and periodically looking up at the large screens at the head of the Ops room. To one side of the TV picture was a large see-through Perspex screen. It had the chart of Gibraltar Bay projected on it and, superimposed, were all the ships and the whereabouts of the various parties involved. A naval rating stood on the far side, constantly updating the data with a luminous pen.

The Information Director stepped up to the situation screen and spoke:

"Please! May I have your attention? Thank you. Can we have the lights up a tad? Ladies and gentlemen, these two men have just come from the target vessel. Carter..." Nick nodded to the dark faces ranged out before him, "and Smith. Carter has been aboard the tanker for a few days. Now, as it is approaching the buoy, I think it's a good time to hear what he has to say. I don't think he'll mind if any of you butt in with questions. Okay, Mr Carter."

There was a podium to one side of the screen so that everyone could see both the speaker and the constantly changing pictures and scene. Nick stepped forward a little nervously and said, "Good evening, or is it night? Err... please call me Nick. I don't really know where to start, or what you want from me. You probably know a lot more about what is going on than I do, so... maybe I should just answer your questions. Before we start, I must point out I was, shall we say, under restraint for most of my time on board, but I did manage to go walkabout on a couple of occasions."

A few people put up their hands, one or two shouted out. I.D2 took charge and interrupted. "Professor, I think we should start with you, please. Fire away."

The professor sat cross-legged; a small man with a head slightly too big for his almost feminine shoulders. Everything he had on looked beige; he was completely bald on top of his head and two great tufts of unkempt grey hair hung like a hat just covering his ears. On his lap were two books, a huge brown file with bits of paper

318

spilling out, and a clipboard balanced precariously on the top. As he spoke, he pushed his round glasses back onto the bridge of his nose. They seemed to sit at a permanent angle as if just about hanging on to the front of his face.

"Yes, I say, Nick, is it? Can you tell me everything you can remember, everything you've seen, or heard, about the nuclear material. Thank you, ma'am, by the way. I don't want to presume to push in, to be first, you know but, I think it's very important, isn't it? The nuclear threat, I mean."

*If I'm nervous*, Nick thought, *this guy is worse.*

"Yes, yes of course. There was, is, a Libyan girl on there. She told me the nuclear material went on board in Tripoli, Libya. Her name's Najia. She saw a dozen or so small drums coming aboard, silver, heavy-looking and they had the letter P on them. She said they were poured into the main cargo tanks. Apparently they did it once they were at sea, for safety reasons. There may have been more, although she only saw a few. The one she managed to read said P, then number two hundred and ten. There was also a heavy box which she thought was full of liquid. Now, I was taken below some of the tanks by the head man, Hachim Hadda. I assume you know about him?" His audience nodded.

"One of the tanks has been transformed into, a training camp, a sort of a firing range, and I think one - if not more - of the tanks further forward may have false bottoms. I mean, it seemed to me that we went under the main tanks. Anyway, somewhere amidships, under the oil tanks, is something radioactive. I heard and saw Hadda with a Geiger counter and he was getting a strong reading in there. I could hear it. Whether it was the heavy box, or some of the drums that were hot, I couldn't tell. He and some of his henchmen attached at least two explosive charges to something behind a screen. But I think these were placed, just in case. He kept hinting that whatever he was planning would be far worse than an explosion, more than a dirty bomb. He also said I would survive. He wanted me to see how magnificent it was. So, my guess is the plan calls for the tanker to remain intact." Nick shrugged, inviting the next question.

The professor was looking down, writing on his notepad. The Information Director was pacing up and down the side of the operations room, chewing on the knuckle of her thumb. She asked. "What is your instinct, Nick? You've met him, spoken to him. Do you believe him? Is he going to blow this thing up, here in Gibraltar roads?"

Nick opened his mouth to speak, then shut it again, shaking his head. He was about to answer when the professor spoke again, "Excuse me, Nick. The heavy box you say was full of liquid. Did she know anything else about that?"

"She did, yes, she did say it took six men to lift. She said it had letters written on it in Arabic and in English, S. N and F. I'm pretty sure that's what she said."

The Professor stood up, dropping his two large books and the folder. There was a man in a suit to his right. The books crashed into his drink on the floor, spilling it up his leg. The professor didn't apologise, just picked up the folder with his notes on and walked out to join Nick.

Professor Fleming looked around the large room for help. "Can we please have the white board down again?"

Nick and company looked a little surprised as the Professor stumbled out to the white board. Then there was a question from an army officer; he introduced himself to the audience for the first time.

"Lieutenant Colonel McNally, SBS. Nick, how many are there, how many players would you say are aboard?"

Nick thought for a moment. "There are three groups, I think. There are Hadda's men, I saw maybe eight... ten, possibly twelve? There could be more of course. They are the fundamentalists, the ones you would expect to carry out terrorist type activities. One of them spouted a suicide speech at me. They are willing; maybe even keen, to die for their cause. Then I saw another group, who I believe don't know anything about what is going on. I got the impression they were being paid to be there, mercenaries. There just in case things go wrong, or maybe they are there for something entirely different, for something after Gibraltar. As I've said, I got the impression Hadda expects to sail away. There were twenty, twenty-five of them. Again I don't know if that was just one watch, one platoon if you like. They were all armed to some degree. By that I mean, I've seen ancient bolt-action-type rifles, some sort of snub-nosed, silenced, machine pistols. I also saw grenades, stun grenades, and Armalites, so they are well prepared."

He looked to his left as the professor helped a Wren put up a whiteboard. One of the suits in the audience, probably government or SIS, thought Nick, spoke. "Excuse me, you said there was three groups?"

"Yes, sorry, I think there are also some crew, ship's crew, who probably don't know what they are getting themselves into. I was very close to the young tanker captain when he was... executed, murdered."

"Did you see who did it?" The man asked.

He thought for a while, hung his head and said. "No... no, I did not."

The chief radio operator made everyone look round when he said, "Er, ma'am, sir. The *Yamm-Amira*... the target, is secured to the buoy. The oil terminal has told the captain he can begin connecting the floating hoses."

She nodded, and said. "So gentlemen, it is imperative we make the right decision here and I can see we have a clear division. But we need to decide soon... do we allow her to unload, then move in, or stall the unloading and go in early?"

There was a heated exchange. It appeared to Nick that there had been some strong disagreements before he arrived. From what he could make out the military wanted to wait until what they called Zero hour, 04:00, when most human beings are at their lowest ebb. The Spaniard, Naldo, on the other hand, wanted to go sooner. Not knowing what the tankers plans were, he wanted to go in early and end it, before they had a chance to do anything. Gibraltar and Spain had the most to lose; their territorial waters were being compromised.

It appeared that the SBS officer, McNally, would have the last say, as it would be his men going in first. He made his point, again: "It would be foolish in the extreme to go in now. Every man and his dog will be wide awake and alert. Nick here has just escaped. They may well think he's dead but you can rest assured everyone on that ship will know that firing has just taken place. We heard from the sniper teams that Nick has already fired a shot. Believe me they will not be tucked up in bed asleep. They have also just moved the ship so all the crew will be up connecting hoses, and engineers will be preparing to transfer the cargo. On top of that there is the obvious safety scenario. A tanker full of some sort of radioactive, contaminated fuel, whether it is petrol or diesel, is not an ideal place for a skirmish. We would have to be setting off all sorts of diversionary explosions. There would also be lots of firing, and from what Nick has just said, not just from us. If we attack while the tanker is full, the chances of causing our own environmental disaster must be... I don't know... magnified tenfold? So, at the moment, until I hear something to make me think otherwise, and as long as the Information Director agrees, we will wait until zero hour."

She nodded and looked like a woman who knew the enormity of the decision she was making. All eyes were on her. She let out a sigh, rubbed her forehead and pinched the bridge of her nose between thumb and forefinger.

"Then... then that is my decision, I have to be led by our Special Services. Unless something changes, we will go with what the Lieutenant Colonel wishes, 04:00. We will let her begin unloading, it should be well underway by the time you go in," she looked at the SBS officer, "but as you say, the less fuel on there, the better."

There was a moment of resignation, and contemplation as they all realised what had to be done.

The noise level rose as small groups gathered and made their plans for the impending attack. Nick's questioning appeared to be over, for now. He seized the opportunity to step down from the limelight. On doing so, he felt a hand on his shoulder.

"Hello again, Nicholas. I said you'd come to Gibraltar, didn't I?"

"Fuck me - it's Miles. I didn't see you back there, hiding in the shadows, but, that's your game isn't it? Faceless, sneaking about in the dark."

Miles ignored the slur. "You got caught then?"

"You could say that. I told you I wasn't cut out for this shit. Where have you been?"

"My dear fellow, I have been exhaustively engineering your rescue. I had to go to Casablanca, then..."

"What rescue? I escaped *my dear fellow*. No thanks to you."

"Nicholas, it wasn't coincidence the sub was there to pluck you from the water. Who do you think-"

"Gentlemen." I.D2 stepped between Nick and Miles. "Gentlemen, I'm glad I put you two together. We would not be so far ahead otherwise. Now, Nick, I have one last endeavour for you. A last request."

# 45

As the briefings continued throughout the Ops room, the professor had been busily writing on the white board. To everyone in the room, his workings were unfathomable. The TV picture, live Perspex screen and the impending events were also far more attention-grabbing.

He'd written number after number, calculation after complicated calculation; he'd rubbed them off and started again. He wrote the Atomic mass as 209u, the Thermal conductivity, Atomic radius, Covalent radius and many more. The tables ended in an equation that meant something only to him, the: Electron Configuration, (Xe) $4f^{14}5d^{10}6s^26p^4$.

Just as the Information Director was issuing her last orders, the professor, with his back to them all, stared at his workings and seemed to reach a conclusion.

He said to no one in particular. "Well... I never! I'll... I... it... might..."

I.D2 stopped and turned to face him. "Professor Fleming. You have something to add, to share with us?"

He turned round, seemingly unaware anyone had spoken to or was listening to him. He just started talking.

"So... so what, what was he, Mr. Hadda, detecting in the hold of the ship? Something in the big heavy box. Something that, if I'm right, had written on it, S.N.F. Now if that was Spent Nuclear Fuel, that would give a reading on the Geiger counter. That could, of course, be used in an RDD - a radiation dispersal device, a dirty bomb. It would be a speculative radiological weapon which combines radioactive material with conventional explosives and Nick, Nick here, saw them putting explosives in with something radioactive. Its purpose would presumably be to create psychological, not physical, harm through ignorance, mass panic, and terror. It is also, we think, under a huge tank full of some sort of fuel." Nick side-stepped from the podium and left the stage to the professor.

"But we don't think that is his aim. So what *are* his intentions? If, on the small heavy containers the girl saw, it didn't say 'P' two hundred and ten but read, P-210 or correctly written $^{210}Po$?" He tapped the figures on the board. "That is Polonium, Polonium 210... it is an Alpha emitter. It could work. It has to be ingested, of course, or breathed in. It is not a radiological hazard as long as it remains outside the body. It acts on living cells, things close to it, like a short-range weapon. Polonium is extremely toxic, weight for weight. It is two hundred and fifty billion times as toxic as hydrogen cyanide!"

He turned and tapped the calculations on the white board again. He was thinking aloud. The room was quiet and all present were absorbed by this strange man's train of thought.

I.D2 eventually spoke. "Go on, Professor. Please, go on." He hesitated, straightened his lopsided glasses and began:

"Well, unlike most common radiation sources, polonium-two-ten emits only alpha particles that do not penetrate even..." He picked up one of his note pads, and tore out a page.

"It would not even penetrate a thin sheet of paper or, or say the epidermis of human skin. Therefore it is invisible to normal radiation detectors. Even hospitals only have equipment to detect gamma rays. But, if... don't you see? If they were to get it into the huge fuel storage tanks in La Linea, it would then go via road tankers around Spain and Portugal to garages, forecourts, as diesel and petrol." His already rapid speech became faster and more excitable as the explanation came tumbling out.

"Then into cars and lorries. Every family, every person who breathed in the exhaust fumes would ingest some like well... like, what was his name? Alexander Litvinenko, the Russian dissident, in London. It took him two weeks to die when a tiny amount was put into his tea. The Times, in its article, I remember said that it was recommended that the coffin with Litvinenko's body should not be opened for twenty two years!"

Nick butted in. "Hadda said something happened in London in 2006 that gave him an idea."

The Professor seemed to come back into the room. He looked into Nick's eyes, then at everyone else in the room. He was excited and pressed home his thoughts.

"Anyone using the fuel, anyone near the exhaust fumes, they could, would die over the weeks, slowly. It is historically called Radium F, and almost impossible for a doctor to spot, you know? They cannot detect Polonium before death because it doesn't emit the penetrating radiation called gamma rays which are encountered with most radioactive isotopes."

He held his hands up for emphasis and continued. "Every car with the contaminated fuel could, in theory, poison every street it goes down, everywhere it stops: traffic lights, schools, even the ambulances taking people to hospital. It would be terrible, but... what a plan. Why... we, you, wouldn't know anything about it for maybe ten days, two weeks? Tens of thousands of people, probably millions, would start to become ill all over Europe. They would be slowly cooked from the inside. They would all get ARS, acute radiation syndrome, the clinical name for radiation sickness. Small amounts no larger than a grain of salt can cause severe radiation sickness. Such is the intensity of the alpha particles, only half a gram of Polonium would be sufficient to raise its temperature by about 500 degrees centigrade! Can you imagine cities like Madrid or Barcelona, for days, weeks? The fumes would reach... well... everywhere, everyone."

"From their point of view, I mean, the terrorist's point of view, it would be perfect. They could have sailed their ship away and out into the Atlantic. They could be thousands of miles away, they would have at least a week's head start. It could be a month before it could be pinned down to one ship, to the one fuel load. It is perfect, just... perfect." His startled and horrified audience just looked at him.

"I'm sorry," he said, "but it is... perfect."

# 46

The professor had thrown a spanner in the works. The luxury of waiting had been taken away. The atmosphere changed from detailing every move, from planning and caution, to speed and action. They had to commit to the Maritime Anti Terrorism Assault as soon as possible. Even the SBS were eager to go early.

The token Spanish officer Naldo insisted the unloading be stopped, but he had no power to order it. It was imperative the oil terminal management did not know what was happening, or the workers might panic and refuse the load. That would alert Hadda, then there was no telling what he would do. Naldo had made a few guarded calls to the oil terminal ashore in La Linea, only to be told if the fuel coming from the tanker had already passed the oil companies quality control tests, then some could indeed go straight onto waiting road tankers. He even asked the head petrochemicals officer if they undertook any radiation tests. The answer was a laugh, and a *"No, por qué?"* Before he hung up, he asked to speak to a senior manager urgently. Whilst waiting, he had an idea and shared it with the English.

*

Whilst bumping down the dusty A1 route out of the rock, the SBS Officer, McNally, spoke with Nick and Smudge. Naldo had attached himself to the group and clung to their every word.

"Nick, I would like you to come along on the drop." McNally registered the doubt on Nick's face, and justified himself. "In a purely observational role, of course. Look, you know where the nuclear waste is. You could take us straight there. You know Hadda, and this girl you spoke to. No one else knows them. I think your coming along could really save lives."

Smudge, still in his dry suit, was listening and said, "He can't, sir. He's scared shitless of heights."

McNally looked round at Smudge and said, "You have to be off, anyway. The lads are going to take you to the *Triumph*. J.D has been so impressed with your piloting that he said you are now AWOL. Seriously, we want you for this one last dive."

*

An hour later, most of the participating groups were assembled in RAF Gibraltar, not far from the main airport runway. Miles had commandeered one of the Royal Marine Commando's fast boats to intercept the pilot boat that had left the tanker and Smudge was putting on a newly prepped re-breather behind a Navy Land Rover. He was about to be rushed away in the dark to join the SBS covert fishing boat to be taken to the submarine, *Triumph*. He'd had his face blackened, was dressed to dive and armed with a waterproof P11 pistol. He was getting hassled to go. He asked for one more minute and had a final word with Nick.

"Listen... I've spent the last week, wondering if you weren't already dead, how I was gonna fuckin' kill you. Now I find out you're alive, I don't get a chance to watch out for your sorry arse again."

"If you're watching me, who's going to look after you? It's those poor SB lads I worry about. Do they know your record for piloting one of those things?" Nick slapped his mate on the back. "I can't believe they let you drive one in the first place."

"Seriously, mate," said Smudge, "be careful, and don't get... involved with all that shooting and revenge shit, will you? Leave it to the Specials. They're actually very good at it."

Nick nodded and said, "Don't fret, man, I've had enough excitement for one week." Then he moved closer, away from the other Clearance Divers, nodded at Smudge's black bubbleless rebreather and said. "See if you can't lose that will you, mate, oppo, chum...?"

Smudge winked back. "I've beaten you to it. The one I had before is still on *Orelia*." He turned and walked off to the waiting SBS.

"Don't forget... breathe out on the way up!" shouted Nick.

*

Hachim Hadda was content sitting in the captain's chair. It was a windy but beautiful night. Alone and on the bridge of his ship, near the end of another successful mission, life couldn't get much better than this. They were pumping the special fuel ashore and the pilot boat had left. It had all nearly gone so horribly wrong with the English trying his luck. But, he'd got what he deserved: shot, drowned or sliced up in the ship's propellers. No trace of him could be found. Najia must have got too close to him. Carter had proved a worthy adversary. Like her, he was difficult to tame and Hachim could respect people like that. She was gone now and he would miss her, for a while.

He had done it. He had pulled off the biggest attack on the west... ever. It had been his idea, his plan and he'd insisted on running it. Well, there was no danger. The name Hadda would become legend. The coming weeks and months would be so exhilarating, he could barely contain his excitement. Soon it would be off to Pakistan with his leaders and they would watch the 24-hour news together. They would drink tea, smoke cigars, worship and laugh. It should start slowly, then build and build, like... like, what was that English expression? Like a snowball, the snowball effect, that was it. The BBC, Sky, and CNN would all be outraged. A few splinter groups would claim responsibility. Governments would call for the perpetrators to be bought to justice. And he, Hachim Hadda, would, like a ghost, disappear again to plan the next mission.

The broad smile was only wiped off his face with the familiar sound of the lift approaching the bridge. The radio crackled and he heard the name *Yamm-Amira*, in a Spanish accent. Hadda didn't move; he waited for his First Officer to take it.

\*

In the darkness they approached the smallest chopper on the airfield, and Nick thought, *that's not ours... is it?*

"I'm going to give you a side-arm, but you won't need it," said McNally handing Nick the standard army-issue Browning 9mm. "We'll be behind everyone, it's just in case... okay?"

Their engine wasn't running but those of the big Chinooks further on were. There were two lines of black-clad men walking out to the twin-engined monsters. To Nick, the noisy whop-whop of the massive rotors bought back memories of the Falklands and Iraq.

They stopped at the relatively tiny matt-black Gazelle. There were two pilots in the front running through check lists and they barely looked round at their passengers. McNally reached into the rear and grabbed a couple of dark green 'ballistic vests'. He handed one each to Nick and Naldo and said, "This is our ride. These are the SRR, the Special Reconnaissance Regiment. They get even less press than we do. The pilot is special ops, and the best there is. We will sit above the whole drop. We'll have a grandstand view."

Nick cast his eye over the chopper; it was crammed with equipment, bristling with aerials, cameras and protrusions. His stomach played its usual trick and turned somersaults just looking at the flimsy-looking aircraft. He wasn't scared, as Smudge put it, but as a diver and given the choice, he would always rather go down than up. But, he wanted to catch up with Mr Hachim Hadda, and see how Najia was, so even a flight in a tiny chopper was not going to keep him on the ground.

# 47

Dave 'Creature' Foot had been designated Special Forces ground commander. He and his team of 23 SBS boys were loaded, blacked-up and ready. He had beefed up his numbers for the drop with 10 Royal Marine Commandos. The big Chinook taxied its way to the eastern end of the runway.

He was delighted and concerned in equal measure to be made boss for the night. But he knew full well the propensity for things to go tits-up was immense. Creature didn't know how many players they would be facing, not even a rough idea. There were mercenaries, of a kind, and some Muslim fundamentalists. 'Some', when referring to a unit of enemy, was a fat lot of good to him; he needed numbers. There were non-combatants on board: the ship's crew, and, possibly, a girl. Apparently she wasn't exactly on their side, but wasn't to be trusted either. There could be a dirty bomb as well, don't forget. So Sergeant, just fuck off, secure the ship, don't kill any friendlies or get radiation poisoning or allow yourselves to be anywhere near any possible suicide bombers. Oh, and don't have any blue-on-blue friendly fire incidents between yourselves and the fly boys! *What the fuck kind of animals did they think his boys were? As if they were going to try and slot members of the SAS? Talk about stating the fucking obvious!*

The huge airframe powered up into the night sky and flew in formation with the second chopper carrying another 30 SAS and Commandos. The two aircraft banked sharply right to head south along the steep, largely unoccupied side of Gibraltar Rock. Creature stood on the rear loading door and looked out at the lights of the Catalan-Bay-Hotel flickering against the dark background. Lucky bastards, they were completely unaware of the mayhem about to ensue, or the possible danger they were all in. He pulled out the tiny picture of his daughter, Libby, on her pink tricycle. Tonight was not the night for getting shot.

His Personal Role Radio hissed and he heard the flight crew say, *"Rendezvous in two minutes. We have a visual on Sea Kings. Still awaiting green light."* Snowy, his sidekick, tapped him on the shoulder and pointed out the faint lights from four helicopters closing on them, *"That'll be the Lynx with the snipers,"* he said. Creature put his photograph away. He looked down at CD, the closest trooper to him. He shook his head and said to Snowy. *"Can you believe this twat? Cot Death is only asleep again. Does nothing rile this man?"*

Snowy adjusted his personal mike. *"Ahh don't worry, when there's a kill in the air he'll come to life. Anyway, he needs his beauty sleep, the ugly bastard!"*

Creature looked down the two lines of men. They all certainly looked the part, armed to the teeth, faces blackened, their gas masks hanging round their necks, ready. Most stared steadfastly ahead, concentrating. On the far side of the fuselage, Boot, his most experienced campaigner, was listening to his MP3 player; he was a Pink Floyd man. Next to him he had placed their officer, Moses. He was bricking himself, it was plain for all to see. His feet were tapping out a rhythm, in a pathetic attempt to look nonchalant, unfazed, unconcerned. He was sweating like a lorry driver on a rape charge and Creature knew he shouldn't even be there. Moses wasn't up to it, but orders were orders. Apparently, he had to learn somewhere. *I don't want him learning fuck all on my watch*, he thought, *especially not how to fuck up the mission or get himself ventilated!*

The rendezvous complete, the eight helicopters turned right again and headed past Europa Point lighthouse and on North to pass Gibraltar town.

"*Sierra Bravo One, aircrew, we have the green light, I say again, we have green. We are still first down. Sierra Alpha Two will be right on our tail, so don't hang about boys! Live-drop in... three minutes. Good luck. Aircrew - out.*"

Creature's heart definitely missed a beat and he wondered, was that right? Was it okay for your heart to do that, miss a beat? He kicked Cot Death and he woke, startled but instantly aware and began his walk down the line of men.

"*Two minutes!*" He looked out the rear loading door and could just make out the following Chinook, her helmeted pilots' heads barely outlined from the glow of their instruments. To each side he could see the much smaller Lynx choppers and he knew that the tiny Gazelle would be above, watching over them. His heartbeat was back down to normal and the usual excitement gripped his stomach. All that was missing now were the loudspeakers blasting out, 'The Ride of the Valkyries,' as in that classic scene from *Apocalypse Now*. Within five seconds of each other, all the choppers he could see went to stealth mode. Flying lights were extinguished and the Lynx broke off left and right and climbed up high.

"*One minute to drop, one minute!*" Everyone in the chopper stood and shuffled either forward or aft to their respective drop point. Creature noticed Moses turn forward, then aft, momentarily forgetting his position until he was shoved in the back by Boot whose job it was to watch over him.

The chopper started to vibrate and shudder as it pointed its nose higher and higher into the sky as it flared to slow down. Creature stood on the tail-end looking straight down at the sea. The helicopter's huge rotor blades bit into the air as they slowed the craft and simultaneously dropped hundreds of feet.

The nose began to level out as the forward momentum slowed to a crawl. Creature looked down... and there it was, the back end of an oil tanker. He clearly saw the guard rails, the bollards, a ladder lying on the deck, then a startled lookout staring straight up at him. The man was just about to raise a weapon when he disappeared from view, cut out by the ship's superstructure.

The huge lumbering chopper hovered to a halt, and the red light over the large rear tailgate immediately turned green. Snowy and Creature kicked the heavy ropes off the rear door until they slapped onto the deck. The two men reached out, grabbed the multi-layered thick rope and stepped out into the night. They swung their legs round, and slid down, controlling the speed with their thick leather gloves. By the time Creature hit the deck there were four other men, about three metres apart, above him. The motivation to move away from the drop was a pair of size 12 assault boots coming down on your head. He took up a defensive position just in time to see the first two men touched down on the for'ard lines. One of them was in danger of becoming entangled with the rotating radar antenna. Two of the men stood with their backs against it to stop it moving. In less than a minute, the first chopper was empty. The RAF aircrew above pulled the quick release toggle on the roof of the helicopter and the ropes plummeted to the deck. The Chinook was immediately leaning its nose down towards the tanker and veering off to safety.

As Creature and his team moved towards the first set of stairs down from the bridge roof, the second Chinook was already above their heads, the ropes thumping down behind them.

*

Probably the best shot in the British Army, Jiz Parker, was 240 meters away from the target ship. Ensconced on board the friendly Danish tanker, he knew the fight was going to go down and wasn't for moving. They had wanted to pull him and use him on a chopper, but that would have meant changing weapons and he was not going to leave his baby. His AS50 fired the largest rifle bullet in the world, he was on a steady platform, and he was ready. He was supremely confident in his and his weapon's ability. He had hit his bulls-eyes consistently at over 2000 yards whilst testing the brand new beast. More than a mile away and he could still take someone's head off; this was going to be a breeze, and it would be the weapon's first kill.

His spotter, the far too talkative Dave Green, was still gabbling on in his ear. Jiz had managed to develop a system whereby he filtered out all the bollocks Dave spouted, and only registered the important stuff. When he said. "Five SBS coming over the port side," Jiz knew it was just a warning, keeping him informed of all friendlies on board, so he didn't shoot any of the sneaky bastards.

Jiz had the stern lookout in his infra-red cross-hairs and could hear the approaching Chinooks as they slowed to a stop above the bridge roof. But he took no notice of the big lumbering choppers. He had been watching the mannerisms of his target. The man had been watching, listening, wondering what the noise was. He saw him look up, he recognised the slow comprehension dawn on him that the choppers were heading for his ship. He may have spoken into a radio on his lapel. Jiz tracked his every move as he spun round and took an Armalite from over his shoulder, cocked it, and bought it to bear on the vulnerable underbelly of the chopper. With perfect timing, the tiny LED light flicked from red to green in Jiz's sights.

Because of the steady north-easterly force four wind, Jiz was aiming just to the left of the man, between his elbow and his shoulder. He stopped breathing, and squeezed the trigger. A kick in his right shoulder and the jump of the weapon was tiny, the recoil almost nothing. The gas operated semi-automatic system had another huge round in the chamber instantly, but he rarely needed it. The round did indeed veer right in the wind, but not as much as he thought. It caught the target right at the juncture of his shoulder joint. A few years ago, with a different weapon and a smaller round, he would've been wounded, but not with the monster shell. The whole upper left side of his chest and arm disintegrated. He was spun round and round. His arm flailed out and spun off across the deck, the hand still clutching the weapon. It looked like a small explosion of reddy-pink, as flesh, muscle and cloth hurled out from the wound.

Jiz was not watching though. The target was down, no longer a threat. He was looking for the next and traversed up and left to the bridge. This target was not so simple, white shirt, gold lapels. If he armed himself, he was going the same way.

# 48

The launch was still there, so the submersible team made use of it. The dive team crouched and took their re-breathers off to leave them on the boat's deck. The big stairs had gone, that would be too easy. Stanley climbed first, his MP5 hung on a harness across his chest. J.D followed looking up at the dark, wet glistening silhouette. Stan always went first. He had an animal-like quality, an almost natural ability to be silent and stealthy, like a big stalking cat.

J.D. followed him up the vertical ship's side, clinging to the rope ladder. As the two men squatted on the deck of the tanker, waiting for the rest of their party, they looked towards the bridge. From the direction of the stern came the instantly recognizable sound of the approaching Chinook. The remainder of his team climbed onto the deck, sought what little shelter there was, and covered each other as they began their move aft towards the accommodation.

J.D looked up. The nose of the Chinook became visible as it hovered over the front of the Bridge windows. Ropes dropped from the for'ard doors, and a man, one of his comrades, was immediately on it and sliding down.

The small party simultaneously threw themselves to the deck. A sharp crack had been audible above the noise of the big chopper. It came from their left and it signalled the beginning. It was a large calibre, probably sniper. *I hope he knows we're here*, he thought.

Hadda was just about to leave the bridge to brief his keen First Officer. Sleep would not come this night he was sure, but a prayer and lay-down would refresh the mind and body. He stood from the luxury of his captain's chair and stretched his arms above his head, suppressing a yawn.

The air pressure in the bridge seemed to vibrate, to increase; it reminded him of a train arriving in a station in the London underground. As he stood still to analyse it he saw a flash of something from high up on a neighbouring tanker. Something was wrong. His First Officer sensed it as well and walked from the navigation table to the front of the bridge.

The vibration grew louder and deeper. Hadda said, "Get the first engineer up here. That doesn't sound..."

The First Officer picked up a hand-held radio just as the armoured glass in the port bridge wing door exploded. Hadda's instincts for self-preservation took over and he hit the deck as half-inch-thick glass ricocheted around the bridge. The F.O was not military trained. He turned towards the shattered glass and lifted the radio, using its aerial to point at the door. Hadda was about to issue a warning, when two 50 calibre rounds slapped into the man's white shirt, tearing his torso from his hips and flinging it past him across the bridge.

Hachim was not easily shocked by blood or trauma but remained mesmerized as his First Officer's legs momentarily defied gravity and remained standing, with no body above them. Then, the knees buckled and crumpled to the floor with a heavy thud, coins spilling out of the pockets. Hadda stared at the bloody, ragged tangle of organs, tissue and bone, unable to tear his attention from the abhorrent yet compelling spectacle.

A hand-held radio skidded across the deck. Hadda crawled on his belly towards it, but it was not on. The battery had been dislodged; he clicked it back into position, and shouted, "Repel infidels, Repel infidels!... Acknowledge!"

He looked up as a series of dull thuds echoed through the roof. Still stunned, he glanced back at his ex-First Officer's lower half and focused on a shiny wet hip bone protruding from a pair of neatly-ironed, blood splattered white trousers.

The sound of two quick gunshots from below galvanised him to move. He slithered down the first few stairs then ran down to the next level and pushed the lift button. Why was nobody answering the radio?

\*

As Nick, McNally and the Spanish Officer Naldo dropped the final few feet onto the bridge roof, all the Special Forces had disappeared below decks. The Gazelle's co-pilot gave McNally a black box that looked heavy. Like his men, McNally was blacked up, and drew his SIG Sauer pistol as soon as he touched the deck. They quickly went down the steps and into the back of the bridge to be greeted with the top half of a man, his face buried in the corner under a switch panel. He looked like he'd been torn in half by some hideous freak accident. Naldo was first to speak as he crossed himself: "Jesucristo, Maria santa, madre de dios!"

"Amen to that," said Nick.

Then they found the man's legs.

\*

Creature led a team of four down one side of a corridor, Snowy and his team cleared the other. They went meticulously, room to room, cabin to cabin. All speech was kept to a minimum. One deck down from the bridge they made their way aft, searching: officer's cabins, showers, heads and dayrooms; all needed to be checked and cleared.

At a cabin marked Navigation Officer, Creature heard a sound. With hand signals, he told the others what he had heard. He grabbed the handle and nodded three times. On the third, he opened the door, felt for the light switch and turned it off. Back-Draught tossed a flash-bang round the corner. He shut the door and the explosion followed, driving the door back onto its hinges. Immediately it was flung open and a kneeling trooper shone the bright light attached to his MP7 into the cabin. It picked out a prostrate figure and held it, the red laser dot on the man's head.

The muffled shout came through his gas mask. "FRONT!" Creature went in and immediately spotted the officer crouched on the floor, stunned. He stepped into the room, leaving the line of fire open. The well-oiled team shouted. "CLEAR LEFT... CLEAR RIGHT!"

Creature grabbed the man by the collar and pushed him face down onto the deck. He put his boot on the back of his captive's neck and shouted. "ONE OUT!" Back-Draught Plasti-cuffed his wrists behind his back. The man barely knew where he was, before he was up, out of the cabin and being shoved between armed men towards the stairs. Two other disorientated crew followed, hand-to-hand to a holding area where they hit the deck again.

Nick stood by the main corridor next to the lift as the terrified officers were flung between waiting soldiers, down the stairs, constantly moving. McNally gave the black box to one of the troopers and told him to keep it with him. Nick asked. "What is that?"

The young trooper who Nick had never seen before answered. "It's a box of tricks, a comms booster for us and a jamming device. Inside a ship with all these metal bulkheads the radio signal is quickly degraded so we boost ours and jam everything else." He then flung another terrified crewmen to one of his buddies down the corridor.

They moved relentlessly on, clearing every compartment. On the floor below, the SAS were doing the same. Eventually they arrived down at deck level and bundled all the bewildered prisoners into the galley.

At the entrance they stepped over a dead black man in desert combats. An expanding pool of blood was soaking into brown paper that someone had taped to the deck to keep the galley area clean. There was an Armalite sticking out from under him. Another body was just inside the door to the galley; he had been shot twice in the chest. A trail of blood and handprints showed where he'd dragged himself into the canteen to die.

Face down, hands secured behind their backs, the shocked captives were not allowed to move or speak. McNally joined Creature at the entrance to the galley and asked, "Have you spoken to J.D?"

"No Boss. He came on at deck level and has gone below." He nodded down at the dead men. "This must've been their work, I've sent ten men to join him, I'm off there now. Can you tell Moses to watch this lot? He's safer up here."

"He's not cut the mustard then?" said McNally with a knowing smile.

As Creature turned to leave he said. "Carter, isn't it? You'd better follow me." Then they heard a burst of rapid fire, and it didn't sound like any of their weapons. Creature broke into a run, closely followed by Nick and Naldo.

\*

Jon Dog and his team were first into the superstructure. JD pulled open the steel door from the tanker's deck to reveal the hallway that led from port to starboard, past the lift and galley. Texas was crouched, aiming his MP5. They both saw the man in camouflage exit the galley with a mouthful of food and a radio held to his ear.

Back home, the SBS did hundreds of hours of live firing in similar CQB (Close Quarter Battle) situations. The soldiers were ceaselessly drilled to make split-second decisions when they used live ammo in the killing house.

Were they seeing *'Friend or Fucker?'* Because of what he was wearing and the radio he was using, Texas decided the running figure was a Fucker. With his weapon set to single shot, he delivered a double tap to the man's chest. The figure fell instantly and almost gracefully, clutching at his heart.

Double Tap is Special Forces terminology for firing two closely grouped shots in succession. The target may be pumped with adrenalin and one shot may not always be enough to put him down. A Double Tap was like being hit with a sledge hammer... twice.

They waited. If anyone else entered the hallway, the same decision would have to be made. It wasn't simply what they were wearing. It was the targets' mannerisms; their level of disorientation, panic or aggression that helped the assault team make that deadly, instant decision. A second man in the same combats appeared. The barrel of an Armalite coming round the corner announced his immediate non-friendly intentions. He never got it aimed before he was hit by multiple shots. His finger squeezed on the trigger as he fell backwards and shot out a light in the ceiling. They waited for any more.

J.D heard the familiar noise of flash-bangs and the shouted orders of his comrades coming from the decks above. Other units were making their way down the central stairs towards the galley.

He ushered his men down the nearest stairwell towards the deep recesses of the ship. More men joined him on the stairwell, amongst them was his good friend Sergeant Creature Foot. Behind him were Nick Carter and the Spanish officer.

JD told his men to hold the stairs and went back up to join the newcomers.

"Back again?" he said to Nick. "You must love this tub." He then turned to Creature and enquired. "Any sign of the boss... this Hadda bastard?" Creature shook his head. They all looked back up the stairs as another flash-bang went off, followed by a number of double taps.

Nick said. "He will probably hold out in the shooting tank. It's like a firing range. Tank four... the fourth one along from the first watertight door."

"Where's the access?"

Nick pointed down the stairs. "Bottom deck, port side. There's a watertight door between each tank. They've made a corridor out of huge piping. It runs under or through all the tanks. Well, as far as tank six or seven, at least. It may go all the way for'ard for all I know."

Creature looked at JD. "I take it the Marines have secured the deck?"

JD answered. "I don't know, but I know what you're thinking. Have them go for'ard and nose about down the cable locker. If this tunnel does go all the way for'ard, it's got to come out up there somewhere, and that could be an escape route for them."

"Or another way in for us?" said Nick. "He has explosives on some spent nuclear fuel and maybe polonium down there. You know that, don't you?"

"Yeah, yeah, I heard," said Creature, "when we've cleared the accommodation, we must get the nuclear lads and Royal Engineers down here. They can tell us how safe it is. I don't want my balls fried by this invisible shit. What is polonium anyway?"

"You don't want to know. And can I just say something else?" said Nick. "Down in those oil tanks, it fucking stinks. I mean it stinks of old crude oil, petrol, all sorts of inflammable shit. You won't be able to use flash bangs in there. The whole ship could go up. It appears to be alright in the firing range. They've clad all the walls in thick wood and it seems pretty clean, but the rest of the tanks are bogging."

The three men looked down the stairwell, to the sound of a foreign voice shouting, and a slamming door grabbed their attention.

JD looked back at Creature. "I've been thinking about that. Is this old rust bucket single or double skinned?"

"They think it's single, but nobody seems to know for sure. Why?" asked Nick.

"We've got some big frame charges on the way with all the special gear as soon as the first Chinook gets back," said JD.

"I like it, I like it," said Creature, "and there'd be no sparks. Can you and your boys get it sorted? We could use them. But, for fuck sake, get the right tank!"

"Tank Four? Have faith"

JD raced back up the stairs to the upper deck. Hot on his heels were Nick and the ever-present Naldo.

# 49

Creature went back down the stairwell where his men were crouched, waiting for him. In a hushed tone he asked: "What d'ya reckon, Boot?"

Boot never took his eyes off the large double doors opposite the stairwell.

"I think it's locked. Davie here had a look under the door with the Snake-Head camera. It's some sort of crew rest-room, maybe the TV room. Lots of chairs laid out like a cinema facing away from this door. There may be some civilians in there, you know, crew, but there are also players in there - with Armalites. There's a second fire exit round there. Mickey 'O' is on it with another assault team waiting for the go."

Creature thought for a second. "Who's got a REM?"

Boot lifted up the Remington pump action 12-bore hanging under his armpit on a bungee cord. It was loaded with plastic Hatton breaching slugs.

Creature pressed 'transmit' on his personal role radio so that Mickey and everyone could hear, "Okay, gas up, Mickey. We go on three. Let's bomb it to fuck, CS as well." There was a rustle of movement all around as everyone pulled up balaclavas and put on S10 respirators. On the bulkhead outside was a red button protected by a thin pane of glass that read: 'Sprinkler-Rec-Room.' Creature smashed the glass. Somewhere, an alarm went off.

Boot stood to one side of the door and waited for the count: 1 - 2 - 3.

He fired the first two rounds at the hinges. The powerful weapon discharged at a range of six inches and blew two large holes in the wooden door. He was leaning forward to fire at the centre handle when somebody let rip from inside. The completely different sound of automatic gunfire rattled through the narrow corridor as the door splintered outwards. High velocity lead mixed with lethal knives of wood, exploded across the passageway. One of the rounds hit his Remington a glancing blow. Unfazed, Boot fired two more shots at the centre handle from the cover of the wall. The door wobbled and fell back inwards.

The shots from inside stopped for a split second as the other assault team fired their shotgun at the other door. It was enough of a distraction to make someone inside hesitate. Creature's team threw in two stun grenades and two canisters of CS gas. They waited seconds for them to explode. Water sprung from the ceiling.

Within a split-second, the flash-bang blinds and deafens. The CS gas simultaneously attacks the respiratory system and the tear ducts. The gas makes eyes pour and induces choking and breathing difficulties.

Boot was about to go in as the second flash-bang exploded. He had been in a room with hundreds of them. The shock and awe was lost on him. There was a man standing behind the splintered door frame; he was just visible as the door went in. He was armed but stunned. Instead of swapping weapons, Boot leaned close and unloaded the shotgun at his head. The plastic round hit him in the ear and he went sprawling into the room. Boot dropped the REM and the bungee dragged it back under his armpit. He stepped into the room, over the man with the earache and shot him twice with his MP5.

They entered in numbers. Creature saw a head behind a large armchair; the barrel of a gun poked above it. He fired through the chair: four shots, closely grouped. A man flew backwards. Creature barely registered other shots either side of him. He stalked, further through the smoke and water. There was another player in his sight line. Under a large old fashioned TV, someone was kneeling, pointing a weapon at the other door. Three or four other red dots zeroed in on him at the same time. He was shot so many times he danced almost to his feet before smashing into the TV and bringing it crashing down.

Ten seconds, five casualties, three prisoners. The room was filled with pungent smoke and fine water droplets from the sprinkler.

Through his gas mask, Creature spoke into his radio, "*Casualties?*" One of his men stepped forward; he had a piece of wood sticking out of his elbow.

"Oooh nasty splinter! Okay, take these three up to the galley. Get yourself seen by the medic. Leave the stiffs. And can someone turn this fucking water off, I'm getting soaked?"

They quickly moved on, down each corridor, down more stairs, entering every compartment every cupboard and every door.

\*

When JD arrived on deck it was teeming with members of 42-Commando. They had just taken delivery of the large container that was under-slung from the Chinook. It was loaded with SBS funny gear. Inside were hydraulic rams for opening metal doors, pneumatic airbags for lifting, explosives and shaped charges of every conceivable type. There was revolutionary underwater burning gear and dozens of odd weapons, some developed by the SBS themselves, and unseen by the outside world.

JD sent some men to the container to retrieve the large frame charges. Fifty metres out to port was HMS *Exeter*, her 4.5 inch gun trained on the bridge. The Royal Marines had lowered the ship's large steps down to the launch and it was being used as a jetty. He could also see the SDV on the surface next to the launch. Smudge was standing on the deck.

Coming up the steps was the Navy's Nuclear Biological and Chemical Defence team. They were already half-dressed in white suits and wearing breathing apparatus and carried large spaceman-type hoods under their arms.

JD had a horrible feeling they could all be just a little bit too eager. *This ship isn't secure yet*, he thought; *things could still go horribly wrong*. He saw Nick running along the upper deck towards him.

"Nick! Nick!" He grabbed his arm. "Are you going for'ard?"

"Yeah, yeah, I'm on it. I've spoken to the C.O in charge of 42-Commando. He's given me some men. I'm meeting them up front."

\*

Nick left JD and ran off for'ard. Every time he looked around, the Spaniard Naldo was behind him. It seemed he had decided to follow him wherever he went. He grabbed the Navy Nuclear Biological and Chemical Defence (NBCD) team and took two of them with him.

A Lt Murr gave him six marines. They went down the for'ard chain locker, searching with torches. At the back of the anchor winch motor room they found a new metal and unpainted watertight hatch in the deck. It had been hidden under an empty wooden box. He knocked the clips off and went down a vertical set of ladders, followed by the group. At the bottom were the black dank bilges of an old unloved ship. For'ard was a mountain of stinking, muddy anchor cable. Aft they found another watertight door with six clips on it.

"This is it, this is it." Nick and two marines undid all the clips and were greeted with the same diameter rusty corridor he had been in whilst escaping.

"This way," he said, and the small party moved aft. The first door they came to had 9 crudely painted on it. Each door's clips were done up tight. They undid them and moved aft. The NBCD boys had a Geiger counter with them and had it on, sweeping all the time.

Nick looked back at them. "Nothing yet Deeps," the eldest said. "Hang on hang on! All of you must take one of these just in case. You too, Royal," he said to the marine corporal. He gave them all a small blue badge that had written on it, 'Personal Radiation Dosimeter.'

"See, it's green? If it turns red, you ain't havin any more kids, cos you'll be firing blanks. Oh, and you'll be a slap-'ead, alright?" He looked at Nick's head and raised an eyebrow. "Well, it won't bother you, obviously. No offence."

Nick put the badge in his pocket and moved on aft, through door 8 then 7 to door 6. He stopped and ushered the guy with the meter forward. It started to click, slowly, as he approached the door, then faster and louder.

"There's summink in there. It ain't dangerous, not from here least ways, but then we have a big thick metal door here. I tell you what though. You wanna be careful going in there, it's borderline." He backed away from the door.

"I'm not going to," said Nick, "you are."

"Hey! What, I ain't going in there, no way!"

"Look, you've got the gear, the breathing apparatus, the suit and the training. Just go as close as is safe and tell me what you see. I've been right up to it and the Geiger counter wasn't running mad at all. I'm alright, look."

He looked Nick up and down doubtfully, "What about your hair?"

"I shave it, you... numbskull. Just go as close as is safe and have a look, okay?"

Naldo was looking worried as well and said to Nick in his broken English, "You go to see bomb? I was bomb disposal officer."

"No, no, too dangerous, for us anyway. It is the radiation that might be too much. You understand radiation?" Naldo nodded but looked concerned.

Two of the marines undid the six clips on the door as quietly as possible. For all they knew, there could be someone on the other side.

The marines opened the door an inch, poking their weapons through. There was nothing but pitch black and the smell of crude oil. They opened the door fully, shining their torches. The next door across the tank leading aft was closed and clipped. Nick knew that door led aft to tank 4 and Hadda's probable last stand.

The two sailors were fully dressed. They breathed their compressed air and with their hoods and gloves on, stepped to the front with the clicking Geiger counter.

He hadn't noticed before but the false base to the oil tank was only about ten feet above the tanker's hull and keel. The low flat area was claustrophobic, dark and menacing. Shining a torch up he could see the massive beams running forward to aft and port to starboard which supported the tremendous weight of the oil tank above. Across, on the far starboard side was the small false wall. That's where the charges were... where the Spent Nuclear Fuel was.

He grabbed the first sailor by his gloved hand, looked through the misted-up glass hood, and pointed out the compartment. The man was sweating and staring at his Geiger counter.

"Go on, get as close as you safely can," whispered Nick. The sailor looked up and nodded. He stepped down and into the base of the tank. The Geiger counter clicked the fastest Nick had heard it. Its forbidding noise seemed like a signal of impending disaster. The two sailors edged towards the container that he had been close to with Hadda and his men. As they shuffled towards the source of the radiation, one of the marines looked at his radiation dosimeter. He showed it to Nick; it was right on the border of green and red.

The two sailors stopped. The small party waiting by the door could see them swinging the Geiger counter left and right. They spoke to each other, their speech muffled under the hoods, and started retracing their steps backwards towards the door. They climbed back into the small tunnel, and the marines quickly shut the metal door as they took off their hoods.

"It's no good," he puffed, "it's no good, Deeps. Even with this gear on, I was well into the red. The Geiger counter here, it was hitting its stops. That is the most it can read. No one can get any nearer than we just did, and we are wearing protective suits, sorry."

"Bollocks! He's done something, Hadda's done something to make it worse."

Nick thought for a second. "Alright, there's nothing more we can do, let's get out of here. Come on, put the clips back on and let's fuck off."

"I will do, I will do it," said Naldo.

They all shuffled back down the narrow tunnel, heads bent low, looking forward to the clean air of the upper deck. As they stepped through the next watertight door the last Marine shouted, "Hey! Where's what's-his-name?"

Nick looked back and the sound he thought was Naldo doing up the clips, had in fact been him undoing them. The door was open.

Nick ran doubled-up back down the tunnel, closely followed by the others.

"Naldo! Naldo! Get back here you crazy bastard. What are you doing? It is too dangerous."

Nick snatched the Geiger counter and pointed it into the tank, its gauge already close to the red. The sailor put his hood back on and edged into the compartment.

Naldo had already disappeared from sight around the metal partition where Nick had seen Hadda and the boy placing the charges.

"Naldo! Get back here, now!" Nicks words echoed round the metal coffin like space. The Spaniard stuck his head round the screen.

"Nick... I live close to this place. My families are all here," he pointed vaguely across the tank. "Here in Palmones, it is only one kilometre away, very close, very close for nuclear. I have to stop this. This is my country, not yours... you don't understand. My twin daughters are asleep just over there. These are my people all around."

"Naldo!" Nick shouted, but he disappeared again. They heard him moving about, then he shouted, "I find the bomb! It is on a... pool... a bath of water... have some iron rods in it. The lid is open to this bath."

"Naldo, shut the lid. It will be waterproof and lead-lined, very heavy... Can you shut the lid?" There was a pause - then a loud thud.

"It is closed. I can tighten to make more closed!"

The Geiger counter in Nick's hand immediately reduced its rhythmic ticking sound, but it was still way too high. He knew everything that had been exposed to the radiation would have soaked up the gamma rays.

"Get out of there, Naldo. You may still be okay."

"No... there is bomb... it... it has timer... and a phone on it. I see it. I can remove it. There is wire... leading to more... wait."

There was silence, then he came back into view with a thin wire feeding between his fingers. He followed it to the metal bulkhead. None of them had seen it in the dark. There was another charge stuck to the wall. They were both set to go together, one to blow the Spent Nuclear Fuel, one to blow the separating wall to the thousands of gallons of fuel. A huge explosion with radiation as a bonus, a crude petroleum, dirty bomb.

"How long was on the timer, Naldo?"

"Wait... Nick... Nick this one... this one has err, how do you say, interruptor de la inclinacion?"

Nick thought out loud, "Interrupter of the inclination... incline, stop the incline... tilt switch? Tilt switch! Do you mean a tilt switch?"

"Si - Yes. A tilting switch. But I can move."

"No! No, don't move it, Naldo." Then Nick had an idea. "Actually, Naldo, if you are sure you can move it, can you place it on the deck? I mean in the middle of the compartment, around midships, away from both bulkheads?"

"I can move. I know this type, Basque - ETA use this one, it is Mercury, it can tilt maybe... five degrees before... You shut door, be safe. Shut door and..."

Before he finished the sentence the sailor in the nuclear suit was out and the Royal Marines were shutting the door. The sailor crawled back into the tunnel removed his hood and said to Nick. "He is going to die, you know that, don't you?"

"No, I know what he means. I've seen these mercury tilt switches before as well and..."

"I don't mean that, I mean the radiation. It'll kill him. He's had way too big a dose already."

They heard a faint cry from within and opened the door again. The crude charge was not far away from them, in the middle of the ship's hull. Nick could now see it was a home-made cutting charge, roughly shaped like a cone. The blast would be concentrated into one spot. Nick had used them to bring down ammo dumps in Iraq. It was simply a matter of pointing the cone at whatever you needed to blast through.

Naldo came out of the container with the second Improvised Explosive Device. He placed it carefully next to the first. He walked near to them, then stopped, leaned forward and vomited onto the floor. Their torch lights shone on his face. He was bright red, as though he had been sunburned.

He looked up and said: "The timer, it say, seventeen minutes, counting down. You go, out of my way, I'm... poisonous. I... I am... sick now." He lifted the shaped charge and placed it onto its short magnetic legs so the blast would be forced down toward the hull.

Nick synchronised his watch, 16 minutes.

# 50

Nick and the marines left the Navy to extricate Naldo from the deep recesses of the tanker. The last Nick saw of him, his neck had swollen and was already restricting his breathing. Nobody could touch him without wearing protective suits and gloves. Once on deck, Naldo was placed on a stretcher by HMS *Exeter's* medical officer and taken to their cleaning station on board the warship.

Nick had no time to witness Naldo's demise, and ran the length of the deck aft to take the nearest set of stairs down below. He could hear a fire-fight. The lower he descended, the more his senses were assaulted with smoke, CS gas, cordite and the sound of rapid gunfire. Three decks down, he stepped over a stretcher that held a black-clad SAS man. The soldier had a drip in his arm and Nick could see the man's trousers had been cut away and a bandage placed around his thigh. Navy medics were working on him. He looked unconscious and Nick noticed he had a large M written on his forehead; he'd been given morphine.

At the bottom of one set of stairs were three dead men. They lay on top of one another. All wore the once-immaculate desert camouflage. Their bodies and uniforms were now blooded, blackened; evidence of the violence of their brush with the Specials. The top mercenary had a gaping hole in his upper chest; his life blood had spread on to his two companions below.

Four decks down, it was crowded with Special Service troops.

"Where is Creature? It's urgent!" He asked one.

The soldier grabbed his elbow and took him down another flight of stairs and along several corridors.

"Wait here!" He shouted through his gas mask.

Nick was constantly wiping tears from his eyes as the remnants of the CS gas seeped around the corridors and compartments of the ship.

Creature appeared, with Boot at his side, he had a small black Geiger counter round his neck. He lifted his gas mask to reveal a flushed face, sweat pouring down into his eyes.

"Well! Is there another way in?" he asked.

Nick explained about the corridor and the radiation in the low compartment for'ard. It effectively put paid to any ideas of an attack from the bows.

"The Spanish bomb officer, Naldo, he went in there. His head was cooked in minutes. I think he's had it," said Nick.

Creature looked at the Geiger counter as it beeped once. "Fuck, couldn't you have brought the IEDs out of there?"

"No. They were in one circuit and one of them had an anti-tamper tilt switch on it. If that went off under any of those tanks... the other one has a mobile phone attached. I had him put them on the deck together so that, hopefully it will blow a hole in the hull. As I understand it, if the fuel rods are kept cool, they'll be fine. They're still in their lead-lined box, so... it was the best I could come up with. It's on a timer." He looked at his watch. "We have fourteen minutes!"

Creature looked hard at Nick. "Shit! So do you think this Hadda, do you think he knows he's beaten, it's all over? The timer is his last resort, to sucker us all in close, then... Ka-Boom. Adiós muchachos!"

Nick nodded, "I guess so. At least he gets something out of this, i.e. us, the tanker, some fallout..."

"I think you're right. There's been no sign of him. He must be holding out forward in tank four. He knows he can defend a long round corridor for ever. It's like, well

357

like, the barrel of a gun... like a funnel. We can't even open the watertight hatch at this end. They just pour fire down it and are sure of hitting a target. But, but when Hadda hears the explosion for'ard, he'll think it's misfired, because he's expecting... well, the end of the world."

Nick nodded. "Yeah, something like that, but all it'll do now we've rearranged it, I hope, is flood that compartment under tank six - and that's the most dangerous. If there *is* a fire it will put itself out by a rapid inrush of seawater. All the watertight doors are closed, but I suggest we clear the decks, now. There are too many on board if she does go up. The ones we can't or don't get off can go astern of the bridge. We did it in the Falklands and it saved a lot of lives. We just have to hope - make sure even - that he doesn't go for'ard and see that we've ruined his plans."

"Any idea's as to how we're going to achieve that?" asked Boot.

"Yeah, one. That black box of tricks that came aboard. Can we un-jam the VHF? If so... I can talk to Hadda – stall him? He'll think we're gonna negotiate," suggested Nick.

"The SBS don't negotiate," said Creature.

*

Smudge was on the deck of the launch, being dressed-in with Jock. JD hurriedly briefed his two divers.

"Smudge, see that frame charge? As soon as you are underneath it, we will lower it down. There's a loose blue line there. Can you see it? Give signals on that, up or down, left or right, okay? Jock, same goes for you. You're going to have to shift your arse across the keel to the starboard side. You've got ten minutes max, so I want you back here in... eight, to be safe, okay? I don't want anyone in the water when either of these frame charges go off, or the one inside tank six goes off, for obvious reasons. Place the charges just above the bilge keel. And

look for the ribs of the ship. You can see some from here."
He pointed up at the vertical ship's side. "The
indentations where there are no metal girders on the
inside... try and put most of the charge there. It will be a
weak point."

Jock just nodded and said, "Aye, can we be away then?"
He had a small underwater scooter that could pull him
along at three knots.

Both men went on gas, dropped into the water and
swam over to the ship's side, where an SBS fast boat was
holding on to the shaped charge. Jock ducked and was
gone, arrowing first for the flat ship's bottom, then
turning up to head to the far side.

The frame charge was about the size of a door. The V
shaped explosive would concentrate the power of the
blast in one area, cutting through metal, brick, or
armoured glass. It was a variant of that used during the
Iranian Embassy siege in London in 1980. It was 200
pounds of power, half TNT and half RDX - a devastating
combination. It had been explained to Smudge that RDX
was the most brisant of all military explosive. Brisance is
the measure of the rapidity with which an explosive
develops its maximum pressure. RDX was fast, and
deadly.

Smudge undid the line and gave a signal to the
surface crew to lower the charge into the sea. All he now
had to do was stick it to the hull and get out of the water,
before he became part of the explosion.

# 51

Hadda was organising his remaining men. He had five of the mercenaries, including the Major, and his six Jihadists. He organised the men to face the only way the invaders could come in, from the stern. His youngest son, Ayman, had arranged the explosives to blow the nuclear material in the base of tank 6, just in case. He'd told his father they could detonate it at any time with the mobile phone. If the invaders tried anything, he, Hachim Hadda, would be the one to decide their fate. Not just that of his men, but of everyone on board.

But this was not how it was meant to end; this was not how he had envisaged the plan. He was confused. How had this happened? He'd heard the invaders' accents; they were definitely English, probably SAS, and he knew they took no prisoners.

Hadda had plans to talk his way out, though. He didn't want to die just yet, or at all, if it could be avoided. He certainly didn't want to die as much as his impulsive son Ayman did. He looked across at his youngest; he was lying behind some sandbags, itching for the fight. Ayman was adamant he would not be taken alive. Hadda knew how much Ayman missed his elder big brother; missed and envied him for being in Paradise.

Hadda's hand-held radio hissed, then came to life for the first time since the Infidels had boarded. He was just about to speak, to ask the whereabouts of the remainder of his men, when a voice he didn't expect came over the radio.

*"Hachim Hadda, Nick Carter, over."* Hadda looked across at Ayman, then at the major, and shook his head. "I don't believe…*!*"

*"Hachim, if you can hear me, I would like to talk to you. There is still a way out for you and your men. Will you open the door? I want five minutes with you. I will come alone and unarmed. You can give me your requests and I can pass them on."*

Hadda looked at the major, who shook his big sweaty head; his son also said no. Hadda put his hand up to them. He hesitated, then spoke into the radio, "Come, now. You will not be harmed, you have my word."

\*

Nick, fully aware of the impending countdown, ran, head bowed, along the same circular corridor down which he had escaped. In the gloomy light, he arrived at the watertight hatch to tank four. There was a weapon pointing through a crack in the door, down the tunnel.

The watertight hatch was opened further by the major and his men. They looked past him, down the corridor, but there was nowhere to hide in a long round pipe. The major grabbed Nick, pulled him into the firing range and, with his massive hands, frisked him. He took Nicks radio and signalled to Hadda that he was okay, clean.

Hadda walked slowly over to Nick, shaking his head.

"Mr. Nick… you are back. You never cease to amaze me. I thought you had surely drowned."

"I don't drown so easily," Nick said. "I am as much fish as human. May I have my radio? I am only permitted to talk to you for five minutes, no more."

Hadda nodded to the major, who reluctantly returned the radio. He put it into his pocket.

Nick tried to speak, but Hadda cut him off. "Before we come to the final solution – whatever that may be – I must ask you a question. Why did you come after me? Why would you come aboard my ship? Once maybe, but twice? Are you some sort of agent, SAS maybe?"

The radio in Nick's pocket vibrated, it was Boot's silent countdown.

It meant... four minutes left.

"No. I am, was... just an innocent sailor. The pendant you took from my yacht. It belonged to my wife. You murdered her."

Hadda smiled. "That? That is a worthless piece. And tell me, I don't remember murdering any English women. Remind me of the occasion."

Nick struggled to contain his emotions. He looked Hadda in the eye, "You wouldn't remember murdering her. She was just one of the hundreds you killed that day in Madrid. She wasn't fully English either. She was half-English. English, Saudi, just another Muslim you decided should join your cause and end their life early. She was pregnant. The only thing I had of hers from that day was that pendant. The one you stole. It's ironic isn't it? It's because of your habit of sneaking about in the night and stealing, it is because of that, your mission here has failed. Nobody else was onto you. This... plan of yours might just have worked if you had kept your grubby little hands to yourself, if you were not just a common thief." Nick spat out the last words accusingly.

The radio vibrated in his pocket... three minutes.

Ayman rose from behind his barricade, raised his weapon and shouted something at his father. Hadda put up his hand to silence him. Nick then saw what Ayman was wearing. It was a bulky waistcoat with wires hanging from it. He could see explosives: the brown packages were wrapped in thin plastic, no doubt packed with nails and shrapnel.

"I see," said Hadda with a slight grin, "now it all makes sense. I understand your determination a bit more. That is why I do not get too attached to any woman, or one wife. But look on the bright side, Mr. Nick, you are about to join her in Nirvana, unless you do exactly as I say. We could all be there together. Wouldn't that be fun?"

"We will never meet again. Eventually, though, I hope to go up. You and your kind are undoubtedly going down,

down to eternal fire and damnation with the other thieves and mass murderers. But before it is decided, as you say you are a gentleman, where is my pendant?"

"It is for Allah to choose. My destiny is as he decides. I'm sorry, but the pendant is again out of your reach, Najia wanted it. And she has... shall we say, gone. And I didn't kill her, Mr. Nick, I believe you did. So again, we see, you are not as innocent as you proclaim."

"You are lying!"

The radio buzzed... two minutes.

"Am I? She's in there," he nodded to Nick's torture hut, "she is where you left her. I will look on her body for it when we are underway, but I promise nothing." He then took out the mobile phone and said. "Tell your people, all I have to do is push this button and.... the second part of my plan will be initiated. This ship will be gone. So, make sure your bosses understand. The first part is done, but as I told you, it doesn't have to be like that. I don't have to detonate. I want to hear the engine start very soon. Then, when we are sailing, I will give you a destination."

Nick looked across at Ayman who looked impatient, or was he... excited? He remembered, he was the bomb maker. Had he told Hadda about the timer? Or was Hadda trying to kid Nick?

Nick stepped back and said. "I will pass your message on. I have to go, I was told you only have," he looked at his watch, "twenty-five minutes to surrender." Hadda indicated to the major to open the door. Nick stepped up and into the round tunnel and pulled the door half-closed. Ayman looked across at him, the boy looked at his watch.

"Unfortunately you are not in as strong a position as you think," said Nick through the crack in the door. "You see, the fuel you have been unloading, it is running, yes, but it goes to the buoy then along the seabed to the tanker on the next buoy. It never made it ashore."

He shut the door, pushed the clip down hard and ran bent forward. He heard the metallic clips behind him and wondered if the major was aiming his pistol at his back.

At the last door into the accommodation, Boot was there to slam it and they both did up the six clips.

As they worked Boot said. "I nearly left you mate, I nearly went. I reckon we've got three minutes."

Nick looked at his watch and said, "Two!" There was a dead man in combats on the floor, the one he knew was called Chooks.

They ran up the stairs, two and three at a time. Up and up, past more dead bodies in the corridors. His eyes began to burn and stream with tears and he struggled to breathe as they ran through the fog of CS gas. Finally at deck level, they burst out into the night. Nick looked right; the deck was deserted. He ran to the ship's side, gulped down the fresh air and looked down. He could see a diver being unceremoniously dragged out of the water and into one of the SBS fast boats. The launch was still alongside. HMS *Exeter* had gone.

Someone shouted. "NICK!" He looked aft and a black-clad figure was beckoning him. Coughing, he ran towards the stern. He looked down at the dark sea to the sound of the big Mercury engine on the fast boat. It rumbled as it went to full power to clear the ship's side.

Right at the stern, behind the towering bridge structure, was a group of SBS men huddled round one figure.

The demolitions man, Back-Draught, was kneeling on the deck with a Magalite torch in his mouth, preparing four wires next to a Shrike Exploder.

Nick looked from Creature to Boot as it dawned on him.

"He doesn't know! Hadda doesn't know... about the timer. It was the boy... the boy set the timer as soon as you boarded."

They all felt the deck shudder and vibrate. A muffled explosion reached them seconds later. Back-Draught looked up at Nick who was bent over, hands on knees puffing.

"Well done mate, we're still here!" He turned back and concentrated on his work, inserting a black and red wire into the green box. "Let's hope that was the shaped charge and it blew a hole through the hull."

"It did," said Nick, hoping, "otherwise I think we'd know about it... or not know about it."

A flood alert alarm went off deep inside the ship, then another.

# 52

Hadda was confused and worried. Was it true they had diverted the fuel to the tanker he now realised had been shadowing them? If so, why? How could they have found out? Then, he thought, *Najia... Najia must have told the English about the polonium*. But he had tried to kill her during his escape. It didn't make sense.

Ayman was close to his side. He looked agitated, scared even. He coughed and had a red mark up his chin. Hadda never showed any of his sons or family any affection. It was a sign of weakness, a frailty. He mistook the look on his young face for one of fear; he was only a boy after all, not quite eighteen.

He forced himself to put his arm around him for the first time ever, and said in Arabic. "Do not worry, my son, we can still get out of this. They will not let this tanker go up here. Even the British are not that stupid. Take that vest off, they will do as we ask - they have to."

Ayman was shocked by his father's words and show of affection.

"Father," he said with a tremor in his voice, "Father, I am not afraid. I long for the moment when I am with my brother, Aalam, and the other holy warriors." He looked at his watch again, "I... if this tanker *were* to explode, could it not also explode the one next to us, with the heat and fire and debris from here? Would that not then still send the chemicals, the polonium into the atmosphere? That would not be a failure. The chemicals would still be breathed in by many, wouldn't it?" Again he checked the time and sought to hug his father even harder.

Hadda looked down at his son and said, "Well, yes, in theory it could but..."

He was interrupted by a loud bang, an explosion, and it was close.

The ship shook, the deck bounced up and down violently, almost knocking them off their feet. It seemed to come from further forward. Hadda took out his mobile and looked at it. The key lock was still on. "Major, prepare yourself. They may be about to try something!"

Ayman was distraught. "That was it. It should've gone, I... I don't understand it!"

He began to sob. "I have failed; we have not done our duty." Big tears ran down his face and he looked up at his father. They could hear the sound of water, powerful, like a vast, violent waterfall.

Hadda was dumbfounded. "What are you talking about? What did you do?" He held his son by his shoulders and shook him. "What have you done? Answer me! Have you... sabotaged this mission?"

Through his tears Ayman reached into his pocket and bought out a small switch. He kept it hidden in his fist. He threw his arms around this father's waist and clenched his hands together. It was the closest he had ever been to him; it felt warm and good. In his palm he pulled out a piece of plastic between two contacts under the switch. He pressed his thumb on the button. It was the happiest moment of his young life.

Ayman held his father tight. The moment was now; he could feel the joy and calmness. He took a deep breath and shouted: "Allahu Akbar, Allahu Akbar!" And released the switch.

His young, frail body was torn apart in the explosion. Locked in a grotesque embrace, the blast sent the two reeling backwards across the room. But the vest had malfunctioned, only half-detonated; the father and son were still alive. Ayman's left leg was gone, along with most of his pelvis. His right arm had vaporised in the reddy-pink detonation, leaving his left hand clutching the stump of his right. There was hardly any blood flowing from him. The heat and closeness of the flash had cauterised the massive wounds and his body had shut down to preserve its vital organs. Ayman's eyes were open; he tried to move, to look up at his father.

Hadda was fatally injured; he knew he was dying. Unable to comprehend what had happened, he looked down at his blackened, disfigured son. Ayman had a haunted grin on his face, the flesh on one side having been ripped away in the blast, revealing the young white teeth and bloody gums. He could smell burnt meat.

Hadda saw the mobile in his hand and stared, knowing it was for something. His blooded finger covered the green button.

The major was standing above him splattered in blood. He had a multitude of large bent nails sticking out of his massive chest. One had pierced his left eyebrow. He pulled it out leaving a jagged dark hole revealing his sinus cavity. The nail was in his hand. He pointed his pistol at them. He looked dazed, angry, he might have been shouting, but Hadda could hear nothing.

To an onlooker like the major, the bloody mess of bodies looked like a nightmare: a twisted freak of nature. The two, once human forms resembled hideous adult conjoined twins. There were three arms visible and two legs, one of the boy's, and one of his father's. Hadda's other leg was broken at the femur and was stuck high up his back; he was lying on his own foot. Only sinew and tissue connected it to his wrecked, blackened body.

Hadda felt cold, but calm, closed his eyes and pressed the button. There was a long delay, then, it seemed as though the world shook. When he opened his eyes again, the major disappeared in a wall of water.

*

Back-Draught had made the final connections to the Shrike exploder. He'd used the small green box to set off his fireworks everywhere from the Arctic to Africa. The four wires were in the spring-loaded terminals. He'd checked the continuity of the circuit by depressing the TEST button. It shone bright and green. Next he pressed PRIME, got the red READY light, and looked up at Creature.

Creature spoke into his headset to the Command Gazelle chopper, somewhere way above them. They in turn sought approval from the depths of the Operations room inside the Rock.

\*

I.D2 and the First Sea Lord watched the tanker on the large screen. The grainy infra-red picture was being fed from a camera on the small chopper. The picture flicked to heat-seeking mode and everyone could see the hot areas of the ship: the engine room, and the funnel.

But their eyes were inexorably drawn toward the group huddled on the stern.

The navy chief radio operator relayed the message to I.D2.

"Ma'am." She couldn't tear her eyes from the picture on the screen. "Ma'am... the ground commander is requesting permission to fire."

All eyes were on her, except for the professor. He was fixated on the picture and stood only three feet from the huge screen.

She didn't speak, she just nodded. The chief needed a bit more; this was a momentous decision and he didn't want a misunderstanding.

"Is that an affirmative, Ma'am?"

She paused again, looked at the chief and said, "Permission granted - fire when ready."

\*

Back-Draught got the nod, shouted, "Fire in the hold!" and depressed the red button.

There was a moment's silence; nobody breathed on the deck as the 400 volts raced down both sides of the ship.

The current exploded an electrical detonator the size of a cigarette which was buried deep inside the lethal mix of military High Explosive. In a billionth of a second, the chemical reaction in both frame charges instantly converted the H.E compound into a rapidly expanding mass of gasses. It caused a blast-wave that travelled at ten miles per second. Even underwater, the temperatures deep within the charges were hotter than the surface of the sun. With the power, velocity and heat focussed on one point by the 'V' shaped charge, the old metal plate that formed the hull of the tanker, melted, shattered and evaporated. The weight of the water followed the door-size hot metal into the cavernous tank.

The cavities inside the human body collapse under such pressures, all those inside instantly imploded. The wall of heat and sound was quickly quenched by the Mediterranean deluge that followed.

# 53

Just before daylight, the Chief Engineer and his team from HMS *Exeter* had the tanker's main engine running. The sailors had disconnected the 36-inch pipe that hung from the tanker and floated out in a lazy snaking arc to the fuelling buoy. The British had paid double the cost of the time at the buoy and paid for the fuel the Spanish never saw. The *Mersk Defender* had already sailed with a mixture of fuel that nobody would ever want.

The *Yamm-Amira* set sail in the dark not long after her, at 06:45, with a skeleton military crew from the *Exeter*. The name of the tanker had been hastily and none-too-neatly painted out in black.

She was the ship with no name, with a dangerous cargo... bound for God knows where.

She had not escaped unseen, and the incident, being so close to the Spanish mainland, threatened to cause the biggest diplomatic breakdown between England and Spain in living memory. The Spanish navy had sent a patrol boat to investigate the explosion on one of their buoys, only to be met by the British navy, refusing them access. The fact that the buoy was in Spanish territorial waters along with the presence of so many helicopters, warships and submarines had not gone down well.

The short border between Gibraltar and Spain was immediately closed and - when the Spanish demanded to speak to their naval representative - that right was also denied them.

By ten o'clock the next morning the British military presence during the operation had disappeared. HM submarine *Triumph* had put to sea carrying the Swimmer Delivery Vehicle, and HMS *Exeter* had sailed with the commandos and many of the civilian extras so that they could be properly de-briefed on the long journey back to England. Two un-marked Hercules took off not long after daybreak, full to bursting point with equipment and personnel.

To the Spanish, it was like banging their heads against a brick wall. The British simply denied anything serious had happened.

*

Nick and Smudge had been ordered by the MoD to sail forthwith, back to England for their debriefing.

Nick had other plans.

While Smudge slept, he altered course South West to head down the Atlantic coast of Africa.

At 15:30 Nick shook Smudge for the First Dog watch at 16:00. He emerged wearily from below wearing a pair of boxer shorts and eating tinned fruit out of the can. Squinting in the bright sunlight, he sat in the cockpit opposite his buddy, and said to Nick, "You look awful."

"Crikey, look who's talking. Did you look in a mirror? You know we have plates, don't you? Lots of them, big ones, small ones, bowl shaped, every kind in fact."

Smudge ignored him. He stood up and looked around.

"Something wrong?" asked Nick.

"I hate to say this but, the land is on the wrong side. Correct me if I'm wrong, but shouldn't it be to starboard? Unless, unless of course we are heading south. Are - we - heading - south?" he looked at the compass. "We are heading south. South is the wrong way for home, isn't it?"

"Well done Vasco Da Smith, we are heading south. That is the way the boat demanded to go."

"Demanded, eh?" He sat down and looked at Nick. "Don't you just hate it when she does that? I have to go back to work. You know other people have what they call jobs, don't you? Well I have one, you see. What happens is, every day, you have to go into this place and... well for want of a better word - work!"

"Shut up, will you. It would take us eleven or twelve days to get back to Blighty anyway. So I figured you deserved some sunshine after your exertions. I'm the skipper, and I say we head eight hundred miles south to the Canaries. Seven or eight days passage, then we'll do some diving and prepare the boat for an Atlantic crossing. By the time they've realised we're not heading that way, it will have all calmed down a bit, you wait and see."

"And the de-brief, what about the de-brief we are required to attend?"

"It's cancelled. I cancelled it. I don't work for the MoD anyway and you deserve some rest and recuperation after putting your life at risk for Queen and country." Nick stood, stretched and went below. "You have the ship, Number One, course two four zero. Shake me at eight!"

"Aye, skipper, aye," Smudge said in his best pirate's voice. "That's it? Discussion over, I take it, and what do you mean, eight? Great, so I have the first and last dog watch, do I?"

Nick ignored him and crawled into his bunk. Smudge never shook him and he slept a full fifteen hours.

The two friends sailed on south, and over the following week, discussed everything that had gone on. Nick's body and mind repaired and gathered strength from the rest and the company. They encountered every type of sailing from hard beats to windward to tearing downwind. They trawled lures and caught fish to eat, they repaired his canoe the SBS had kindly returned and finally changed the port engine fan belt during a bout of windless calm. After eight days and four hours, at 11:00, Smudge shouted, "Land ahoy!" They were at Gran Canaria.

When they tied up in Las Palmas de Gran Canaria, Nick cajoled Smudge to help him load up the yacht with the stores required for his thirty-odd day solo trip across the Atlantic. They worked hard during the mornings, then, in the heat of the afternoon, went wreck hunting. The evenings were spent in bars around the marinas, discussing the Cuban wreck or pouring over charts for other possibilities. In the end they decided Nick should sail towards the Caribbean Island of Antigua and Smudge would do some more research back at work. Smudge would maybe fly out to join him when things had calmed down at home. Nick found a small dive store that sold everything, including the $CO_2$ absorbent, pure $O_2$ and mixed gases he would need to commission his newly acquired re-breather.

The Friday that Smudge was due to fly, Nick went to an internet café in Las Palmas and hesitantly checked his bank account. What he saw astonished him. All the money Miles had mentioned was sitting in his account. He hadn't had so much money since his last saturation dive years earlier. He printed out the balance and kept looking at the slip of paper as he walked amongst tourists on his way back to the boat. He felt uneasy about the money, but accepted he'd earned it, and knew he needed it.

Feeling flush, he gave Smudge the cash for his ticket, which he none too gracefully accepted. On the quayside, and with the taxi waiting, they said their goodbyes. Smudge refused to let Nick go to the airport, sniffing, "I hate tearful goodbyes!"